GOOD AT GAMES

This Large Print Book carries the
Seal of Approval of N.A.V.H.

GOOD AT GAMES

JILL MANSELL

THORNDIKE PRESS
A part of Gale, Cengage Learning

GALE
CENGAGE Learning·

Farmington Hills, Mich • San Francisco • New York • Waterville, Maine
• Mason, Ohio • Chicago

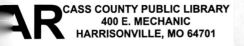

GALE
CENGAGE Learning®

LIBRARY OF CONGRESS CATALOGING-IN-PUBLICATION DATA

Names: Mansell, Jill, author.
Title: Good at games / by Jill Mansell.
Description: Large print edition. | Waterville, Maine : Thorndike Press, 2016. |
  © 2000 | Series: Thorndike Press large print romance
Identifiers: LCCN 2016003244 | ISBN 9781410489203 (hardcover) | ISBN 1410489205
  (hardcover)
Subjects: LCSH: Large type books. | Domestic fiction. | GSAFD: Love stories.
Classification: LCC PR6063.A395 G66 2016b | DDC 823/.914—dc23
LC record available at http://lccn.loc.gov/2016003244

Published in 2016 by arrangement with Sourcebooks, Inc.

Printed in Mexico
1 2 3 4 5 6 7 20 19 18 17 16

To Cino
With love

CHAPTER 1

Suzy fell in love with Harry Fitzallan the moment she showed him her husband's sperm sample.

The sample didn't really belong to her husband, of course. Chiefly because she wasn't married.

It wasn't a sperm sample either — it was a McDonald's cup containing the dregs of her strawberry milkshake. But when your brother's just been stopped for speeding and he really, *really* doesn't want to lose his license — well, sometimes you just have to improvise, do the best you can with what you've got.

Oh, and if she was being honest, it wasn't actually love at first sight either. Still, it was undeniably a healthy attack of lust.

"Oh, terrific, this is all I need." Rory Curtis, who never swore, let out a low groan as the police car moved smoothly in front of him, flashing its you've-been-caught sign, the driver indicating with a leisurely wave that Rory might like to pull over onto the hard shoulder.

"Bastard!" Unlike her elder brother, Suzy Curtis was partial to a bit of profanity. "Honestly, what is it with these people? Why can't they do something useful, like catch burglars? When are they going to stop harassing innocent motorists who —"

"This is bad news." Brusquely, Rory interrupted her tirade. "I've got points already. There goes my license." He exhaled heavily. "How can I do my job without a car?"

He was a worrier and a workaholic. Suzy, who wasn't, could feel his agitation as he braked and pulled over. She fiddled with the milkshake cup in her lap, quite tempted to take her own frustration out on it and crush it in her fist like an empty Coke can. Except if she tried this, she'd only get milkshake drips all over her navy agnès b. skirt.

Rory slowed to a reluctant halt behind the police car, and they watched the policeman climb out.

Suzy gasped, instantly diverted and whistling in astonishment because the sight of him was so unexpected. "Blimey, I'd have his babies any day."

"You could start right now." Rory's jaw was tense, his tone resigned. "It might distract him from booking me."

There was no getting away from it; this police officer was absolutely gorgeous. Suzy, clocking every delicious detail from the bright blue eyes that crinkled at the corners to a body that was, quite frankly, excellent in every respect, had to make a conscious effort to close her mouth. After all, there's nothing remotely attractive about a girl who drools.

Her fingers curled helplessly around the milkshake cup. Next to her in the driver's seat, Rory's breathing quickened, and a vein on his temple began to throb. As the policeman strolled toward them, Suzy fleetingly imagined having his babies. She glanced thoughtfully down at the cup in her hand and removed the straw.

"That's it, I'm booked," fretted Rory, massaging his aching forehead.

"Shhh, let me just give something a try." Suzy patted his arm, threw open the passenger door, burst out onto the grass shoulder, gazed at the most beautiful policeman she'd ever seen in her life . . .

. . . and burst into a torrent of tears.

He looked taken aback. "Oh, now —"

"Please, Officer, please. I *know* we were

9

going a tiny bit fast, but —"

"A tiny bit fast? Ninety-seven miles per hour, according to our radar."

"But every second counts, and this is our last t-t-try," Suzy sobbed. "Six years of agony, four lots of IVF, and we just can't afford any more tries. Officer, I'm begging you . . ." Trembling, she held up the brightly colored milkshake cup advertising the latest Disney movie. "We have thirty minutes to get to the hospital. The doctors are all there, standing by. I've had all the injections . . . This is my very last chance to have a baby, and if you don't let us go this minute" — she clutched the cup to her heaving bosom — "they're all going to die!"

Suzy blinked, her lips bravely pressed together, unconcealed anguish in her eyes. Well, that was that. Couldn't say she hadn't given it her best shot. Heavens, he was gorgeous.

Calm down now, she reminded herself. *Whatever happens, I absolutely* must not *flirt with him.*

"You mean . . ." Perplexed, he pointed at the cup, then at Rory in the driver's seat. "He . . . into a milkshake cup?"

Suzy prayed he wouldn't ask her to take the lid off. Strawberry, bit of a giveaway.

"Well, it has to be put into something." It

came out as an indignant wail. "What would you use, a wineglass?" She bit her lip and brushed the tears from her eyes. "Oh, look, I'm sorry, forgive me; it's all been such a terrible strain. They have a room set aside at the hospital, for the men to . . . but my husband can't . . . Um, it's all so impersonal, you see . . . He prefers to do it at home. Go on, take a look if you don't believe me!" Going for broke, Suzy took a step toward him, eagerly offering him the cup. "But please, whatever you do, don't drop it. Those are my babies in there."

As he hesitated, the passenger door of the patrol car swung open, and the second officer hauled himself out. He was fattish, fiftyish and wheezy, with a face the color of a baboon's bottom.

Hmmm, no danger of inadvertent flirtation there.

"Problem?"

"Oh, please, please let us go," begged Suzy, her face crumbling once more — but not unattractively so. "Don't you understand? Every second counts!"

The good-looking one glanced over his shoulder at his colleague. Then turning back to Suzy, he nodded at the car.

"Better get a move on, then. No time to lose."

"Oh, thank you, thank you, Officer!" Suzy was so overjoyed she almost threw aside her milkshake cup and flung her arms around him. Instead, she confined herself to imagining how it would feel to fling her arms around him. All that scratchy blue serge against her warm naked body — heavens, there was definitely something about a man in uniform. "You don't know what this means to me!"

"Good luck." He gave her a regretful smile, as if — under other circumstances, of course — he wouldn't have minded discovering for himself how her warm naked body might have felt clasped masterfully to his blue serge chest.

"You're not even giving them a ticket?" The ugly one looked disappointed.

Ignoring him, Suzy said, "You must tell me your name."

"Fitzallan."

"I meant your first name."

"Oh." He smiled, blushing fractionally. "Harry."

Rory was holding the passenger door open for her. Feeling as if they were Bonnie and Clyde about to make a nifty getaway, Suzy slid into the car and buzzed down the window.

"If we have a boy, we'll name him after

12

you," she yelled, waving to him as they sped away.

A fortnight later, on the last day of July, Suzy piled the employees of Curtis and Co. into the bar of the Avon Gorge Hotel to celebrate a record-breaking month of business. She had even managed to persuade Rory to take a couple of hours off from working himself into an early grave and have a couple of hard-earned drinks instead.

The rest of them had more than a couple. Suzy, who had exceeded her sales target by 300 percent, launched happily into the tequila. Martin Lord, her fellow agent, matched her drink for drink. When Donna — their hugely efficient Gothic secretary — spotted a noisy crowd from Slade and Matthews, a rival agency in Clifton, Martin soon had them engaged in a raucous game of Truth or Dare.

"Dare!" roared their opponents when Martin refused to strip down to his socks. "One lap around the terrace with Suzy on your back, singing 'My Way' and whipping you with a leather belt."

"Dare?" Martin grinned. "That's been my fantasy for years."

"Don't you dare drop her," Rory warned as Suzy, joining in, hitched up her skirt and leaped onto Martin's back. "She's my star saleswoman."

"Not to mention a brilliant singer." Leaning forward, Suzy lovingly ruffled her brother's dark hair. "Donna, I need a bit of help getting started. Give me a C minor."

Donna, patting the pockets of her long black dress, said, "Haven't got one."

"Never mind, I'll have a Marlboro instead." Precariously, Suzy tilted sideways, grabbed a half-empty wine bottle from the table, and whisked a lit cigarette from Martin's fingers. "All I need now is a pair of spurs. Hi ho, Silver, off we go, watch out for those tables . . ."

Everyone was cheering madly, but it was a dare too far for Martin, who had drunk seven tequila slammers on an empty stomach. He swayed, ricocheted off the edge of one of the tables, and lost his balance before Suzy even had a chance to burst into song. Which was just as well, probably, since her singing voice was woefully off-key.

"Aaargh!" As she toppled backward, she dimly wondered if her bottom was up to the task of cushioning the blow. She felt herself falling in slow motion. Her arms reached only fresh air. Behind her, a chair clattered to the ground, and a pair of strong arms, appearing out of nowhere, caught her

14

as she fell.

Amazed, Suzy gazed at the unfamiliar hands clasped firmly around her waist. Someone with reflexes like greased lightning had rescued her from a truly horrible fate, and she couldn't even see his face. Furthermore, her thighs were still wrapped around Martin's waist.

Which was embarrassing, and not what you'd call elegant.

Slowly, Suzy disentangled her legs. By a stroke of luck, she had managed to hold on to both the cigarette and the bottle of Pouilly-Fumé. To steady her nerves, she took a deep drag on one and a glug of the other. Thankfully, in the right order.

Then she turned around to see who had hurtled so magnificently to her rescue.

For a moment she didn't recognize him, so strongly associated was he in her mind with scratchy blue serge. Then Suzy saw the way his eyes crinkled at the corners, and every detail of their last meeting came flooding back: Hatless this time, his dark hair was curlier than she had realized. The eyes were as blue as ever. And now that he was wearing a pale yellow polo shirt and fitted jeans, she was able to appreciate the finer points of his body, which was fat-free, well-toned, and clearly up to the task of lift-

15

ing sizable weights when the occasion arose.

Well, sizable-ish. Nothing wrong with being 130 pounds.

"I really hate to say this," said Suzy, "but it looks like I've been caught out."

"Does really," Harry Fitzallan agreed, his expression sorrowful. "Smoking, drinking, piggy-back racing, not to mention your husband over there, watching you gallop around on another man's back."

The tequilas she had so recklessly downed earlier were making Suzy's head spin. She said, "Actually, he's not my husband. He's my brother."

"In that case, I really hope that wasn't his sperm sample you were in such a hurry to get yourself inseminated with."

"What can I say? I told a big lie." Suzy tried hard to look suitably ashamed. "It was strawberry milkshake."

"And there was me, thinking I was being such a nice guy." Harry gave her a rueful look. "Doing the decent thing and all that. I kept thinking about you, you know. Afterward. Hoping it would work out for you and your husband . . ."

"But when I *do* have a baby," she told him earnestly, "I absolutely promise to name him after you."

He raised a skeptical eyebrow. "You can't

even remember my name."

Suzy, who could, waved her arm and declared, "I shall call him Constable."

It came out as Conshtable.

Harry smiled. "You're drunk."

"I know, I know." She nodded vigorously, entranced all over again by the astonishing blueness of his eyes. "But as Winston Churchill once said, 'When I wake up in the morning, you'll still be beautiful.' "

"He almost said it. Well, he almost said something vaguely like that."

"So what happens now? Are you going to arrest me?"

"What for? Being drunk in charge of a Marlboro?"

He watched her try to flick the inch and a half of ash into an ashtray and miss. Suzy shook her head and tossed back her long tawny hair, narrowly avoiding setting fire to it.

"Come on, you know what I'm talking about. Perspiring — no, no, *con*spiring to pervert the course of justice . . . that's what I did, wasn't it?" Oh, it was so easy to repent your sins when you knew you weren't going to be punished! "Oh, Officer, how can I ever make it up to you?"

Harry grinned. "Let me just check something out first. Are you married?"

"Me, Officer? Crikey, no." Swaying a bit, Suzy located her almost-empty glass on the table and solemnly held it up. "Totally single, that's me, Officer. As single as this tequila."

"In that case," said Harry, "you could always come out to dinner with me tomorrow night."

Yes, yes, yes!

Triumphantly knocking back the last few lukewarm drops of her drink — *clunk* — Suzy congratulated herself on an excellent result. It was like selling a fabulous house within hours of it going on the market. *But this is even better,* she thought happily. *A date within a matter of* minutes. *Damn, I'm good.*

Uh-oh. Lifting the empty glass up to the light, she realized that her mouth was no longer leaving prints around the rim. And if her lipstick had worn off, that meant her face had more than likely gone shiny too. Not to mention her hair being in need of a damn good brushing.

Basically, it was time for her midevening tidy up.

"You know what I hate?" Harry's head was tilted to one side, his tone conversational. "I hate it when I ask a beautiful girl out to dinner and she doesn't say anything.

18

Just stares at her glass. So do I take that as a no?"

"Wait here." Suzy reached for her bag. "Don't go away, don't move a muscle." By way of explanation she waggled her fingers in the direction of the ladies' room, which was out in the hall by the reception desk.

"I don't even know your name," Harry protested. "At least tell me that much." He looked worried as Suzy moved toward the double doors. "You're not going to run out on me, are you? Do that Cinderella thing and disappear?"

What, leave behind one of her beloved black patent Manolos? Was he joking? They'd cost a fortune!

"I'll be back in two minutes." Suzy blew him a kiss. "Promise."

She'd been right about the shine factor. Relieved that at least her eye makeup was still intact, Suzy pulled out her makeup case and began to repair the damage. Matte powder first, to restore much-needed order to her hectic complexion. Lipstick next — no lip brush, she couldn't be bothered with all that — then a slick of lip gloss for that extra-pouty finish. Lip gloss was a nightmare, of course, if you were planning on kissing someone, because (a) all men cringe at the very thought of it, and (b) if they do manage to overcome their fear, you both invariably end up with glossy chins.

Suzy rolled it on anyway because (a) it looked sexy, and (b) she had no intention of kissing Harry this evening.

I might be a bit drunk, she thought with pride, *but I can still play hard to get.*

Oh no, let him wait.

Until tomorrow night, at least.

The door to the ladies' room crashed open less than a minute later. Suzy, bent double in front of the ornate gilded mirror, vigorously spraying the roots of her just-brushed hair with hair spray to give it oomph — and experiencing a bit of a head rush — let out a shriek, as for the second time that evening she was grabbed unexpectedly from behind.

So to speak.

Heavens, it was like déjà vu, only really happening. Except this time the hands doing the grabbing were bigger, hairier, and . . . um, there appeared to be quite a few of them.

"One, two, three, *heave,*" bawled one of the crew from Slade and Matthews. Rather ungallantly, Suzy felt. The walls of the bathroom began to spin as she was thrown over a burly shoulder.

"Right, I've got her. Mike, you bring her bag. Si, get the door open. Hold on, my lovely, you're coming with us."

"Don't want to," Suzy gasped, her out-of-control hair flopping over her face as she clung on for dear life.

"No choice, darling. Truth or Dare, that's the game, and this is what we were dared to do."

Si held the door open. Denzil, Suzy's kidnapper, propelled her through the doorway. Mike brought up the rear, clutching her handbag in one hand and the can of hair spray in the other.

Suzy, jiggling up and down on Denzil's sturdy shoulder as they raced through the lobby, panted, "You don't understand, I have to go b-back. I'm in the middle of arranging a d-d-dinner date."

They were outside the hotel now, heading up Princess Victoria Street and attracting curious glances from passersby. Suzy prayed her panties weren't on display.

Denzil gave her bottom a reassuring pat.

"With a policeman. We know, Rory told us. That's why we had to kidnap you, darling. To save you from yourself."

"But he's g-gorgeous!"

"He's not; he's a traffic cop." Denzil was scornful. "Imagine if you married him. He'd

21

arrest you every time you squeezed the toothpaste tube in the middle, or left a tea bag on the side of the sink."

"You don't understand," wailed Suzy. "He's not like all the others. And he has these incredible blue eyes."

They had reached the Clifton Wine Bar, where a tremendous Friday night party was in progress. Still carrying Suzy in a fireman's lift, Denzil pushed his way into the noisy, heaving throng.

"You stay here with us, darling. Trust me, it's for the best. Never tangle with policemen; they've all got a thing about handcuffs." By way of consolation, presumably, he patted her bottom once more before lowering her — somewhat bumpily — to ground level. "Besides, think what it'd do to your street cred."

They were joined minutes later by Rory, Martin, and Donna.

"Was he still there when you left?" With her free hand, Suzy clutched her brother's arm. The other remained firmly locked in Denzil's grasp.

"Who, the boy in blue?" No great drinker, Rory was as befuddled after two pints of lager as the rest of them after ten. "I think he might have been." He frowned at Suzy. "Why, was he bothering you?"

"He was asking me out!"

Brothers, honestly. Sometimes couldn't you just kick them?

Rory grimaced sympathetically and gave her shoulder a clumsy consoling pat.

"Bad luck. Still, never mind, we didn't tell anyone where we were going. He'll never find us."

Denzil's hand remained clamped around Suzy's wrist for the next hour.

Until nature called.

"If you think you're dragging me into the men's bathroom with you," Suzy told him, "well, you're just not, OK?"

Denzil pulled a twenty-pound note out of his wallet.

"Be an angel and get the next round, then." He broke into a slow, leery smile. "Hey, you're gorgeous, you know that?"

"Yes."

"What are you doing working for that brother of yours, when you could be working for us?"

"Denzil, I like it there."

"Fancy being headhunted?"

"No," Suzy said patiently.

"Come on, you know you're crazy about me. We'd be fantastic together."

"I'm fantastic where I am, thanks."

Nature was by this time hammering on

the windows and bellowing through a megaphone, demanding to be taken notice of.

"I'm breaking my neck here," Denzil told her — romantic or what? "Go order some drinks, there's a good girl. I'll be back in no time at all."

It was a good thing he was a real estate agent and not a prison officer, thought Suzy as she slipped out of the wine bar and hurried back down Princess Victoria Street, her high heels clacking on the cobbles like castanets.

Please be there. Please, please *still be there . . .*

But, of course, when she reached the bar at the Avon Gorge Hotel, he wasn't.

CHAPTER 2

The funeral of Blanche Curtis, mother of Rory, Julia, and Suzy, was arranged to take place at Canford Crematorium in Westbury-on-Trym at midday on the last Tuesday in August.

Two days before the funeral, Jaz Dreyfuss — Suzy's ex-husband — said, "Would you like me to come?"

"Can if you want." Suzy shrugged. "But she didn't like you."

"Of course she didn't like me. You'd never have married me if she had." Jaz broke into a grin. "You always told me it was your ambition in life to run off with a man your mother would really hate."

Suzy was standing on a chair in the middle of her sitting room, surveying her reflection in the mirror above the fireplace and waiting for Fee to finish pinning up the hem of her dress.

"Poor old Blanche, what a way to go," said

Jaz. "Wherever she is now, I bet she's furious."

This was true. The same thought had occurred to Suzy. After a lifetime hooked on adventure, Blanche would surely have had her heart set on a death with more pizazz to it. More oomph. Waterskiing down the Amazon, maybe, then being ambushed and gobbled up by crocodiles. Or crashing out of the sky in a hot-air balloon and plunging into an Alpine crevasse.

As a way of dying, either of these would have been far more Blanche's style.

Anything would have done, basically, so long as it was colorful and dramatic and had panache.

Except it hadn't happened that way at all. Instead, Blanche Curtis had succumbed peacefully, at home, to a massive coronary in her sleep. Not a crocodile or an icy abyss in sight.

"There, all done." Fee spoke through a mouthful of pins. "Take it off carefully, and I'll hem it for you."

"You're an angel." Suzy was deeply grateful. Show her a house and she could sell it, but sewing was one of life's mysteries. And while Blanche would definitely approve of the red velvet dress she had bought especially for the funeral, she was liable to start

26

pounding on the lid of the coffin in outrage if Suzy turned up at the cemetery in a skirt that was an unflattering length.

As Suzy peeled off the dress and passed it to Fee, the front door banged.

Leaping down from her chair, Suzy looked joyfully at Jaz and yelled, "Maeve's back!"

Moments later, the sitting room door was flung open, and Maeve McCourt, her wet-look purple raincoat glistening with rain, appeared in the doorway. She held out her arms and declared, "My poor baby, come here!"

Suzy was across the room in a flash, hugging Jaz's housekeeper and being hugged in return until they were both out of breath.

"Look at you, practically naked in your bra and panties," Maeve chided. She reached into her vast purple shoulder bag and whisked out a family-size box of Kleenex. "Crying your eyes out and getting rain all over yourself from my raincoat — that's a sure way to come down with pneumonia. There, there, my darling, you cry as much as you want to. Just make sure you've got something warm on first."

"This isn't a bra and panties," said Suzy, wiping her eyes and sniffing loudly. It was actually a white Donna Karan cropped tank top and matching micro shorts. "And I'm only crying because I'm glad to see you."

It was true. These were the first tears she'd shed since learning of Blanche's death. Slightly guiltily, Suzy realized that she was closer to Maeve than she'd ever been to her own mother. If anything should happen to Maeve, she would be distraught.

"Let's get you out of this." Amid much creaking of plastic, Jaz helped with the removal of the coat. "Why don't you two sit down and have a chat about things? Was it a good vacation then, Maeve?"

Maeve, who had been visiting her enormous extended family in Dublin, gazed fondly at Jaz and said, "Great, love. The very best. I'll tell you all about it later. Are you two off now?"

Fee and Jaz were both heading tactfully for the door. Fee held up the red velvet dress.

"Have to finish this."

"And I've got a meeting," said Jaz. "I'll be back by eight."

There was no need to elaborate; they knew the kind of meeting Jaz meant.

"Good lad." Maeve nodded approvingly, knowing full well that it drove him mad.

"Don't do that." Jaz sighed. "If you call me a good lad again, I shall have to hit you."

"Hah," said Maeve, winking at Suzy and

28

Fee. "I'd like to see you try."

"You should have let me know about Blanche earlier," Maeve scolded when the other two had left. "You know I'd have come straight back."

"And ruined your break." Suzy gave her a look. "That's exactly why we didn't tell you. I've been fine, really." She smiled. "Still, I'm glad you're here now."

Maeve gave her another perfect hug, the kind Suzy had spent so much of her childhood missing out on. This one lasted for several minutes, which was heavenly and just what she needed.

At last, Maeve broke away and said cheerily, "Now then, my darling, I picked you out a little present this morning! Just a little something to cheer you up."

You could love someone to bits, Suzy had long ago discovered, yet still inwardly cringe when they opened their mouths and certain words came trilling out. Mentally, she braced herself, while Maeve bent over her bag and got down to some serious rummaging. Maeve's passion for thrift shops wasn't so much the problem as her tragic taste in "little presents," which she bought at the drop of an orange knit cap.

"Maeve, you shouldn't have," said Suzy,

although this was advice that Maeve — sadly — continued to ignore.

"Nonsense! The moment I spotted it, I knew it was right up your alley." Maeve gave her a kiss and watched with pride as the tissue paper fell away.

It was a brooch. A huge Perspex brooch with a photograph of a young Donny Osmond inside. Donny was baring his teeth in one of those unforgettable Osmond smiles and holding out a bunch of red roses that looked suspiciously fake.

Fresh tears pricked the back of Suzy's eyes. She was touched by the gesture but still mystified.

Why? Why is this brooch right up my street?

"Doesn't he have the most gorgeous eyes?" Maeve said happily. "It was like fate, I'm telling you, finding it there in that shop."

"Fate . . . ?"

"Sure, and weren't you only telling me last week about that policeman fellow you thought was the bee's knees? What was it you said at the time?" Maeve raised her eyebrows, willing her to remember. When Suzy shrugged and shook her head, she went on. "You said he had a pair of eyes to die for, gorgeous blue eyes, so you see, I thought at once it was the perfect omen." She held up one finger. "And then the rest of it began to fall into place."

"Go on," said Suzy, fairly sure that Donny and his five hundred brothers had had big *brown* eyes. Not that she was old enough to remember.

"OK, so now, Donny Osmond was a pop star, and you're crazy about pop stars!" As she held up a second finger, Maeve was triumphant. "Wouldn't you call that another omen?"

"I'm crazy about pop stars?"

"Hey, you married Jaz, didn't you?"

So that was what that bit was about. Suzy hid a smile. Something else that drove Jaz mad was being called a pop star.

But she could see that Maeve was bursting to tell her the third omen.

"I married Jaz. Of course I did. What else, Maeve?"

"Look what he's holding! Red roses! And here's you all ready to bury your mother!"

"I didn't order red roses for her wreath," said Suzy.

"Ah, but you'll be wearing that red velvet dress, though, won't you?" Maeve clapped her hands together, delighted with her own foresight. "And don't the roses in the brooch exactly match the color of the dress? I'm telling you, they'll go together like a dream."

That was it. Suzy knew she'd have to wear the brooch. It was like a mother being given a badge to wear by her five-year-old, bearing the message: *World's Greatest Mommy!!!* All you could do was pin it on, cross your fingers, and pray — hard — that everyone would understand.

"I love it." She gave Maeve another hug. "And I love you."

"I'll make us a cup of tea, and you can tell me everything," said Maeve. Sternly, she added, "As soon as you've put some clothes on."

"But I'm not cold," protested Suzy.

"It's not proper, dancing about in your drawers in front of Jaz."

"I wasn't dancing. And they're not drawers. Anyway, I swim in Jaz's pool in a bikini, and you don't kick up a fuss about that."

"Completely different," Maeve declared.

"Completely daft, if you ask me."

"Look, you don't see Fee running around half naked in front of Jaz, do you? Because it isn't right, that's why. It's called observing the proprieties," said Maeve. "And not acting like a wanton trollop."

"Maeve, you know how fond I am of Fee. She's been great to me, and I love her to bits. But we have exactly one thing in common, and that's that many moons ago we were both silly enough to marry Jaz. Admit it," said Suzy. "Apart from that, we're not what you'd call alike."

Maeve glanced pointedly at her tanned breasts, spilling over the low-cut Donna Karan sports top. "You mean you're a wanton trollop and she's not."

At the age of eighteen, Jaz Dreyfuss had rented a garage from Fee's father. He and his band needed somewhere to practice without being yelled at every ten minutes to turn it down. The garage was over a hundred yards from the house, and Fee's father was as deaf as a post, so the amount of noise they made didn't bother him in the least.

It had driven Fee to distraction, their pounding beats totally drowning out her beloved Enya tapes, but since Jaz and his fellow band members were paying for the use of the garage, she could hardly complain. And although she'd only seen him from a distance, she couldn't help thinking that the lead singer — Jaz, of course — didn't look too bad at all. In a scruffy, long-haired, multi-earringed kind of way.

Unable to concentrate on her own gentler music, and easily distracted from the banking exams for which she was supposed to be studying, it wasn't long before Fee found herself wandering across to the garage while the guys practiced. Once you got used to their brand of heavy rock, some of the songs weren't bad. Sometimes she took mugs of coffee over for them, wrapping the handles around her fingers like brass knuckles and spilling half the contents before she even reached the garage, but refusing to use a tray because the one time she'd tried it, Ken, the drummer, had put on his I'm-the-Queen voice and trilled, "Ay say, a tray, how frightfully *naice.*"

Jaz had been the only one who hadn't fallen over laughing. While Fee had blushed furiously, he'd flicked back his long blond hair and said sympathetically, "Ignore them. They're pitiful. Just a bunch of ignorant cretins."

She had fallen helplessly in love with him on the spot.

During the months that followed, Fee made herself indispensable to the band. She became a one-woman café, providing bacon sandwiches and endless mugs of tea. She lugged amplifiers into and out of the van, cleared away the empty lager cans, and painstakingly sewed the band's new name — Fireball — on to the backs of their denim jackets in flame-like shades of red, orange, and ocher. She also spent hours sticking up

34

the posters she had designed herself, promoting forthcoming gigs in and around Bristol.

"It's embarrassing," Ken complained one night, after a sell-out performance at the Pig and Whistle. "We're a hard rock band, and we've got a roadie who looks like a Girl Guide." He gestured at Fee in her crisply ironed blouse and sensible skirt, her glasses glinting as she haggled with the pub manager over their fee. "I mean, she's a bank clerk, for Chrissake. How rock and roll is that?"

"Some bloke last week asked me if she was our groupie." Vince, the bass guitarist, joined in. "Jaz, I'm serious, she's fucking up our image. People are starting to mock us."

"You ungrateful bastards. What's the matter with you?" Jaz was fairly drunk, but he defended Fee as he always did. "We'd be nowhere without her. She's keeping this show on the road practically single-handed."

"Don't tell me you fancy her," jeered Vince.

"Of course not," lied Jaz. Because he did, quite. "I'm just saying, she does a bloody good job."

It was Jaz's dream to become famous, so it became Fee's dream too. But instead of trusting to luck like the rest of the band, who felt that — rather like love at first sight — being spotted and signed to a label should somehow just miraculously happen, Fee sent copies of Fireball's six best songs to every A&R manager at every record company in London and told them that if they thought the tape was good, they should see the band playing live.

SellOut Records signed up Fireball a fortnight later.

"Makes a change from the van, doesn't it?" said Jaz, arriving at Fee's house the following evening in a chauffeur-driven white limo. "C'mon then, are we going out on the town or what?"

"You've arranged all this for me?" Running her fingers through her dark red hair, her eyes like saucers, Fee was both astonished and overjoyed.

Jaz grinned and took her trembling hand. "Why not? You're worth it."

"Where are we going?"

"Bloody everywhere, seeing as it cost me eighty quid and now I'm broke." Jaz was rueful. "That's the trouble with these record companies, they don't shower you with money the moment you sign the contract. Sadly, you have to earn it first."

They drove down to Burnham-on-Sea, ate fish and chips and drank Blackthorn Cider

— paid for by Fee — in the back of the limo, and later made love among the sand dunes, while the chauffeur stayed in the car and listened to Radio 2.

It was the happiest night of Fee's life. Having spent the last six months being quietly envious of the miniskirted girls who flocked around Jaz and all too often disappeared into the back of the van with him, she now knew that what she'd been missing out on all this time was every bit as wonderful as she'd imagined.

Even if the sand was a bit . . . well, sandy.

"I can't believe this is happening," Fee whispered afterward, lying back and gazing up at the stars.

"Me neither. We're going to be the biggest band in the world." Jaz reached for the bottle of Blackthorn he had brought along with him. "And it's all thanks to you."

This wasn't quite what she'd meant, but Fee didn't mind. Tears of happiness filled her eyes.

"I love you." There, she'd said it. She knew she wasn't supposed to, but who cared?

"We could be playing Wembley before Christmas. Imagine jetting off around the world — hearing your stuff on the radio . . . going to the same parties as Bono."

Fee bit her lip. She really wished she hadn't said it now. A cool breeze swept across her bare legs, breaking her out in goose bumps.

"What? You've gone quiet," said Jaz. He put his warm hand on her thigh. "Don't you think it'll be great?"

"Oh, yes."

"Aren't you excited?" Frowning, he half sat up. "Don't you like Bono?"

"Does it matter if I do or not? I'm not going to be the one meeting him." Tipping her head away so he couldn't see, Fee wiped her eyes. "But I'm excited for you, really I am."

With his fingers on her chin, Jaz gently tilted her face back toward him.

"Why are you crying? Do you think I did this tonight for a bet, or something?"

"No. Well, not a bet, exactly. But maybe as a kind of thank-you," admitted Fee.

"As in, thank you for getting us a record deal?" Jaz smiled down at her. "Oh dear. You must have a pretty low opinion of me."

"Wrong," said Fee. "I have a high opinion of you and a low one of me."

He couldn't bear to think of her being unhappy. They owed her everything. And she was worth twenty of the blond mini-skirted bimbos who eyed him so hungrily

38

each time he stepped onto the stage.

"Well, stop it." Jaz stroked her dark red hair away from her face. "You're my girl-friend now. You and me, we're a couple. A team."

He meant it too. The more people sneered and said it wouldn't last, the more absolutely determined Jaz became to make sure it did. And when Fireball's first single rocketed to the top of the charts, he celebrated by drinking a bottle of Jack Daniel's and asking Fee to marry him. Fee, no longer working at the bank, busied herself finding them somewhere to live. With the money that had started to roll in, they acquired a huge Victorian town house on Sian Hill in Clifton, with stunning views over the Suspension Bridge and the Avon Gorge. The neighbors, a retired army colonel and his wife, were horrified when they discovered who was moving in next door to them. They were even more horrified when Jaz and Fee held a housewarming party for five hundred guests, and the colonel found a couple of dozen passed out in his garden the next morning.

In the three years that followed, Fireball had another four number-one singles, plus two chart-topping albums. The parties got wilder, and Jaz's drinking spiraled out of control. When Fee tried to tell him to slow down, he called her a spoilsport. When she threatened to leave him, he gazed at her through bloodshot eyes and said coldly, "Don't lecture me. I'm not a kid."

The colonel and his wife had had enough. They put their house on the market, but by this time, Jaz's exploits were so legendary that nobody else wanted to buy it.

"He's going to sue you," said Fee, reading the letter from their neighbors' lawyer, "for devaluing his property."

It was ten o'clock in the morning, and Jaz was drinking Stolichnaya, poured into a can of 7UP so that Fee wouldn't notice and start nagging again.

He closed his eyes. "How can I get this bloke off my back?"

"You could buy the house," Fee suggested.

Would that solve all his problems? Somewhat hazily, Jaz decided that it would.

"OK, let's do it. You sort it out."

On their fourth wedding anniversary, and at her wits' end, Fee gave him her ultimatum.

"You're always drunk. I can't carry on like this. Either you sort yourself out or I'm leaving you."

"Nag nag nag." Jaz sighed. "And you

wonder why I'd rather be with my friends than with you."

Trembling, Fee stood her ground. "You're killing yourself. Will you stop drinking? Please?"

He pulled a face. Why did she always have to *do* this? "I don't want to stop. I'm having fun."

Looking down at Jaz in bed, Fee said sadly, "Are you sure?"

Fee moved out of the house . . . and into the one next door. This raised a few eyebrows, but since it suited her purposes and was convenient, she ignored them and carried on regardless. To occupy herself, she set about having the place converted into luxury apartments.

Jaz, vaguely put out by his wife's defection, decided she'd only done it to annoy him. To get his own back, he taunted her with a succession of groupies, pretty young girls with bleached blond hair and adoring smiles.

"If you're trying to make me jealous," Fee told him wearily one day, "it isn't working. I feel sorry for them, and I feel sorry for you. I certainly don't feel sorry for me."

CHAPTER 3

Curtis and Co., Real Estate Agents, occupied a prime position in the heart of Clifton. With ten minutes to spare before her next appointment, Suzy was perched on the edge of her desk licking the icing off a white chocolate éclair from Charlotte's Patisserie when Jaz stuck his head around the door.

"Is that how you recruit your customers nowadays?" He grinned and waved briefly at Donna, tap-tapping away at her computer.

"Certainly is." Suzy bit into the éclair. Her eyes sparkled as she licked cream from her fingers. "Want to buy a house, sir?"

"Thanks, but I've got plenty already, what with me being so rich."

"You can never have too many houses, sir."

"Go on then, I'll take a dozen," said Jaz. "Actually, I'm on my way to the gym. Maeve asked me to drop by and invite you over for dinner tonight. She's doing one of her specials."

Suzy raised a skeptical eyebrow. "Maeve *asked* you?"

"OK, slip of the tongue. She told me. And you aren't invited around, you're coming around," Jaz amended. "Seven o'clock, don't be late." He paused. "You all right?"

The funeral was tomorrow. Hence Maeve's concern, bless her. Suzy nodded.

"I'm fine."

"Actually, you're not," he told her cheerfully. "You've got icing on your chin."

"Now I remember why I divorced you," said Suzy, picking a pen off her desk and throwing it at him.

"I've worked here for six months now," said Donna when Jaz had left, "and I still don't know how you two first met."

"No? It was all thanks to my mother actually. Which annoyed her no end." Suzy crossed one leg over the other and jiggled a high heel. "We were in the car having this massive argument, and I jumped out. As you do. So she drove off and left me, like a lemon, at the side of the road."

"Where were you?" Donna interrupted, clearly trying to picture the scene.

"On the M4. Somewhere between Reading and Swindon."

"God, the *highway* . . ."

"Anyhow, I was crying my eyes out. My shoes were still in the car, and I didn't know what on earth I was going to do next. Then a white Porsche pulled up ahead of me and Jaz got out. He was on his way back from London — it was pretty miraculously one of his sober days — and he asked me if I'd broken down. So I howled for a bit and told him all about the fight with my mother, and he offered me a lift home."

"Cool," said Donna, impressed. "Nothing like that ever happens to me."

"So on the way back, he found out that I lived in Bristol too, only a couple of miles from him. And he was so sweet, when I kept blubbing and saying I never wanted to see my hateful mother again, he offered to take me back to his place until I'd calmed down."

"Double cool." Donna sighed. "And then I guess he just seduced you."

Suzy's smile was wry. "Well, I like to think I seduced him, but what can I tell you? I was eighteen." She shrugged. "I *thought* I was in love with Jaz Dreyfuss."

"Weren't you?"

"Lust." Suzy paused, struggling to be honest. "Or more likely in love with the idea of getting out of my mother's house for good."

Mystified, Donna said, "Couldn't you

have just moved into a studio apartment?"

"I could have, but it wouldn't have irritated her nearly so much."

Donna was struggling to find a speck of romance among the debris. "But you liked him, surely?"

"Oh, of course I did, I fancied him rotten." Smiling, Suzy remembered that feeling in the pit of her stomach, like an aviary full of hummingbirds. "He was lovely to me, he was gorgeous-looking, he was rich and a famous rock star . . . crikey, who wouldn't?"

"And he liked you." Donna was hopeful.

"Oh, he liked me all right. Almost as much as he liked drinking."

"Was it really awful? I can't imagine what he was like."

"Jaz?" Suzy paused; this was something else she remembered only too clearly. "Well, he drank. And drank. And drank and drank and drank. And then he drank some more. What you have to understand is that back then I was quite innocent in that respect. I'd never known an alcoholic before. For a while, I didn't realize how bad it actually was. Half the time, I just thought he was lying around unconscious because he was a rock star and . . . basically, that's what rock stars *do.*"

Donna blinked her heavily mascaraed

eyelashes. "And then you married him."

"I was nineteen. People shouldn't be allowed to marry when they're nineteen and hell-bent on getting back at their mothers. They should have pretend marriages," said Suzy, "like little kids have pretend shops, with Monopoly money and packets of candies and little plastic tills that go *ding.*"

"It must have been glamorous, though," Donna persisted. "Jetting off all over the world, brilliant vacations, meeting famous people."

Suzy gave her a you-must-be-joking look.

"There's nothing glamorous about living with a drunk. It wears you down. And it drives you absolutely mad, knowing that it *could* be brilliant, if only he didn't drink. Jaz was lovely when he was sober," Suzy said sadly. "I can't tell you how many fights we had about it. One night I actually got down on my knees and *begged* him to stop. I'd booked him into a clinic, the taxi was waiting outside, and Maeve was threatening to carry him down three flights of stairs and throw him into it . . ."

"And?"

"He refused to go. We couldn't force him. It was hopeless."

"So you left him," said Donna.

Suzy nodded.

"A week later, I'd had enough. However I felt about Jaz, I couldn't live with him anymore. Oh, and you should have heard Julia and my mother. Between them, they must have said 'told you so' at least a million times. Worst of all, they automatically assumed I'd go running home to them. Tuh, I'd rather have stuck needles in my eyes than do that." Suzy shuddered. "Anyway, I was pretty miserable, as you can imagine. So I moved in next door, into the apartment above Fee's. She was brilliant."

"And Jaz stopped drinking," said Donna.

"Good grief no, nothing so flattering." Suzy swung her legs, idly drumming her heels against the side of the desk and pushing back her hair. "If anything, he drank *more.* So that was it, our marriage was over, and I was single again. I went out on a few dates, half hoping it would make him jealous and kick-start him into getting his act together, but he was beyond all that. He couldn't have cared less." She paused and checked her watch; the client was late. "Anyhow, six months later, I'd started seeing this guy named Marcus, and one night, we bumped into Jaz in the bar at the Avon Gorge. He said he was glad I was happy and didn't I think it was about time we got a divorce? And Marcus said he thought that

47

was a great idea, so Jaz put his lawyers onto it. He told me he had to go over to the States for a couple of months to work on an album but that by the time he got back, it would be all done. We didn't fight about money," Suzy explained. "It was all very amicable. So Jaz disappeared, the divorce went through, and ten weeks later, he came back . . . and that was when we found out he hadn't been working on an album at all. He'd booked himself into detox without telling a soul — some clinic in the middle of the Nevada desert. And he did it," said Suzy. "He actually did it. And he hasn't had a drink since."

"Just like that," Donna marveled, her kohl-rimmed eyes wide. "Easy."

"Not easy at all. But he'd made the decision for himself, without being bullied and blackmailed into it. And look at him now. If there was anyone I'd have said could never do it in a million years, it'd be Jaz. But he did."

"And what happened to Marcus?"

"Oh, *him*." Suzy's tone was dismissive. "He was only after me for my alimony. I chucked him a couple of months after Jaz got back."

"Weren't you ever tempted? You know, to try again with Jaz?"

"There was never really the opportunity." Sighing, Suzy said, "It wasn't long before he developed that malignant growth on his arm."

Donna's eyes almost popped out.

"Malignant growth? I didn't know he had a malignant growth!"

Suzy pulled a face at her. "I'm talking about Celeste."

The weird thing about putting a funeral notice in the paper was not having the faintest idea who would turn up. It was like sticking up posters advertising a rave, thought Suzy, and waiting to see what happened . . . Would the place be besieged by ten thousand teenagers ready to party, or would five grungy hippies pile out of a van, mumbling, "Hey, man. Like, where's the action?"

Still, there'd been a pretty decent turnout today. The chapel was full and no grungy hippies had turned up, which had to count as a bonus.

Not that this had cheered up Julia, her incredibly proper older sister, who could always be relied on to find something new to be offended about. Although, strictly speaking, Suzy amended, the thing currently upsetting her wasn't new at all; it must be thirty years old at least.

Behind them the rest of the mourners sang "All Things Bright and Beautiful." According to Julia, this had been one of their mother's favorite hymns. Next to her in the front pew, Suzy knew, Julia was casting furious sidelong glances at her, tanned and voluptuous in her skin-tight red velvet dress.

"For heaven's sake," she hissed agitatedly between verses, "take it *off.*"

"I can't," Suzy whispered back. Now, which would bother her most? "There's a big jam stain underneath."

"Cover it up, then. With your jacket. Otherwise, everyone's going to think you've gone mad."

"It's my mother's funeral, and I can wear whatever I like." Suzy gave her Donny Osmond badge a reassuring pat and glanced over her shoulder at Maeve and Jaz, several pews behind.

"Stop *ogling.*" Julia gave her a sharp dig in the ribs. "You're not a Japanese tourist."

"I haven't the faintest idea who some of these people are," Suzy marveled. As the organist led them with a flourish into the final verse, she peered past Maeve, trying to make out the features of a shadowy figure standing right at the back of the chapel, next to the double doors.

All Suzy could see was someone in a big trilby-style hat and a long dark coat. The hat was tilted forward at such an angle that it wasn't even possible to tell whether the mourner was male or female. Deeply frustrated, Suzy resisted the urge to stick her fingers in her mouth and give a shrill whistle, forcing whoever it was to look up. Anyway, she didn't need to do that, the service was almost over. Any minute now they'd all be filing outside and Thingy-in-the-Trilby would be lining up to shake her hand and offer the usual condolences.

And learning who they were was bound to be a big letdown anyway, like unwrapping a thrilling-looking Christmas present and discovering it was a vacuum cleaner. If Trilby's a man, Suzy decided, he'll turn out to be one of Blanche's hairdressers. If it's a woman, she'll be someone who once worked in the local convenience store.

". . . the Lord God made them *all,*" bellowed the vicar, concluding the final chorus. There was a moment of silence, broken only by one of Julia's semi-stifled sobs, then the organist began to play something altogether more subdued, and the vicar held a solicitous arm out to his front row, indicating that they should lead the way out.

Rory went first. Then Julia, dabbing at her

eyes with a black lace-trimmed handkerchief. Suzy, last out of the pew, found it hard to believe it was still possible to buy handkerchiefs edged with black lace. Julia must have trimmed the damn thing herself.

Then she cheered up, diverted by the thought that now she could start matching up faces with who had been who in her mother's life.

That middle-aged woman over there, for instance, noisily blowing her nose . . . Ah, yes, seen her before. She's a member of the bridge club.

And what about that young, rather good-looking guy hovering next to the fire exit? Hang on, wasn't it her mother's milkman? Good heavens, was it usual for milkmen to attend their customers' funerals?

And *sob*?

Oh well, that was Blanche for you, thought Suzy as she progressed slowly down the aisle. People who didn't know her that well thought she was great; she'd always been far better at cultivating new friendships than old ones.

Ah, they'd reached the double doors. Suzy searched rapidly among the stragglers at the back for Trilby.

Without success.

Whoever was under that dashing hat had

already gone.

The post-funeral gathering, held at Blanche's house in Sneyd Park, went on well into the evening.

"That bridge club of mother's can certainly put it away," Rory told Suzy as he squeezed past, armed with fresh supplies of Scotch.

Suzy discovered Julia panicking in the kitchen. To cheer her up, Suzy said, "Have you seen Margot from across the street chatting up Mum's lawyer? Honestly, that woman's not safe to be let out."

"I can't find any oven gloves. Where does Mummy keep the oven gloves?" Julia, stressed out and tearful, was counting the minutes before she could take her next Valium. "The vol-au-vents are burning, and I can't get them out of the oven, and I just want everyone to go home and leave us in peace."

Poor Julia. The funeral had been a huge ordeal for her, Suzy realized. As well as the grief, there was all the funeral etiquette to be abided by.

"Come on, sit down." Feeling sorry for her elder sister, Suzy steered her gently onto a chair, poured her a glass of wine, and switched off the oven. "Don't worry about the food; they've had more than enough. I'm going to start kicking everyone out now. And there's no reason why Douglas *has* to read the will tonight — we'll send him home and schedule a meeting at his office for the end of the week."

Douglas Hepworth came into the kitchen with Rory at that moment. Having overheard her words, he blinked nervously at Suzy from behind his owlish glasses and made the mini shrugging gesture he always made when he was anxious about something.

"Ah, to be honest, I'd rather get it sorted out tonight. Your mother specifically requested it . . . Ummm, there is a reason . . ."

More mini shrugs. Suzy decided it was his way of unsticking his polyester shirt from his plump, perspiring shoulders. Douglas wore the look of someone who'd really rather not be here this evening. Clearly, something was up. Determined to go out with a bang, Blanche had no doubt made some weird arrangements for her estate. Suzy could just imagine the terms and conditions her mother would have had such fun compiling. If Julia wanted to inherit her share of the money, for instance, she'd first have to roller-skate naked down Park Street . . . and Rory would have to drive around Clifton in a battered truck, wearing a knit cap and gorilla slippers . . .

Or would Mum make me do that?

Then again, maybe it wasn't anything to do with terms and conditions. It could be Douglas's unhappy task to inform them that they weren't getting anything at all, that their mother had left the lot to a tribe of Amazonian Indians.

Or a blind-donkey sanctuary.

Nothing was impossible where Blanche was concerned.

"It's nine o'clock." Rory checked his watch. "Suzy's right; they can start making a move."

"But that's so rude," wailed Julia.

"Has she not left us any money?" Suzy asked Douglas, who was also surreptitiously glancing at his watch.

"Oh, no . . . I mean, yes . . . don't worry." Shrug shrug. "It's nothing like that."

One of the butch bridge club women popped her head around the door.

"Any chance of another couple of bottles of single malt?"

Julia, the perfect hostess, wiped her eyes and rose obediently to her feet. Suzy placed a hand on her shoulder and guided her back down onto the chair.

"I'm so sorry, did you miss it?" She smiled

her most charming smile at the woman in the doorway. "We called last orders ten minutes ago. The bar's closed."

One by one the guests kissed and hugged everyone in sight, told one another they'd given Blanche a send-off she would have been proud of, stumbled into an assortment of cars and taxis, and roared off into the night.

"I'll make some coffee," said Rory when the last of them had been dispatched. He closed the front door and loosened his black tie.

"If you'd excuse me for just one moment," Douglas said damply, pulling his cell phone out of his pocket, "I need to make a quick call."

He retired discreetly to the conservatory. Julia, heaving a massive sigh of relief, said, "Give me five minutes to freshen up," and headed upstairs in the direction of the bathroom.

The air in the drawing room was opaque with cigarette smoke. When Suzy flung open the French windows, it tumbled out like an avalanche of ectoplasm. In contrast, the night air was cool and clear, and a light rain pattered down through the trees.

Kicking off her high heels, Suzy stepped

outside onto the paved terrace, felt the first raindrops land on her face and throat, and set off down the garden.

Just a quick circuit, to clear the industrial quantities of smoke from her lungs and brace herself for whatever Douglas had in store. And it gave her feet a chance to cool down too. It had, after all, been a long day spent in particularly ruthless stilettos.

In fact, now that she'd taken them off, her feet were so grateful they seemed to want to dance around like spring chickens.

Skip, skip.

Ah, that was better. You could almost say her feet were cock-a-hoop.

Skip, skip.

Free as birds, *skippety skip,* happy as — *CRUNCH.*

"Oh God oh God oh God," howled Suzy, feeling sick.

Cringing and holding her left foot as far away from the rest of her as possible, she hopped up and down on the path and hung on to the overhanging branch of a weeping cherry for support.

"What is it?" an alarmed voice blurted out of the darkness. A figure stepped out from behind the trunk of the cherry tree. "Are you hurt?"

A pair of warm hands grabbed hold of

Suzy's arms. Which was lucky. Otherwise, she would have keeled over in shock.

"I'm not hurt. I stepped on a snail." Suzy's heart was racing. "What about you? Are you a burglar?"

"No."

"Who then?"

A moment's silence. Broken by "Can't you guess?"

Baffled, Suzy said, "Of course I can't guess."

"OK, look, why don't we sort you out first?" It was a female voice, husky and awkward. "I'm sorry, but I can't concentrate on anything while you've got bits of snail stuck to your foot."

She had a point, whoever she was. Hopping around in the blackness, Suzy managed to unclip her suspender and peel off the sheer stocking in one go. Shuddering with revulsion, she flung it — snail remains and all — into a nearby hydrangea bush. Then, leaning back against the rough trunk of the cherry tree, she peered more closely at her intruder.

It was too dark to see her face, but there was certainly something familiar about the silhouette.

And the long coat.

"You were at the funeral this afternoon."

She saw the head dip in agreement. "Yes."

"You left before the end."

"That's right."

"Why?" Suzy was fascinated by the clicking noises made each time the girl nodded — what was she wearing, maracas for earrings? "And why didn't you come back to the house afterward with everyone else?"

"I didn't think I should."

"I'm sorry; I don't get this at all."

"I didn't want to cause any trouble, upset you any more than you were already . . . I mean, the last thing any of us needs is a big dramatic scene in front of an audience."

The girl's voice was unsteady, almost fearful. Totally flummoxed. Suzy ran through a few unlikely scenarios in her mind. Suddenly recalling the plot of a movie she had seen the other week, she exclaimed, "Good grief! Are you trying to tell me my mother was a *lesbian*?"

This question was greeted by an astonished silence. At least, Suzy hoped it was an astonished one. It was possible, of course, that it was the kind of disappointed silence emitted by someone who didn't expect you to guess the right answer so soon.

Eek, Blanche a lesbian. Surely not.

The mysterious clicking noises began again, but this time, the girl appeared to be shaking her head from side to side.

Well, that was a relief anyway.

"I can't believe this. You must know who I am."

"Well, I'm sorry," Suzy protested, "but what am I supposed to be — Psychic Suzy, Mind Reader Extraordinaire? Look, we could do it with charades if you want. You start with your name. First word, how many syllables? Hang on, somebody's coming . . ."

At the sound of approaching footsteps she swiveled around. The next moment a bright flashlight shined directly into her eyes. Dazzled and blinking, Suzy held up one hand to shield herself from the light.

And a stunned male voice said, "I don't believe it. *Jesus!*"

This situation was fast becoming too weird for words. Suzy felt her heart begin to flap like a parrot in a cage. She might be blinded by the flashlight, but she recognized that voice at once.

"Harry?" Shock made her babble. "Heavens, of all the gardens in all the world you had to walk into this one. Harry, I haven't the faintest idea what you're doing here, but you're interrupting a *really* important game of charades. You can be on my team, OK?"

This had to be some kind of elaborate

setup, Suzy decided. A ploy to meet her again. Unless . . . and bearing in mind that he was, after all, a policeman . . .

"Hang on, is this an undercover operation?" Suzy swung back to face the girl. "Do you work with Harry?" She smiled. "Or are you an international drug smuggler?"

Harry held up a phone.

"I've been waiting for you to come back to the car." He was addressing the girl, Suzy realized. "He just called a couple of minutes ago. It's time to go in."

Going in, that definitely had an undercover ring to it. Maybe the girl was a fellow officer after all.

Next to her, Suzy heard the girl take a deep breath.

"Right." She turned to face Suzy. "I'm Lucille."

"What?" Suzy mentally ran through the possibilities, charade-wise. Loo. Seal. Well, that would have been dead easy.

"Lucille Amory."

Suzy gazed blankly at her. It was clearly meant to mean something, but she couldn't for the life of her imagine what.

"I'm sorry, I'm usually terrific at names. Could you . . . ?"

"Your sister," Lucille said awkwardly.

Suzy laughed. "What?"

61

Her sister's name was Julia, for heaven's sake.

Harry, clearing his throat, said, "I think maybe we should go in."

CHAPTER 4

It wasn't until Suzy was standing aside to allow Lucille through the French windows ahead of her that she realized where the clicking had been coming from. Hundreds of tiny beads, threaded among the dozens of plaits in her hair, made contact with one another every time the girl moved her head.

Lucille's skin was the color of Taster's Choice made with double cream. Her eyes were chestnut brown. She looked nervous but stunning, like a young model making her debut on the catwalk.

"This is a joke, right?" Suzy glanced from Lucille to Harry and back again. "Did Jaz set this up?" Far-fetched, admittedly, but Jaz may have thought they could do with a practical joke to lighten the mood.

But if he had, wouldn't Lucille be screaming with laughter by now instead of trembling uncontrollably and looking as if she'd quite like to burst into tears?

She's got eyelashes like Bambi, thought Suzy. *Now how fair is that?*

The door was flung open, and Julia appeared. Her gaze shifted from Suzy's legs to Harry to Lucille. "Who are these people?"

Glancing down, Suzy remembered that she had one bare leg and one stockinged one. When she moved, she felt the redundant suspender flapping attractively against the back of her thigh.

"This is Lucille. Our sister, apparently. Technically, she's a half sister. And all this time we thought darling Daddy was such a saint. Oh well, good for him. That's what I say." Suzy paused briefly and gestured at Harry. "And this is Harry. He's a policeman. I'm afraid I don't have a clue what he's doing here. Unless, of course, he's our brother." Eek. "Oh God, you aren't, are you?"

Harry was giving her an odd look.

"Lucille's my friend. I'm just here to give her some moral support. Believe me, when we came here tonight, I had no idea I was going to see you."

"Daddy would never have an affair," Julia quavered, outraged. "*Never.* This girl's lying through her teeth!"

"Your father didn't have an affair," said Lucille. "Blanche was my mother. Look, I'm sorry; this isn't easy for me either." Catching her breath, she looked with ill-concealed longing at the drink clutched in Julia's thin hand. "I really thought you knew."

Suzy realized it was true the moment Douglas Hepworth broke the silence. Bustling past them into the drawing room with his briefcase clutched importantly in his pudgy hand, he ignored Julia's thunderstruck expression, plonked himself down in the leather armchair, and said brusquely to Lucille, "Good to see you, glad you could make it. Right then, if everyone's here, I'd like to begin."

It was will reading in the style of a smash and grab. Douglas, keen not to let himself become embroiled in the repercussions of finding out that one's family was . . . well, bigger than you'd always thought, confirmed in less than three minutes that Lucille Amory was indeed Blanche Curtis's daughter and that the estate was to be divided equally between her four children.

Then like Superman — *whoosh* — he was gone.

Well, thought Suzy, *like Superman, only fatter and without the red panties. Then again, who am I to talk, with one seven-denier barely black leg and one simply bare one? Talk about*

65

uncoordinated.

"This is ridiculous. I don't believe this is *happening,*" sobbed Julia.

"Me neither." Lucille laced her fingers together in her lap. "I mean, I wasn't exactly expecting a wild welcome, but . . ." Her voice trailed away.

"You hadn't expected to have to break the news to us yourself," Suzy supplied, feeling sorry for her. "Let's face it; it was pretty amazing news to have to break." Although it was, at the same time, absolutely typical of Blanche. "Ummm . . . if it isn't a rude question, how old are you?"

"Twenty-six. And a bit."

"You were born when I was eight." Rory had been the diary-keeping type as long as he'd been able to write. He thought for a moment. "Mother took off on one of her trips then. I remember she was away for six months."

"So much for adventuring through the South American jungle," Julia interjected bitterly. "She wasn't up the Amazon at all, was she? She was knocked up. Oh, for heaven's sake, Rory, are you going to fill up my glass or do I have to drink straight from the bottle?"

Suzy felt as if her brain had grown too big for her skull. There were a million questions to ask. "Where do you live?"

"Here." Lucille was clutching Harry's hand for support. "I mean, in Bristol. Bishopston."

Just a few miles away.

God, imagine!

"And you were adopted," said Suzy.

"No. My dad brought me up. Mum just . . . ummm, visited us every now and again."

"Your father's black?" Julia looked horrified.

"No, pale green. Of course he was black."

"Did *our* father know?" said Rory.

Lucille shook her head.

"But you thought we knew." Suzy was struggling to understand.

"I was curious. After your father died, I asked if I could meet you. Mum said she'd told you all about me" — her gaze flickered in Julia's direction — "but you decided it would be easier all around if we didn't meet."

Indignantly, Suzy said, "Well, that was a big lie. We hadn't any idea!"

"I'm sorry, I'm sorry. I just don't want this to be happening." Julia flapped her hands in distress. "We're talking about a whole double life here. Our mother has spent the last God knows how many years involved with a . . . a . . ."

"Black man," Lucille said evenly. "Dad came to this country from Mauritius thirty years ago."

"Couldn't be bothered to come to the funeral, though, could he?" Julia retaliated bitterly.

"That's because he's dead. Otherwise," said Lucille with a flash of spirit, "I'm sure he would have *bothered*."

"Look, I'm sorry about my sister." Suzy rushed to make amends. "She's a bit . . . you know. Cares a lot about what the neighbors think."

"Are you calling me a snob? I am *not* a snob." Julia was by this time quivering with outrage.

"Oh, yes you are." Suzy smiled at Lucille. "She is, she's horrendous. Julia tried to bribe a TV crew once because they'd caught her on camera coming out of Walmart. She almost died of shame when it appeared on the local news."

"I was taking a shortcut," Julia insisted through clenched teeth. "You can't seriously imagine I'd *buy* anything from Walmart."

Suzy beamed. "See what I mean?"

"This is ridiculous; we aren't here to discuss me." Julia seethed visibly; she hated being made fun of. "Let's face it, Lucille's here for one reason and one reason only. The moment she gets her hands on the money, that'll be it. We won't see her for dust, will we?"

This was what Julia clearly hoped would happen. Embarrassed by his sister's breathtaking insensitivity, Rory said awkwardly, "Hold on now. That's entirely up to Lucille."

"If that's what you want to happen," Lucille said stiffly, "then fine. It really isn't my mission in life to embarrass all of you and bring shame on your family." There was an edge to her voice as she uttered these last words. There were also tears in her eyes. Suzy impulsively reached for her arm as Lucille rose to leave.

"Please, you can't go. Julia doesn't mean to be rude." Well, she probably did. "It's been a shock, that's all. And I don't even know why any of us *are* shocked, because this is so bloody typical of Blanche. A bit of drama, a good old showdown — wasn't that all she ever wanted? So long as it was one where she wasn't around to take the flak."

"Don't you dare talk about her like that," Julia burst out. "You mustn't speak ill of the dead!"

"Why not? It's true. If she's watching us now, she'll be loving every minute of this.

And why *didn't* she tell us we had a sister?" Suzy demanded hotly.

Except they already knew the answer to that one. Julia's horrified reaction was all the proof they needed. Blanche had always reveled in being the center of attention, but only on condition that it showed her in a flattering light.

"And then she left." Suzy finished telling Jaz and Maeve the next morning, in the kitchen at Jaz's house. Reaching across the table, she helped herself to a handful of grapes. "It was a bit embarrassing actually. I tried to give her a hug to make up for Julia being such a cow and got one of my earrings caught up with some of the beads in her hair. Harry had to untangle us." She pulled a face. "And then it got more awkward because it felt like the end of a disastrous date. I asked Lucille for her phone number and she said, 'Look, you don't have to try to be nice. Why don't we just leave it to the lawyer to sort out.' "

"Sounds more like one of my disastrous marriages," Jaz observed with a grin.

"But I *do* want to see her again. I mean, imagine, all this time I've had a sister I didn't even know about! I always wanted a nice sister, not a bossy, neurotic older one

70

like Julia. And think what it must have been like for Lucille, growing up in the same city and thinking that we didn't want to meet her."

"What's she like?" Jaz looked interested.

"Beautiful."

"Nothing like you then."

Suzy kicked him efficiently under the table.

"Ouch."

"You know I'm gorgeous. She's just got it in a different way. Taller, thinner, real cheekbones, that kind of thing."

"And this Harry fellow — the one you were so keen on — he's her boyfriend?" Maeve was standing at the head of the table, briskly chopping her way through a mountain of tomatoes.

Suzy shook her head.

"Just a friend, apparently. They grew up next door to each other in Stockwood. I did manage to tell him that I hadn't run out on him at the Avon Gorge the other week, I explained about being kidnapped and mentioned in passing that I wasn't seeing anyone else at the moment. I was rather hoping he'd ask me out." Suzy popped another grape into her mouth. "But he just frowned and said, 'I hardly think this is the time or the place.' Which was a bit of a bugger. Still, never mind," she concluded brightly. "He can always get my number from Lucille."

"So subtle, so shy, so retiring." Jaz eyed her with amusement. "You really should be a real estate agent."

Suzy glanced at her watch.

"Speaking of which, I'd better make a move. I'm showing a gynecologist around that new apartment in Guthrie Place at nine fifteen."

"What does she do for a living?" asked Jaz.

"I just told you." Suzy was busy tucking her pink shirt into the waistband of her white skirt. "Gynecologist. Funny kind of a job for a woman" — she mimed peering up something with an imaginary flashlight — "but there you go; I suppose it takes all sorts."

"I meant Lucille."

"Oh." Hurriedly, Suzy smoothed her skirt over her hips and reached for her jacket. "No idea. She didn't say."

Nobody had been more amazed than Suzy herself when she had taken to selling property like a Scot takes to porridge. Having plowed her exams in spectacular fashion — because who needed exams; she was marrying a rock star! — she had emerged two years later from the wreckage of her marriage to Jaz dazzlingly ill-equipped for . . . well, pretty much anything. Taking pity on her, but not at all sure that it was a smart business move, Rory had offered her a job at the agency, and — not at all sure that it was her cup of tea, but touched by his concern — Suzy had accepted.

Happily, they were both proved wrong. Meeting prospective clients and matching them to the perfect home came so naturally to her that within three months Suzy was outperforming the senior agent — who promptly threw a tantrum and left. Rory promoted Suzy, crossing his fingers hard and praying she wouldn't get bored.

She didn't. The buzz of successful selling had Suzy in its grip. She made the clients laugh, startled them sometimes with her honesty, charmed them so naturally that they half fell in love with her, and never for a moment lost her infectious enthusiasm for the job.

"Well?" said Rory when she erupted into the office at ten thirty.

"Sold to the gynecologist with the creepy rubber gloves." Waving her cell phone in triumph, Suzy threw herself onto the nearest swivel chair and did a victory twirl. "She

73

offered two three five, and the Clarksons accepted."

"She wasn't bothered about the bathroom?" Rory was impressed; the Clarksons' poky bathroom had put off a number of clients. "I thought she'd go for that second-floor apartment on Pembroke Road."

"She was going to, but I told her that if she bought Pembroke Road, she'd be living above a family with three teenagers. She doesn't need a massive bathroom, but she definitely wants peace and quiet." Suzy beamed. "I said, OK, this one costs a few grand more, but think what you'll save on earplugs and expensive psychiatric treatment. And she laughed and offered me a job as her receptionist."

"Dr. Witherton?" Donna looked up from her computer. "Actually laughed? My friend Hazel works on one of her wards at Frenchay. According to her, Esme Witherton is seriously scary. Rumor has it, she hasn't laughed since nineteen seventy-six."

"Tuh, only because nobody's told her any good jokes. She loved my one about Bill Clinton and the tea bags." Rory looked horrified, and Suzy shrugged modestly. "I'm a genius, that's all. So" — elaborately casual now — "any messages while I was out?"

"The agent from the Halifax wants you to

call him back." Donna consulted her note-pad. "And the Ferrises want to see the house on Bell Barn Road this after —"

"I meant nice messages," protested Suzy. "*Interesting* messages. Date-type messages from gorgeous men, preferably policemen. With bright blue eyes. Named Harry. Come on," she wailed, "he must have called!"

"Ummm, no. Although, hang on." Suzy's heart soared for a nanosecond. "The agent from the Halifax is named Barry." Donna's expression was innocent. "That's nearly the same, isn't it?"

"No, it is not. Barry Bagshaw has acne and BO and eyebrows like a murderer. He's about as gorgeous as a bucket of sick, and he has a *very* tedious one-track mind."

"Sex?" said Donna.

"Worse. Structural subsidence."

"Oh. So what makes you so sure this sexy policeman of yours is going to get in touch?"

Suzy looked smug.

"He will. I know he will. He has to — he's my next boyfriend."

Rory, who had an appointment with a desperate would-be vendor on Julian Road, picked up his briefcase and car keys and said drily, "Poor devil, he just doesn't know it yet."

■ ■ ■ ■

By seven o'clock that evening Harry still hadn't phoned.

"I don't understand it," she told Fee, hurt. "He knows he likes me. How could he not like me? What's the matter with him? Why doesn't he just call me up and ask me out?"

Fee had never gone back to banking. As a way of acknowledging all the hard work she'd put into the band, Jaz had insisted on continuing to support her financially while she did all the things she most wanted to do. And there were so many things Fee wanted to do, from charity work to part-time education, that she was always busy, making the most of her new life.

Fee was off to one of her beloved evening classes — archaeology, by the look of the books she was stuffing into her burlap haversack.

"Maybe he's working."

"He could still *phone.*"

"Why don't you phone him?"

"Too forward. I wouldn't want him to think I was pushy." Suzy frowned. "Besides, he didn't give me his number."

"Slipping," Fee observed, throwing her haversack over her shoulder. "So what are your plans for this evening?"

"Oh, I don't know." Suzy thought for a moment, then brightened. "Maybe I'll give my new sister a call."

CHAPTER 5

"Hi, Lucille? It's me, Suzy! I wondered if you'd like to meet up tonight, maybe go out for something to eat, get to know each . . . ?"

Leaning forward with the phone balanced between her ear and her shoulder, Suzy was carefully repainting her toenails a dazzling shade of violet. She paused and listened to Lucille's reply.

"Oh. Oh, I see. Well, that's a shame but never mind. Another time. How about tomorrow? Oh, right, you're busy then as well, are you? Maybe over the weekend, then. Ummm . . . you wouldn't happen to know offhand what Harry's phone number is, I suppose? Only he wrote it down for me the other week, but I lost it."

At the other end of the phone, Suzy detected barely concealed amusement.

"No, you didn't lose it," said Lucille, "because he never gave it to you in the first place." She hesitated for a second, clearly struggling with her loyalties. "Look, don't tell him I told you this, but Harry bet me a fiver you'd ask me for his phone number."

"You're kidding! The nerve of the man," Suzy exclaimed.

"Yes, well, that's kind of the way he is with girls. He's just so used to them hurling themselves at his feet . . . oh, you know how some men can get."

Interestinger and interestinger.

"You mean he's a good-looking bastard who treats women like dirt." Suzy's stomach did a quick, pleasurable squirm. Good-looking bastards had always been her big weakness, they were such a challenge.

Like Jaz, of course.

Well, who'd want a wimp?

"Harry can be a bit . . . arrogant, I suppose." Lucille sounded apologetic. "I mean, he is lovely, but —"

"Ah, just give me the number." Suzy smiled, touched by her concern. "And don't worry, I can look after myself."

You couldn't blame the girls for hurling themselves at him, Suzy thought, opening the front door an hour later.

There was no getting away from it. He was gorgeous.

"I'm sorry," she told Harry, "but I have to

ask you this. Your eyes. Are they real?"

"They look it, don't they? But they actually aren't." He opened them wide and rolled them from side to side. "They're made out of papier-mâché, PVA glue, and the tops from dishwashing liquid bottles. I saw it done on the Disney Channel."

Suzy studied his eyes closely. He wasn't wearing colored contacts. Phew, thank goodness for that. She couldn't be with a man who'd stoop to colored contacts.

And — double hooray — he was looking a lot more cheerful now than he had last night.

"I hope Lucille didn't think I was only calling her for your number," Suzy told him. "Do you think she thought that? I really did want to see her, you know. She said she was busy tonight *and* tomorrow night . . . D'you know if that's true?"

Suzy had her doubts about this. To be honest, Lucille had sounded evasive.

But Harry nodded. "Oh yes, she's working."

"Well, that's a relief. And a coincidence," Suzy exclaimed, "because I wanted to ask you what Lucille does. Hang on, working in the evenings, let me guess . . . she's a nurse?"

"Right, OK, bit of an awkward situation,"

said Harry after a pause. He pushed his fingers through his dark, curly hair. "The thing is, Lucille didn't want to tell you what she does."

"But that's just mad! I'm a real estate agent, for heaven's sake." Suzy looked amazed. "There aren't many jobs more embarrassing than that."

Wooop-wooop, shrilled Harry's car as he aimed his key at it.

"What Lucille does isn't embarrassing. She's just terrified of you thinking she's only latching on to you for one reason." Taking Suzy's hand, Harry led her across the road. "Look, she's not going to be thrilled with me, but why don't we pay her a visit? Doesn't it drive you crazy," he went on, "not being able to park in front of your own house because jerks like this leave their *idiotic* cars blocking *your* drive?" As he spoke, he gestured with contempt toward the bright red Rolls carelessly parked across the entrance to the driveway. "I mean, talk about sad. What kind of poser would want to drive around in a car like that anyway?"

The Silver Shadow had been a present from Jaz on her nineteenth birthday — even though for the life of him he couldn't remember buying it.

Suzy, who loved her car like a baby, said,

81

"I know, pathetic isn't it! Actually, it's mine."

"Oh well, occupational hazard," said Harry, his blue eyes twinkling as he gestured down at his shoes. "When your feet are this big, every now and again, they're bound to end up in your mouth."

Big feet, eh? Suzy looked innocent. She'd heard all about men with big feet.

The Pineapple Bar, on the waterfront, wasn't one of Suzy's regular haunts. A drastically renovated old building of many levels, overlooking the Baltic Wharf, its ground-floor bar heaved with teenagers and reverberated to the sound of club music. Nightmare, thought Suzy, feeling incredibly ancient — at twenty-four — as she followed Harry up the staircase.

"Does Lucille work behind the bar? I don't understand why she didn't want me to know that. Nothing wrong with bar jobs."

"Stop talking," said Harry over his shoulder. "And keep up."

The second floor was even busier, the smoky air filled with the shrieks of fifty or so overexcited girls out on a hen night mobbing a male stripper. A rhinestone-studded G-string went sailing through the air, to a roar of encouragement.

"Don't look," Harry said bossily.

"I really hope Lucille isn't a male stripper in her spare time. How many more stairs?" complained Suzy as he led her toward the next flight.

"Sorry. This place used to be a warehouse."

She was starting to pant like a Saint Bernard.

"Is Lucille really up there, or is this a cruel joke?"

"Oh, she's there. I can hear her."

All Suzy could hear were the deafening screeches below them of the girls having a bachelorette party, yelling, "Get 'em *off off off!*" at the stripper. And he'd done that already, surely?

How many rhinestone G-strings could one man wear?

Onward and upward they went. *Heavens,* thought Suzy giddily. *I could do with crampons and oxygen. Not to mention a couple of Sherpas.*

"There she is," said Harry at last, pointing to a lone figure at the far end of the room. And he was right. There was Lucille, perched on a stool with a guitar, playing and singing some Sheryl Crow–type song.

She wasn't exactly causing a stir. Nobody else on the fourth floor of the Pineapple Bar was taking any notice. When Lucille reached the end of the song, Suzy and Harry were the only ones who clapped.

"It's my break now," said Lucille, putting aside her guitar and eyeing Suzy defensively. "I suppose this was Harry's idea."

She was wearing torn black jeans and a tiny scarlet cotton camisole. Her beaded hair — appropriately enough, given their location — was fastened up on top of her head pineapple fashion. Harry, returning from the bar with their drinks, said, "It's Malibu night. I got you both a Malibu and Coke."

"Why? Because they were two for the price of one?" Suzy looked indignant. "I hope this doesn't mean you're a penny-pinching cheapskate."

"It means this bar only sells Malibu," Harry told her patiently. "If you want anything else you have to go downstairs."

Oh. That was all right then. Suzy forgave him. Even though she couldn't stand Malibu.

"And yes," Harry went on, addressing Lucille, "it was my idea to bring her here."

"I don't know why you wanted to keep it such a secret," Suzy exclaimed. Although she did, of course.

Well, it was pretty obvious.

"Look, it must be bad enough as it is, having me crawl out of the woodwork," Lucille said frankly. "Going, 'Hi, guess what, I'm your sister!' and claiming my share of your inheritance." She gazed steadily at Suzy. "So it's hardly going to improve matters, is it, if the next thing I do is whip out my guitar and say, 'Oh, and by the way, I'm a singer — hey, didn't you used to be married to Jaz Dreyfuss? Maybe you could introduce me to your ex!' "

"You wouldn't do that," said Suzy, taken aback.

Oh God, would she?

Lucille looked faintly exasperated.

"*I* know I wouldn't. But you don't know me at all, do you? You might think I'm building up to it, angling for an introduction . . . you know how it is, some people will do anything for the chance of that big break. Well, anyway," she went on, "I just want you to know that I'm not that kind of person. In fact, I'd rather you didn't tell Jaz what I do. Less awkward all around."

Suzy shrugged. "OK, if that's what you want."

It made a change, certainly. In her experience, getting to meet Jaz was most struggling musicians' mission in life. Amazingly — in Suzy's view — they didn't regard him

85

as a has-been, a washed-up old alcoholic. To them, Jaz was still the genius who had written one of the bestselling rock albums of all time. It was quite touching really. Even now, a day seldom passed without at least a couple of demo tapes from eager wannabes either arriving in the mail or being pushed hopefully through his door.

Total waste of time, of course, because Jaz never listened to them. His life these days was a music-free zone.

"She doesn't push herself," Harry announced, "that's her trouble. She's a bloody good singer."

"So bloody good that I get ignored in pubs all over the city." Lucille's tone was dry. The next moment a balding manager-type appeared at their table, bossily tapping his watch.

"We don't pay you to sit around gossiping."

Breaks around here evidently weren't allowed to last longer than three minutes. *What a dump,* thought Suzy.

Lucille drained her glass and stood up. When she saw Suzy removing her jacket and settling back to watch, she said, "Oh God, you don't have to be polite."

"I'm never polite," Suzy said happily. "I wouldn't stay if I didn't want to, I can promise you that. I just can't imagine where you get it from, this being all musical — none of our family can sing for toffee. Well, *I* think I can, but everyone else assures me I can't. Jaz says I sound like Edna Everage being garroted with her own tights."

Lucille reached down for her guitar. "My dad was a singer."

"Oh, wow!" Suzy was impressed. "You mean he was famous?"

Lucille smiled.

"No, it wasn't his job. He just sang for fun. Actually, he drove a taxi for a living."

A taxi driver. Gosh. Try as she might, Suzy couldn't imagine the double life her mother had led over the years, flitting between the wealthy, serious-minded scientist and the — less wealthy, presumably — singing taxi driver.

It took Suzy less than fifteen minutes to clear the entire fourth floor of the Pineapple. Each time Lucille reached the end of a song, Suzy clapped and cheered with noisy enthusiasm and stared so meaningfully at the rest of the customers, daring them not to join in the applause, that in no time at all they were nudging each other, knocking back their drinks, and sloping off downstairs.

By ten o'clock Lucille's audience had shrunk to Harry, Suzy, and two mildly bemused bartenders.

"Isn't she brilliant?" Suzy stuck her fingers in her mouth and whistled shrilly with appreciation as Lucille finished with a dreary-sounding song by PJ Harvey. Not catchy enough for Suzy's taste, but now clearly wasn't the time to be critical. "She's my sister, you know! Fancy me having a sister who can sing like that!"

"Fancy *her* having a sister who can turn off an audience like that," observed the taller of the two bartenders. "Especially before she's even had a chance to take the hat around."

"Is that what happens?" Appalled, Suzy clapped her hands over her mouth. "Oh God, oh God, I didn't think! Quick, where's the hat? Let me put something in . . . How much does she usually get?"

"Don't worry." Lucille materialized at her side as she searched frantically for her purse. "They're teasing you. I get paid."

Suzy looked unconvinced. "Much?"

"Not much. Actually, a pittance. But I get by. And next week I start at the Bar HoopLa on Whiteladies Road."

"You get by," Suzy echoed doubtfully. Honestly, there were still so many questions she wanted to ask. She was tempted to draw up a ten-page questionnaire, a bit like a tax return, listing every single thing she was bursting to know. "Do you do anything else, apart from the singing?"

"I do some dog walking," said Lucille. "It's good. Flexible."

"She walks my brother's dog," Harry added. The phone in his jacket pocket began to ring. "Damn, I hope that isn't work."

"Dog walking," said Suzy, shaking her head. "Do you know, that's something I've never understood. How can people own dogs and call themselves dog lovers when they can't even be bothered to take their animals for a walk? I mean, how hypocritical can you get?" She ranted on, beginning to get carried away. "What's wrong with these people? If they loved their dogs they'd *want* to walk them, wouldn't they? But oh no, that would be too much like hard work! Why bother to take your dog for a walk when you can sit on your fat backside and pay someone else to do the dirty work for you? Talk about *bone idle* . . ."

"Right. Right," said Harry, nodding into his phone. He held it out to Suzy. "For you."

Suzy looked at it. "How can your phone be for me?"

He wasn't smiling. "Trust me, it is."

Warily, she took the phone from him. "Hello?"

"Name?" demanded a peremptory male voice.

Oh Lord, not the chief constable!

"Myfanwy. Er, Myfanwy Shufflebottom," said Suzy. She made alarmed eyes at Harry, who shrugged and sat back, looking sorry for her.

"OK, now, you just listen to me. Every morning I take my dog for a run across the Downs. He probably covers three miles. And every evening I take him out on another run, this time for maybe four or five miles. But during the day, I do have to work, and because my dog is an Irish wolfhound, he enjoys as much exercise a day as he can lay his paws on. Which is why, *Ms*. Shufflebottom, I pay a dog walker to visit him at lunchtime and take him out for an hour." He paused, then concluded, "Furthermore, I do not have a fat backside."

"What can I say?" said Suzy. "I apologize. From the heart of my shuffly bottom."

The male voice drawled, "I should think so too."

And then he hung up.

Suzy listened in disbelief to the dial tone. "He hung up."

"Surely not," said Harry with a grin.

"Who was he?"

But Harry, clearly enjoying himself, simply shrugged.

Suzy found the number of the last call received and pressed Return. It was picked up on the second ring.

"Hello?"

"Who *are* you?"

She heard him laugh. "A dog lover, Ms. Shufflebottom. Or perhaps I could call you Myfanwy?"

Her fingers tightened around the phone.

"Look, I'll tell you my real name if you'll tell me yours."

More laughter. For heaven's sake, thought Suzy indignantly, how irritating was it when people *did* that?

"This is rather like the dormouse saying to the elephant, 'I won't step on you if you won't step on me,' " said the man on the other end of the phone. "You see, I already know who you are."

Suzy's ear was tingling. She was loving every second of this. The smart thing to do now, of course, would be to hang up. Ha! That would show him what kind of —

"Bastard!" wailed Suzy, staring at the phone in disbelief.

Startled, Lucille said, "What?"

"He hung up again! He bloody hung up

on me before I could hang up on him! That is *so* unfair." She swung around to Harry, who was trying hard to keep a straight face. "Was it your boss?"

"No, thank God." Harry exchanged an amused glance with Lucille. "It was my brother, Leo."

CHAPTER 6

Lucille refused their offer of a lift home; she had her bike with her. Harry and Suzy, waving good-bye, watched her pedal off into the night with her pineapple hairdo bobbing and her guitar strapped to her back.

"She's very independent," said Suzy.

"Oh yes."

"I feel like the new owner of a puppy from Battersea Dogs & Cats Home. Desperate for her to like me. Do you think she does?"

Harry shrugged, then smiled.

"I don't know. Lucille's wary, but she's no puppy. Give her time." He slid his arm around Suzy's shoulders as they headed for the car. "If it's any comfort, I like you." He gave her a quick squeeze. "A lot."

They pulled up, less than ten minutes later, outside Suzy's apartment. Eyeing the rakishly parked Rolls, Harry said, "Couldn't you just sell it and buy a Porsche?"

Suzy loved her Rolls because nobody expected her to drive one. When you were twenty-four, with tumbling tortoiseshell hair, long legs, and breasts that frankly shouted "Hello, boys!" you conformed to a certain stereotype. People automatically pictured you driving some sporty little number, something sleek and curvy and with a propensity for getting its top off.

But that had never been her dream. When, barefoot and abandoned, she had first been rescued by Jaz from the hard shoulder of the highway all those years ago — well, six years ago, though it seemed more like fifty — he had asked her what her favorite car was, and she had told him. And six months later, on her nineteenth birthday, he had bought her the Rolls.

It had been love at first sight. Plus, of course, it had lasted a lot longer than the marriage.

"When I have to pay to leave my car in a parking space," Suzy told Harry, "I like to get my money's worth."

"Right, well, early start tomorrow. I'd better make a move." He revved the engine slightly and glanced at his watch.

Suzy, who hated it when men pulled up outside her apartment and switched off the ignition, was impressed.

"OK. So, do I get a good-night kiss?"

Harry leaned across and kissed her briefly on the cheek. Then he smiled. Oh, that heartbreaking smile!

"Have you enjoyed yourself tonight?"

"So-so," said Suzy. "Average. *Comme ci, comme ça.*" She paused. "Would you like to come in for coffee?"

"Better not."

"Fine." Suzy approved of this too. She liked it when they said no. So long as she knew they wanted to really. Saying no because they actually *didn't* want to . . . well, that would have been the pits.

As she reached for the door handle, Jaz's front door swung open. Jaz, wearing only a pair of jeans, whistled through his teeth, gazed into the distance, and called out, "Cat, hey, cat, come on in now, puss puss puss."

"Your ex-husband," Harry remarked.

"Er, yes." The ex-husband who didn't even *have* a cat.

Jaz peered across at the car, did an oh-so-surprised double take — good job he'd never yearned to be an actor, thought Suzy — and shouted across, "Hey, Suze, is that you? Coming over for a drink?"

"A drink? I thought he didn't drink." Harry sounded startled.

"He doesn't. I do." Suzy knew exactly what Jaz was up to.

"Hey, come on," said Jaz. "It's early. Just one drink."

"Are you and he still . . . ?"

"No," said Suzy, "we're not."

"Both of you," Jaz called out easily. "I meant both of you."

"Do you want to?" said Suzy.

Harry hesitated, then shrugged. Casually.

"OK. Why not?"

Suzy smiled to herself. It worked every time. Nobody turned down the opportunity to meet Jaz.

"The bad news is," she told Harry, "you'll have to meet Celeste too."

Celeste, Jaz's girlfriend, was the bane of Suzy's life. With her short white-blond hair, huge china-blue eyes, and dinky size-six figure, she had that irritating Barbie-doll look about her — and an even more irritating habit of constantly reminding other people how dinky and fragile she was.

Suzy, who *liked* being a long-legged, curvy size twelve, was tired of Celeste's endless derogatory comments regarding her weight. She couldn't understand what Jaz — who in the past had always had such excellent taste in women — possibly saw in her.

Well, that wasn't strictly true. She did know. Because Celeste had a trump card she played to the hilt. She might spend her life bitching about Fee and Suzy, and she might teeter around in fluffy mules with completely ludicrous satin bows in her hair, but she was also — cue that card! — a recovering alcoholic, just like Jaz.

And Jaz had apparently convinced himself that Celeste had saved his life. Now, as far as he was concerned, she was his talisman, his lucky charm.

When actually, as Suzy so often pointed out to him, Celeste was nothing but amazingly self-centered, a gold digger, and a total pain in the neck.

"We met at an AA meeting," Celeste told Harry, as if he didn't already know. The whole planet, Suzy thought wearily, must have heard this story by now. "I just walked in, and there was Jaz. Not that I even recognized him at the time, I was in such a state. I'd only been sober for a couple of days. I was going through hell. After the meeting, I just broke down and cried in the street — I was *that* close to running into the nearest pub. But Jaz saw me crying and came over. He got me through the crisis." She nodded for emphasis, and the massive

97

pink bow on top of her head bobbed around like a pair of rabbit's ears. "We talked all night. It was like there was this incredible *connection* between us. I mean, Jaz had been sober for almost four months, but he was still struggling too. If it hadn't been for him, I know I'd have started drinking again. And he feels the same way about me. We supported each other, Harry, d'you see? Whenever one of us weakened, the other had to be strong. And we did it, didn't we, darling?" Her wide blue gaze fixed lovingly on Jaz. "We saved each other's lives."

It was the loving look that got Suzy most of all. Whenever she saw it — which was, sadly, *often* — she had an overwhelming urge to stick two fingers in her mouth and make loud gagging noises. Why was it that other women could see through Celeste in a flash, yet men fell for her nauseating charms every time?

Lucille wouldn't be taken in for a moment, Suzy thought with pride. *If she were here now, she'd see Celeste for the celebrity-hungry bimbo she is.* She watched Harry falling for her nonsense hook, line, and sinker — oh well, he was a *man;* what could you expect? — and topped off her wineglass from the bottle of Pouilly-Fumé Jaz had opened for her.

Harry, needless to say, had taken the diplomatic route and settled for coffee.

"Don't worry about Suzy. She does it on purpose," Celeste told Harry as the neck of the bottle clunked against Suzy's glass. "She loves to goad us. I think it must give her a cheap thrill."

"Pouilly-Fumé?" Suzy raised an eyebrow. "Hardly cheap."

In Celeste's favor, at least there was no pretense, no shilly-shallying around. Since she made no secret of her disdain for Suzy, they were free to taunt each other with abandon. Suzy enjoyed these insult-flinging sessions immensely; she just wished Jaz wouldn't roar with laughter at the pair of them and call them his double act.

"Anyway," she went on, "after being married to Jaz for two years, I deserve a few thrills. And why shouldn't I have a drink? We don't *all* have to suffer for the rest of our lives, do we, just because you two are on the wagon?"

"If someone were about to throw themselves off the Suspension Bridge," Celeste said to Harry, "she'd help them over the barrier."

"This is the real world," said Suzy. "People do drink. You either lock yourselves away from temptation or get used to it."

"She has no idea." Celeste gave Harry's arm a consoling pat. "Take no notice. It's sheer ignorance."

"Oh, this is good." Suzy seized on this with glee. "You're the one who thinks Tuesday is spelled with a *ch* and I'm the one who's ignorant! *Plus,*" she went on, "if Jaz doesn't want his guests drinking in front of him, why does he keep alcohol in the house?"

Harry's head was swiveling between Suzy and Celeste like a one-man Wimbledon audience. Jaz, standing in front of the fireplace, grinned broadly and let them get on with it.

"You should try giving the drink a rest yourself," Celeste told Suzy. "All that extra weight would just drop off you, I'm sure."

"What a coincidence, I was just thinking the same thing," Suzy retaliated sweetly, "about you and mascara."

Because Celeste went through gallons of the stuff. *Gallons.*

Harry, leaping gamely into the breach like the good police officer he was, said, "So, Celeste, do you work?"

"Me? Heavens, no!" Celeste laughed prettily. "Being Jaz's girlfriend is a full-time job."

"In other words," said Suzy, "she's bone idle."

Even Jaz couldn't let this pass.

"You mean unlike you," he commented drily, "who worked like a *Trojan* throughout our marriage."

"That was different," Suzy shot back. "You were drunk all the time! You *needed* looking after."

"And you were Florence Nightingale?" Celeste turned to her in triumph. "From what I've heard, all you ever did was eat chocolate and go shopping. Although frankly, I'm amazed you could ever find clothes big enough to fit you."

Harry coughed loudly and began to look alarmed.

"Don't worry," Jaz reassured him. "They're always like this. So where did you two go tonight?"

Clearly relieved to hear a sane voice, Harry said, "The Pineapple Bar."

"To see Lucille," Suzy chimed in. "She was working there."

"Really? Doing what?"

"Bartender," Harry said swiftly.

"I suppose she drinks as well." Celeste sounded pitying. "I don't know. I just wish people could realize there's more to life."

"Like wrapping ribbons around their heads and trying to pass themselves off as boxes of chocolates?" said Suzy. "Actually, she walks dogs too. Who knows — if I ask her nicely, maybe she'll take you out."

"I just feel so sorry for her." Celeste fluttered her eyelashes sympathetically at Harry, then shrugged and sipped her lukewarm coffee. "Imagine the disappointment of meeting your long-lost sister for the first time and discovering it's *you*."

CHAPTER 7

"I didn't realize you two hated each other that much," said Harry, when the front door had closed behind them.

"Oh, we don't *hate* each other." Suzy flapped her hand dismissively. She and Celeste loved to goad each other, but the great thing was that neither of them ever took offense. "I just wish Jaz could have found himself someone . . . better."

Harry looked doubtful. "Are you still in love with him?"

"No!"

"Sure?"

Honestly, thought Suzy, *what's the matter with people? Why do they always think that?*

"Of course I'm sure," she said patiently. "And before you ask the next question, no, I am *not* jealous of Celeste."

Harry considered this for a couple of seconds.

"OK, maybe not. But is Celeste jealous of you?"

They had reached his car. Suzy turned to face him, her mouth tilting — gosh, all by itself! — up toward his.

"You sound like Columbo," she murmured. "And nobody's even been murdered."

"Hmmm." Reaching toward her, Harry carefully lifted a tendril of dark blond hair out of her eyes. "Yet."

Jaz knew her too well. He had left the door unlocked.

"Well?" said Suzy, bursting back into the drawing room. "What d'you think?"

"It shouldn't matter what we think," Jaz told her. "It's what you think that counts."

"Except I can't always be trusted to get it right," said Suzy, "on account of me having such terrible taste in men. I mean, look who I once married."

Jaz laughed. Celeste, picking idly at the silver nail polish on her toes, said, "I thought he was OK. Cute."

"*Cute?*" Suzy gazed at her in horror. "That's a nice thing to say about a puppy. It's a *terrible* thing to call a grown man."

Celeste shrugged and tried again. "OK, he's good looking in a pretty kind of way.

Like the guy in that movie we saw on TV the other night." She gave Jaz a nudge. "Really old movie . . . ooh, what was his name? He played a fairground worker, and you told me his friend in the movie used to be in some band."

"*That'll Be the Day.* David Essex," said Jaz, not quite daring to meet Suzy's eye.

Innocently, Suzy said, "So the friend who used to be in some band was . . . Ringo Starr?"

"That's the one!" Celeste nodded happily.

"And this band he used to be in. Was it by any chance the Beatles?"

"Right again! Honestly, you're like a total nerd, aren't you, when it comes to old music?" Celeste's tone was admiring. "It's almost as if you're forty-six, not twenty-six."

"I'm twenty-four," said Suzy.

"Oops, sorry. I don't know why I always think you're older. Must be the clothes." Celeste shrugged. "Anyway, what I'm trying to say is that Harry looks like the other one, the cute one. That David Wessex."

Back to cute again. Terrific. Suzy turned impatiently to Jaz for support.

"So how about you?"

"Well, some people *have* said I'm cute." Jaz grinned and stopped teasing her. "OK. The truth? He seems like a nice bloke.

But . . ."

Holding her breath, Suzy watched him wiggle his hand in a noncommittal fashion.

"You don't think he's for me? Is that what you're saying?" she demanded indignantly. "For heaven's sake, you couldn't be more wrong! He's *perfect.*"

Jaz gave her a quizzical look. "Really?"

"Really."

"In that case, fine."

He wasn't going to argue with her, Suzy realized.

Time to go home.

She had lied, of course. Harry wasn't perfect.

But he was *almost* perfect. *Say 90 percent,* thought Suzy, gazing up at the darkened bedroom ceiling. *Which, these days, is frankly about as good as it gets.*

Oh, it was no good. She couldn't sleep. Rolling over onto her side, she flicked on the bedside light and grabbed the TV remote control. This was one of those tired body, racing brain scenarios — Suzy knew from experience — that meant she didn't have a hope in hell of getting to sleep.

Something was bothering her.

And that something was the missing 10 percent.

The crucial 10 percent, preventing Harry Fitzallan from being perfect.

And the reason it was bothering her so much, Suzy realized, was that she didn't have a clue what could possibly *be* lacking.

Crikey, didn't Harry have it all? Good looks? Great body? Intelligence? Wit? Charm?

So why, *why* did she keep finding herself secretly wishing that he could be a little bit more . . . a bit more *something*?

It was no good; her mind remained blank. Harry was certainly missing something, but she didn't know what. Sincerely hoping it wasn't his willy, Suzy aimed the remote at the TV and flicked through a few cable channels.

MTV was showing one of Jaz's old videos, featuring him playing live in concert at the Birmingham NEC. *When had that been? Five years ago? While we were together,* thought Suzy, *because I was there at that concert. And while Jaz was downing at least two bottles of Stolichnaya a day, judging by the look of him.*

The camera spun into dizzying close-up, and the next moment, Jaz's heavily lidded brown eyes filled the screen. Amazingly, despite the fact that he was clearly struggling to focus and needed to hang on to the mike stand for support, he was still giving a mesmerizing performance. Inebriated he might be, Suzy observed, but the star quality was still there.

That was the thing about Jaz, of course. He'd always had charisma by the bucket-load. How else would he have gotten away with it for so long?

The camera panned back again. As the climax to the song approached, Jaz ripped off his loose white shirt. Lithe and bare-chested, wearing only dark blue leather trousers now, he moved to the very front of the stage. The audience, going wild, reached out to him. Jaz paused, tossing his sweat-drenched blond hair out of his eyes. He held up one arm, smiled that trademark lopsided smile of his and —

"Oh, sod off." Still annoyed with him, Suzy pressed a button on the remote with an executioner's relish. Bloody Jaz, why should she watch him anyway, when he'd just been so mean to her? And how dare he criticize Harry, she thought indignantly, when he refused to take any notice of her opinion of Celeste?

After zapping her way through a couple of dozen more channels, Suzy settled finally for a documentary on face-lifts, in which a scary woman with skin like stretched plastic wrap was whining, "The thing is, I simply can't bear the thought of losing my looks."

But the TV couldn't hold Suzy's attention. OK, maybe Jaz hadn't actually criticized Harry in so many words, but the implication had been there all the same.

That she Could Do Better.

Honestly, what a nerve.

Then again, thought Suzy, *what else are we meant to expect from someone like Jaz? Someone who finally cleans up his act, kicks the booze, turns into the kind of brilliant human being you'd always wished he could be while you'd been married to him . . . and then goes and bloody wastes it all on someone as ridiculous and utterly pointless as Celeste?*

Suzy switched off the TV, closed her eyes, and mentally ran through the list of appointments she had lined up for tomorrow.

Then she smiled to herself, wondering what Harry would have to say if she told him that sometimes she daydreamed about sleeping with Jaz and accidentally on purpose letting Celeste find out.

Not because she wanted to sleep with Jaz, particularly.

Just for fun.

It was only a harmless fantasy, after all. You were allowed to do things like that in your fantasies.

For a start, it would wipe the kittenish, look-who-I've-got, aren't-I-clever smile off Celeste's face and put an end to all that unbearable smugness.

And second, Jaz had always been pretty spectacular in bed, even when he was plastered. If he was that good drunk, Suzy had often pondered, what in heaven's name was he like when he was sober?

Well, you couldn't help wondering, could you?

The Lennoxes were both out at work all day. Eager to sell their five-bedroomed detached house on Mariner's Drive as quickly as possible, they had handed the spare keys over to Suzy and assured her that she was free to show prospective buyers around whenever she liked.

"Smart front door," Mrs. Lacey-Jones noted with approval when they pulled up outside the house in Suzy's Rolls.

"Very." Suzy nodded too, glad that the Lennoxes had taken her advice. The first rule of house selling was still to repaint your front door. Preferably a glossy dark blue. And polish up any brass hardware. Because first impressions count, and people decide whether they're interested in a property within half a second of clapping eyes on it.

Rather like when you clap eyes on a new man.

Inside, their footsteps echoed across the polished oak floor. Colonel Lacey-Jones strode about in his equally glossy brogues with his hands clasped behind his back. His military mustache twitched with approval at the sight of the garden through the drawing room windows. Mrs. Lacey-Jones, who also had a hint of a military mustache, not to mention a bottom every bit as broad and tweedy as her husband's, said, "Jolly nice decor." She ran a hand over the Georgian writing desk to her left. "You can tell the house belongs to a good family."

"Oh, yes, and they're absolutely charming," lied Suzy. Stuck up and patronizing, more like. Still, sensing that Mrs. Lacey-Jones would be impressed, she said, "Esther Lennox is the head of the WI."

"Really? Oh, but I've *met* her!" Mrs. Lacey-Jones, clearly delighted, bustled up the stairs after her husband. "Marvelous, marvelous woman! Now look at this wooden paneling, Herbert. Excellent. Ah, now which bedroom would this be?"

Having reached the first door along the landing, her hand was already grasping the doorknob.

"Actually, it's a bathroom." Suzy consulted her list of details. "South facing, large and sunny, free-standing bath, you're going to just love it —"

"AAARGH!" screamed Mrs. Lacey-Jones as the door swung open.

"Call the police!" Colonel Lacey-Jones bellowed, pushing past her and grabbing the nearest weapon at hand, which happened to be an onyx-handled lavatory brush. "Go on, Daphne, dial 999 — I won't let them get away!"

"Oh my God," moaned the girl in the bath, covered in goose bumps and trembling with fear. "Don't do it. Please don't call the police . . ."

As she shook, the chains wrapped around her wrists and ankles rattled against the sides of the enamel bath. The man in there with her scrambled to his feet and reared up like a grizzly bear, causing Mrs. Lacey-Jones's pale eyes to bulge almost out of her head.

"What the fuck's going *on* here?" he roared.

Having recognized the girl from the formal graduation photograph in pride of place on the mantelpiece downstairs, Suzy smiled brightly and said, "We'll probably look back one day and laugh about this."

Colonel Lacey-Jones, lavatory brush still

held menacingly aloft, turned and gave her an incredulous stare.

"Well," Suzy amended, "maybe not quite yet."

CHAPTER 8

"The poor girl was in shock," Suzy told Donna back at the office an hour later. "She shares a house in Hotwells with six other people — it's a total privacy-free zone. Her boyfriend lives at home with his parents and five brothers and sisters. They were just desperate for a few hours alone together."

"And that's what they like to do in their spare time, is it?" Donna wrinkled her nose in bemusement. "Blimey, some people. Going at it while you're chained to the bath. I mean, how can that be comfortable?"

Suzy shrugged. She felt sorry for them.

"They weren't doing anyone any harm. Well, until Mrs. Lacey-Jones walked in on them and almost had a heart attack on the spot." Ruefully, she added, "Plus, of course, they've blown my chance of a quick sale."

"Will you tell the Lennoxes what happened?"

"Oh, yes, great idea: tell the head of the

Women's Institute that while she and her husband are out of the house, her daughter sneaks in and cavorts in their bath with twenty feet of dog chain and some guy hairier than a gorilla. No thanks."

"Well, that's something," said Donna.

Rummaging in her desk drawer for an emergency packet of malt balls, Suzy found one, ripped it open with her teeth, and added sadly, "Although it looks as if the daughter's going to have to break it to them."

Donna winced in sympathy. Her mother had once spotted her making out with a boy at a bus stop, and that had been bad enough.

"Really?"

"Well, the last thing Mrs. Lacey-Jones shouted as she stormed out of the house was, 'I know your mother, you little trollop. Just wait until I tell her about this.' "

"Isn't there anything you can do?" Donna looked hopeful.

Suzy, who had already tried and failed, crunched up a malt ball and said, "Yes. In future, always knock on the bathroom door, no matter how empty the house is."

Returning to the office at five o'clock, Suzy found Rory at his desk rattling off letters into his Dictaphone. Martin Lord, his emerald-green silk tie askew, was scribbling appointments in his overcrowded diary.

"Hi." Suzy swung her bag onto her chair. "I've just shown Marcus Egerton the apartment on Alma Road, and he's put in an offer for one fifty. Did Donna tell you about it this morning?"

"She did." Rory switched off his Dictaphone. "And I've had a call from Mrs. Lennox, withdrawing her house from our books."

"Oh, damn." Suzy sighed. "Thought she might."

"She was in a bit of a state."

"Imagine what kind of state her poor daughter's in!"

"Ever been chained to a bath, Suze?" Martin Lord grinned at her. "I'll give it a go if you will."

The fact that Martin had a gorgeous wife named Nancy and two adorable small children didn't stop him from flirting shamelessly with anything remotely female. It did nothing for Suzy but by all accounts worked wonders with the clients. Martin was a charmer, a ladies' man through and through.

"I tell you what," offered Suzy. "Why don't I chain you to a bath? Then Nancy could pour boiling oil all over you, from a

116

great height."

He grinned.

"Doesn't sound very erotic. Warm baby oil, maybe."

Suzy, waggling her fingers at him, said, "Live maggots."

"Chocolate spread."

"Cows' entrails."

"Cointreau-flavored whipped cream, straight from the can." Martin raised an eyebrow, James Bond–style. "Ah, now we're talking."

"Ants," Suzy countered with relish. "No, superglue. No, no, *witchetty grubs* . . ."

"Oh, Nancy phoned earlier, by the way. While you were out." Donna looked up from her computer screen. "She said to remind you to be home by seven."

"Damn." Looking bemused, Martin asked, "Why?"

"It's your wedding anniversary."

"*Damn.* We're supposed to be going out to dinner." Martin banged his forehead. "I said I'd book a table at Neil's Bistro."

Suzy marveled at his selfishness.

"How can you forget your anniversary?"

"I didn't forget. I knew it was today. It just slipped my mind. *Hell.*" Martin sighed. "What do I do now?"

"Go home, I'd imagine," said Rory.

"I've got an appointment with a client at eight o'clock."

There was a shifty look in his eyes. For appointment-with-client, red-hot-date-with-pouty-blond, Suzy guessed. Martin was mad about blonds. Nancy, of course, was a dazzling brunette.

This, as far as Suzy was concerned, pretty much summed men up.

"No problem." Whipping out her organizer, she called his bluff. "Give me the details, and I'll meet your client for you."

Martin hesitated, then shook his head.

"It's OK. I'll reschedule."

Ha! Talk about a dead giveaway.

"Really, it's not a problem. I insist." Suzy's tone was soothing. She held her pen poised above the page and tilted her head innocently to one side. "Come on now, what's the client's name?"

And is it a he or a she? Oh really, a she? Good heavens, what *a surprise!*

"All right, all right." Martin heaved a sigh of reluctance. "The name's Hallen."

"Mrs.?" Suzy inquired with a bright smile. "Miss? Or Mzzz?"

You no-good, cheating adulterer.

"Mr.," said Martin. "And he'll meet you outside the property on Parry's Lane at eight sharp."

"Bugger." Suzy groaned aloud the moment the door had swung shut. Through the glass she watched Martin, emerald silk tie flapping, race across the road, hurrying to reach Lloyd's flower shop before it closed up for the night. Gloomily, she said, "I'd never have offered if I'd thought for one second he really did have a client."

"I'd do it," said Rory, his tone apologetic, "but I've got something else going on."

Suzy smiled at him. It would be too much to hope that her workaholic brother had a hot date. Since his divorce, Rory appeared to have given up on women completely; these days, he had about as much social life as a lettuce.

Less, actually, since at least a lettuce stood a fighting chance of ending up one evening in a candlelit restaurant.

"Doesn't matter. I'm not seeing Harry tonight anyway." With good-natured resignation, Suzy chucked her organizer into her bag and slid off the desk. "So what are you doing then, something nice?" She gave Rory a look of encouragement. Well, you could always live in hope.

"Shower's sprung a leak." Rory was busy shoveling papers into his briefcase. Lifting his head, he pushed his glasses back up over the bridge of his nose. "Plumber's coming around."

"And is this plumber a Miss, a Mrs., or a Mzzz?" asked Suzy.

"His name's Albert. He's in his sixties; he has no hair and three teeth," Rory told her patiently. "None of which he ever cleans. But he knows his way around an *S* bend."

"Oh well." Suzy broke into a grin. "Whatever turns you on."

The property on Parry's Lane was one of the most exclusive currently on Curtis's books. Suzy, who didn't like it much, pulled into the driveway just before eight and quickly checked her reflection in the rearview mirror.

Right. Enthusiasm required, and lots of it. Just because she wasn't wild about this kind of sixties-style architecture — all flat roofs, clean lines, and blank, department-store-size windows — it didn't mean she couldn't persuade someone it was the best thing since Baileys ice cream.

She was redoing her lipstick when the lights of another car swung up the drive behind her. Running her fingers quickly through her hair, Suzy reached into the glove compartment for her rape alarm, slid it into her jacket pocket, and jumped out of the car.

A slate-gray, M-reg Volvo. Oh, marvelous, how thrilling was this man going to be?

But when he climbed out, Suzy saw that, gosh, he actually *was* quite thrilling. A vast improvement on his car, anyway. Tall, at well over six feet, he was probably in his mid-thirties. And he had hair, which was always a bonus. Straight dark hair and nice ears — she'd always had a bit of a thing about ears — and teeth white enough to gleam in the dark, although, of course, that could mean they were false.

Still, the eyes were nice, and they had to be real, at least. And beneath the dark suit lurked a pretty fit, athletic-looking body.

Excellent.

What's more, thought Suzy, *hooray, I'm wearing my lucky jacket!*

"Mr. Hallen?" Moving toward him, she stuck out her hand. "I'm Suzy Curtis. I'm afraid Martin wasn't able to make it this evening so I'll be showing you the property instead."

"Oh, right. That's fine." As he shook her hand, he regarded her with amusement. "I hope I'm not putting you out."

What a smile. What a mouth. There was no getting away from it, thought Suzy. Selling a house to someone you liked the look of was definitely easier than doing business

121

with some facially challenged troll.

Plus, it was a lot more fun.

"Putting me out? Not at all." She flashed him a brief, dazzling smile of her own — *See? I can do it too.* "Now, did Martin tell you that the owners have relocated? The house has been empty for a fortnight, but they've left the carpets and curtains, which will be negotiable." Jangling keys, Suzy found the right one and fit it into the front door. "They're asking four fifty, but realistically, I'd think an offer of four twenty is as much as they can expect. Now then, here we are. Let's get some lights on. Have you seen many properties yet?"

"No." He shook his head and glanced around the hall. "This is the first."

"And have you a place of your own to sell or . . . ?"

He smiled again, acknowledging the delicacy of the question.

"I sold my house in London last year. Since moving back to Bristol, I've been renting. Now, with the business sorted out, I thought it was about time I bought somewhere."

Suzy nodded, relieved. She liked that answer. What she was less keen on was when some man suddenly burst into noisy tears and blurted out the story of how his wife was divorcing him and refusing to let him see the kids. This one didn't look the type, but you could never be sure. It wouldn't be the first time she'd been caught out.

The kitchen lights flickered on to reveal acres of polished steel units and a gleaming black marble floor.

"God," said Mr. Hallen.

"I know. It's a bit Starship *Enterprise.*" Suzy watched him pace around the kitchen. She saw his broad shoulders stiffen as he paused at the sink. "Is everything OK?"

"Fine, fine." Hearing her high heels behind him, he swung around and put out a restraining arm. "No! *Don't look —*"

CHAPTER 9

Suzy looked.

Well, you have to, don't you?

And there, frantically struggling to clamber out of the sink — and failing dismally — was a spider the size of a Millie's cookie.

"Oh, you poor thing. I bet you've been stuck in there for days!" Scooping it up into her hand, Suzy pushed open the window behind the sink and carefully shook the spider out. "There, off you go, sweetheart. I always worry when I do that," she added over her shoulder. "I mean, do they find their way home, back to their families? Or will his wife and children spend the rest of their lives wondering whatever happened to Dad?"

As she spoke, Suzy turned to face her potential client. Was it her imagination or was Mr. Hotshot-Hallen suppressing a bit of a shudder?

"Well, I'm impressed. I thought you'd run

a mile at the sight of a spider," he said drily. "Most girls would."

Not to mention you, Suzy thought with secret delight.

Aloud she said, "I'm not most girls."

"I'd noticed. Still, it must come in handy." He nodded in the direction of the window out of which she had dropped the spider. "Saves all that screaming and jumping up onto chairs and having panic attacks."

"Then again, sometimes it totally back-fires. Shall I tell you something *really* embarrassing?" Leaning against the sink, Suzy confided, "I once got a call at two o'clock in the morning from an ex I still liked. He asked me around to his place to deal with a spider. Of course I knew what he *really* wanted, so I jumped into the shower, threw on some makeup, and drove over to his apartment with nothing on under my coat. And there was the spider, on the ceiling directly above his bed. And when I'd gotten rid of it for him, my ex thanked me and showed me to the front door and called me a brick."

He laughed.

"I hope you posted it back through the mailbox after that."

"Oh, I would have gone, like a shot, but that's the thing about spiders. They're like policemen, never around when you need them. You aren't interested in this place, are you?" Suzy said suddenly.

He raised an eyebrow.

"Is it that obvious?"

"You haven't even looked in the cupboards."

"Sorry."

"Do you want me to show you the rest of the house," Suzy offered, "or not bother?"

He shook his head. "There's no point. I don't like it."

"Me neither," said Suzy.

"And I'm sorry if I've wasted your time." His mouth twitched. "Still, at least we rescued the spider."

"Actually," said Suzy, "we didn't. *I* did."

"You think I was scared, don't you?"

"Yes."

"I wasn't."

"The customer is always right," Suzy told him. "Of course you weren't scared."

He pushed his hair out of his dark blue eyes and smiled down at her.

"I don't know — this could be against the rules — but would you have dinner with me?"

Golly, talk about a fast worker.

From now on, thought Suzy, *this is* definitely *my lucky jacket.*

126

"Are you married?" As she spoke, she glanced at his ring finger. Nothing. Hooray!

He smiled and shook his head. "You?"

"Oh no. Definitely not married."

"Seeing anyone?"

"Nooo." Suzy crossed her fingers behind her back. After all, how involved with Harry was she, really? They'd only been seeing each other for a week and a half. Three dates so far: a few drinks, an Italian meal, and a trip to the cinema to see a movie Harry had hated. They hadn't even slept together yet. That didn't count as seeing someone, did it?

Besides, you didn't lightly turn down an invitation to dinner from someone as down-right gorgeous as this.

"Dinner would be great," Suzy said happily.

There was a long pause.

Mr. Hallen sighed. "Oh dear."

"Oh dear what?"

"I'm disappointed."

"Disappointed?" She blinked up at him, startled. "In the house, you mean?"

He was shaking his head.

"In . . . in *me*?" Suzy swallowed, her voice beginning to wobble.

He gave her a look that bordered on the sympathetic.

"You don't know who I am, do you?"

In her jacket pocket, Suzy's fingers groped for her rape alarm.

"I didn't set out to deceive you," he went on easily. "As a matter of fact, I did wonder if you'd recognize my voice."

The trouble is, thought Suzy, *he doesn't sound like a mass murderer or an escaped lunatic.*

With her free hand, she pushed her hair out of her eyes.

"Recognize your voice? No, why would I?"

"We have spoken on the phone."

Phone, phone . . .

By this time thoroughly confused, Suzy said, "You mean you called Curtis's?"

"Not then, but perhaps I should explain." He paused, then said steadily, "When I spoke to your colleague, Martin Lord, he must have misunderstood me. My name isn't Hallen; it's Fitzallan."

"Oh. *Oh!*"

In an instant, everything became clear. Suzy clapped her hand over her mouth.

"You're Harry's brother!"

He nodded in agreement. "Leo."

"The one with the dog!"

"Baxter," Leo Fitzallan said gravely.

"You don't look a bit like Harry." Suzy's

128

gaze was accusing.

"Sorry. I didn't know it was compulsory. If we're being honest," he pointed out, "you don't look much like Lucille."

"Hang on." Suzy frowned. "Why didn't you tell me straightaway who you were?"

There was that devastating smile again . . . but Suzy was no longer quite so sure she trusted it.

"Like I said, this wasn't planned," Leo Fitzallan told her. "But sometimes you see an opportunity that's just too good to pass up. Jameson's Restaurant OK with you? Or we could try Le Gourmet." As he spoke, he ushered her toward the front door. "You see, for the past ten days or so, my brother has talked about nothing but you. He's well and truly smitten. You must know that."

Yes, thanks, thought Suzy. *I* had *noticed.*

Aloud, she said stiffly, "We get on very well together."

"Hmmm."

"Hmmm what?"

"I was interested." Leo sounded amused. "To find out how you felt about him."

Suzy's eyes widened with indignation.

"Oh, that's great. So inviting me to Le Gourmet was just a big trick, was it? A cunning plan, to see if I said, 'Ooh no, thanks so much, but I couldn't possibly go out to dinner with someone else; my boyfriend wouldn't like it.' "

His expressive eyebrows said it all.

"Well," drawled Leo, "it was worth a try."

She locked the front door of the hideous house behind her.

"OK, well, I'm sorry this place wasn't your cup of tea. If you'd like to pop into the office I could give you details of other properties that —"

"Your car or mine?" Leo interrupted.

"Excuse me?" Suzy was already climbing into the driver's seat of the Rolls.

"For dinner."

"At Le Gourmet?"

"If you like."

"Gorblimey, guv, you're a proper gent and no mistake." Reaching across, Suzy clicked open the passenger door. She dropped the Eliza Doolittle accent and smiled up at him. "Come on, we'll go in mine."

Miraculously, there was a parking space right outside Le Gourmet on Whiteladies Road. As she expertly reversed into it, Suzy said, "Anyway, I'm not having dinner with you because I fancy you rotten."

"No?"

"No. We're here purely because I'm a real estate agent and you want to buy a house."

130

They hadn't prebooked. Every table in the restaurant was full. If they waited at the bar and had a drink, the manager told Leo, they could be seated in half an hour.

Once they were settled in the bar, Suzy twirled the stem of her wineglass and continued, "You see, this is what my job's all about. I need to find out exactly what you're after. Then I have to persuade you to let me find it for you."

Particularly when we're talking close to half a million pounds . . .

"And is that what you're good at?" said Leo.

"It's what I'm best at."

She watched him smile to himself as he studied the menu. Sensational cooking smells were drifting up from the kitchen; her stomach began to rumble like a volcano.

"Along with parking large cars in small spaces," Leo observed. "And tackling large spiders. Not to mention talking your way out of speeding tickets."

Amazed to find herself turning pink, Suzy said, "Oh, so Harry told you about that."

Leo, his tone grave, replied, "As I said, we're talking seriously smitten. Harry has told me everything about you. And I do mean everything." He paused. "I even know about" — longer pause — "the music."

131

She bristled, instantly on the defensive. There was that acerbic eyebrow going up again. Honestly, why did people love to sneer so much?

If you had a speech impediment or a deformed foot, Suzy thought defiantly, no decent human being would dream of poking fun at you. But dare to be just the teeniest bit different in your musical tastes and the whole world feels free to make fun of you, openly criticizing your choice and generally laughing themselves sick at your expense.

Leo, it appeared, was no exception.

Charming.

Just because she enjoyed songs with a jolly tune. And a nice cheerful beat.

"I happen to like ABBA," said Suzy.

"And 'Macarena.' "

"One of the all-time greats."

"And 'YMCA.' "

"So?"

"And 'Agadoo.' "

" 'Doo-doo, push pineapple, shake the tree,' " Suzy said promptly.

Half sang, actually. She couldn't help herself; it was one of those involuntary reflexes, like breathing.

Funnily enough, Jaz had always told her she should have married the lead singer from Black Lace.

"And the soundtrack from *Saturday Night Fever,*" Leo persisted.

He was seriously beginning to get on her nerves.

"Look, I could *pretend* to like k. d. lang and Schubert and Jamiroquai," Suzy protested. "But I just don't. I like what I like, and I like stuff that makes me feel happy. So to each his own, OK? You don't smirk at my record collection, and I won't smirk at the lapels on your suit, or the fact that you drive a Volvo."

There was nothing wrong with his lapels, but seeing as he was only a man, she was pretty sure he wouldn't know that.

And he definitely drove a Volvo.

"Touché," said Leo Fitzallan, raising his glass of wine.

"You might have terrible taste in houses as well." Suzy stuck her elbows on the bar, warming to her theme. "You might go for hideous Southfork-type properties, with really tacky decor."

The waiter, discreetly approaching, murmured to Leo, "May I take your order, sir?"

"I'm sorry, we've been talking too much." Suzy gave him an apologetic smile. "I haven't even looked at the menu yet. Could we have another few minutes?"

The waiter nodded and left.

Leo, studying the menu, said, "The smoked duck sounds good." He glanced up and added mildly, "No, I don't go for really tacky decor. And I prefer Victorian properties."

"Top price, four fifty?"

"Maybe five."

Five hundred thousand pounds, thought Suzy. Business must be good. What had Harry said his brother was involved in? Oh yes, a chain of fast-food outlets, that was it. Leo was Britain's answer to Ronald McDonald, according to Harry.

"And where do you want to live? Clifton? Sneyd Park? Stoke Bishop? Leigh Woods?"

Leo shrugged. "I'm not bothered. I just want to see a house and fall in love with it."

Suzy smiled. She knew exactly what he meant. And she approved. Some clients were only interested in properties that "fit the bill," that were "the sort of thing we're after." Others wanted a house they could fall in love with. Such a property wasn't necessarily the sensible choice, but the moment you clapped eyes on it, your heart went *ziiing* and you knew this was the one you Had to Have.

The first kind of client was by far the easiest, of course, but the second was so infinitely more rewarding.

At that moment, Suzy was seized by inspiration.

"I've got somewhere fabulous to show you. It could be the house of your dreams." Putting down her wineglass, she delved into her bag and pulled out her appointment book. "Can you make it tomorrow?"

"No, I'm —"

"The next day?"

"— in New York," Leo finished. "For a week." He glanced at his watch. "I have to leave in just over eight hours."

Biting her lip in frustration, Suzy felt her stomach rumble with hunger. She saw the young waiter edging toward them again. She breathed in the heavenly garlicky cooking smells emanating from the kitchen . . .

Do it, do it now!

"OK." She abruptly slid off her bar stool. "Let's go."

CHAPTER 10

"Haddock and fries and mushy peas," Suzy announced, jumping back into the driver's seat and lobbing two hot parcels into Leo's lap. "And I got you an orange Fanta. Is that all right?"

"Perfect. Who needs Chateauneuf-du-Pape when you can have orange Fanta?" Leo unwrapped one of the fragrant parcels and offered her a fry. "Jesus, what's *that*?" He shuddered as the sound of a thousand Irish feet began to boom through the in-car speakers.

Proudly, Suzy said, *"Riverdance."*

Oh, that music, it was stirring her blood already! All the little hairs on the back of her neck were leaping to attention.

"At least you can't dance to this in public," remarked Leo.

Maybe not, Suzy thought, *but you should see me in the privacy of my own bedroom, jigging away in front of the full-length mirror.*

Then again, perhaps it was just as well he couldn't.

"Is this how you normally do business?" said Leo, as they sped across the Downs.

"It's called seizing the moment." Actually, it was called intuition. "I'm giving you first refusal on a house I think you'll really like. If we leave it until after you get back from the States, it could be too late."

"Don't tell me," said Leo, his tone dry. "There's someone else mad about the place and if I don't put in an offer tonight they'll snap it up."

"Not at all. Nobody else has even seen it yet." Reaching over, Suzy pinched another fry. "But I just think you might kick yourself if that happened."

The corners of his mouth lifted a fraction. "Harry told me you were a great sales-woman."

"I have a talent for matching people up with the right properties," Suzy told him happily. "It's my specialty. That's what makes me great."

"Actually, this fish is pretty good." Leo looked up, alarmed. "Good grief, what's that noise?"

She grinned. "Don't panic. Just my tragi-cally empty stomach."

Once they were inside the house, Suzy turned on the oven and threw her untouched parcel of haddock and fries in to keep warm. Forty minutes later, when she had given Leo the full guided tour — including the floodlit garden — she led him back to the kitchen, took the parcel out of the oven, and began to devour the contents.

With a passion.

"Sorry, I'm starving. Well? What do you think?"

"I like it. A lot. I think this could be just what I'm looking for. But," Leo went on slowly, "you can't seriously expect me to put in an offer now. Of four hundred and eighty thousand pounds. For something I haven't even seen in daylight."

"Come on, where's your sense of adventure?" Suzy protested. "It's even better in daylight! You won't believe the view."

Leo watched her jump up, race across the kitchen, pull open a cupboard, and take out a bottle of Heinz tomato ketchup.

"So this is where you grew up."

Suzy pulled a face.

"Well, that's debatable. I probably only grew up when I divorced Jaz." She shook the bottle like a grand prix winner and dolloped sauce generously over her fries. "But this is where I lived."

"And were you happy here?"

"Happy? Oh yes." Suzy smiled slightly. "Despite my mother."

Leo took another look around the ground floor while she demolished the rest of her meal. Returning, he leaned in the doorway with his hands in his pockets and watched her stuff the empty wrappers into the kitchen trash.

"I'm definitely interested, but I'd have to see it again. Properly, in daylight."

Spoilsport.

"OK."

"We'd better be making a move. I have to be at Heathrow by seven."

"Right." Suzy switched off the lights in the kitchen. "I'll take you back to your car."

The Volvo was still there, parked in the darkened driveway of the hideous house at the top of Parry's Lane. Pulling up behind it — thankful it hadn't been stolen — Suzy jumped out to shake hands with Leo Fitzallan in true real-estate-agent fashion.

As she reached into her bag in search of a business card, a bird swooped down from one of the trees lining the drive, missing her head by inches.

"Here we are. Call me when you're back from the States. If you're still interested and the house hasn't been sold, we can fix — God, what *is* that?"

The dark shape flitted past her again, even closer this time.

"A bat," said Leo.

"Aaargh!" Letting out a strangled scream, Suzy seized the straps of her handbag and swung it around her head. Spiders were OK, spiders she could handle, but *bats.* Ugh, they were *something* else. They had sharp little teeth and flappy, pointy wings and their mission in life was to get themselves tangled up in your hair. Ducking, panicking, and dimly aware that undignified whimpering noises were emanating from her throat, Suzy swung the bag frantically, like an Olympic hammer thrower going for gold.

Except the knack with Olympic hammer throwing is knowing when to let go. Before she could stop it happening, the leather straps had wound themselves embarrassingly around her neck and the bag — with its heavy metal clasp — made violent contact with the front of her face.

Clonk went the clasp against her nose, and Suzy let out another shriek, this time of pain.

"Owww! My *node*! Oh *no* . . ."

As her hands flew up to her face, she felt the telltale warm trickle of blood. Oh, brilliant. Great. A nosebleed. Just what a girl needs when she's wearing her lucky lilac jacket and a white Donna Karan camisole top.

At least the bat had gone. With any luck she'd hit it for six into next door's garden.

God, I knew *I hated this house.*

The blood began to gather speed, the trickle turning into a flood. Reflexively, to save her clothes, Suzy flung her head right back. The blood, promptly altering course, slid down the back of her nose and throat. When she tried to breathe, the air came out in a kind of panicky bubbling snort.

She wailed, "Help, help, I'm drowning!"

It came out as "I'b drowdig!"

"Here." Leo pulled a clean white handkerchief out of his jacket pocket. Suzy jammed it — *wumph* — over her nose and mouth. Within seconds it was crimson. Her nosebleeds had always been fast and furious.

"Open by bag — ged the keys." She pointed to her handbag on the ground, then to the house, remembering that the previous owners had left a couple of guest towels in the downstairs bathroom.

Thankfully, Leo didn't argue. Within

141

seconds he had found the keys, unlocked the front door, and switched on the lights. Still spluttering, but desperate not to drip blood on the hall carpet, Suzy followed him in and made a lunge for the bathroom.

She blanched at the sight of herself in the mirror above the pristine white sink. Oh yes, very *Interview with the Vampire.* And despite her best efforts, there was plenty of blood on her favorite top.

Pinching the bridge of her nose hard and mopping up with one of the lime-green hand towels, she leaned against the sink. Leo, behind her in the doorway, said, "Is it broken?"

Suzy shook her head gingerly. Then, moving the towel away from her mouth, she spat a mouthful of blood into the sink.

Oh dear, elegant or what?

"No. I've always been a bit prone to nosebleeds. It'll stop in a minute."

The owners of the house had thoughtfully left a roll of toilet paper behind as well. Tearing off a couple of sheets, Suzy rolled them up and stuffed one — even more elegantly — up each nostril. Meeting Leo's gaze in the mirror — was he making a heroic attempt not to laugh? — she explained, "Don't want to drip all over my car seats."

Leo straightened up. "What's that noise?"

Aware that she was snuffling like a Pekingese, Suzy said, "Me, probably. Trying to breathe."

"No, outside."

The next moment they heard footsteps racing on the gravel. The front door, already open, was flung violently back on its hinges.

"OK, nobody move!" bawled a male voice behind them. "Put your hands up! Stay right where you are!"

As Suzy turned slowly around, the sodden toilet paper plug dropped out of her left nostril. It came to rest in her blood spattered cleavage. She saw the look of horror in the eyes of the policeman in the doorway.

"Are you all right, miss? Don't worry, you're safe now." Whipping out a pair of handcuffs, he grabbed Leo's wrists and twisted them behind his back. "Jesus, what's he *done* to you?"

"Really, he didn't . . ." Suzy began as a second set of footsteps echoed in the hall.

"Better radio for an ambulance," barked the first policeman over his shoulder.

"She doesn't need one," Leo said calmly.

Suzy heard an astonished voice gasp, *"Leo?"*

The first policeman, his tone grim, said, "Know him, do you?"

"Quite well, actually," said Leo.

Suzy summoned up a reassuring smile as the second policeman appeared in the doorway. Well, as reassuring as she could manage with ribbons of blood and saliva dripping from her teeth.

"Hello, Harry."

Harry insisted on driving her home in the Rolls.

"The neighbors phoned us to report a break-in. They knew the house was empty. They heard a commotion in the front garden . . ."

"Bats," said Suzy.

"Not at all. They thought it was burglars. They did absolutely the right thing."

"I mean, there was a bat flying around my head. I panicked and tried to hit it away with my handbag. Caught my nose instead."

"So you said." Harry pulled up outside her house. He turned sideways in the driver's seat, his expression troubled. "What I don't understand is what you were doing there at that time in the first place. I mean, it's hardly normal, is it? Showing people around houses at eleven thirty at night?"

"You do what you have to do." Suzy shrugged. "See an opportunity, seize an opportunity."

Harry sniffed. "And why does it smell of

fish and chips in this car?"

"Because we stopped for fish and chips on the way." Patiently, Suzy explained, "We're putting my mother's house on the market. From what Leo was saying, I guessed he might be interested. He's off to the States in a few hours and I really wanted him to see it before he left." She blinked, her patience beginning to slip. "Harry, please stop *looking* at me like that. When a client has that amount of money to spend on a house, you do whatever it takes to sell him one. Leo's registered with three other agencies besides ours. I'd like Curtis's to be the one he ends up doing business with. You can understand that, surely?"

"Oh yes, I can understand that. Money talks," said Harry, "and my brother's loaded." He paused. "So? Did he make a move?"

"A move?"

"Come on, don't look so innocent. You know what I'm talking about."

Astonished, Suzy wailed, "Of course he didn't make a move! For heaven's sake, this was *business.*"

Harry, his voice level, replied, "And you've just told me that you'll do whatever it takes to seal a deal."

Phew, jealous or what?

145

"Now you're just being ridiculous." Suzy shook her head in disbelief.

"He's my brother," said Harry. "I know what he's like. To be honest, I'm amazed he didn't try to take you out to dinner."

"Well, I didn't have dinner with him."

True, *just.* Phew again.

"Only fish and chips," muttered Harry.

"And I paid for them." At that moment a police car drew up behind them, its headlights beaming into the car. Grateful for the reprieve, Suzy swung herself out of the passenger seat. "Your lift's here. Thanks for driving me home. I'm sorry you think I've spent the evening doing my damnedest to seduce your brother." She abruptly stuck out her hand. "Keys please."

Harry looked taken aback. "Suzy, I didn't mean —"

"No, no, that's absolutely *fine.*" She could feel the muscles tensing up in her jaw. "I'm going to have a bath now. Good night."

CHAPTER 11

Domesticity had never been one of Suzy's great strengths. The next morning before work she popped next door to find Maeve, alone in the kitchen, singing to herself and energetically frying sausages and mushrooms.

Suzy hovered in the open doorway and looked helpless. "Maeve, how do I get blood out of a white top? I can't remember if I'm supposed to boil it, or cover it in salt."

"D'you think I was born yesterday?" Maeve chided over her shoulder.

"Maeve!" Suzy broke into a huge grin. "I don't know what you mean."

"Bring it over here and I'll deal with it later," said Maeve, as Suzy had known she would. Dancing gleefully up behind her, she planted a kiss on the older woman's tissue-soft cheek.

"Thanks, Maeve. You're an angel. Ooh, and those sausages look fab."

"They're not fab at all. They're not even sausages." With an expression of disgust, Maeve gave them a prod with her steel spatula. "They're those vegetarian things. For Celeste."

"Made with what?"

"Pfff. From the taste of them, the sawdust sweepings off the floor of the butcher's shop."

Eyeing the sausages with reduced enthusiasm, Suzy said, "Should you be frying them like that, if they're for Celeste?"

Celeste was a low-fat person.

"Celeste is in bed, the idle baggage." Maeve snorted. "What she doesn't know won't hurt me. Shift your big bottom, now." Nudging Suzy out of the way, Maeve switched off the gas burner and reached for a pile of plates. "Go fetch that white top of yours, why don't you, so I can take a look at the damage."

Like a magician, Suzy produced the bulging carrier from behind her back. With a flourish she whisked out the offending articles.

"Jesus, a bloodbath." Maeve clucked. "The mischief you young people get up to these days, I don't know."

The truly great thing about Maeve, Suzy thought, was her utter unshockability. You

148

could walk into the room with a pickax sticking out of your head and Maeve would say, "Will I be getting you a couple of aspirins, love? And how about a nice cup of tea to wash them down?"

At that moment Jaz and Fee came in, having finished their early morning stint in the pool. Fee, in a vibrant turquoise tracksuit, was rubbing dry her short, straight, sensibly cut hair. Jaz, still dripping wet and barefoot, was wearing a dark blue toweling robe.

"Sixty lengths." He greeted Suzy with a grin. Then, noticing her blood-soaked clothes: "Christ, what have you been doing? Practicing open-heart surgery on yourself?"

"Good job I didn't come here looking for sympathy." Suzy touched the faint blue bruise on the bridge of her nose. But Maeve was taking a vast dish of kedgeree out of the oven, followed by a tray of cooked-to-perfection bacon. Unable to resist such sublime smells, she pulled out a chair and sat down. "Actually, I was with Harry's brother when it happened."

"So Harry's got a brother, has he?" Jaz, sprawling opposite her and tipping his own chair back on its hind legs, said, "What's he like?"

Hmmm. There was a sixty-four-thousand-dollar question if ever she'd heard one. Suzy hesitated for a moment, but the urge to talk was too strong. And — for better or for worse — she'd always been honest with Jaz.

Mentally bracing herself, she said, "He seems nice."

"Nice?"

"Older than Harry," Suzy elaborated, fractionally. "By five years."

"Go on."

She shrugged.

"Bit taller, I suppose. Six two, six three."

"Really. And would you say he was, by any chance . . . better looking?"

Jaz was giving her one of his knowing, crooked smiles, as if they all knew the only thing she really cared about was a man's looks. Which wasn't true at all, Suzy thought crossly. Looks *weren't* all-important; of course they weren't.

Just because she'd never been able to bring herself to actually go out with an ugly man . . . that didn't necessarily mean she was shallow, did it?

After all, you wouldn't go out and deliberately buy an ugly sofa.

Anyway, Leo wasn't better looking than Harry. Harry was beautiful. You could never in a million years call Leo beautiful.

"Actually, he's pretty ugly," Suzy lied. "Big, dark, mean, and terrifying."

150

"You mean he punched you?" Startled, Jaz nodded at her bruised nose.

"No, he did *not*."

Over breakfast she related the events of the night before, culminating in her parting words to Harry.

"So that's it," Suzy concluded. "I stormed into the house. He roared off in the police car." She shrugged and forked up a mouthful of kedgeree. "Looks like it's curtains for me and Harry."

"Well, if you ask me, it's for the best," Jaz said comfortably.

"I didn't ask you." Suzy glared at him.

He ignored this.

"Put it this way. If you two had a fistfight, the chances are, you'd win."

"We aren't going to have a fistfight. As of today, I'm officially single again."

"There's always this Leo fellow," said Maeve, pouring out more tea. "And he has plenty of money, from the sound of things. That's not to be sneezed at."

Suzy had a vivid mental image of Leo holding out wads of twenty-pound notes while she sneezed all over them.

"Maeve, shame on you," Jaz chided. "Insinuating that Suzy would be interested in a man with money. Honestly, the very *idea*."

He started to laugh. Suzy didn't even bother to reach across the table and stab him with her fork.

She knew it wasn't the money that attracted her to Leo Fitzallan.

When she had realized that Harry was great but there was something missing, preventing him from being perfect, she hadn't been able to put her finger on what it was.

She had just wished he could be a bit more . . . *something*.

Now, with a start, the answer came to her.

She had wished he could be a bit more . . . like Leo.

Eek.

"I'm sorry," said Harry.

He was sitting behind her desk, wearing a faded denim shirt and jeans, looking penitent and smelling gorgeous. When Suzy moved toward him he stood up and held out a bunch of creamy yellow stargazer lilies from the florist around the corner.

Donna, clearly impressed, said, "He was waiting outside when I arrived to open up. Do you want me to put them in water for you?"

Suzy took the stargazers and looked at Harry.

"I wasn't expecting to see you again."

"I know." He looked ashamed. "I behaved like an idiot last night. Forgive me?"

"Harry —"

"Look, I'm on duty tonight, but we could have lunch," he said eagerly, "couldn't we? Tell me what time to pick you up, and I'll take you somewhere nice. If you like, we could go to Le Gourmet."

Oh, terrific. Meeting the maître d' again, that *would* go down well.

"I have to work through lunch today." This was true, at least. Suzy glanced down at her feet. Water was dripping from the stems of the flowers onto her shoes. "Harry, I don't know . . ."

"Please," he broke in urgently, "I don't want us to break up over this. I overreacted, that's all. I'm never jealous as a rule. It was just seeing you there with Leo."

Donna diplomatically seized the dripping lilies. "Let me deal with these. There's a vase in the back room."

"You have to understand," said Harry, when Donna had disappeared. "Leo isn't the easiest person in the world to have as a brother. He does what he likes, takes what he wants, and doesn't give a damn about anyone else. He's a ruthless bastard, you know. That charm thing is just a front with

Leo. The moment he has what he's after, he loses interest."

Suzy suppressed a shiver of . . . what? Excitement? *Oh, help.*

"Harry, all I want to do is sell him a house."

"You might think that now." His tone was bitter. "But you don't know him like I do."

"OK, maybe not. But I still think you're overreacting." Suzy glanced at her watch. "Look, I really do have a ton of work to get through."

"I was eighteen," Harry went on, ignoring her, "when I fell in love with Sophia. We were crazy about each other. I asked her to marry me. We got engaged. I'd never been so happy in my life."

He paused.

A long, significant pause.

"And?" Suzy felt obliged to ask, although it didn't take Columbo to figure out the rest.

"Leo was working in the city. Making a heap of money, driving a flashy car. He came home one weekend, met Sophia . . . and decided he wanted her." Harry's expression was grim. "That was on Friday night. By Sunday morning, it was mission accomplished. Sophia told me the engagement was off. She was in love — so she *thought* — with Leo."

154

Suzy felt sorry for him. It was a rotten thing to happen. But then again, these things did happen. All the time. You just had to put it down to experience, get on with your life, and not let it haunt you for the next goodness knows how many years.

"But you got over her," she said, to encourage him.

"Oh, I got over her." Harry looked up, his blue eyes bleak with pain. "Sophia was the one who couldn't get over Leo, when he dumped her six months later."

Ooh, *wicked* Leo.

"Why did he dump her?"

"Who knows? Just got bored, I guess. As soon as the novelty wears off, he moves on to the next conquest. He's never been able to resist a challenge."

"And Sophia was gutted." Suzy wondered briefly if Harry had tried to get back together with her, and been given the cold shoulder. That would explain his enduring bitterness.

"Sophia slashed her wrists," said Harry.

"Oh."

"Then she overdosed a couple of times. Spent the next three months in a psychiatric unit."

"Oh *dear*."

Inadequate, of course, but what else could

she say?

"When she came out, she got involved with a bad crowd. Within weeks she was hooked on heroin. She turned up on Leo's doorstep one night, begging him to take her back."

"What did he do?"

"Called the police." Harry paused. "Sophia was arrested and held overnight in the cells. The next day they let her go. She caught the Tube to Leo's apartment in Hampstead, posted a note under his door — he was at work at the time — then went back to her apartment and took heroin for the last time."

Aware that she was clutching at straws, Suzy said hopefully, "You mean she kicked the habit?"

"No," said Harry. "I mean she took a massive overdose and killed herself."

As the door swung shut behind Harry, Donna emerged from the back room clutching the blue glass vase of stargazers.

"I've arranged them and arranged them. Thought I'd better stay out of the way until he'd gone."

"Do I have to run through it again, or did you hear everything?"

"Oh, I heard it. Every word." Donna

arched her Gothic eyebrows. "I even heard the sloppy kisses."

"They weren't sloppy," Suzy protested. "They were lovely."

"So anyway, you made up. Everything's all right again. I must say, he is gorgeous."

This was high praise coming from Donna, who preferred her men long-haired and sporting Herman Munster makeup.

"I know." Suzy tried not to sound smug.

"Mind you, I can understand why he doesn't trust you with his brother. What were you doing with him last night anyway?"

"Don't wiggle your eyebrows at me like that. Nothing sleazy." Suzy looked offended. "Just trying to sell him a house."

"And what's he like, this big bad Leo?"

The good thing about Donna was you could tell her anything. And, unlike Jaz, she didn't retaliate with stuff you didn't want to hear.

"What can I say? Dangerous to know, clearly." Suzy felt her heart begin to race again, and shrugged. "Tall, dark, rolling in it . . . and a complete and utter bastard."

"Oh dear," said Donna with a grin. "Exactly your type."

"Any luck with the Hallen guy last night?"

Martin, dropping into the office at lunchtime, found Suzy eating a Heath bar and brushing her hair.

She looked up at him. "Do you by any chance mean the Fitzallan guy?"

"Oh. I thought Fitz was his first name." He glanced at his cell phone. "Battery's getting low. What about the place on Parry's Lane — was he up for it?"

"Hated it." Suzy put down the half-eaten chocolate bar and reached for her own phone. "How did you get on?"

Martin looked blank. "Get on with what?"

"Dinner. Last night. To celebrate your wedding anniversary."

"Oh, that. It was OK."

OK? Such enthusiasm.

"Romantic?" prompted Suzy.

"Suze, get a grip." He gave her a how-thick-are-you look. "I was with Nancy. She's my *wife*."

Suzy gave up. She dialed Lucille's number and listened to the phone ringing at the other end.

"Hello?"

"Hi, it's me. Are we still on for tonight?"

"Oh . . . well, yes." Lucille sounded pleased. "If you're sure you want to."

"Of course I want to! We can get to know each other better. Bowling first," said Suzy happily — she loved bowling — "then a couple of drinks, then on to a club. I'll pick you up at seven o'clock."

Lucille hesitated. "You don't have to. I can meet you there."

"Don't be daft; let me give you a lift! I haven't seen your apartment yet, have I?"

"Look, it's not exactly Kensington Palace. Don't expect too much." Lucille sounded awkward.

"Are there bats flying around your living room?"

"Er, no."

"In that case," Suzy assured her cheerfully, "I can cope."

CHAPTER 12

Emerging from the shower at six thirty, Suzy heard a knock on her front door.

Celeste held out a shopping bag. "I brought these over for you. Maeve said she managed to get the blood out."

"Great, thanks." Suzy took the bag.

Celeste didn't move. "Can I come in?"

"Why?"

"I'm sooo *booored,*" wailed Celeste, like a petulant six-year-old.

"Oh God, come on then." With a sigh, Suzy moved to one side. "But I'm going out in twenty minutes."

Brightening at once, Celeste said, "That's all right. I can help you decide what to wear."

I'd rather die.

"I already know what I'm wearing."

Celeste tilted her head prettily to one side. "Yes, but you don't always choose the right thing, do you?"

This was good, thought Suzy, coming from someone currently decked out in a sugar-pink baby-doll nightie, silver-flecked Barbie-size cardigan, and fuchsia-pink high heels with pompoms on the front. She made her way back through to the bedroom, where her black long-sleeved T-shirt and black jeans were laid out on the bed.

"See?" said Celeste with an air of triumph. "That's exactly what I mean. Dull, dull, *dull.*"

"Why are you bored?" Ignoring her, Suzy took off her toweling robe and began to dress. "Where's Jaz?"

"AA." Celeste pulled a face.

"Shouldn't you be going with him?"

"God, I'm so fed up with AA meetings. They're the most boring things in the world. Anyway, I don't need them anymore." Celeste threw herself onto the bed and watched Suzy ease herself into her jeans. "Have you ever thought of going on a diet?"

"I thought about it once, but I wouldn't want to end up like you."

Pulling the T-shirt over her head, Suzy smoothed it down over her hips and tucked it in. She regarded her reflection in the mirror with satisfaction. "Anyway, I've never had any complaints. Why don't you go to the movies with Maeve if you're bored?"

"It's her night out at the Jumping Prawn." Petulantly, Celeste pleated the edge of a violet pillowcase.

"She wouldn't mind you tagging along." Eyeing the baby doll nightie, Suzy said, "They enjoy a good laugh."

"What, and spend the evening being groped by a bunch of toothless geriatric Irishmen? No thanks."

"How about Fee?"

"Evening class. Bloody archaeology. I ask you, how can she be interested in all that old stuff?"

"Have a nice quiet evening in then," said Suzy. Honestly, this was worse than trying to deal with a six-year-old. "Paint your nails, have a bath, watch a video." *Play with your dolls, make a necklace out of Cheerios, do some coloring.*

Celeste stuck out her bottom lip. "Don't want to."

Bending over, Suzy began vigorously brushing her hair. "You know your trouble, don't you?" She looked at Celeste, upside down. "You don't have any friends."

Celeste sighed. "They all got jealous when I started seeing Jaz." She rolled over onto her front and looked hopefully at Suzy. "So where are you off to?"

"Bowling."

"Who with?"

"Lucille."

"Can I come with you?"

"No."

Standing up, Suzy flipped her hair back. She crossed to the dressing table and got vigorous with the bronzing powder.

"Oh, *please.*"

"No."

"Go on," cried Celeste, "let me come with you. I'm so bored I could die! Anyway," she added persuasively, "Lucille would love to meet me."

When Celeste got going, there was no stopping her. Freshly bronzed, Suzy leaned closer to the mirror and spun the top off her mascara.

"No."

"Suze, don't be *mean.* I love bowling! Please say yes, please please please . . ."

"Oh, for God's sake." Suzy sighed. "All right then." She chucked the tube of mascara back into her makeup case and selected a lipstick. "You can come with us." She looked sternly at Celeste's jubilant reflection in the mirror. "But not dressed like that."

Celeste, in the passenger seat of the Rolls, had her bare feet stuck up on the walnut dashboard. Having changed into a sherbet-yellow microskirt and a sawn-off Little Miss Mischief top — clearly her version of dressing down — she was now busy repainting her toenails. The smell of the polish clashed violently with her perfume. Buzzing down both windows, Suzy glanced first at Celeste's toes, then at the rectangular Chanel bottle clamped between her knees.

"That's *my* nail polish," Suzy said.

"I know." Brush poised, Celeste sat back to admire her handiwork. She wiggled her Day-Glo pink toes happily. "I saw it on your dressing table. Pretty, isn't it?"

"I only bought it yesterday!"

Suzy was indignant. Borrowing things without asking was something of a specialty of Celeste's.

"Hey, relax. I'm not stealing it from you. I've finished now, anyway." Celeste screwed the top back on the bottle and rolled her eyes. "Honestly, all this fuss over a bit of nail polish."

Suzy slowed down as they reached the top end of Gloucester Road, where Bishopston bordered Horfield. She peered at the house numbers, squinting her eyes against the glare of the evening sun.

"That's the one. With the brown door," Suzy announced at last.

"Yuck." Celeste wrinkled her nose, "It looks horrible."

"Lucille's got the attic apartment."

"Even horribler."

"Yes, well. It would be nice if you didn't tell her that."

Suzy parked the car a short distance up the road and they made their way back to the house. There was a scruffy, overgrown front garden and the wooden gate was hanging off its hinges. She rang the bell for the top-floor apartment and stuck her hands in the pockets of her jeans.

After what seemed like ages, Lucille opened the door.

"Good grief." Suzy's mouth fell open. "What's going on? What happened to you?"

Lucille had been crying. Her eyes were red and there were mascara stains on her cheeks. Her white T-shirt was marked all over with big grubby handprints and badly torn at the neck.

"I'm sorry. I can't come b-bowling." Her voice was low and unsteady. "Something's . . . come up."

"Who did this?" Suzy pointed to her T-shirt, aghast.

"My landlord."

"Jesus! Where is he? In your apartment?"

Lucille, her knuckles white as she clutched

165

the peeling door frame, shook her head. She indicated a closed door in the dingy hall behind her.

"He's in there. Ummm . . . unconscious."

Celeste let out a yelp.

"Did you shoot him?"

"No."

"Stab him? With a kitchen knife?" Celeste's eyes widened. "Through the heart?"

Despite everything, Lucille managed a weak smile.

"No. Nothing like that. He's just drunk. Out for the count and snoring like a train. Look, I'm fine, really. I'm sorry about the bowling, but I'll call you tomorrow —"

"You will not," declared Suzy, pushing the front door open. "Look at the state of you! You can't stay here."

Lucille sighed and let them in. "I know that."

Upstairs, her small sitting room was awash with shopping bags stuffed with clothes, piles of books and CDs, and a bundled-up duvet.

"I've spent the last hour getting my stuff together." As she spoke, Lucille peeled a series of posters off the walls and rolled them up. "I'd offer you a coffee, but I've already packed the kettle. I want to be out of here before he wakes up."

"I don't blame you," said Celeste with a shudder. "This place is *grim.*"

"And speaking of grim," Suzy announced, "this is Celeste."

"I guessed." Lucille spared her a brief smile before bending down to unplug the speakers from her stereo. "Jaz's girlfriend, right?"

"Fiancée," Celeste corrected, smugly fluttering her left hand at Lucille. Three hefty diamonds sparkled in the dusty sunlight slanting through the attic window. "Twenty thousand pounds, this ring cost. I told him not to spend so much, but he said I was worth it."

"Tell us what happened," said Suzy.

"Oh, it was *so* romantic. We were walking down Princess Victoria Street, and I just *glanced* in the window of that jeweler's on the corner —"

"Celeste, give it a rest." Suzy shook her head in despair. "I was talking to Lucille."

"He's a fat drunken pig," said Lucille, winding the wires from one of the speakers slowly around her fist. "He called me downstairs to his apartment, said we needed to have a talk about the rent. When I went down, he told me he knew I fancied him, he'd seen the way I looked at him, and why didn't we come to some arrangement that

167

would suit both of us? Then he grabbed me and started trying to kiss me. The more I struggled, the harder he tried to pin me down on the sofa." She shuddered at the memory. "His hands were all over me. He smelled awful. He told me he'd been fantasizing about me for months, and I was almost sick on the spot."

Horrified, Suzy said, "Did he . . . ?"

"No." Lucille shook her head. "Thank God. I managed to break free and he tried to chase me around the room. He lunged forward, tripped over his case of lager, let out a roar, and crashed facedown onto the sofa. And that was it. He didn't hit his head or anything. He was just out cold."

"God, how awful." Celeste wrinkled her nose. "You didn't fancy him at all, then?"

"Funnily enough," Lucille replied with commendable patience, "no."

"So what happened next?"

"His face was squashed against the cushions. I turned him onto his side, so he could breathe." Her voice began to wobble. "Then I came up here and started to pack."

"Should have let him suffocate," said Suzy. She briskly pushed up the sleeves of her black top. "Right, well, we'll help you — oh, don't cry, it's all over now." She rushed on as fresh tears began to roll down

168

Lucille's smooth brown cheeks. "I know it must have been terrible . . ."

"I'm not upset because of him." Lucille was wiping her eyes and looking utterly bereft. "I'm crying because this was my home . . . and now here I am packing up all my stuff . . . and I don't have a clue where I'm g-going to *go.*"

CHAPTER 13

Celeste, who had been admiring her reflection in the mirror hung above a cracked, glued-together bookcase, said brightly, "There's a Salvation Army hostel on Ashley Road. I expect they could take you in. Mind you, they might make you wear a bonnet and bash a tambourine."

"I didn't want to bring her along this evening, really I didn't," Suzy apologized to Lucille.

"What?" Celeste's pale blue eyes opened wider than ever. "All I did was make a sensible suggestion."

"See the front of her T-shirt?" said Suzy. "What it should say is Little Miss Thick-as-a-Plank. Could you bear to have her as a next-door neighbor, d'you think?"

Lucille blinked. "You can't . . ."

"Look, you're my sister. And I'd really love it if you'd move in with me."

"*You* might love it," Celeste put in, "but

170

what about Lucille? Why would she want to live with you?"

Suzy ignored her. She touched Lucille's arm. "Please say yes."

"It's kind of you to offer, but I feel a bit . . ."

"Sick at the thought of it?" said Celeste.

"We can at least give it a go," Suzy urged. "I mean, you do need somewhere to stay. And I've got a spare bedroom. If you'd rather have your own place, then fine, but you still need somewhere to sleep until you find it."

Lucille shot her a look of gratitude. "This is really nice of you."

"Then you will?" Suzy's face lit up. "Brilliant!"

But Lucille was still looking reluctant, shaking her head. "The trouble is . . ."

"Oh, please don't start worrying about money. I won't charge you rent!"

"The trouble is, it's not just me."

"Who else then?" said Suzy, bewildered. "Oh my God, don't tell me you've got a baby!"

Lucille smiled weakly. "Worse than that, I'm afraid."

"Blimey." Celeste sounded amazed. "What could be worse than a baby?"

"Come see," said Lucille.

She led them out of the living room, across the landing and into the minuscule kitchen.

"Look out the window."

Together, Suzy and Celeste peered down into the tiny, unkempt back garden. In the center of the scrubby lawn stood a cheap yellow plastic sun lounger. And across the sun lounger was sprawled a large — actually a *very* large — dog. Sensing movement above, he raised his head from its resting place between his front paws, gazed up at them, and slowly wagged his tail.

"His name's Baxter," said Lucille.

"He's huge," marveled Celeste.

Leo's dog, Suzy realized.

Hang on . . .

"So what was Baxter doing while you were being attacked by your landlord?" she asked Lucille.

"Sunbathing. He's the world's most useless guard dog," Lucille admitted. "Violence isn't Baxter's thing at all. To be honest, he's a total wimp. I'm looking after him for Leo," she explained, "until he gets back from the States."

"Go on then," said Suzy. "You've twisted my arm."

Joyfully, Lucille said, "Are you sure?"

"Come along." Suzy turned away from the

172

window. "The sooner we finish packing up, the faster we'll be out of here." She broke into a grin. "Good thing I've got a big car."

It took them less than an hour to clear the apartment of Lucille's belongings. Finally, everything was loaded into the Rolls.

Baxter thumped his tail good-naturedly when Lucille opened the back door leading out into the garden and called his name. He climbed off the sun lounger, loped over to them, and — by way of introduction — tried to stick his head up Celeste's skirt.

"He's lovely," Lucille assured them. She closed the back door, then hesitated. "I'd better just check on Les, before we go. Make sure he's still alive."

In the front room, which stank of alcohol and BO, Les hadn't moved. He was snoring loudly, and his filthy green shirt was open to the waist, revealing a mountainous stomach that shuddered like a blancmange every time he drew breath.

"He attacked you," said Suzy. "You should report him to the police."

Lucille shook her head.

"More trouble than it's worth. I'm out of here now anyway. That's good enough for me."

"Seems a shame, though," said Celeste,

"to let him get off scot-free." Her expression thoughtful, she glanced out through the grimy back window.

"We could always trash the place." As she patted Baxter's head, Suzy gazed without enthusiasm around the room, which was, frankly, disgusting. "Then again, who would notice?"

"Is he really out cold?" Bending over the back of the sofa, Celeste pinched the back of Les's pudgy hand, hard. There was no reaction.

"What are you thinking?" said Suzy.

"Wait here." Celeste darted out of the room. They heard the back door open. Moments later she was back, dragging the grubby sun lounger into the living room by its wheels.

"Celeste, are you mad? We don't want his sun lounger," said Suzy with a shudder.

"Come on, there are three of us. We can do it." Pushing the sun lounger up against the sofa, Celeste braced herself behind his head and shoved her arms under Les's fat shoulders. "You two take a leg each. OK. One, two, three, *heave* . . ."

Les snorted like a rhino as they hauled him over onto the filthy groaning plastic. He waved one arm and muttered, "Not last call yet, issit? Giss another pint, mate."

Then he subsided into unconsciousness once more.

"Now what?" whispered Suzy.

"I think the front garden, don't you?" Celeste grinned, reached for her bag, and fished out the bottle of Day-Glo pink nail polish.

Leaning over and undoing the last straining buttons on Les's shirt, she painstakingly painted *FAT UGLY BASTARD* in unmissable capitals across his white hairless chest.

Alarmed, Lucille said, "Can we do this?"

Celeste looked at the almost-empty bottle of nail polish, pulled a face, and chucked it over her shoulder.

Suzy, grabbing the bottom end of the sun lounger, discovered that thanks to the wheels it was surprisingly easy to maneuver. She smiled first at Celeste, then at Lucille.

"Oh, I think we should. Don't you?"

The finishing touch, once Les was installed in his front garden in full view of passersby, was inspired by Baxter. Watching him cock his leg against the gate, Celeste took a half-empty bottle of lukewarm Evian out of her bag and tipped it carefully over Les's denim-clad groin.

Envious that she hadn't thought of it herself, Suzy said, "You know, sometimes I could almost like you."

A bus trundled past. They watched the passengers peer down at Les, nudge one another, and laugh.

"Funny you should say that," Celeste replied cheerfully, "because I never think I could almost like you."

The car was piled high with Lucille's belongings. Celeste, in the passenger seat, had shopping bags piled up beneath her feet and on her lap. Lucille and Baxter, together with a couple of dozen more bags, were squashed into the back.

"I love looking at other people's stuff." Celeste, rummaging happily through one of the bags balanced on her knees, pulled out a cosmetics case. "It's so great finding out what they're really like." She flipped the case open. "I mean, take a look at this . . . Rimmel, Miners . . . God, Lucille, why d'you buy such cheap makeup?"

"Set the dog on her," Suzy told Lucille. With her free hand she snapped the cosmetics case shut, almost taking Celeste's fingers off. "And you, don't be so nosy."

"All right, all right, don't get your panties in a twist." Celeste was unperturbed. She peered into the nearest bag, poked about a bit, and dragged out a pocket-size photo album. "Hey, what about this, then? Your mother and Lucille's father — look at those

176

hairstyles!"

"Put it *back*," hissed Suzy, exasperated.

"And what are these?" Dropping the photo album back into the bag, Celeste grabbed a handful of tapes, all identical, and with just the name *Lucille* printed in uneven silver lettering on each of the cases.

"They're nothing. None of your business," said Suzy.

From the backseat, Lucille said abruptly, "Could you please leave my stuff alone?"

"All my hard work" — Celeste shrugged — "and this is the thanks I get."

Suzy looked at the cassettes, still clutched in Celeste's hand.

"Are you going to behave yourself, or do I have to stop the car and push you out?"

"You sound like the old bloke who used to drive our school bus," grumbled Celeste. Splaying her fingers, she pointedly dropped the cassettes back into the shopping bag. "There. Happy now?"

"Ecstatic," said Suzy.

Celeste waited until they turned onto Zetland Road. While Suzy's attention was taken up with avoiding a pensioner on a moped, she liberated one of the cassettes and slid it into her own bag.

It wasn't stealing, for heaven's sake. She was only borrowing it.

CHAPTER 14

Jaz would be back soon. Celeste lay back in the bath, envisaging what he was doing now. More often than not, following a meeting, those who didn't have to rush off retired to one of the cafés nearby for a coffee and an informal chat. These chats drove Celeste to distraction. It was like being forced to listen to a bunch of fat people discussing their diets when you only weighed seven stone and had never needed to count a calorie in your life. It was like listening to people telling you about their own dreams, like listening to paint dry . . .

Oh, it was all fascinating stuff as far as Jaz was concerned, because AA had saved his life. Celeste understood that, and she was grateful, of course she was, but her patience was starting to wear alarmingly thin. In fact, she was beginning to think that if anything could turn her *into* an alcoholic it was being forced to attend any more of those bloody boring meetings. Truly, it was enough to drive the saintliest teetotaler to drink.

Closing her eyes, letting the bubbles wash over her narrow shoulders, Celeste recalled the night when she and Jaz had first met. She smiled to herself at the memory, at the flukiness, the sheer *chance* of it. That, though, was what life was all about, surely? Spotting an opportunity and making the most of it.

She had always had a crush on Jaz Dreyfuss. Photographs of him, painstakingly cut from magazines, had covered her bedroom wall from the age of fifteen onward. While her school friends had drooled over Take That and Boyzone, Celeste had remained true to Jaz. She loved his music, his wildness, and his gorgeous brown eyes. Better still, he lived in Bristol and so did she, which had to shorten the odds against them one day clapping eyes on each other, enabling Jaz to fall in love with her at first sight.

To Celeste's great disappointment, this seemed destined not to happen. At every opportunity she had dressed herself up to the nines, caught the bus across the city to Clifton, and hung around the streets and outside bars waiting to accidentally bump into him. But she never did. And the next thing Celeste knew, Jaz had disappeared off the scene completely. When he reemerged, a couple of months later, it was to announce that he had been through rehab and had now stopped drinking, hopefully for good.

Celeste was pleased for Jaz's sake, but it was bad news for her. If he'd given up the booze, there was no longer much point in her hanging around Clifton's many pubs and bars.

It was the end of her beautiful dream. She stopped going to Clifton and instead started going out with an apprentice butcher named Alan, from Brislington.

And then, two months later, it happened.

Typically, Celeste was wearing her awful office clothes and no makeup. But Alan was no longer worth putting on makeup for, and she didn't care what he saw her looking like. The romance had by that time well and truly worn off.

Waiting at the curbside as darkness fell, Celeste stuck her cold hands in her pockets and silently cursed Alan for being late. Six o'clock he was supposed to pick her up from work and there was still no sign of him. And now, to add insult to injury, her view of the approaching traffic had been blocked by some selfish idiot parking his flashy car right where she didn't want him to park . . .

Her heart skipped several beats as she realized who was driving the car. Holding her breath, Celeste watched Jaz Dreyfuss climb out, lock the doors, and, head bent, make his way rapidly across the road.

Without stopping to think, Celeste followed him. As she reached the pavement on the other side, Alan's white van trundled into view. Celeste ducked down behind the row of parked cars so he couldn't see her, and scurried — like Groucho Marx — along the pavement after Jaz.

When he headed up the steps of an anonymous gray building, Celeste didn't hesitate for a second. Jaz was out of sight, but she could hear his footsteps echoing along the corridor to her left. She followed the sound of the footsteps, then rounded a corner and stumbled to a halt. Jaz was there, waiting outside some kind of hall . . . and he appeared to be waiting for *her* . . .

Giddy with excitement and trepidation, Celeste gazed at him in a kind of stupefied silence. Would Jaz be furious with her for following him? Would he yell at her, tell her to go away? And what was he doing here anyway? Through the glass in the door she could see a motley collection of people pulling up chairs . . . oh no, don't say Jaz had gone and gotten himself involved with some religious group?

But he didn't seem angry. In fact, he was smiling at her. Almost, Celeste realized, in an encouraging way.

"First time?" When he spoke, his voice was gentle.

"Y-yes."

"Coming in, then?"

Seize the moment. Spot an opportunity and grab it. Or spend the rest of your life kicking yourself.

"Yes." She began to tremble. *Please don't let it be one of those weird cults where you have to have sex with dozens of ugly men. There's only one man in this building I want to have sex with . . .*

"You're shaking," Jaz told her. His warm hand closed around her icy one. "It's OK. Don't worry, you'll be fine."

He was right, of course. And to Celeste's intense relief it wasn't some nutty religious cult he was dragging her into. As soon as the first woman stood up to announce that her name was Glenda and she was an alcoholic, Celeste had known what she had to do.

"My name is Celeste, and I'm an alcoholic." Addressing a group of strangers had been nerve-racking, but that had worked to her advantage. Throwing herself into the role, she had blurted out, "I can't carry on like this. I have to stop drinking. It's wrecking my l-l-life." The tears had come easily, pouring down her cheeks. She had given a stupendous performance.

And afterward, when the meeting was over, she had rushed from the room like a teenager bolting from school.

Returning to his car minutes later, Jaz had found her sobbing on the pavement as if her heart would break.

"I can't do it," wailed Celeste, burying her face in her hands. "I can't, I c-can't!"

"Yes, you can." He pulled her upright and gazed down at her white, tearstained face. "I'll take you for a coffee. You can tell me all about yourself."

"You don't want to hear," Celeste mumbled. "I'm a hopeless case." Her chin trembling, she looked fearfully up at him. "I pour vodka on my cornflakes."

"Wrong," said Jaz. "You used to pour vodka on your cornflakes. You don't anymore."

She shook her head. "Why should you care anyway?"

"Because we're all in this together." With one finger, he carefully wiped away her tears. "And if I can stop drinking, you can

183

too. Come on, sweetheart, get in the car."

And that had been that. A lifetime of being irresponsible and pleasing no one but himself had meant that Jaz had never actually cared for anyone else before. Delighted to discover that he was now in a position to help another human being, he had thrown himself into the task of helping Celeste.

In the bath, Celeste smiled to herself and lazily soaped her arms. She heard the front door slam downstairs. Oh yes, she had spotted her opportunity and grabbed it with both hands, and she'd never for a moment regretted it. Hankering occasionally for a nice glass of red wine and not being able to have one was a small price to pay for living with Jaz. Never having been much of a drinker anyway, she was more than happy to make that sacrifice.

The bathroom door opened, and she smiled at Jaz.

"You're back. How did it go?"

He came and sat down on the side of the bath.

"Jeff's wife is pregnant. They're thrilled." He paused. "Dave thinks his girlfriend's going to leave him."

"Poor old Dave." *Serves him right for being so boring,* Celeste privately thought. Her gaze roamed over Jaz's body, so fit and lean and gorgeous in his black sweatshirt and cream jeans. He was everything she'd ever wanted, her dream come true.

"And Jeff said didn't I think it was about time I got back into the business," Jaz went on, his voice level.

Celeste looked at him. This was a subject that had arisen before. In Jaz's mind, alcohol and the music business were inextricably linked. They went together. Since drying out, he had given up work completely, refusing to record an album, or tour, or even attempt to write any more songs. She knew he was worried that a return to his old life might mean he wouldn't be able to resist the temptation to start drinking again.

"You don't have to go back to work. Not if you don't want to." Gently, Celeste squeezed his arm. She didn't want him to resume his career anyway. They were happy together and they had more than enough money . . . the thought of Jaz plunging back into the wild rock-and-roll lifestyle made her nervous. Not just because of the drink, but because of the groupies . . .

"Don't worry; I won't let them pressure me into it."

Jaz smiled faintly. Three and a half years, he knew, was a considerable break by anyone's standards. And he was torn, because he *did* want to get back to work. It didn't matter that the royalty checks were still rolling in — he couldn't spend the rest of his life doing nothing.

"You're healthy," said Celeste. "That's all that matters. Jeff just likes to stir things up. He's jealous because you've got more than he'll ever have."

A vacation was what they needed, she thought. A couple of weeks away from it all, relaxing on a private beach in the Seychelles, that would do the trick.

"Forget Jeff." Jaz changed the subject. "What did you do this evening?"

"Actually, I've been quite busy," Celeste gaily announced. "Helping your new next-door neighbors move in."

"Come on then," Suzy said two hours later. "I'll show you mine if you'll show me yours."

"It might make you feel a bit funny," Lucille warned.

"It won't, I promise. I'm interested. Oh, this is so great!" Suzy waved her arm happily around Lucille's new bedroom. "*Tons* more fun than bowling. I've never had a roommate before."

Giving in, Lucille reached over the side of the double bed and hauled up the bag

186

Celeste had tried to investigate earlier.

"Wait, I'll go get mine." Suzy leaped off the bed. "We'll take turns, start from the beginning, see how we compare."

Lucille had been right; it did feel a bit funny looking at photographs of your own mother suddenly being somebody else's mother. In a strange house, smiling into the eyes of a strange man, proudly showing off a strange baby . . .

Except it wasn't a strange baby, Suzy had to keep reminding herself. It was Lucille.

"You had *hair*," she said accusingly, nudging Lucille with her forearm. "And look at you, you were *gorgeous*. Well, I'm sorry, but this isn't very fair."

"You were lovely too," Lucille protested, pointing to a snapshot of Suzy at six months, lying in her baby carriage.

It was a valiant lie.

"I looked like a Sumo wrestler and I was as bald as an egg until I was two. According to my mother, I was the ugliest baby in Bristol." Suzy sighed and turned to the next page of the album. "Happily, I blossomed. By the time I was three, I was *totally* gorgeous."

"Not to mention modest," said Lucille, her head bending over the photos. "Is this your dad? He looks nice."

"That was taken at Julia's birthday party. She was ten, I think. Going on fifty," Suzy added with a smile. In the photo, a group of girls clowned for the camera while Julia, her pristine blue party dress teamed with white knee-length socks, stood stiffly at attention, clutching her father's hand.

"Where's Mum?" Lucille noticed that Blanche wasn't featured in any of the photos taken on Julia's birthday.

"Don't know. Probably with you," said Suzy. She pointed to one of the photos in Lucille's album, of Lucille splashing in a paddling pool while Blanche looked on. "And there's your dad." She peered more closely at the smiling, dark-skinned man sitting next to Blanche. "Wow, he was handsome."

They carried on leafing through the albums, following each other's progress through childhood, comparing clothes, hairstyles, and vacations. On the beach at Bournemouth with Lucille, and in a pool on the Algarve with Suzy, their mother wore the same yellow daisy-patterned bikini.

"That was the villa we stayed in," Suzy pointed out.

"And that was our caravan," said Lucille. "In Mudeford."

Suzy experienced a pang of guilt.

"Didn't you ever wish you could go abroad?"

Lucille looked astonished.

"We had brilliant vacations. As long as Mum was there, I was happy. Nothing else mattered."

Suzy was still trying to imagine Blanche roughing it in a tatty caravan park.

In Mudeford, Dorset.

Actually enjoying herself.

It was hardly the Zambezi, was it?

Suzy shook her head. "She must have really loved you and your dad."

Proudly, Lucille said, "Oh, she did. And we loved her."

Weirder and weirder. From the sound of things, Blanche had been a better mother to Lucille than she'd ever been to her legitimate family. Actually, it explained a lot — not least the toy parrot from Paraguay — *allegedly* — which she had later spotted on the shelves of the souvenir shop at the Bristol Zoo.

"All those years," Suzy murmured, "she was sharing herself with — my God, there's *Harry*!" Glad for the diversion, she pounced on the next photo in the album, of two teenagers on bikes pretending to push each other off. Lucille, her hair cropped short

189

and her brown eyes bright with laughter, was wearing a Frankie Say Relax T-shirt and pink shorts. Next to her, Harry wore tight black jeans and a billowing crimson, pointy-collared shirt. He was grinning broadly, and his hair, which was long and curly, looked suspiciously blow-dried.

"That was his Duran Duran period," Lucille confided. "He's going to kill me for this."

Suzy had to ask.

"Did you two ever . . . ?"

"No. We were best friends, that's all."

"Are there any more like that?" Suzy began to eagerly riffle through the cellophane-encased pages. "Yes! Oh, this one's brilliant! What was going on here?"

"New Year's Eve party at Harry's house. We must have been sixteen." Lucille bent her head over the page, pointing out each of the people in the photo. "That's Pearl Harris; she had a major crush on Harry. That one's Shauna. She threw up in the goldfish bowl about five minutes after this picture was taken. I'm dancing with Ben Grigson — he kept trying to undo my shirt . . . and Harry's chatting up Ben's sister. I can't remember her name, but she never did find her shoes. We fished them out of the pond in the back garden six months later."

Suzy, following her finger, exclaimed suddenly, "And that's . . ."

"Leo."

Fascinated, Suzy peered at the tall figure on the far right of the picture. Leo must have been twenty or twenty-one then. He was leaning against the wall, clasping a drink and watching the proceedings with a faint supercilious smile on his lips. Some things never changed, Suzy realized. Then, as now, Harry had been the pretty one and Leo the more chiseled and mature of the two. He wore a striped rugby shirt and chinos and an air of older-brother boredom.

"He didn't want to be there," Lucille said wryly. "But he had to stay and make sure we didn't accidentally burn the house down."

Unable to resist it, Suzy said, "Did you ever . . . ?"

"Oh, *please.*" Lucille started to laugh. "Leo was Harry's big brother. I was Harry's scruffy little friend. As far as Leo was concerned, we were just a couple of silly kids. I was scared stiff of him."

At the mention of Leo's name, Baxter had lifted his head. Suzy reached over the side of the bed and gave his ears a consoling rub.

"What about now?"

191

"Oh well, old habits die hard. He's still Harry's terrifying big brother." Lucille shrugged. "I've never even thought of him in that way."

Smiling, she tucked a row of beaded plaits behind one ear.

"But if you did?" Suzy persisted.

"I just wouldn't. Come on. He's way out of my league."

What?

"I never think that." Suzy looked amazed. "It never occurs to me that someone could be out of my league."

"That," Lucille replied, "is because you're a confident, successful businesswoman. You live in a great apartment, you drive a Rolls, you wear wonderful clothes . . ."

"And I have an irresistible personality," Suzy prompted.

"Oh well." Lucille spread her hands. "Goes without saying."

"Plus a totally fabulous body."

"Exactly," said Lucille with a slowly spreading smile.

"But don't you see? So do you!"

"I walk dogs for a living," Lucille said patiently. "I sing in pubs and clubs and get ignored totally. If I'm not ignored, I'm heckled by drunks. It doesn't do wonders for your confidence, you know."

Suzy rolled onto her side, trying to imagine it. If a drunk was daft enough to heckle her, she would launch herself at him, drag him by his ears into the nearest bathroom, and stuff his head down the toilet.

Then again, she wasn't Lucille.

She couldn't sing either.

Well, only like a scalded cat.

Glancing back at the photo of the New Year's Eve party, she changed the subject.

"I showed Leo Mum's house last night."

"So I heard. He mentioned it this morning when he dropped Baxter off on his way to the airport." A dimple appeared in one of Lucille's cheeks. "Bit of an eventful evening, by all accounts."

"He seemed interested." Realizing the ambiguity of this statement, Suzy added hastily, "In the house, I thought."

"Well, he sounded keen to me."

"I wondered if it might be too big for him, what with all those bedrooms. But it didn't put him off."

"Oh, Leo wouldn't worry about that," said Lucille. "He's going to need somewhere big, isn't he? Him and Gabriella are bound to want loads of kids."

Gabriella.

Kids.

Loads . . .

Suzy felt her stomach tighten abruptly and do a kind of swoop of disappointment.

God, I really hate it when this happens.

Bugger, bugger, bum.

Aloud, she said casually, "Who's Gabriella?"

"Didn't Leo mention her?" Lucille looked surprised. "Oh, she's *stunning.* She and Leo have been together for, ooh, must be a year now. They're getting married in December."

CHAPTER 15

"Harry, no, stop it! When I said come in for coffee," Suzy explained, "I did actually *mean* coffee."

"Come on, we've had such a fantastic evening," murmured Harry, his mouth nuzzling her neck. "You can't do this to me. You know you want to as much as I do."

"Yes, yes, of course I do. But listen, Harry, I make it a strict rule never to sleep with a man until I've known him for at least six weeks."

That put a stop to the nuzzling. Harry drew back, astonished.

"In heaven's name, *why*?"

Hooray, she could breathe again.

"It stops me from being a tart." Suzy smoothed down her skirt, shook back her ruffled-with-passion hair, and flicked the switch on the kettle. "And it's nice! You have time to look forward to it . . . all that gorgeous anticipation . . . Now, proper coffee or instant?"

She was reaching for the coffeepot. Harry, who couldn't be bothered with anticipation — gorgeous or otherwise — said, "Instant." He shook his own head in bewilderment. "But six *weeks.*"

"And being stopped for speeding on the highway doesn't count." Suzy guessed he was busily counting backward.

"*Damn.*" Harry sighed. He leaned back against the kitchen wall, his face a picture of disbelief. "So you're telling me you actually persuade other blokes to go along with this?"

"They don't have to. I can't force them," Suzy told him cheerfully, "can I? Some stick around and some don't. Which is fine by me too. If they like me enough, they'll wait. If all they're after is a quickie and another notch on their bachelor bedposts, well then . . ." She shrugged, unperturbed. "They're no loss."

She meant it. She really meant it, Harry could tell.

Aloud, he said, "But I'm still allowed to kiss you?"

"Oh, yes." Suzy's smile was dazzling. "You're definitely allowed to kiss me. Two sugars or three?"

Harry watched her pile three sugars into

her own cup, then hover a heaped spoonful inquiringly over his.

"Just one."

"See?" exclaimed Suzy. "How could I sleep with you when I don't even know if you take sugar in your coffee?" With an air of triumph she waved the spoon at him. "I mean, wouldn't that just be the pits? Talk about sleazy . . . ugh!"

Harry, not used to being turned down, smiled and slid his arms around her waist. It was the most ridiculous rule he'd ever heard of. And rules were made to be broken, weren't they?

Slowly, he kissed Suzy's neck and whispered, "One sugar. There, now you know."

Behind them the kitchen door burst open, and Baxter, his claws clicking like castanets on the red-and-white-tiled floor, bounded across the kitchen to greet them. Springing apart from each other, Suzy and Harry braced themselves for violent impact.

Lucille gasped, slithering to a halt in the doorway. "God, sorry. I didn't realize you two were . . . ummm . . ."

"Having a coffee," said Suzy, clinging on to the red marble countertop and submitting to Baxter's enthusiastic welcome. She grabbed the jar of Taster's Choice and waved it at Lucille. "Can I make one for you too?"

Suzy heaved a sigh of relief the moment Harry had gone. "Saved by the dog."

"Oh Lord, this isn't going to work out, is it? Me living here." Lucille looked worried. "I feel terrible, like a giant contraceptive. I'm really cramping your style."

"Please. I *want* my style to be cramped."

Kicking off her high heels and throwing herself onto the sofa, Suzy explained her six-week rule to Lucille.

When she had finished, Lucille looked almost as horrified as Harry had done earlier.

"What, *never*?"

"Well, never say *never*." Suzy wiggled her toes. "We're all allowed the occasional lapse. Sometimes these things take you by surprise." The corners of her mouth began to twitch. "You get carried away and . . . it just happens."

"But not with Harry."

"Well, not yet," Suzy agreed.

Lucille was looking troubled. "Then again you haven't exactly had the chance, have you? Thanks to me."

"Don't worry about it — oh, tell me what happened on *EastEnders* tonight! Did

Peggy find out yet about the affair?"

Effortlessly, Suzy changed the subject — but Lucille had certainly had a point when she'd made her last remark about Harry. Oh dear, it wasn't looking promising, was it? After all her talk about the thrill of the wait, where *was* that sense of mounting excitement, the shuddery, bungee jumping adrenaline rush of anticipation? Gone on vacation, by the feel of things. Walked off with its hands in its pockets like a bored teenager.

It simply wasn't happening, Suzy realized with a pang. By now she should have reached the stage where she couldn't wait to rip Harry's clothes off.

And she hadn't.

That first lightning bolt of lust on the hard shoulder of the M4 had fizzled and faded. You couldn't make a spark happen if it was no longer there.

A box of matches, Suzy thought sadly, *that's what I feel like. A box of matches that's been left out in the rain.*

And the saddest thing of all was she knew why it had happened.

Harry was too keen.

It was as simple — and ridiculous — as that.

Sensing that she wasn't really paying attention to the *EastEnders* update, Lucille said, "He really likes you, you know. I haven't known Harry this keen for years. Not since . . ."

Oh Lord, Suzy thought.

Alarmed, she said, "Don't say Sophia."

Lucille gave her a what-can-I-tell-you look. "Sorry, but it's true. He's really smitten."

Not wanting to hear any more, Suzy rolled over onto her front, picked up the remote control, and aimed it at the television. When you were crazy about someone, there was nothing better in the world than being told they were crazy about you too.

But when you weren't, all you felt was slightly sick.

I'll have to break up with him, she decided. *It's the only decent thing to do. And the sooner the better. Dragging it out just isn't fair to Harry. I'll be doing him a favor.*

Oh dear, it all sounded horribly reminiscent of having your dog put down. Feeling terrible for even thinking it, Suzy glanced guiltily across at Baxter, sprawled on the cobalt-blue rug in front of the fire. He returned her gaze without flinching, one hairy eyebrow raised in a quizzical "So you'd have me put down, would you?" fashion.

"Oh," exclaimed Lucille, "I forgot to tell you about the ad I put up in the convenience store window. I've had three more phone calls this evening from people wanting me to exercise their dogs. Isn't that great?"

Suzy, still busy wondering how she was going to go about breaking up with Harry, said, "Brilliant! I'll buy you one of those grass sleds for your birthday. You can take it up to Ashton Court park, harness hundreds of dogs to it, and let them pull you for miles. Think of all the exercise it'll save, not to mention the money you'll make."

"Speaking of birthdays," said Lucille, "it's Harry's next week. Did he tell you?"

"What? Oh . . . yes, yes he did." Of course he had, Suzy remembered. It was on the seventeenth, exactly a week from today. And thank goodness Lucille had reminded her.

Like the feeling you get when you realize you have a genuine reason to cancel that dreaded visit to the dentist, Suzy experienced a surge of guilt mingled with relief. That was OK then; she couldn't possibly break up with Harry so close to his birthday — that would be a really rotten thing to do.

So — *phew* — she could stop worrying about it for now.

He was working nights for the rest of this week, Suzy told herself, so it wasn't as if

201

they'd see that much of each other anyway. No, all she had to do was treat Harry to dinner somewhere nice next Tuesday evening, buy him a funny card, and pick out a present. Nothing too extravagant, that might build his hopes up. Then again, nothing stingy either, because that would be too mean for words. Just something neutral. Like a nice sweater.

Then, a couple of days later, she could casually ease herself away . . .

Arriving home from work the following Monday, Suzy spotted a tall, familiar figure leaning against a car parked outside her house.

Correction: leaning against a grubby gray Volvo.

"Look!" Glancing over her shoulder, Suzy alerted her backseat passenger to the situation. "Look who's here!"

Baxter, his vast head stuck through the open window, was grinning his manic Jack Nicholson grin and letting his ears billow in the breeze behind him. When he saw who Suzy was pointing out, he let out a yodeling howl of joy and did his level best to squeeze the rest of his 150-pound body through the seven-inch gap.

Hoping her face wasn't too end-of-the-day shiny, Suzy pulled up behind the Volvo and reached behind her to open the rear door. Whimpering with impatience, Baxter exploded out of the car at last and hurled himself besottedly at Leo.

Suzy, emerging at a more leisurely pace from the driver's seat, lifted up her sunglasses and slowly smiled at Leo from under them. She'd seen Diana Dors do this in a movie once. Jolly effective.

Provided, of course, you didn't have a shiny face.

"Well, he certainly seems to like you," she told Leo.

"Cupboard love. He can smell the potato chips." Leo took a small bag out of his shirt pocket. Ecstatically, Baxter guzzled the contents in one go. "Oh well, tracked him down at last." As he rubbed Baxter's ears, Leo explained, "The flight landed at Heathrow at three o'clock. I drove back here, went straight over to Lucille's place to pick up Baxter . . . and got an earful of extremely colorful abuse from her landlord."

"Oh, what a shame," said Suzy. "So he's still alive, then."

Leo said, "After that, I called Harry. He told me Lucille was staying here with you."

"That's right."

"And you took Baxter in as well. Good of

you." He frowned. "But I've been ringing the doorbell and no one's in. Where's Lucille, and why is Baxter with you?"

It was the first time Suzy had seen him in daylight. And considering he had come directly from the airport following a transatlantic flight, Leo was looking unfairly good. His white polo shirt and faded Levi's were creased, of course — how could they not be? — but his tanned face glowed with health and his dark blue eyes, which crinkled at the corners whenever he smiled, were bright and alert. He had sportsman's eyes, Suzy decided. They didn't miss a thing. Even more unfairly, although he wasn't wearing mascara and she was — *loads* of it, actually — his eyelashes still managed to be longer and thicker than hers.

He had sportsman's stubble too, she observed. Funny how it could look so unappealing on a girl's legs yet so gorgeous on a man's chin.

Now where was the justice in that?

"Lucille's got herself loads more dog-walking business," she told Leo. "She's taken a gang of salukis to the Downs for a six-mile run. I said Baxter could spend the afternoon with me in the office. We've become excellent friends — he adores the backseat of my car."

Oops, provocative remark. Suzy held her breath, waiting for Leo to raise an amused eyebrow and drawl, "Who wouldn't?"

When he didn't, she couldn't decide whether to be disappointed or relieved that he wasn't that tacky.

Instead, checking his watch, Leo said, "Will Lucille be gone for long?"

"Should be back any minute now." Suzy waved her keys at him. "Come in for a drink."

The hot afternoon sun had streamed in through the closed south-facing windows, turning the apartment into a furnace. Having flung open the windows, they moved out onto the wrought iron balcony overlooking the back garden. Suzy brought out two tumblers, a jug of mineral water with lime slices and ice cubes bobbing on the top, and a couple of dog chews for Baxter.

It was a bit of a bugger, Leo being spoken for. She hadn't meant to think this, but the thought kept popping — practically of its own accord — into her head. Then again, thought Suzy, maybe it was just as well, especially if Harry's still a touch sensitive about having his girlfriends decide that, actually, they prefer his older brother.

In an attempt to move on to more neutral ground, she started asking him about his trip to New York.

Within minutes, Leo said gently, "Stop it."

"Stop what?" Suzy felt herself going pink.

"You know what. I've told you before. Don't mess Harry about."

Damn, thought Suzy, it had happened again. She'd been flirting with Leo without even realizing she was doing it.

Still, he could have been more tactful; no need to make such a drama out of the situation. Pointing it out like that was hardly chivalrous.

Stung, she said, "Guilty conscience?"

Leo's dark blue eyes narrowed. "What?"

"Harry told me," said Suzy. "About you and Sophia."

Was it her imagination or did the tension in his shoulders subside? There was a long pause, then Leo said, "Thought he might. Well, maybe you're right."

"Maybe? Come on," she chided. "You ran off with his girlfriend. Then you dumped her and she killed herself. I mean, you can understand why he was upset with you."

Slowly, Leo's gaze ran over Suzy, taking in the tight, white, scoop-necked T-shirt and pink skirt, her bare brown feet propped up on the balcony rail, and the expensive sunglasses pushed up on top of her head, keeping the tumbling tawny mane of hair off her tanned face.

Nothing escaped his notice.

Finally, he said, "And maybe you can understand why I don't want you to upset him."

The cheek of it, Suzy thought indignantly. *You're the one who screwed Harry up in the first place, and now I'm the one being made to suffer for it.* Men, honestly. They were enough to make you want to spit.

Except she mustn't spit at Leo. Mustn't lose her temper either. *I have to be lovely and charming and nice,* thought Suzy, fishing a slice of lime out of her glass and biting into it so hard all her salivary glands went *eek* and shriveled up in shock.

Oh no, she had to be nice to Leo. Because he was a potential client, and she very much wanted to sell him a house . . . any house, but especially her mother's.

And you didn't persuade people to buy a property worth hundreds of thousands of pounds by antagonizing them.

Nor, in this case, by flirting with them.

Even by accident.

"Anyway." Brightly, Suzy changed the subject. "I gather congratulations are in order. You're soon to become a father!"

This had the desired effect. Leo's eyebrows shot up, and he almost choked on his drink.

"What?"

Flicking her slice of lime over the balcony into the garden below, Suzy waited politely for him to finish spluttering.

"Gabriella, isn't that her name? You didn't tell me you were getting married! According to Lucille, your future wife wants *loads* of children."

The doorbell rang before Leo could reply. Downstairs, Suzy found Harry on the doorstep in uniform. His patrol car was parked by the front gate.

"Oh God, you haven't come to arrest me again, have you, Officer?" She said it loud enough to be heard by the two elderly spinster types tottering past, their expressions rigid with disapproval.

"Only if you've been very, very naughty," Harry informed her, equally loud and with a broad grin on his face. Oh dear, it was at moments like this that she remembered why she'd been attracted to him in the first place. There were no two ways about it: he was funny, and he was definitely gorgeous. *Why,* Suzy thought frustratedly, *why can't that be enough?*

"Leo's here."

"I know. He called me, remember?
208

Thought I'd just drop by to see how every-one is."

Just drop by to make sure I'm not having torrid sex on the kitchen table with your brother, thought Suzy. She watched another car pull up, farther along the road.

Amazed, she said, "Blimey, it's Julia."

"I called into the office," Julia announced, coming straight to the point as usual. "Rory told me about that girl moving in with you. For heaven's sake, are you out of your tiny *mind*?"

CHAPTER 16

Following her elder sister up the staircase, Suzy said, "That girl? You mean Lucille? She's my sister, Julia. Our sister. Why shouldn't she stay with me?"

"You know nothing about her, that's why. She could be all kinds of trouble! And what's that police car doing right outside the house? What are the neighbors going to think?"

Harry had gone on ahead while Suzy waited on the doorstep for Julia. Now, watching Julia's stilettos go clickety-clack up the stairs — heavens, her legs were thin — Suzy said, "Jaz and Celeste are away on vacation. And the Fraser-Harts are at work. Lucille isn't going to smash up the apartment and make off with my TV, if that's what you're worried about."

"You hope," Julia replied, her tone grim. She entered the sitting room and stared without enthusiasm at its occupants.

"You remember Harry," said Suzy. "Lucille's friend. You met him at —"

"I know where I met him," Julia snapped.

"And this is Leo, his brother. Leo, this is my sister, Julia. Oh, and this is Baxter, Leo's dog. He's been staying with us for a few — no, Baxter, get *down*. Don't . . ."

"Aaargh!" screamed Julia, flattening herself against the wall. Entranced by this new game, Baxter leaped up and rested his front paws on her shoulders. All they needed now was some music, and they could dance.

"Get him off my shirt!" Julia squealed. "It cost ninety five pounds — oh my God, if he licks my face I shall be *sick.*"

Clearly working hard to keep a straight face, Leo came to the rescue. When order had at last been restored, Suzy said apologetically, "Julia isn't crazy about dogs."

"I'm not crazy about a lot of things." Never afraid to speak her mind, Julia straightened her shirt and gazed pointedly at Harry and Leo. She turned to Suzy. "Can't you see what's happening here? First the girl, then her friend turns up" — Julia gestured dismissively at Harry — "then we get the friend's brother, not to mention the friend's brother's *dog* . . . It's just absurd! Before you know it you'll have poor relations stacked up like refugees in every room."

At this, Leo raised an eyebrow. Harry reached for the jug of iced water and said, "Does anyone else want another drink?"

Suzy, hearing a faint click, said firmly, "Julia, don't do this —"

"I came here to talk some sense into you." Julia held up her arm like a traffic cop. "And you're jolly well going to hear me out! It's bad enough that this girl's crawled out of the woodwork, but you can't let her take over your life. Just get Mum's house sold, pay her off, and get rid of her."

"Julia —"

"Or the next thing you know," said Julia, "she'll be demanding a share of the business."

Behind her, framed in the doorway, Lucille said, "For your information, I want nothing from the business."

Julia swung around, unrepentant.

"And for *your* information," she mimicked icily, "I don't believe a word you say. As far as I'm concerned, you're nothing but a leech, hell-bent on destroying us — and I'm not going to let it happen."

"Out," said Suzy, gesturing for Lucille to move out of the way and steering Julia forcibly toward the door. "Out, out, *out.*"

"She's the one you should be saying that to," Julia hissed, "not me."

"By the way," Leo announced, gazing steadily at her, "I'm thinking about it."

Julia's lip curled at the sight of him in his crumpled clothes, with his faintly insolent smile and sixteen hours' worth of stubble on his face. She loathed stubble, it was so working class. She loathed it almost as much as she loathed men who couldn't be bothered to iron their shirts.

"You're thinking of leaving?" she sneered. "Well, don't let me stop you."

"Actually," Leo said mildly, "I meant I'm thinking of buying your mother's house."

"That took the wind out of her sails," said Suzy, gazing out of the front window and watching Julia stomp furiously back to her car.

"She really hates me." Lucille sighed. "Maybe I should move out."

Suzy looked at her in surprise.

"She really hates lots of people. Don't let it worry you."

Lucille, clearly troubled, shook her head. "You can't expect me to just ignore her."

"Listen, you're new to this sister business." Patiently, Suzy explained. "I've had *years* of practice. The thing about sisters is you *don't* have to be polite to them, you *can* ignore them, and you never, ever, *ever* let them upset you. If they do," she went on, reminiscing happily, "you can always creep into their bedroom at night and cut off their bangs."

At this, Lucille had to smile.

"You're my sister. Does that mean I'm allowed to do that to you?"

"Ah. Not unless you want to wake up the next morning with an indelible-ink mustache."

Harry's walkie-talkie crackled into life as Leo and Baxter left.

"I have to go too," he told Suzy with regret.

At the bottom of the staircase he kissed her.

"I love you, you know."

Oh, help . . .

"No, you don't," Suzy assured him. "You just want to sleep with me."

"Well, that too." Harry grinned. "I'll see you tomorrow night."

"Eight o'clock. Don't be late."

"Did I mention it was my birthday?"

"Only about thirty-five times."

"Shall I tell you what I'd really like as a present?"

He looked so gorgeous in his uniform.

Almost irresistible.

Almost.

"How about a calendar?" said Suzy, pulling open the front door. "Then you'll be able to work out when those six weeks are up."

Oh dear, was it mean, saying that? By then she would be long gone. It was like a judge promising a prisoner that when his case came up next month, he wouldn't send him to the gallows, safe in the knowledge that he was actually retiring next week.

Except it wasn't like that at all, Suzy consoled herself. Of course it wasn't. Harry would get over her in no time. There were hundreds of pretty girls in Bristol who would be only too happy to have sex with him.

More than only too happy.

After all, when you fancy a Mars bar and the shop's sold out, you don't have a nervous breakdown about it, do you?

You just help yourself to a nice Snickers or a Heath bar instead.

In the office the following morning Donna said, "You've got someone else interested in Sheldrake House." She pointed to a slot in Suzy's diary. "I penciled him in for midday. He said he'd meet you there."

"What's his name? Is he on our books?" Suzy peered across the desk.

"Dr. Price. And no, he isn't. But a buyer's a buyer," said Donna, sensing her lack of enthusiasm. "And he sounds as if he knows what he wants."

To turn it into a nursing home probably, Suzy thought, *which isn't what I want at all.* The prospect of the beautiful house she had grown up in being converted into a rest home for incontinent geriatrics wasn't exactly a cheery one. It deserved better than that.

Maybe this afternoon she should give Leo another call.

Suzy heaved a gusty sigh. It was still a bit of a bugger, Leo turning out to have a fiancée.

Then again, if he weren't marrying this Gabriella — and what a show-offy name that was — the chances were that he wouldn't be interested in buying Sheldrake House.

Suzy was the first to arrive at the house, just before midday. Unlocking the heavy front door and stepping into the hall, she breathed in the comfortingly familiar smell of the home in which she had grown up.

Would it still smell like this in a year's

time, when other people were living in it? Not if this Dr. Price turned the place into a rest home, that was for sure. It would just smell of air freshener and eau de wee.

The sound of tires crunching on gravel propelled Suzy over to the front door. A gleaming white Audi pulled up and a pretty girl in a white broderie anglaise sundress jumped out. Baby-blond hair, gleaming like satin in the sunlight, swung around her shoulders. She had a neat, tiny figure. White ballet-type pumps on her feet. No makeup whatsoever, and no jewelry either. She didn't need makeup, Suzy realized. She was . . . how old? Twenty-one, twenty-two, maybe? And stunning. Totally stunning. Sparkly eyed and friendly looking. The kind of girl you couldn't help but take to on sight.

Dr. Price's girlfriend?

His — *ahem* — personal secretary?

Or his daughter?

Granddaughter, even?

"Hello, I'm Suzy Curtis." Descending the steps, Suzy held out her hand in greeting. "Well, we're on time! Trust the man to be late."

The girl laughed. "Absolutely. Hi, nice to meet you. Gaby Price."

Naturally, she had the perfect handshake. Cool, not too firm, not too limp.

"Well, how shall we do this?" said Suzy. "Make a start now? Or wait until Dr. Price gets here?"

"Oh dear, brace yourself." The girl smiled broadly at her, revealing the kind of pearly teeth a four-year-old might possess. "I'm afraid I'm Dr. Price."

Suzy gazed at her in disbelief. "You can't be!"

Gaby Price said teasingly, "Women can be doctors too, you know."

"Oh please, I didn't mean that!" Embarrassing or what? "But . . . the receptionist who took your call this morning . . . she said you were a *he.*"

Heavens, was Donna on drugs or something?

"Ah. My secretary called your office and made the appointment," said Gaby Price. "I have a male secretary."

"But you look so young!" Suzy couldn't help it; she couldn't wait to find out which moisturizer this girl used. "I mean, how old do you have to be to be a doctor?"

"I'm fully qualified, I promise you," said Gaby Price with a mischievous smile. "And since you ask, I'm twenty-nine."

Up close, her complexion was flawless. This girl-woman doctor, thought Suzy, wouldn't know a pore if it came up and grabbed her by the throat. In fact, she was a walking miracle. The incredible poreless woman.

Still dazed, she said, "You look about seventeen."

"It's not always an advantage." Gaby's tone was rueful. "Particularly when you're trying to exert a bit of authority on belligerent patients who don't want to hear what you have to tell them."

Suzy was fascinated. She was bursting to ask a million questions. But Dr. Price was already glancing at her watch. Clearly, her time was both valuable and limited.

Switching into efficient businesswoman mode, Suzy stepped to one side and ushered the girl-woman — *whatever* — ahead of her into the house.

"Right, let's get on with it, shall we? And before we start, I'd better explain that this house is pretty special to me. You see, it was my mother's —"

"Oh, I know all about that." In the cool, oak-paneled hall, Gaby Price laid a reassuring hand briefly on her arm. "Leo told me the whole story." She smiled, gazing around with unconcealed pleasure. "This is where you grew up."

CHAPTER 17

"I felt like such an idiot." Suzy groaned, streamers of Scotch tape dangling from her teeth and fingers as she fought a losing battle with Harry's birthday present. That was the trouble with metallic wrapping paper; instead of obediently staying where you put it, it much preferred to do its own slithery thing. "God, she must have thought I was a complete — *ouch!*"

"Here, let me."

Lucille, fresh from the shower and wrapped in an orange satin robe, deftly removed the Scotch tape strips from Suzy's fingers, leaving her free to finish peeling away the strip that had stuck itself painfully to her bottom lip. Collapsing onto the floor next to Suzy, she gripped the delinquent parcel between her knees. Within seconds it was taped into submission.

"You know what you should be?" Relieved that the hideous task was at last completed

— and even gladder that her lip wasn't bleeding — Suzy gave her a hug. "One of Santa's Little Helpers, that's what."

"But does it matter if Gabriella thinks you're a complete idiot?" said Lucille. *Completely* idiotically, in Suzy's view. "I mean, so long as she likes the house. And you're pretty sure she did like it, aren't you?"

"Well, I can usually tell."

Getting on with the business at hand, Suzy flipped open the card she had chosen for Harry. Nothing slushy, heaven forbid. In the end, she had gone for something the polar opposite of slushy. Permafrosty, perhaps.

"That's good news then, isn't it?" Lucille sounded encouraging.

"Of course it is. I just keep cringing at the thought of her going back to Leo, saying, 'Blimey, that Curtis girl's a few wasps short of a picnic, isn't she? Are you sure you want to do business with a company like that?' "

This was a big fib, of course, but Suzy couldn't bring herself to tell Lucille the true reason — that seeing as she had a bit of a crush on Leo Fitzallan, she really didn't want him to think of her as a stupid, idiotic type of person.

"You're underestimating Gabriella. She's lovely," said Lucille.

Lovely, Suzy thought. *Hate that word.*

Unclicking her pen — but sadly not her brain — she scrawled *Yours sincerely, S Curtis* across the bottom of Harry's card.

"Oops," said Lucille with a grin.

"Oh, *bum.* Now I'll have to go out and buy another one." Suzy glanced up at the clock in dismay. "Half past seven . . . and I haven't even started getting ready yet!" Punctuality was her big thing; she hated being late.

"You jump in the shower. Don't worry, I'll get you a card," said Lucille.

Phew, that was a relief. The shops were all closed by now. Lucille was evidently the organized type who kept a stash of all-purpose cards for emergencies.

"You've got spares?" said Suzy.

Lucille levered herself upright.

"No, but the all-night gas station will."

It was one of those squirm-makingly awkward moments. By the time Lucille arrived back at the apartment it was three minutes to eight. All dressed up and ready to go, Suzy gazed at the card Lucille had chosen on her behalf.

"Happy Birthday to the One I Love," proclaimed the curly gold lettering on the front, intertwined with forget-me-nots and butterflies.

It was even worse inside.

There was a poem.

"They didn't have a huge selection," said Lucille. She added brightly, "It's all right, though, isn't it?"

My Heart Is Yours Forever
You Mean Everything to Me
Together We'll Be Happy
for All Eternity.

Feeling a bit sick, Suzy swallowed hard. Her own lousy taste in music was nothing compared with Lucille's taste in birthday cards.

The clock on the mantelpiece chimed eight.

"Go on then, sign it," Lucille urged.

"Ummm, isn't it a bit over the top?"

"Don't be so fussy. I told you, they didn't have a lot to choose from."

Oh God. Lucille looked as if she was about to start taking offense. Suzy hurriedly reached for the pen.

"What shall I put?"

"Love from Suzy." Lucille rolled her eyes, amazed at her stupidity.

Love. From Suzy. Oh well, it was only a word on a card, wasn't it? People didn't read it and automatically assume that you *did* love them, did they?

Mentally crossing her fingers, she quickly signed as instructed.

"There, all done. Thanks for getting it for me." Suzy couldn't help picturing Harry's face when he opened the card. Maybe she could turn it into a huge joke. Crikey, she hoped he wouldn't sue the pants off her for breach of contract when she broke up with him in, ooh, roughly forty-eight hours' time . . .

"I can't believe it's going so well between you," Lucille said happily. "My oldest friend and my newfound sister. I mean, how amazing is that?"

With a jolt, Suzy realized why she hadn't been totally honest, Harry-wise, with Lucille. It was precisely *because* Lucille was so thrilled by the idea of the two of them as an item that she hadn't had the heart to come clean. Inwardly, Suzy winced. Breaking up with Harry was probably going to disappoint Lucille more than it would him.

Ten minutes passed.

"He's going to love his present," said Lucille, giving the silver-wrapped parcel an enthusiastic pat.

I should hope so too, thought Suzy, who had paid a ludicrous amount of money for the Ralph Lauren lilac cashmere crewneck sweater. It was one of those guilt buys, of course. No newly dumped ex-boyfriend of hers was going to be given the chance to call her a cheapskate.

And now it was twelve minutes past eight. For heaven's sake, Suzy thought indignantly, was there *anything* more annoying than people who couldn't be bothered to turn up on time on their birthday?

Aloud, she said, "If he's not here by quarter past, he won't be getting his present. I mean, where *is* he? He's *late.*"

By eight thirty, there was still no sign of Harry. Planning to break up with someone was one thing, Suzy rapidly discovered, but being stood up by them was quite another.

Tired of stalking up and down the sitting room, Suzy paused in front of the huge oval gilded mirror above the marble fireplace. She looked terrific, didn't she? In her new strappy tangerine silk dress and with her hair fastened up with silver combs? She was wearing seven-denier stockings, two hundred pounds' worth of Manolo Blahnik stilettos . . . even a brand-new bra and matching panties in topaz yellow lace. Which was a pretty generous gesture on her part, Suzy felt, considering she hadn't even been intending to let Harry see them.

And her makeup was perfect.

Swinging around, Suzy said, "Tell me, am I the ugliest thing you've ever seen? Do I look totally hideous?"

"Yes, awful." Lucille was stretched out across the sofa, idly flicking through the TV channels. Grinning, she said, "All right. You look fantastic."

Suzy spread her arms in amazement.

"I *know*. I know I do! So what I *also* want to know is why hasn't the fucker turned up?"

By nine o'clock Suzy had had enough.

"Right, that's it." Picking up Harry's painstakingly wrapped birthday present, she flung it across the room. "Harry Fitzallan is now *officially* a bastard."

Lucille patted the cushions on the sofa next to her.

"*Titanic*'s about to start."

"I can't stay in!" wailed Suzy. "I won't stay in! I spent *hours* getting ready to go out —"

"Well, twenty-five minutes," said Lucille, to be fair.

"— and I'm jolly well *going* to. Otherwise, all this" — Suzy gestured to her hair, her makeup, her seven-denier stockings — "will be *wasted.*"

"OK," said Lucille.

"If only I had someone to go out with." Suzy heaved a sigh and looked soulful. "Someone who could cheer me up, someone really kind and lovely . . . Did I ever tell you, by the way, that you are absolutely my favorite sister?"

Lucille thought for a moment. "No."

"Well, that is so weird, because you are, you really are! In fact, you're my most favorite sister in all the world . . ."

"Would you like me to come out with you tonight?"

Suzy leaned across the sofa and enveloped her in a bear hug. "I thought you'd never ask!"

Disentangling herself, Lucille stood up and indicated her baggy tank top and khaki combat pants. "Give me ten minutes to get changed." Over her shoulder, she added, "And give Harry another call."

"He doesn't deserve one. Anyway, I'd much rather go out with you."

"Just try," said Lucille. "It's his birthday, after all. Imagine if he turned up five minutes after we'd left."

"Serve him right!" Suzy exclaimed indignantly. It was what she was hoping would happen. Then he'd know how it felt to be left high and dry.

Partly to placate Lucille — and to pass the time while she was getting changed — Suzy gave Harry-the-Bastard's cell phone one last try. It rang, then switched to voice mail. She dialed his apartment. No reply. Finally, she rang the police station where Harry was based, just to check — again — that he hadn't been called in on some emergency.

He hadn't, surprise surprise. Even more irritatingly, the desk sergeant who had picked up the phone on both occasions sounded as if he was smirking all over his fat, ugly, red face.

Suzy had never met him, but he *sounded* as if he had a fat, ugly, red face.

"Still no luck, eh? Sorry, love, can't help you. Looks like he's forgotten he was meant to be meeting up with you. Want to leave a message, love? Would you like me to tell old Harry boy what you think of him for standing you up?"

Suzy could hear snorts of laughter in the background, plus a few ribald comments. She was clearly providing in station entertainment for the whole shift. Without bothering to reply, she hung up just as Lucille reappeared in a black top and a short white skirt that showed off her long legs.

"No luck?" Lucille nodded at the phone,

sounding worried. "Maybe something's happened."

Ha, thought Suzy, *chance would be a fine thing.*

"People always think that, and it's never true. All that's happened is Harry's decided not to turn up tonight."

It was probably his childish idea of revenge, Suzy thought, his way of paying her back for refusing to sleep with him.

"He could be ill," Lucille pleaded. Catching the look in Suzy's eye, she added, "I'm not just trying to make up an excuse."

She was, of course, but Suzy didn't blame her. Harry was her best friend. It was Lucille's job to defend him and come up with endless completely feeble excuses.

There was just one drawback . . .

"He's got one of these, I've got one of these" — Suzy tapped her phone dismissively — "and he hasn't even bothered to call me. Let's face it: there is no excuse."

At Henry Africa's Bar, on Whiteladies Road, they bumped into Adam Pettifer and his team from the Pettifer Agency on Blackboy Hill.

"Are all real estate agents like this?" gasped Lucille two hours later as Adam, whisking her between the tables, gave her

229

an impromptu salsa lesson.

"No," said Suzy. "Some of them can actually dance."

"Oh, come on, cheer up." Lucille had to shout to make herself heard above the chatter and music in the packed bar. "There's a phone over there. Give him another call, if you want to."

One of the Pettifer's team was being served at the bar. Turning, he yelled, "Suzy! Another one for you?"

Suzy smiled and nodded, determined to get into the swing of things. Of course she didn't want to phone Harry. The whole point of leaving her cell phone at home was so she *wouldn't* spend the evening waiting for it to ring.

Or be tempted to keep trying Harry's number.

Peeved wasn't the word for how she was feeling. Honestly, the sheer nerve of the man. How *dare* Harry stand her up?

At midnight they piled out of Henry Africa's and set about trying to flag down a cab. When — for some curious reason — no taxi driver seemed keen to transport eight noisy, well-oiled real estate agents and a dog-walker-cum-singer across Clifton, Suzy threw up her arms and declared, "This is hopeless. We'll just have to walk."

"Screw walking." Adam Pettifer seized her by the waist. "We're going to do this in style. We'll . . . salsa!"

They danced their way along Alma Road and Buckingham Vale.

"Ow, my *feet,*" wailed Suzy, hopping and clutching Lucille's arm for support as she pulled off first one shoe, then the other.

Lucille was still worried about Harry.

"What if he turned up at your house just after we went out?"

"Let's not spoil the evening thinking about Harry." Suzy attempted without success to stuff her stilettos into her handbag. Hopeless, much too small. Grabbing Adam's arm, she jammed them instead into the pockets of his Armani jacket — one on each side, like panniers on a donkey.

"It's bloody miles to your place," Adam grumbled as they crossed Pembroke Road.

"Stop moaning. Have I ever thrown a bad party?"

He gave her a clumsy hug.

"You're a doll, you know that?"

A *what*?

"I know," said Suzy, nodding vigorously.

"You seeing anyone at the moment?"

They were taking a shortcut along Vyvyan Terrace. Behind them, Lucille and the rest of Adam's staff were still singing, twirling and salsaing on and off the edge of the pavement like a team of Gene Kelly clones doing "Singin' in the Rain."

Well, quite like a team of Gene Kelly clones. So long as you didn't look too closely and kept your fingers stuffed in your ears.

". . . at the moment?"

Suzy realized she hadn't been paying attention. "Sorry, what?"

Grinning, Adam repeated slowly and clearly, "Are you seeing anyone at the moment?"

"No." Absolutely definitely not.

"Great! Would you like to go out with me?"

"No thanks," said Suzy.

For a second he looked disappointed. "Sure?"

"Sure."

"OK." Adam shrugged and lowered his mouth to her ear. "But I can stay tonight, can't I? Nothing meaningful, just for the sex."

"Look, it's really kind of you to offer," said Suzy, "but it's still no thanks."

"That's too bad." He draped a friendly arm over her shoulder and whispered, "Lucille's pretty gorgeous too, isn't she?"

Suzy hid a smile.

"Oh yes."

"Would she like to have sex with me tonight, d'you think?"

"Probably not, no."

Adam heaved a sigh. "This is hopeless. At least promise me you've got loads to drink at your place."

"Don't worry." Suzy's tone was reassuring. "We've got the lot."

"Because I will be needing to drown my sorrows." Adam swayed and looked mournful.

Suzy, giving his arm a consoling pat, said, "I think they've already drowned."

At last they reached Sian Hill. Ahead of them, lit up against the inky night sky like a Las Vegas casino, the Suspension Bridge stretched across the cavernous Avon Gorge.

Better still, they were almost *home*. As she fumbled in her bag for the door keys, Suzy wondered if her feet would ever recover. Her seven-denier stockings certainly wouldn't; they were in shreds.

"Who's that?" said Lucille suddenly.

Suzy looked up.

"What?"

"There's someone outside the house. Sitting on the front steps."

Harry. It had to be Harry, the birthday boy himself!

Come to grovel, Suzy thought with satisfaction. *Come to grovel and apologize and beg me to forgive him.*

Aloud she said happily, "This should be good."

"Be nice to him," pleaded Lucille. "It is his birthday, after all."

"Not anymore it isn't." Suzy glanced at her watch; half past midnight. She tucked her arm through Adam's, leaning against him as they made their way up the hill. This was definitely going to be fun.

"Hang on," said Lucille, stopping dead and pointing across the road. "Isn't that Leo's car?"

It was. And Leo, having spotted them, was climbing out of it. As the figure on the doorstep simultaneously rose to his feet and began to trot toward them, Suzy realized that it wasn't Harry at all. This was a middle-aged man she'd never seen before in her life.

"Suzy Curtis? Are you Suzy Curtis?"

A jolt of fear shot through Suzy. She shuddered, her fingers tightening helplessly around Adam's elbow.

What's going on?

Moving at speed, Leo reached her first.

"Where have you been?" he demanded brusquely. "Your phone's switched off."

Feeling numb, Suzy pointed at the house. "I left it at home. Oh God, where's Harry? What's happened to him?"

"Suzy Curtis? Mike Platt from the *Evening Post*. You're Harry Fitzallan's girlfriend?"

Behind her, Lucille gasped. Feeling sick, Suzy yelled, "Yes! Yes! Just tell me what's going on!"

"He's in Frenchay Hospital." Leo's voice was clipped. "It's pretty bad, but he's conscious. Fractured skull, broken leg and arm, a few broken ribs, cuts and bruises. The doctors say he'll recover, but it's a miracle he's still alive."

"Oh my God . . ." Shivering violently now, Suzy was dimly aware of Adam Pettifer draping his jacket around her shoulders. The rest of the group hovered uncertainly in the background, not knowing what to do. One of Suzy's shoes fell out of the pocket of Adam's jacket, onto the pavement. Leo bent and picked it up.

"He's been asking for you."

"What was it, a car accident?"

A muscle twitched in Leo's jaw. "You could say that."

The reporter from the *Evening Post* shoved Adam out of the way and thrust a small tape recorder under Suzy's nose. "Harry Fitzallan is a hero, Suzy! He risked his own life to save two young children from a terrible death. How do you feel about that?"

"Come on," Leo said curtly, "I'll drive you to the hospital." He glanced at Lucille. "You'd better come too."

"He saved two children?" Stunned, Suzy said, "How? I mean, when? I mean, how . . . ?"

"Just before eight this evening. He was on his way over to see you."

"He could get the George Medal for this," gabbled the reporter, his tape recorder outstretched as Leo ushered them both across the road. "Hey, Suzy, before you go, how are you feeling right now? You must be very proud!"

CHAPTER 18

"There'll be plenty more of that at the hospital," warned Leo as they drove away at speed. "The press has really latched on to this one. They're already bidding for interviews."

"Never mind that." Next to him in the front seat, Suzy clamped her trembling, ice-cold hands between her knees. "Tell us what happened."

"Well, as I said, Harry was on his way over to you. He stopped for gas at the station on Beaumont Road. There was a woman at the next pump with her two kids in the back of the car. A girl of six and her baby brother." Having set the scene, Leo paused for a second. "Meanwhile, just around the corner — although Harry didn't know it at the time — two teenagers were mugging an old woman. She was an easy enough target — they snatched her handbag and ran off — but a passerby saw them and gave chase.

When they reached the gas station they saw he was catching up with them. Harry and the woman were paying for their gas by this time. Harry saw them try his car, but he'd taken his keys in with him. The woman, though, had left hers in the ignition. So they jumped into her car and started it up."

Suzy gasped. "With the children still in the back."

Leo nodded. "Exactly. Harry tore out of the shop. The woman was in hysterics. Harry tried to stop them by standing in front of the car, but they accelerated toward him. They were trying to run him over. He couldn't jump out of the way — there wasn't room. All he could do was throw himself onto the hood. He had to cling on to the windshield wipers. Harry yelled to them to stop, but they didn't. They were laughing like hyenas, he said. Throwing the car from side to side, trying to force him off. And all the time he could hear the kids crying and screaming in the back."

"He could have been killed," Suzy whispered.

"Of course he could have been killed." Leo's tone was grim. "And you haven't even heard the rest."

Closing her eyes, Suzy said, "Go on."

"They drove — at speed — down to the

docks. God only knows how Harry managed to hang on for so long. Then they smashed through a fence at Baltic Wharf. The car was heading straight for the river. Just before it went over the edge, the teenagers jumped out. Harry was still on the hood. The car tipped over as it went into the water and landed on top of him, breaking his leg, arm, and ribs and fracturing his skull."

Hang on, something wasn't right here, surely?

"No . . . you've lost me." Suzy shook her head, puzzled. "So who got the children out of the car?" And why on earth, she wondered, had that reporter been burbling idiotically on about the George Medal? Not being funny or anything, but all Harry had really done here was leap onto the hood to avoid being run over. Of course, jumping in front of the car in the first place had been a brave thing to do, but *heroic*?

As if sensing her traitorous thoughts, Leo turned his head briefly and glanced at her. "Harry did."

"But hang on, you said . . ."

"I know, but he still managed to get them out. God knows how," said Leo. "Basically, I suppose, because there was no one else around to do the job. The two teenagers had run off. There were a few pensioners, apparently, who saw the whole thing, but they couldn't help. And every second counted."

Suzy looked at Lucille, whose eyes were wide with shock. Since she appeared to have lost the ability to speak, Suzy carried on. "So Harry rescued both children? But *how*?"

"He managed to force open one of the doors, pulled the girl out, unclipped the baby from his child seat . . . The police arrived just as he reached the riverbank with both children in his arms. The moment they were taken off him, he collapsed. The ambulance crew couldn't believe it when they arrived and examined him. According to the doctors, what Harry did was practically superhuman." Leo paused for a moment. "So where were you tonight until half past twelve? And who was that guy you were draped over?"

"Nobody. Just a friend." Caught off guard by the abrupt change of subject, Suzy felt herself going red. Defensively, she swiveled around, in need of support from Lucille. "He was just a friend, wasn't he? They all were. Harry didn't turn up, so we went out — and that's all there is to it!"

"Harry didn't turn up so you went out," Leo echoed, like a disdainful judge addressing the court. Not quite beneath his breath, he murmured, "My, my, we *are* the loyal type."

"Well, what was I supposed to think?" Nettled, Suzy's voice began to rise. "Oh dear, Harry's a bit late, he must be scrabbling around in the mud at the bottom of the river, pulling innocent children out of hijacked cars?"

"She tried to phone him," Lucille put in, "loads of times."

"Harry guessed it was you." Leo glanced at Suzy as he pulled into the entrance of Frenchay Hospital. "He heard his phone ringing in his pocket. Unfortunately, he couldn't answer it — he was busy hanging on to a pair of windshield wipers at the time."

"OK, *OK*," Suzy retaliated, flicking her hair crossly out of her eyes as he parked. "But I still didn't go out and pick up another man for the night."

"No, more like six or seven," Leo drily observed. "And before we go in, you may want to take something off. Harry might have a fractured skull" — his gaze flickered over her — "but even he's not going to believe that jacket belongs to you."

Knowing there were photographers hanging around was making Suzy twitchy. She didn't mean to be shallow and vain — after all, Harry was the one whose picture they were clamoring for — but it was hard to relax when you suspected you looked like something out of a disaster movie, the socialite rescued from the depths of the jungle after three weeks of eating other people's legs, with her hair and makeup all over the place but her pearls intact.

Not that there was any chance of stopping to repair the damage, anyway, with Leo frog-marching her along echoey corridors like a prison guard. Suzy's bare feet in their shredded stockings were making slapping noises on the unforgiving concrete floor — for heaven's sake, she sounded like a seal in the zoo.

Hurrying to keep up, Suzy attempted to restore some kind of order to her falling-down hair. And — yes, hooray! — she had a lipstick in her teeny tiny handbag. Nudging Lucille, who was carrying the bag for her while she struggled with her hair, Suzy mouthed *lipstick* and mimed plastering it onto her lips.

Glancing over his shoulder, Leo drawled, "Just this once, try not to think only of yourself."

Indignantly, Suzy said, "I just want to look my best for Harry."

"Hmmm." Clearly not fooled for a second — damn, she hated it when that happened — Leo turned right and said abruptly, "We're here."

Suzy stumbled to a halt behind him. It was definitely too late now to look her best. She settled for biting her lips, pinching her cheeks — *ouch* — and sucking in her stomach instead.

Oh, and putting on her stilettos . . .

"I'll have my shoes now." She held out her hands.

Leo raised his eyebrows. "Why are you looking at me?"

"Because you've got them," said Suzy. She pointed to the pockets of his leather jacket. "I took off Adam's jacket and you put it in the trunk of your car. And I said, 'Shoes,' and you said, 'Right.' Which I took to mean that you had the situation under control. That you would carry my shoes, seeing as my feet were too blistered for me to wear them."

Having listened with apparent polite interest, Leo now shook his head.

"Sorry. Got our wires crossed here. I thought you wanted me to check that both shoes were *in* the trunk."

Talk about a blatant lie. He'd done it on purpose, Suzy realized. To teach her some

243

obscure sort of lesson. Deciding that Leo Fitzallan wasn't nearly as nice as she'd once thought, she straightened her shoulders, thrust out her hand, and said, "Give me the car keys then, and I'll go back and get them."

This was a bluff, of course. Born of sheer bravado. Even on the cool concrete floor her feet felt as if they'd been dipped in chili sauce and set on fire. She would have cried, probably, if Leo had tossed her the keys.

Thankfully, Lucille came to the rescue.

"Stop it, *both* of you." She shook her head in disbelief. "All this sniping about a pair of shoes — this is just ridiculous!"

"Tell that to Zsa Zsa Gabor here," murmured Leo.

I can't believe this is happening to me, Suzy marveled. *The man's a Rottweiler. How could I ever have liked him?*

"Right," said Lucille. "You two stay here and fight if that's what you want to do. I'm going to see Harry."

As they stood there, at the entrance to the ward Harry was in, a nurse slipped past them and pushed her way through the rubber doors. An antiseptic smell came rushing out at them, filling Suzy's nostrils and triggering an ancient memory she preferred to forget.

Suzy glanced down at the faint scar running along the inside of her arm. When you were seven years old, sliding down the banisters at school was something you were dared to do. And she'd done it — except that the barked reprimand of the headmistress had made her lose her balance, and underneath the staircase had been a sharp-edged metal sculpture.

Falling onto the sharpest edge of all — just typical of her, as the headmistress had wearily pointed out — Suzy had sliced open her arm in spectacular fashion. Blood had sprayed everywhere and the headmistress had been forced to rush her to the hospital.

The pain had been excruciating, but that wasn't what Suzy remembered now. All of a sudden she was seven again, having her arm stitched together in the emergency room and crying, crying endlessly for her mother.

She was even able to recall the sympathetic look on the doctor's face as he had asked her where her mother was.

Suzy closed her eyes momentarily, remembering her half sobbed, half hiccuped reply.

"She's gone a-away again. To Afri-ca-ca-ca."

The next moment her eyes snapped open as a brisk female voice barked, "Now, now, gentlemen, no smoking in this hospital."

The nurse had pushed open the door to the waiting room. A great cloud of smoke billowed out, followed by a gaggle of sheepish-looking photographers and reporters.

"Well?" Lucille looked at Suzy. "Are you coming or not?"

It was all right for Lucille. She had shoes on and braided hair that was impossible to mess up.

Heroically, Suzy didn't voice these thoughts aloud.

Instead, she said, "Of course."

The rubber doors bounced shut behind them, and the photographers — recognizing Leo from earlier — swung into action. The nurse, who clearly moonlighted as a bouncer on her nights off, waded into the fray and extricated Suzy and Lucille.

"Ow!" yelped Suzy as a size-twelve brogue landed on her bare toes.

"Plenty of time for that later, gentlemen," the nurse declared bossily. "These people are here to see Mr. Fitzallan, and I'm sure they'd appreciate it if you'd give them room to breathe."

Actually, this took Suzy back a few years as well, to the time when Jaz had been at the height of his popularity. As his wife, she had become accustomed to the attentions of the paparazzi. Sometimes it had been fun and sometimes it had been a pain in the neck. Either way, she'd never left the house unprepared.

But being the wife of a rock star was one thing. Being the girlfriend of a policeman was quite another.

Anyway, this was neither the time nor the place. Anyone visiting an unlit hospital ward in the middle of the night would look like an idiot in dark glasses.

Suzy smiled, ignored the cameras, and said nothing while the nurse ushered them along the corridor and into a side ward.

"He's exhausted," the nurse warned them. "Ten minutes and no more."

CHAPTER 19

Harry, lying in bed hooked up to a cacophony of drips and machines making beeping noises, opened his eyes.

"Suzy. You're here. And Lucille."

The nurse discreetly withdrew. Leo moved over to the far wall and leaned against it, his hands stuffed into the pockets of his leather jacket, his expression unreadable.

"Oh, Harry." Flinching slightly as she moved toward him — that contact with the size-twelve brogue had *crushed* the toes on her right foot — Suzy held out her hands in dismay. "What did they do to you?"

He looked like a cartoon of an accident victim. His left leg was in a cast. So was his right arm. Bandages were wrapped around his head and there was a skin-stitched gash along his left cheekbone. Even his chest was bandaged, Suzy saw when he raised his good arm. If Dennis the Menace fell down a mountain and got crushed by a ten-ton truck, he would end up looking exactly like this.

Although not so good-looking, of course. Because Dennis the Menace wasn't Harry the Bastard.

Except Harry wasn't Harry the Bastard anymore, was he?

He was now, officially, Harry the Hero.

"I'm sorry about tonight," said Harry.

"Don't even *think* that!" Bending her head, Suzy kissed him. "You're here, you're still alive. That's all that matters."

Behind her, from somewhere over by the far wall, she detected a barely audible snort of derision. Happily, the turban of bandages around Harry's ears appeared to have muffled his hearing.

"I bet you were cursing me, thinking I'd stood you up." He smiled up at her.

"Well, we did wonder."

"I'd never stand you up."

"I know," said Suzy. Because what else could she say?

"What happened to your feet?" said Harry. In his semi propped-up position he could just see them.

"My shoes hurt. I took them off. Ummm . . . how are you feeling?" She knew it was a stupid question.

"Oh, lucky to be alive."

Stupid question, Hollywood answer. Harry the Hero gave her hand a squeeze, held it against his cheek and kissed it.

Very Hollywood.

This time even he must have heard the snort of amusement from over by the far wall.

"You saved those children's lives," said Suzy, slightly desperately.

"All in a day's work." Harry smiled modestly, then shrugged and winced. "Blasted broken ribs. Are the press still outside?"

"Yes. They took some pictures."

"Don't give them too much," said Harry. "They're bidding for exclusive rights, did you know?" His expression grew less weary, more animated. "You wouldn't believe the amounts of money they're talking about."

Suzy thought she probably would. When she and Jaz had broken up, the offers from the tabloids to kiss and tell had been enough to make anyone's eyes water. Thankfully, her eyes had been watering quite enough already — she had cried nonstop for six weeks — so she hadn't been remotely tempted to sell her soul in exchange for an eight-page spread.

Lucille, who had diplomatically hung back until now, sensed that Suzy was at a bit of a loss. Moving forward she said, "Poor Harry.

250

Some birthday this turned out to be."

"Oh God!" Appalled that she had forgotten, Suzy clapped her hand over her mouth. "Happy birthday!"

Great, brilliant, well done, *Suzy. Happy broken leg, happy broken arm, happy fractured skull . . .*

"We've got your cards and presents at home," Lucille told Harry.

"Don't worry. I've got everything I could want." Harry kissed the back of Suzy's knuckles again. "You're here, that's all that matters. And those kids are still alive." He paused, considering this. "Actually, that's a great line. When you go, you could tell that to the press."

The door opened, and the nurse appeared, tapping her watch.

"Time's up, I'm afraid. Mr. Fitzallan needs to rest."

"Big day tomorrow," Harry said briskly. "They've scheduled the press conference for ten thirty."

Suzy was speechless. Harry was turning into a media expert before her very eyes. Before you knew it, he'd be commissioning Andrew Morton to write his biography.

"Everybody out now." The bossy nurse ushered them through the door. "Time for Mr. Fitzallan to use his bedpan."

Oops, thought Suzy. *That's not very romantic. Better not mention that at tomorrow's press conference, Harry.*

He gave her a long, lingering kiss goodbye. Which, frankly, she could well have done without in front of Leo's sardonic gaze.

"See you tomorrow," said Harry. "Ten o'clock sharp, OK?"

"But —"

"I need you here with me. And wear something . . . you know, to knock 'em dead."

"Harry, I don't —"

"That black lacy top thing," Harry said helpfully. "The one that goes . . ." With his good hand, he made the appropriate scooping gesture. Low-cut, basically, and leaving not a lot to the imagination. "Oh, and on your way out . . . don't forget to mention that bit about me getting what I want for my birthday."

Blimey, wondered Suzy, *whatever might he hanker for next? World peace?*

It was on the news the next morning. Suzy, switching on to see if Harry had merited a mention, was astounded when she realized the GMTV reporter was doing a live link from the grounds of Frenchay Hospital.

She dragged Maeve over from next door and yelled up the stairs to Fee to come see this.

"I'm standing outside the ward now, speaking to one of the nurses who has been helping to take care of this truly heroic man," confided Martin Swizzle, straight to the camera.

"That's Harry they're talking about." Suzy felt an odd sensation in her chest, like polystyrene expanding. It was impossible not to feel proud.

"Details are sketchy so far. We have to wait for the press conference later this morning." Martin deftly drew a plump, pretty little nurse farther into the shot. "But perhaps Pat here could tell us a bit more about Harry Fitzallan. For instance, we know he's twenty-seven years old. So, Pat, what does he look like?"

Pat giggled, slightly hysterically. "Well, Martin, we think he's the best-looking man we've ever seen! He's really gorgeous, like a movie star or something! All the girls are drooling over him —"

"Not literally, I hope," Martin Swizzle interjected with a swift smile to camera. "That would be unhygienic."

"To each their own," Maeve announced, blowing on the hot tea Suzy had made her.

"Your Harry fellow's a looker, I'll grant you that, but if it's a real man you're after, you can't beat Barry Manilow."

Maeve was mad about Barry. She sent him Christmas cards, cakes, even the occasional sweater. Not hand-knitted. Ones she'd picked up in Oxfam.

"I thought Michael Flatley was your favorite," Suzy protested.

Maeve looked scornful. "Ah, he's nothing but a big show-off, flaunting his bare chest and acting like he's so great."

"What about Len Goodman?" said Fee.

"Well now, I'll grant you he's a lovely man. Then again, this one isn't so bad either." Maeve nodded happily at Martin Swizzle, who was now interviewing the wife of one of the other patients on Harry's ward. She hadn't spoken to Harry, as such, she was explaining enthusiastically, but she'd passed his room and glimpsed him through the crack in the door and he'd seemed utterly charming.

"Well, hopefully, I shall be speaking to Harry Fitzallan later on today," Martin announced when the woman had finished gushing — hopefully, not all over his shoes. "And maybe also his girlfriend, Suzy Curtis, who arrived at the hospital in a distraught condition last night."

A photograph flashed onto the screen of Suzy, shoeless and with her stockings disintegrating around her ankles.

"God!" groaned Suzy, covering her eyes.

"Suzy, ex-wife of the notorious rock star Jaz Dreyfuss, spoke only briefly to waiting journalists last night. As she left the bedside of her lover —"

"Lover!" Suzy let out a shriek of outrage.

"— she announced that yesterday had been Harry Fitzallan's birthday but that he hadn't minded in the least missing out on the traditional celebrations . . . because what better birthday present could anyone wish for than those two young children's lives?"

Although Martin Swizzle was nodding and gazing with utter sincerity into the camera, Suzy suspected that he was secretly longing to stick his fingers down his throat and make pretend sick noises.

It was certainly what she was tempted to do.

"Ahhh!" Maeve sighed as another photograph appeared on the screen, of the two children Harry had saved. "Look at their little faces!"

"Never mind that," said Suzy, spilling coffee all over her knees as she scrambled to her feet. "Look at my face. I'm supposed to be at that press conference in two hours and I'm a mess!"

"Don't forget, Harry wants you to wear that black lacy top," said Lucille.

"It's an evening thing! I'll look like a hooker," Suzy wailed. "I can't wear that!"

"You mean the one that puts your bosoms out on show?" Maeve sounded delighted. "Don't worry, love, I've got just the thing."

By the time Suzy emerged from the bathroom, Maeve was back. "I bought it for my sister in Dundalk, two pounds seventy-five from the St. Peter's Hospice shop, but she won't mind you borrowing it, seeing as it'll be in all the papers. There now, won't that look grand against the black? And you'll be able to cover up all that exposed flesh!"

If that was what it was for, Suzy wondered why she hadn't packaged it up and sent it to Barry Manilow instead. But as she took the scarf from Maeve and dutifully admired its yellow-and-mauve zigzag design, she knew there was to be no wriggling out of this one. She would have to wear it.

She would rather cut off her own arms than hurt Maeve's feelings.

And, looking on the bright side, at least it didn't have pictures of cartoon cats splashed all over it.

The phone rang.

"I've just had a call from Mr. and Mrs. Taylor," said Rory, who never watched early morning television. "You're free this morning, aren't you? They want to take another look at the house in Alma Vale so I said you'd meet them there at ten."

"Ah." Suzy told him why she couldn't make it.

"But I'm tied up, and Martin's got a full list. *Blast,*" Rory said, which was as near as he ever got to swearing.

Covering the receiver, Suzy said to Fee, "Are you busy this morning?"

Fee, who was clearing away the coffee cups, shook her head.

"Panic over. Fee says she'll do it. And I'll be back after lunch."

Triumphantly, Suzy hung up. Fee looked at her. "What did I say I would do?"

"Act as getaway driver. Rory's robbing a bank at ten o'clock." Suzy scribbled down the address and the name of the clients.

Fee said brightly, "Great! Will he mind that I never go faster than twenty-five miles an hour?"

"He'll be thrilled. It means you'll never be stopped for speeding by good-looking policemen." Suzy handed her the details. "Actually, all you have to do is call into the office, pick up the keys, and meet these

257

people at this address. They're ditherers," she reassured Fee, "so don't worry about getting an offer out of them. They're the kind of people who need fifteen trips to the store before they'll buy a set of eggcups."

CHAPTER 20

The conference room at the hospital erupted into a tumultuous round of applause as Harry was wheeled in. Cameras had been set up on tripods all around the room. In the center, seventy or eighty hospital-issue chairs were occupied by journalists from more radio stations and newspapers than Suzy knew existed. When the doctor in charge of Harry's care had finished parking the wheelchair in its designated position, Suzy was allowed to sit down next to him. The flashbulbs were still going off. Harry gave her hand a reassuring squeeze and smiled his dazzling smile at the cameras. Suzy crossed her legs and hoped her Kurt Geigers were in the shot. She didn't want people to think she spent her whole life wandering around bedraggled and barefoot like some stoned-to-the-eyeballs hippy.

"Take that scarf off," Harry hissed out of

the corner of his mouth. "I told you, it looks terrible."

"Can't," Suzy murmured back, because anything was better than grinning inanely at the massed ranks of cameras. "They'll think I'm going to get up and strip."

The hospital administrator overseeing the press conference held up her hands for silence.

"Thank you, ladies and gentlemen. Dr. Hubble will now run through Mr. Fitzallan's injuries, treatment, and prognosis. Following this, Mr. Fitzallan will read a prepared statement describing his experiences yesterday evening. Then we shall take questions from the floor." She paused for effect. "Finally, the children rescued by Mr. Fitzallan will be brought in by their mother to meet him properly for the first time and express their gratitude for what he did."

More applause, then the room grew silent. Despite inwardly cringing at the woman's tone, Suzy felt pride welling up once more. There was no getting away from it; Harry had done a very brave thing. He was a true hero.

And Dr. Hubble fancied him like mad, Suzy was almost sure. Slender and exceptionally pretty, she rested a hand on Harry's shoulder as she spoke warmly of his terrible injuries and incredible strength of will. Only a man in superb physical condition, she went on to explain, could withstand so much damage and overcome such severe pain in order to not only save himself, but also put himself through the tremendous ordeal of rescuing two children from a submerged car.

"We in the medical profession," she concluded, "are skeptical about miracles. But I have no hesitation in stating that Harry Fitzallan is — at the very least — a man in a million."

Harry shook his head modestly as applause rang around the conference room once more. Blushing and smiling, Dr. Hubble sat down. The administrator announced, "Ladies and gentlemen . . . Harry Fitzallan!"

It was like the London Palladium, thought Suzy. She half expected a troupe of cancan dancers to launch themselves onto the stage, flashing their frilly bloomers and yelling *yeeha!*

"I'm just an ordinary guy," Harry said simply. "I did what anyone else would have done. I'm a policeman, so it's my job anyway." He waited for a second, gazing out at the sea of journalists. "But if I wasn't a policeman it would still have been my job."

He'd rehearsed this, of course, over and over again. But it was still good. Suzy felt hot tears well up in her eyes. The only funny thing was Harry's voice, which was weaker and huskier than it had been twenty minutes ago when she'd first arrived at the hospital. It was the kind of voice people used when they called work to say they were sick. Even if they'd sprained an ankle, they still seemed compelled to do that croaky voice thing in order to convince the boss that they really did deserve the day off.

Doggedly playing down the fact that he might have done anything the teeniest bit heroic — which naturally had the opposite effect — Harry related the events of last night and earned himself a spontaneous standing ovation.

Then it was time for the question-and-answer session. Suzy felt a trickle of perspiration crawl snail-like down her spine.

"Suzy! How d'you feel about what Harry did?"

Harry gave her a loving — yet self-deprecating — look. He wasn't British for nothing.

"Disappointed, actually," said Suzy. "I thought after he'd rescued the children and swum ashore, he could have at least chased after the car jackers and put them under arrest."

Ha, she could be British too.

Everyone laughed. Especially Harry. Croakily.

"I'm sorry." Leaning over — and wincing a bit, en route — he planted an apologetic kiss on her cheek. "I let you down."

The cameras flashed on all sides; so this was what it was like to be Nicole Kidman and Tom Cruise.

"I couldn't be prouder of him," said Suzy.

"So how serious is it between you two?" called out a journalist in the third row.

Eek, ask me another one, quick!

But the silence was lengthening.

Nobody, it seemed, was prepared to ride gallantly to her rescue.

"Um." Suzy rubbed her damp palms together. "Well, we're very happy, thanks."

"Any plans for the future?"

Plans? OK, let's see: up until last night the plan was to finish with Harry before the weekend, because actually I was getting a bit bored with him.

Suzy tried to imagine saying these words aloud. Crikey, this crowd would string her up and disembowel her faster than you could say "razor-sharp scalpel."

Dr. Hubble would probably volunteer to

263

do the job herself.

Heavens, she couldn't say *anything* like that.

Going for the neutral reply — wise move — Suzy smiled and said pleasantly, "No, no plans."

Beside her, Harry raised his good hand.

"Excuse me. Sorry to interrupt, but I wonder if I might say something here?"

This was, of course, a rhetorical question. Harry was the undisputed star of the show. Obligingly, the audience quieted, waiting for him to speak.

He could probably recite "Humpty Dumpty," thought Suzy, and earn himself a round of applause.

"As some of you may already know," Harry began, "yesterday was my birthday."

Laughter. Everyone knew that.

"Thanks to events beyond our control, Suzy and I weren't able to celebrate the occasion in . . . well, in quite the way I'd planned."

Ribald whoops of approval greeted this remark. Out of the corner of her eye, Suzy couldn't help noticing that Dr. Hubble was looking tight-lipped.

Harry shook his head and smiled the self-deprecating smile that in less than fifteen minutes had practically become his trade-mark.

Hugh Grant, watch and learn.

"Sorry, sorry . . . I didn't mean it like that. What I'm trying to say is, I didn't get the chance last night to say something to Suzy that I've been wanting to say for some time. So, with your permission, I'd like to take the opportunity to say it now." He paused, took Suzy's hand, and went on huskily, "Phew, this is scarier than hanging on to a car by its windshield wipers. OK, here goes. Suzy, you know how I feel about you. You're the best thing that ever happened to me. And I know I'm nothing special, just an ordinary guy . . . but I love you more than anything . . . What I'm trying to say is, will you marry me, Suzy? Would you do me the honor of becoming my wife?"

Suzy heard the blood drumming like a thousand tom-toms in her ears. Loudly, but sadly not quite loudly enough to drown out Harry's words.

Everything seemed to be happening in slow motion too. But, again, not quite slowly enough.

You could have heard a pin drop in the conference room. All eyes were upon her.

Oh no, this isn't fair. I'm trapped! I need an ejector seat! How can I say yes?

265

Except, except . . . how could she possibly say no?

OK, keep calm, deep breaths. Basically, there's no way in the world I can say no. Not here in public, like this.

Right, so all I have to do is say yes but not mean it. And explain to Harry in private later that I can't possibly marry him, I only said yes to spare him the ultimate humiliation.

"OK," said Suzy. *Oops, loads more enthusiasm than that.* Hurriedly — and at the same time mentally crossing her fingers — she said, "Yes, Harry. Yes, I'll marry you. Of course I will!"

After that, wheeling in the children whose lives Harry had saved came almost as an anticlimax. The toddler, Mikey, clung to his mother's skirt, and the six-year-old, Lauren, was clearly overwhelmed by the attentions of so many photographers. Their mother, tearful and almost speechless with gratitude, hugged and kissed Harry and told the reporters over and over again that it was a miracle and Harry was an angel who had fallen to earth.

Even Harry had the grace to look embarrassed by this.

Suzy sat through the rest of the press conference in a daze. Her life was spinning crazily out of control. The wedding — Harry had already assured everyone — would take place *soon. Of course* they wanted a family of their own . . . three, maybe four children, God willing. And yes, of course Jaz Dreyfuss would be invited to the wedding — he and Jaz were great friends, they got on like a house on fire . . . And the ring? Oh, nothing flashy, probably a platinum-set diamond solitaire.

Suzy had planned to tell Harry the moment they arrived back on the ward that he needn't buy her a ring because there wasn't going to be any wedding.

But when they reached Harry's room, someone else was already there waiting to speak to him.

Waving — quite literally — a checkbook.

"Hi! Terence DeVere, from *Hi!* magazine!"

Clearly, this was his little joke.

"Great, *great* story," the man went on. Flicking back his groomed hair, he beamed at Suzy.

"The feel-good story of the year, I'm telling you! Just the kind of thing our readers go for. OK, cards on the table. Initial in-depth interview. Exclusive rights to cover the wedding. And honeymoon pictures, of course. Total, two hundred and fifty thousand pounds. So, do we have ourselves a deal?"

Suzy felt as if she were on a plane having trouble with cabin pressure. Her ears were popping, and there was no sign of the flight attendant with the big silver tray of hard candies.

Harry leaned forward in his wheelchair and shook Terence DeVere's pudgy pink hand.

Grinning broadly, he said, "Oh yes, we definitely have ourselves a deal."

Having battled with disinterested pub landlords to get Jaz and his band their first bookings when they were unknown, Fee wasn't afraid of anyone.

But while she wasn't what you could call afraid of Rory Curtis, she was certainly in awe of him. It was all right for Suzy to describe him as a big old pussycat — she was his sister. As far as Fee could make out, Rory was brusque, uptight, somewhat humorless, and basically a bit daunting.

Still, no need to feel daunted today.

Rory was on the phone when Fee pushed open the door to the office of Curtis and Co. Correction, he was on the phone, scribbling notes with one hand and simultaneously tapping into a computer with the other. A ferociously hard worker — Fee knew this from Suzy — Rory never did one job when he could do three. Suzy might provide the style and the panache, but he was undoubtedly the one who supplied the sheer hard slog that kept the business afloat.

This, of course, was the reason his brief marriage ten years earlier had failed. And Rory had given that side of things a miss ever since.

Over at her desk, Donna was on the phone. Waiting for one of them to become free — and secretly hoping it would be Donna — Fee waited and watched Rory's dark eyes narrow with exasperation behind his glasses as, glancing up at the computer screen in front of him, he realized he'd deleted something he hadn't meant to delete.

"OK. Two o'clock. Bye." Rory hung up, clattered a few computer keys, heaved a gusty sigh, ran his fingers through his straight dark hair, scrawled a note in his diary . . . and looked up at Fee. "Oh, hi. Bringing the keys back? Thanks for doing that — tell Suzy she owes you a drink."

Fee handed him the keys to the house in Alma Vale. "No need. I enjoyed it."

"Time wasters." Rory threw the keys into his desk drawer. He had no time for time

269

wasters, but in this business, you had to humor them.

"Actually," said Fee, "they want to buy it."

Rory's eyebrows shot up. "You're kidding! They actually put in an offer? A lousy one, I suppose."

Fee took the folded-up particulars out of her shirt pocket. "It says here three hundred and twenty thousand. They offered three hundred, but I told them the vendors had already turned down three hundred and ten. So they decided to go with the asking price. I said I'd tell you, and you'd call them back when you'd spoken to the sellers." Feeling the beginnings of a blush crawling out from under her russet bangs, Fee said, "Was that OK?"

"OK?" Rory actually broke into an incredulous smile. "It's a miracle!" The smile vanished. "Unless it's a joke, of course. Did Suzy put you up to this?"

"No," said Fee equably. "Why don't you call them, if you don't believe me?"

"I believe you. But I'd still better call them. Ummm . . . there's coffee in the machine." Distracted, Rory was already reaching for the phone. "Help yourself."

Fee made coffee for the three of them. By the time she'd finished, Rory had hung up.

"You're a genius," he told her.

"You're not." Feeling brave, Fee nodded at the flashing computer screen. "I don't think you meant to do that, did you?"

Rory sighed and pushed his fingers through his hair again, ruffling it up at the back.

"I wasn't meant to be doing it in the first place, but we're pretty snowed under. Donna's up to her eyebrows, and I've got clients lining up for appointments . . ."

Over at her desk, Donna waggled her jet-black, painted on eyebrows and pulled a face.

"He's a slave driver, that's what he is."

It was Rory's ruffled-up hair that did it. It made him look less intimidating, more vulnerable.

And quite a lot like a parrot. Shyly, Fee said, "I could give you a hand if you like. Help out with the backlog. I'm not busy this afternoon, and I know how to use a computer."

She'd never seen a man look so relieved.

"You're a lifesaver," Rory declared. Hastily, he added, "I'll pay you, of course."

"Don't be daft." Fee felt herself going pink all over again. "I'm happy to help out."

CHAPTER 21

"Harry, this is out of control. It's just . . . mad."

For the first time, Suzy had managed to get him on his own, by wheeling him outside into the tiny rose garden separating Harry's ward from the one next to it.

It was sunny and still hot for mid-September. Suzy pushed up the sleeves of her black lace top and put on her serious face.

"We have to talk about this. Be honest, you weren't planning to ask me to marry you last night."

"I was," said Harry.

"But we've only known each other for three weeks!"

"Nearly four."

"Harry!"

"Anyway, that's what makes it so romantic. It's a whirlwind affair."

"It isn't *any* kind of affair," wailed Suzy.

"Affairs are when you're sleeping with each other. And we aren't doing that."

"I meant it when I said I loved you." Harry looked mystified. "We're fantastic together, you and me. And now all this has happened . . . it's like a dream come true! It's the opportunity of a lifetime! We'd be crazy not to make the most of it."

Suzy shook her head.

"Harry, please, listen to me —"

"No, *you* listen." He gripped her hand, his eyes as bright as sapphires. "I'm a policeman. I earn an average wage. Signing that deal with *Hi!* gives me as much money as I'd make in ten *years* of patrolling the streets. Think about it, Suzy. It's not even as if I have to do something horrible to earn it — all they want us to do is get married! And go off somewhere exotic on honeymoon! For pity's sake, what's so terrible about that?"

"But it's mercenary and calculated and . . . and it's not *real,*" shouted Suzy. "And I don't love you, and I don't *want* to marry someone I don't even love!"

"Oh well," said Harry, "now you're just being selfish. Have you even bothered to *think* about the kids?"

"I don't want to have kids!"

Not yet anyway, thought Suzy, *and not with you.*

"I'm talking about Mikey and Lauren." Harry gave her a sorrowful look. "They're part of the deal too."

"What?" Suzy shook her head; she couldn't for the life of her imagine what he meant. Unless . . .

Oh, good grief. Don't tell me we have to adopt *them.*

"Their mother's divorced and on welfare. They live in public housing, and they've never had a vacation in their lives," said Harry. "When we get married, Lauren's our flower girl, and Mikey's a ring bearer — bit young, I know, but that can't be helped. So they get ten grand, and their mother can afford to take them to Disneyland . . . *Hi!* wasn't bothered about them, you know." He sounded aggrieved. "But I insisted. For the sake of the kids."

Suzy still couldn't believe this was happening to her. She had once, years ago, painted herself — literally — into a corner. In her kitchen, to be precise. To get out, she'd been forced to climb onto the washing machine, teeter along the windowsill, leap across to the fridge, then swing herself *around* the open kitchen door and out into the safety of the hall.

274

This time, clearly, it wasn't going to be so easy to escape.

And I didn't paint myself into this corner anyway, she thought. *Harry's done it for me.*

It was emotional blackmail, nothing less.

"All my life," Harry went on softly, almost to himself, "Leo's been the successful one. He always got everything he wanted — the career, the money, the girls — and I've felt inferior to him. Second rate." He shook his head defiantly. "But now I've got a chance to even things up. The money, the girl — you — *and* I'm a hero into the bargain. Don't you see, Suzy? What was it that guy from *Hi!* said? This is the story that's going to capture the hearts of our nation. And it's going to change *my whole life.*"

Suzy couldn't speak. But she had to.

"I don't love you."

"Give it time," Harry pleaded. "OK, maybe you don't think you love me now. But I can make it happen, I know I can."

"You can't," said Suzy.

"Why not? What have I ever done wrong?"

This, for a start.

Struggling to be honest, Suzy said, "It's not you, it's me. Harry, you're a nice person." She fiddled with the ends of the scary yellow-and-purple scarf in her lap. "I think it's just that you're too nice."

"Oh well, that's easy enough to sort out." Harry flashed her the smile that had earlier melted the hearts of every female in the conference room. "I'll just have to be really horrible to you instead."

Lucille arrived to visit Harry two hours later.

"You look cheerful, for a man with barely an unbroken bone in his body." Greeting him with a kiss, she tipped the contents of a shopping bag over Harry's bed. Nectarines, bars of chocolate, a bottle of Gatorade, and several paperbacks tumbled out.

"Anything else you need, just let me know," said Lucille. "Although I expect Suzy's gotten you loads of stuff already. Is she here?"

"Hiding in my bedside cabinet." Harry grinned. "No, she had to get back to work. She'll be over again later."

"I brought your cards and birthday presents too." Lucille emptied out a second bag. "Those are from me, these are Suzy's. So how did the thingy go . . . the press conference?"

"Brilliant." Harry told her everything that had happened, leaving out the bit with Suzy afterward in the rose garden. He was confident he could overcome her qualms; his proposal had come out of the blue, that was all. As soon as Suzy was over the shock, he knew he'd be able to win her over.

"You're kidding! That's *fantastic* news," squealed Lucille, her beaded hair flying as she threw her arms around him in delight.

"Ouch," Harry said mildly as one of the beads went *clonk* against the stitched-together gash on his left cheekbone. But his blue eyes were sparkling, and his smile was broad. "I know it is."

Rory couldn't believe he'd been so rude. It hadn't even occurred to him at the time that he was being rude. But, mentally replaying his brief conversation with Fee Driscoll as he drove back to the office at five o'clock, he now cringed at his own boorishness.

Fee had been generous enough to help them out and in return he had said, "Tell Suzy she owes you a drink."

Rory winced again. How utterly crass could you get? He could just imagine Fee's remarks on the subject when she saw Suzy tonight.

Which was odd, because normally he was too busy thinking about the business to worry about what anyone else might think of him.

Rory pulled up at the toll booth, fed his

money in, and set off across the Suspension Bridge. The sun was still bright, glittering on the river below, and he could see plenty of people sitting out on the terrace of the Avon Gorge Hotel.

That's what I'll do, thought Rory. *Get back to the office and announce that we all deserve a drink.*

He would show Fee that he appreciated her efforts, take them all down to the Terrace Bar, and buy a few rounds. Maybe even buy a couple of bottles of celebratory champagne.

After all, Fee had sold a house to the Taylors, the original clients from hell.

Yes, thought Rory, pleased with himself. *That would be a nice touch.*

Suzy was perched on the edge of her desk swinging her legs when Rory came into the office. Donna was still heroically working away behind her computer and Martin was hanging up sets of keys.

"OK, we are done for the day. We're off to the Terrace Bar, and the drinks are on me," Rory declared. He peered around the door leading to the back room. "Where's Fee?"

"She left half an hour ago. Had some stuff to do before she goes out this evening," said Donna.

"Oh." Damn. Rory wished he'd looked around the door before making his announcement. They wouldn't let him back out of it now.

Donna tapped a pile of letters in her out tray. "She did brilliantly. We've almost caught up."

Rory swallowed. That just made things worse. "Well . . . if it's not convenient, we could always make it another time . . . ?"

Donna and Martin immediately looked outraged; he might have known it would never work.

"Oh no, we couldn't," Suzy announced, jumping down from her desk. "Come on, let's go. I definitely need a drink."

The next day Harry's picture was splashed across every paper. If he had been ugly, it would still have been a terrific story, but Harry's movie-star looks were what had really tipped the scales.

If there was anything the public liked better than a hero, it was a drop-dead gorgeous hero, Suzy realized, awed by the scale of the coverage. According to the hospital administrator in charge of Harry mania, the switchboard was being inundated with calls from well-wishers offering congratulations, get-well messages — and sometimes much more. There were plenty of amateur physical therapists out there, it seemed, all eager to offer services of an astonishingly personal nature if Harry required a bit of help getting his poor battered body back into full working order.

Suzy just wished he'd take a few of them up on it.

If one more person told her how lucky she was, she might be tempted to plunge a hypodermic needle into them.

"Ooh, you're so *lucky,*" said one of the auxiliary nurses who worked on an adjoining ward. She had popped in to Harry's room to tell him how wonderful he was and ask for an autograph. With his right arm in a cast, Harry had had to sign his name with his left hand — a wobbly affair that looked as if it had been done by a three-year-old.

Suzy smiled dutifully. Just as well there wasn't a hypodermic needle in sight.

"I know."

"I'm the lucky one," said Harry. "Getting to marry the girl of my dreams."

Suzy's smile grew fixed, like a beauty queen's. *Now remind me, where do they keep the sick bags?*

"You make such a perfect couple," the nurse assured them. "Think of the beautiful children you'll have!"

The middle-aged receptionist popped her frizzy head around the door.

"Visitors, Harry. Your brother's here to see you . . . Can I get you another cup of tea or is that one still warm? And how about a nice chocolate cookie to go with it?"

Suzy couldn't help marveling at the service Harry was getting. As far as she could make out, all the other patients on the ward had to wait for the rickety cart to be trundled around three times a day, with a teapot the size of a beer barrel dispensing stewed brown liquid into bile-green NHS cups.

Not like Harry, whose tea was freshly made for him every twenty minutes by the besotted receptionist and brought to him in a smart navy-and-gold Marks & Spencer mug.

"You spoil me, Doreen," he told her with a smile.

Doreen, simpering madly back at him, said, "If *you* don't deserve a bit of spoiling, love, I don't know who does."

CHAPTER 22

The side ward was already awash with get-well cards stuck all over the walls, but when Leo strode in, his gaze flickered almost instantly to the one card Suzy would have preferred him not to see.

Oh, what a surprise.

She felt her nails digging into the palms of her hands as he scanned the dreadful poem inside.

"Suzy's birthday card," Harry said proudly. Just in case Leo had forgotten how to read.

"So I see." Leo's eyebrows were raised. His mouth twitched with derision. "Very . . . touching."

"We're getting married," Harry announced. With even more pride, if that was possible.

"Evidently." Leo gestured toward the untidy pile of newspapers on the windowsill. He paused, then said, "Congratulations."

Suzy felt her toes curl up inside her shoes, but she forced herself to smile jauntily at Leo. "Thanks."

"I hope you'll both be very happy," said Leo, who clearly didn't.

"Oh, we will be." As she said it, Suzy heard a voice she recognized, out in the corridor.

"I'd have asked you to be my best man at the wedding," Harry told Leo, "but the guy from *Hi!* . . . well, he's pretty keen on the idea of Jaz doing the honors. He says sorry, he knows you're successful, but you're just not as famous as Jaz."

Harry was clearly enjoying himself; this was his moment of glory. But inwardly, Suzy cringed. Harry had met Jaz once, for all of thirty minutes, and now he was going to ask him to be his best man.

Her own ex-husband, for pity's sake!

"I completely understand." Leo sounded amused. "I'm a nobody. Suzy's ex is a recovering alcoholic rock star. You'd be mad not to choose him as your best man."

The door swung open, and Gabriella burst in.

"Can you believe it? Harry Fitzallan, you're looking handsomer than ever! That has to be the most dashing scar I've ever seen" — she indicated the curved gash along Harry's cheekbone — "and every woman in the country is fantasizing madly about being rescued by you!"

Suzy was tempted to hold up her hand and say, "Actually, every woman in the country but me."

Gabriella's was one of the voices she had heard outside in the corridor a moment ago. The other had belonged to Dr. Hubble.

"And you're the one who's got him," Gabriella told Suzy with a grin. "That must feel sooo great. I'm so happy for you, really I am . . . it's just the best news ever!"

She meant it, Suzy realized, as Gabriella first gave her a hug, then Harry. There was none of the cynicism in her voice that there had been in Leo's.

Curiously, she said, "Do you know Dr. Hubble?"

"Monique? Oh yes, we went to med school together! We shared boyfriends." Gabriella laughed. "We even shared a cadaver once in anatomy class. Me and Monique go way back!"

Suzy could just picture it. Two teeny tiny girls, both spectacularly pretty *and* medical students to boot. It was enough to give a noisy, 130-pound real estate agent a complex . . .

Except nobody gives me a complex, Suzy

reminded herself, *because I'm not the complex-suffering type.*

For a start, she had real curves, which was more than either of these two sparrows possessed.

And *I've got four exams.*

Furthermore, like it or not, she had Harry.

"Oh, by the way, about your mother's house," said Gabriella. "I mean, it's gorgeous and we love it, but we do have a few more lined up to see before we decide." She touched Suzy's sleeve. "I hope you don't mind."

"Of course not," lied Suzy, minding enormously. Having been so convinced that they'd both loved her old home, she now couldn't help feeling . . . well, a bit snubbed.

It was like hearing a childless couple coo admiringly over your baby, but when you actually offered it to them for adoption, they backed off hurriedly, saying, "Oh no, we wanted one prettier than that."

"You never know," Harry said cheerfully, "the way things are going, I might end up buying the place myself."

This was another lie, of course. Harry was only showing off, indulging in a bit of one-upmanship with Leo. But Suzy was grateful anyway. It was nice to have Harry on her side, sensing her hurt and leaping to her defense.

Metaphorically speaking, of course. It would be a while before Harry was going to be capable of leaping anywhere.

"Here we are, Harry." The receptionist was back, easing her way past Gabriella and Leo. "A lovely cup of tea," she cooed, "made just the way you like it. And a couple of plain chocolate cookies." In a stage whisper she added with pride, "They're Millie's."

Behind her, Gabriella rolled her eyes expressively at Suzy and mouthed, *Ooh, Millie's.*

Which almost made up for her earlier slur on Suzy's mother's house.

"I have to go." Checking her phone, Suzy saw that the messages were starting to stack up.

"OK." Harry held his good arm out to her. "You said Jaz and Celeste were due back today, didn't you? If Jaz wants to come visit me," he said casually, "that's fine."

Big of you, Harry.

Suzy had to lean across the bed to kiss Harry good-bye. It couldn't just be a peck either. She felt compelled to throw herself into it with just-got-engaged-to-a-superhero abandon.

She hoped Gabriella and Leo, behind her, weren't getting a grandstand view of her fuchsia-pink panties.

"Love you," whispered Harry, gently stroking her overheated cheek.

"Love you too," Suzy forced herself to murmur back.

Oh, but why, why *am I having to force myself to say it? Why can't I just love you anyway? It would make life soooo much easier.*

"See you again *very* soon," Gabriella said warmly when Suzy turned to leave. "Imagine, we'll be sisters-in-law! Won't that be great?"

Suzy didn't need to look at him to know that Leo's expression was derogatory. Even his aftershave smelled cynical. He thought she was the one who was milking Harry's hero status for all it was worth.

Leo despised her, Suzy realized. And since he clearly wasn't going to buy Sheldrake House, she didn't see why she should carry on being polite to him for a moment longer.

To Gabriella she said, "I can't wait to be your sister-in-law, but I'm not looking forward to being Leo's."

Lucille was jogging across the Suspension Bridge, exercising a pair of Highland terriers in rhinestone collars, when she recognized the jogger heading toward her from the other end of the bridge.

Jaz Dreyfuss was wearing sunglasses and a black tracksuit. Lucille whistled encouragement to the hopelessly unfit terriers and ignored him as they approached each other. She knew Jaz because everyone knew Jaz, but he didn't have a clue who she was.

But as their paths crossed, almost exactly at the halfway point, Jaz murmured, "Hi, Lucille."

To the dogs' collective relief, Lucille stopped running. "Very good. How do you do that?" She rested her hands on her hips and smiled. "Or did someone tattoo my name across my forehead while I was asleep?"

Jaz took off his sunglasses and leaned back against one of the stone pillars. Just back from Antigua, he was very tan.

"Beautiful girl, head full of beads, professional dog walker . . . call me psychic, but I just thought there couldn't be too many of you in Clifton."

"Who says I'm a professional dog walker?" countered Lucille. "These could be mine."

She and Jaz simultaneously gazed down at the two panting, overweight terriers, their rhinestone collars twinkling in the sunlight.

Jaz, eyebrows raised, looked at Lucille.

"Oh well." Lucille conceded defeat.

"Maybe not."

"So how's it going then?" said Jaz. "What's it like, living with my ex-wife?"

Lucille said mischievously, "Can't you remember?"

"The state I was in?" His expression was rueful. "Not really. All a bit of a blur, to be honest. Although I seem to remember being shouted at a lot."

"Suzy doesn't shout at me. We're getting on really well." Lucille paused. "You know she's getting married?"

Jaz looked astounded.

"You're joking! Who to?"

"Harry."

"Bloody hell! You can't take your eyes off that girl for five minutes . . . When did this happen?"

If he hadn't already heard, Lucille wondered if she should be telling him. Suzy might have wanted to break the news herself. Feeling awkward, she fiddled with the dogs' leashes.

"Haven't you seen the papers?"

"We've been on vacation." Jaz shook his head. "I never look at the papers when I'm away. We got home an hour ago, Maeve was out, I felt like a run . . . Bloody hell!" he exclaimed again. "What brought all this on? Don't tell me she's pregnant."

Lucille's white running tank was sticking damply to her midriff. Embarrassed, she loosened it and glanced at her watch.

"I've got to get these dogs home. If I'm late, their owner'll send out a search party. No," she added hurriedly, "she isn't pregnant."

"But that's as much information as you're willing to pass on right now," guessed Jaz. He winked at her. "Because you don't want this to be the day Suzy starts shouting at you."

Relieved that he wasn't about to start interrogating her, Lucille said, "She'll be home by six."

"Tell you what. Why don't both of you come around to dinner." Jaz checked his watch. "Say, sevenish? Unless you have other plans."

Lucille, who hadn't, said, "OK."

"Great. We can get to know each other." With a fleeting grin, Jaz replaced his sunglasses. "And I can hear exactly what Suzy's been up to the moment my back's turned."

After an hour-long bath, Celeste wrapped herself in a stunning new turquoise silk robe and sat down in front of her dressing-table mirror to do her face. Rummaging through the drawers in which she kept her makeup, searching for the Max Factor iced-pink lipstick that would go so brilliantly with her Antiguan tan, she came across the cassette she had liberated from Lucille's bag a couple of weeks earlier and promptly forgotten about.

Only mildly curious, Celeste now dropped Lucille's tape into the cassette player she kept handy in order to be able to listen to music while she put her makeup on.

"Bloody hell," she exclaimed aloud, when she heard what was on the tape.

Jaz walked in moments later.

"What is *that*?" He listened in disbelief to the noise emanating from the cassette player.

"Something embarrassing." Celeste giggled. "Isn't it awful?"

"Don't tell me you bought it!"

"Of course not."

"So where did it come from?"

Still smiling, Celeste switched the tape off. "I just . . . found it." Happily, vagueness was her stock-in-trade. "What's the matter with you, anyway? You look as if you've just bumped into Elvis."

Too distracted to give the terrible tape another thought, Jaz said abruptly, "Suzy's getting married."

"Surely not." Having unearthed the ice-pink lipstick, Celeste carefully applied it to her pouting mouth. "Who'd want to marry Suzy?"

Jaz had once, of course, but he'd been paralytic at the time. It wasn't his fault.

"That bloke. Harry What's-'Is-Name."

"Must be mad."

"*She* must be mad," Jaz said hotly.

"Why should you care?" Celeste blotted her lips with a tissue. "Not jealous, are you?"

"Of course I'm not jealous," Jaz snapped.

"Good." Celeste spoke lightly, but her stomach had twisted itself into a tight knot. Everyone else thought it was so great that Jaz and Suzy could be divorced and still get on well together.

Celeste wondered if they'd feel quite the same way about the situation if it were *their* partner still flirting with his flashy, extrovert, up-for-anything ex-wife.

"They're coming over tonight," said Jaz.

"Who, the happy couple?"

"Suzy and Lucille." Jaz belatedly realized that it hadn't occurred to him to invite Harry along. And Lucille hadn't mentioned it either.

"Oh." Celeste glanced at the silent cassette player, her ice-pink mouth twitching with private pleasure. "Right. That'll be nice."

CHAPTER 23

Maeve, arriving home from a productive tour of Clifton's thrift shops an hour later, filled them in on all the details. She had kept every edition of every newspaper to show Jaz and Celeste what they had missed while they'd been away.

"It's like a fairy tale, wouldn't you say?" She jabbed happily at the front page of the *Express*. "Isn't that just the most gorgeous photo you ever saw? Did you ever see a couple so happy?"

You mean like Bill and Hillary Clinton, Jaz wanted to say. That *happy*?

It was only a photograph. It didn't mean anything. The camera lied. Jaz knew that better than anyone. After all, how many times had he been caught by the paparazzi looking perfectly sober when in reality he'd been out of his tree?

"And here's Harry with the two children he saved. And there he is with the bandages

293

off his head . . . See, that's better, isn't it? Will you look at those lovely glossy dark curls? He's up for all manner of bravery awards," Maeve told them with enormous pride.

"Sure you wouldn't like to marry him yourself, Maeve?" said Jaz.

"What, and have Suzy chasing after me with a frying pan in one hand and a steak knife in the other? She's in love, bless her. You can see it in her eyes." Pointing to yet another photograph, in the *Daily Mail* this time, Maeve dragged an Oxfam bag onto her lap and happily pulled out a man's vest. "I bought this for Harry. Isn't it a find? Thought he might like to wear it for the wedding."

The vest was emerald-green satin, with maroon Lurex stripes. Even Elton John might have winced a bit at the sight of this one.

Yesss, there is a God, thought Jaz.

"I'm sure he will," he told Maeve. "It's . . . perfect."

Celeste was poring over one of the pictures taken at the first press conference.

"What on earth was Suzy thinking of here?" In amazement she pointed to the yellow-and-purple zigzag scarf. "I knew she had diabolical taste in clothes, but this is ridiculous."

The corner Suzy had found herself painted into was getting smaller by the hour. Having fully intended to be totally honest with Jaz, she rapidly encountered a couple of problems.

First, Lucille was sitting there listening to every word.

Second, Suzy's hackles had risen the moment she'd seen the look on Jaz's face when he'd opened the front door.

It was the kind of look a father might give his daughter when she tells him she's chucking her job in high finance and running away to join the ecowarriors.

It was definitely the kind of look that made Suzy want to kick him.

Smirking, he said, "Oh, Suzy, you cannot be serious," like John McEnroe. "Pleeease tell me this is all a windup."

If Jaz had been nice about it, Suzy realized later, and Lucille hadn't been there, she would have told him exactly that. The truth, the whole truth, and nothing but the truth. Instead, thanks to his patronizing attitude — and her own pride — she found herself saying breezily, "Oh, I know. I'm *totally* messing up my life. I'd *so* set my heart on marrying yet another clapped-out alcoholic rock singer and instead, I end up with some *really* good-looking superhero. Oh dear, oh dear, major calamity. Where *did* I go wrong?"

"Beautiful house," said Lucille, ignoring Suzy's tirade and gazing around the massive marble hallway. She peered up at the modern, stained glass chandelier at the head of the staircase.

"She's getting the hang of you," Jaz told Suzy with a grin. "At the first sign of an argument, change the subject." To Lucille he said, "Good move. Come on through. Did you manage to get those flabby dogs home in one piece?"

"Their owner had bowls of chopped-up hamburgers waiting for them." Lucille shrugged. "What can you do? I'm just the dog walker. When I tried telling her she shouldn't feed them so much, she told me I was heartless and mean."

Celeste, drifting out to meet them, said, "And all you're doing is trying to help. I know how you feel — Suzy's exactly the same when I suggest she should go on a diet." She paused for effect and smiled at Lucille. "Hello again. And you have to live with her. I bet you wish now you'd gone to the Salvation Army hostel, like I said."

"Maeve!" shouted Suzy, heading for the

kitchen from which sublime cooking smells were drifting. "Pour me a massive drink!"

Over dinner, and with Maeve's encouragement, Suzy grew into her role of besotted bride-to-be. She was damned if she was going to let Jaz jeer at her.

"We thought Thornbury Castle for the wedding," she announced.

Maeve sighed. "So romantic."

"Harry wondered if you'd like to be his best man," Suzy told Jaz.

He looked horrified. "You must be joking. I don't even know him!"

"OK, but you could give me away."

"Sounds more like it." Jaz grinned. "Giving away my ex-wife, handing her over to the next poor sucker."

"Like selling an old car you don't want anymore," Celeste joined in. "Hardly able to believe that someone is gullible enough to be taking it off your hands."

"Stop it now," Maeve scolded. "When's it going to be, love?"

"Oh, as soon as Harry's out of his casts. *Hi!* wants to feature it in its Christmas issue."

"What I don't get," Jaz said, "is you told me you were never going to marry again. You swore you never would. And now . . . this."

"Of course I said that. Blimey, I'd just come out of the marriage from hell." Suzy rolled her eyes at his stupidity. "But everything's different now. I met Harry, and we fell in love with each other. He's perfect for me."

"He is, he is," Maeve agreed dreamily. "He's like a real life James Bond. When that reporter phoned yesterday to speak to Jaz about it, I told him his paper should set up a fan club and sell T-shirts with Harry's face printed on them. He thought that was a grand idea."

T-shirts.

Harry the Hero T-shirts.

Suzy suppressed a shudder of alarm.

But Jaz was smirking again. He clearly found the idea ludicrous.

"Jaz had a fan club once," Suzy told Lucille, her tone conversational. "Of course, that was years ago, before he became a washed-up has-been."

Jaz had chosen the music that was murmuring quietly in the background. Noticing that Lucille was familiar with the track currently playing — her lips were moving silently along with the vocals — he said, "D'you like Nina Simone?"

Lucille looked startled, almost guilty. "Ummm . . . yes."

"Oh dear, you've got taste." Jaz pulled a sympathetic face. "It can't be easy for you, sharing an apartment with Suzy."

Glad to get off the subject of weddings and fan clubs and T-shirts with Harry's face on them, Suzy said, "Has it ever occurred to you that I could be the one with taste and the rest of you are all just hopelessly tone-deaf?"

"So who are you going to have singing at your wedding?" said Jaz. "The Smurfs?"

Suzy shrugged, feeling sorry for him.

"The thing is, you think that would be oh-so-terrible. But I don't. I think it'd be great."

"But you're into real music." Jaz turned his attention back to Lucille. "That's a relief anyway. Tell me who else you like."

"Ooh," cried Celeste, jumping up from the table. "I know!"

Bemused, Lucille said, "Chris Rea, Van Morrison, Mary J. Blige . . ."

"Hang on, it's here somewhere. I brought it down earlier." Celeste was over by the stereo now, riffling through a pile of loose tapes. "Ah, here we are! This is the kind of music Lucille *really* likes . . ."

Lucille watched, mystified, as the Nina Simone CD was abruptly ejected and a cassette slotted into the tape deck.

Moments later her skin began to crawl as the opening notes flooded the room.

Triumphantly, Celeste upped the volume.

"Tuh," said Suzy. "Call that music? Sounds like Björk, trapped in a trash can."

"Turn it off," croaked Lucille, breaking into a sweat.

"Björk, trapped in a trash can, having her teeth pulled out by a mad dentist." Suzy started to laugh. "Oh well, if this is *real* music, I'm glad I'm a pleb. Give me New Kids on the Block any day."

Recognizing the tune — such as it was — Jaz frowned and said, "This is the thing you were playing upstairs earlier. I don't get it. Why would —"

"It's you, isn't it?" Celeste turned joyfully to address Lucille. "That's you, singing. I wasn't sure at first, but it's definitely your voice." She giggled. "Do tell. Did you write the song as well?"

Lucille leaped up from the table, raced across the room, and snatched the tape from the machine so fast it unraveled like knitting.

"You had no right to do that," she shouted at Celeste. Crimson blotches of embarrassment had sprung up over her neck and shoulders and she was shaking with rage. "How dare you . . . how dare you! You *stole* that tape . . ."

Belatedly putting two and two together, Suzy said, "If you don't give her a slap, I will."

"You're not serious," said Jaz. "That wasn't really you?"

Maeve said diplomatically, "Well, I liked it. I think you have a grand voice, love. Very . . . original."

Celeste looked bewildered. She held up her hands in surrender. "I didn't mean to upset you, truly. It was just a joke."

Lucille was longing to slap Celeste, but she was here as a guest in Jaz's house. Innate good manners — much to her disgust — got the better of her and kept her tightly clenched hands down by her sides. Only the gentle rattle of the beads in her hair betrayed the fact that she was still trembling.

In a low voice, Lucille said, "It's not funny, OK? If you ever touch any of my things again, I'll kill you."

"Now, now, girls." Maeve held up a serving spoon. "Who's for another helping of coq au vin?"

"Anyway," Suzy said hotly, "what Maeve said just now was right — Lucille *does* have a grand voice. It's *true,*" she added, because Jaz was giving her one of his looks. He clearly thought he was going to have to do the decent thing — lie through his teeth and tell Lucille her tape was a work of towering genius.

Lucille sat back down. "Look," she said firmly, "can we just forget this?"

"No, we can't," Suzy countered, even more firmly. She turned back to Jaz. "I don't know what that tape's all about, but Lucille's a fantastic singer."

"I'm sure she is." Jaz really wished Suzy wouldn't do this to him.

"I mean it. Better than that Nina Simone girl any day." *Well,* Suzy silently amended, *any day apart from the one Lucille had made that weird tape.*

"Yes, yes," murmured Jaz.

"She's a professional," Suzy went on, exasperated. "She sings in clubs and bars. The only reason I didn't tell you before was because Lucille made me promise not to. She's a very modest person . . ."

"I'm not surprised," Celeste murmured in an undertone.

"Oh, *do* shut up." Marching around the table, Suzy stopped at Lucille. "Right, well, this is easily solved."

"Oh no it isn't," said Lucille.

"Don't be such a wimp." Suzy held out her arms and tried to yank her to her feet. "Go on, sing!"

"I will not," hissed Lucille, hanging on to her chair for dear life.

"Suzy," Jaz said wearily, "leave the girl alone. Please."

"I want you to hear her! How else can I prove I'm telling the truth?"

"You don't have to. We believe you."

"Yes, but —"

"Lucille, do you want to sing for us?" Jaz asked reasonably.

"No," said Lucille, her knuckles white where she was still clinging to the chair.

"There, you see? She really doesn't want to." Jaz gave Suzy his I-mean-it look. "Now put her down this minute."

To Lucille's immense relief, she did.

"This is ridiculous." Suzy sat down and helped herself to more mashed potato from the oval dish in front of her. "Lucille didn't want you to know she was a singer because she didn't want you to think she was some kind of groupie."

"Not groupie," said Lucille. "I didn't mean groupie." She turned to look at Jaz. "I just thought you might feel . . . you know . . ."

Jaz nodded. He knew exactly what she was trying to say.

"It's OK." He gave her an encouraging smile. "But I still can't figure out the tape.

What happened there?"

The colored beads rattled as Lucille shook her head.

"I was an idiot. This bloke heard me singing one night at the Pineapple. He said I had talent and persuaded me that what I needed was a demo tape to send to people in the business. For two hundred pounds he said he'd produce it for me in his recording studio." She paused, embarrassed. "He was very flattering and I was daft enough to believe him . . . even when the recording studio turned out to be a broom closet under the stairs in his house. Of course, when he sent me the tapes a week later, I realized it was a scam. The backing track was out of sync with the vocals, the acoustics were diabolical, and the tapes were so warped and distorted, you could barely tell it was me. Of course, when I went around to his house he called me a lying bitch and slammed the door in my face."

"Bastard!" yelped Suzy, outraged. "You should have gone to the police."

"I'd paid him in cash. There was no way of proving the tapes had been made by him. Anyway, I felt quite stupid enough already." Lucille's smile was crooked. "It didn't do a huge amount for my confidence. I thought if I had been any good, he wouldn't have buggered up the tapes in the first place."

"So why did you keep them?" said Celeste.

Lucille shrugged. "It's hard to throw away something you've paid two hundred pounds for."

Celeste, who had that afternoon thrown away a three hundred pound Voyage cardigan that had gone droopy around the neckline, said, "OK, but I don't understand why you just gave up. Why didn't you try again, find a better recording studio run by people who know what they're doing?"

And charge thousands of pounds rather than a measly couple of hundred, thought Lucille. She had sold her television, worked extra barmaiding shifts, and lived on boiled rice for a fortnight in order to scrape together that "measly" amount of money.

"I don't know," she told Celeste. "I suppose I just couldn't be bothered."

"Are you going to eat any more of that?" Maeve was gesturing toward Suzy's plate. "Or shall I bring in the pudding?"

Suzy barely noticed her plate being whisked away. Lucille hadn't confided in her about this before.

"Jaz has a recording studio," she announced.

Jaz briefly closed his eyes.

"He *does*," Suzy went on brightly, giving

Lucille a huge nudge when she didn't react. "Down in the basement. Just sitting there doing nothing . . . imagine that!"

Thanks a lot, Suzy, thought Jaz.

"Would you have any of that extra-wide Scotch tape?" Lucille asked Maeve, who was now collecting up the rest of the plates. "I need something to cover Suzy's extra-wide mouth."

"Oh, don't get all uptight on me now," Suzy complained. "You need a recording studio and Jaz has one — it's the answer to a prayer! The least he could do is let you borrow it."

"Raspberry pavlova and sticky toffee pudding," Maeve announced as she left the dining room. "So if you've belts to unfasten, unfasten them now."

"Go on," Suzy urged Jaz. "Don't be mean!"

"I'm so sorry about this," said Lucille. "You see now why I tried to keep it quiet."

Jaz smiled. Just about. "It's not your fault."

"It's not my fault either," Suzy exclaimed. "I *did* keep quiet about it! If you want to blame someone" — she gestured indignantly across the table — "blame Celeste."

Jaz picked up his tumbler of iced mineral water. What a dinner party this was turning out to be. And what a position Suzy was putting him in.

He didn't want to be the bad guy, regarded as cold hearted and mean. But he hadn't so much as set foot in his recording studio since coming out of rehab.

Just the thought of taking down the key and unlocking the door made him feel as if he needed a drink.

CHAPTER 24

Could there possibly be anything nicer in the world than a Heath bar?

Alone in the office, Suzy lovingly peeled off the wrapper and admired the dappled chocolate covering. Then she bit into it, her teeth sinking through the toffee, her head twisting from side to side in order to bite off that first heavenly mouthful . . . oh, and they were sooo much better straight from the fridge . . .

"Ahem."

Suzy's eyes snapped open, and she spun around guiltily. Damn, she'd been so carried away she hadn't even heard the door open and close behind her.

And, double damn, it had to be Leo Fitzallan.

"Mmff . . . shorry . . . mergh . . ."

"Bitten off more than you can chew?" inquired Leo with a slight smile.

Suzy's mouth was full — OK, *over*full —

and the toffee was welding itself to her teeth like quick-setting cement. Waving her hand apologetically, praying the melted chocolate wasn't about to spill out and dribble attractively down her chin, she chewed and swallowed, chewed and swallowed, threw the rest of the Heath bar onto her desk and chewed and swallowed again.

Oh dear, not very glamorous.

"Sorry," said Leo. "I obviously interrupted a special private moment."

And swallowed again.

Hooray, didn't even dribble!

"There." Suzy executed a quick curtsy. "All gone. Now, how can I help you?"

He was wearing Givenchy aftershave — none of your Tommy Hilfigers or Calvin Kleins for Leo Fitzallan, thank you very much — and an expensively cut dark suit. Suzy wondered if he had chosen the bottle-green shirt and blue and amber tie himself, or whether Gabriella had picked them out for him.

Probably Gabriella. A man who drove a gray Volvo would never be that adventurous. And the dark blue in the tie exactly matched his eyes.

Definitely Gabriella.

"I thought maybe we should call a truce," said Leo. "How does that sound to you?"

Blimey, Suzy thought, *like a miracle. Quick, give the man a bottle of water and see if he can turn it into Chardonnay.*

Aloud she said, "So what's brought this on?"

"My brother's happy with you. By Christmas you and I'll be related. The last thing I want is a family feud. Easier all around if we bury the hatchet now," Leo said easily. "Put the bickering behind us. What d'you say?"

He was even more attractive, Suzy realized, when he was in a good mood. During the last few days all he'd seemed to do was scowl, sneer, and generally radiate disapproval, which was sexy enough in its own way, of course, but it really was amazing the difference a few laughter lines could make.

"I agree." Her mouth curled up at the corners. "That's it then. From now on, we're going to be completely lovely to each other. And I'll just have to find someone else to bicker with."

"So long as it isn't Harry," said Leo.

"Harry isn't the bickering kind." Suzy smiled sunnily at him and perched on the edge of her desk. "This feels quite weird, actually. I'm not sure what we're supposed to do now. If this were *Friends* we'd be giving each other a group hug."

For a split second something indefinable flickered in Leo's eyes. The next moment it had gone. He pushed his fingers through his ultra-straight dark hair, heaved a sigh and shrugged as if searching for inspiration.

"Now I'm here, I suppose I could always buy a house."

"*Great* idea. You could buy a couple!" Going along with the joke Suzy reached behind her on the desk; grabbed a handful of sales details and waggled them at him. "Here, go mad . . . buy six!"

"No thanks, just the one," said Leo. "Sheldrake House."

Stunned, Suzy realized he was serious. "My mother's house? You mean . . . you really *want* it?"

"Well," said Leo, "I'm prepared to make an offer."

"How much?"

He shook his head thoughtfully, playing the part of the shrewd businessman.

"Let's see, the asking price is four eighty. What would you be prepared to accept?"

Quick as a flash, Suzy said, "Four fifty."

"OK. That's what I'll offer."

Suzy jumped down from her desk. She stuck out her right hand and said joyfully, "Done."

As they were shaking hands on the deal, Donna swung back through the door with the pint of milk she had popped out to get. When she saw Suzy and Leo, she stopped dead in her tracks and said, "Oops."

"Donna," said Suzy, "we're shaking hands, not making out. This is Leo, Harry's brother." A huge grin spread unstoppably over her face. "And he's going to be buying Sheldrake House."

"Great," said Donna, "but you'd better have a look at the back of your skirt."

Suzy twisted around, peering over her shoulder. When she saw what Donna had been pointing out to her she wailed, "Oh *no*!"

Her beautiful, *beautiful* sunflower-yellow skirt . . .

Donna said helpfully, "It looks like you sat on some dog poo."

It did indeed.

"My Heath bar." Suzy groaned. Turning, she saw the melted chocolate and toffee remains on the edge of her desk. Mournfully, she added, "Just as things were going so *well*."

"You'll have to go home and change," said Donna.

"Typical. Just when my car's in for service." Suzy sighed. "I don't have a coat with

312

me. It's a busy Saturday afternoon in Clifton. And I now have to walk home with people pointing and laughing at me behind my back because they think I've just sat in some dog poo. Well, this is going to be great. I can't *tell* you how much I'm looking forward to it. In fact, I may —"

"My car's just across the road," said Leo. "Would you like me to give you a lift?"

"Yes, I would. Thank you," Suzy told him gravely. "I thought you'd never ask. And if you could just bring the car over to this side of the road, that would be great."

Well, it was worth a try.

"Don't push your luck," said Leo.

Outside on the pavement, Suzy searched in vain for the gray Volvo.

"Is this a trick?" She shot a suspicious glance at Leo. "Your car isn't here."

"It is." He nodded at the dark green Porsche parked opposite, then casually slid his arm around Suzy's hip. His hand came to rest lightly on her bottom, and tingles of electricity promptly zapped their way down the backs of her legs.

Suzy didn't know which shocked her the most: the car or Leo's hand on her bottom.

"Is it covered?" she murmured as they crossed the road.

Solemnly, he looked behind him and said,

"No one else can see a thing."

"When did you get this car?" Suzy was glad to spot a road map of Britain in the front — she'd be able to sit on that and spare the passenger seat. "Yesterday?"

"Six months ago."

"I didn't know you had a car like this. I thought you were Volvo man!"

Why on earth didn't he get one of those stickers announcing that his other car was a Porsche?

"Baxter is Volvo dog," Leo explained. "He doesn't like this one. It's too cramped." Smiling to himself, he added drily, "Don't tell me I've gone up a notch or two in your estimation."

Suzy, settling herself on the opened-out road map and buzzing down the passenger window, said happily, "You did that already when you made an offer for Sheldrake House."

The journey back to Sion Hill took all of a minute and a half, but Suzy was grateful to have been spared the walk.

"That's brilliant. Thanks." She unclipped her seat belt as Leo pulled up outside the house. "Shall I give you a call later when I've spoken to our lawyer about the sale?"

"Actually," said Leo, "I wouldn't mind being invited in for coffee."

Surprised because she'd expected him to shoot off but pleased because now he could give her a lift back to the office as well, Suzy said, "Right now you're my favorite client. You can have pretty much anything you like!"

Lucille was out. Suzy left Leo to make the coffee while she changed out of her wrecked yellow skirt and into a neon blue one. While she was in the bedroom, she quickly redid her lipstick, which had worn off, and gave her neck and wrists a few extra squishes of Gio.

When Suzy emerged, Leo had made the coffee and was standing by the windows overlooking the back garden.

He turned at the sound of her footsteps, and the look in his eyes made Suzy's heart suddenly beat faster.

Much faster.

"What's wrong?"

"Oh, I think you know," said Leo.

"I don't. Tell me."

"Tell you?" One eyebrow went up. "How I feel about you?" His voice was low, almost hypnotic. "Are you sure you want to hear this?"

Suzy stared at him, unable to believe this

was happening. Adrenaline, rushing out of nowhere, flooded her body. Did she want to *hear this*?

"I think I'd better," she said unsteadily.

Leo nodded.

"You know it's there, don't you? This thing between us. It kills me to see you with Harry, when all I want is to have you for myself."

Suzy couldn't speak. Actually, she could barely stand, her legs were so weak. Her knee joints felt as if they'd been filled up with mercury.

"So what are we going to do about this?" Leo went on.

"Ummm . . ."

Softly, he said, "I know what I want to do about it."

This is how it should be, thought Suzy, having a bit of trouble breathing as Leo began to slowly move toward her. *This is how Harry should make me feel. But he doesn't, he just* doesn't . . .

Leo stopped, three feet away from her, and held out his arms. There was that look in his dark eyes again, the look that affected Suzy like a drug.

Overcome with impatience, she closed the gap between them, slid her hands around Leo's neck, tangled her fingers in the silky depths of his hair and closed her eyes in ecstasy as, at last, their mouths met.

Oh, oh, *oh,* what a fabulous kiss. Suzy, in a daze, gave herself up to it totally. If there was an Oscar for Most Fabulous Kisser, Leo Fitzallan would win it, hands down.

When he began to pull away, a low moan of protest escaped from Suzy's throat. It was a don't-stop-now moan, and to make sure he got the message, she wound her arms tighter around him, pressed herself still closer to him, began to move . . .

"Oh dear," said Leo, managing to break contact despite her best efforts and taking a step backward.

" 'Oh dear' what?" Suzy gave him a don't-worry look, ready to reassure him.

"Smile," said Leo. "You're on *Candid Camera.*"

"What?"

"Not literally." He sighed as Suzy's head began to swivel around like a Dalek's. "But I found out all I needed to know."

"About what?" The next moment, her eyes widened in alarm. "My God, you mean . . ."

"Faithfulness just isn't your strong point, it seems. Engaged for four whole days," Leo drawled, "and prepared to cheat on Harry already. After promising *me* that you'd never do anything to hurt him. Oh, Suzy,

317

I've met some heartless women in my time, but you really are in a league of your own. You just don't care who you hurt, do you?"

CHAPTER 25

Oh, oh, this was monstrous! It had all been a scam, Suzy realized, her skin crawling with shame and outrage. Those mesmerizing looks Leo had been giving her had meant . . . absolutely nothing. All that guff about the magical *thing* between them, and how it killed him to see her with Harry . . .

He just made it up to trap me!

He wasn't really a fabulous kisser at all; he was nothing but a cheat.

A sneaky, despicable cheat, at that.

It was at moments like these that Suzy understood *exactly* why Harry was so desperate — for once in his life — to outdo his brother. How awful must it have felt to grow up in the shadow of someone with the answer to everything? Someone who never put a foot wrong, who had the Midas touch when it came to money and the James Bond touch when it came to the opposite sex?

Utterly galling, thought Suzy. That was

how it must have felt.

Leo Fitzallan was going to despise her whatever she said. But if she told him she was only going along with the so-called wedding plans because Harry had begged her to, he would despise Harry as well.

The words *hanged, sheep,* and *lamb* sprang to mind.

Oh God, here goes.

"Look, I'm sorry, I don't know why I did it, but please please *please* don't tell Harry," Suzy begged. "He'd never forgive me, and I do love him; truly I do! And I swear I'll never do anything like that again!"

It was a mortifying process, but under the circumstances, Suzy felt it was the least she could do. Red-faced with shame, she could scarcely bring herself to look Leo in the eye.

Worse still, her brain was still frantically replaying every second of that stupendous kiss. Her lips still tingled helplessly at the memory of his mouth on hers. They hadn't been able to quite take in the fact that none of it had meant what they'd thought it had meant.

See? thought Suzy. *I'm not the only gullible one around here. You fell for it too.*

Aloud, defiantly, she said, "Are you going to tell Harry?"

Leo hesitated, then shook his head. "No,

I'm not. But you don't get any more chances, you have to understand that. From now on, you behave yourself. Because if I find out you've done *anything* to upset my brother —"

"OK, OK." Suzy gestured in frustration for Leo to give it a rest. She was tempted to ask him how he thought Harry might react if he found out who'd been kissing his fiancée in the first place, but basically, there didn't seem much point. Leo would be bound to have the perfect razor-sharp answer. Arguing with him was like deciding to represent yourself in court because you couldn't afford a lawyer, then discovering at the last minute that you were up against the country's most rapier-tongued prosecutor.

"I mean it." Leo's dark eyes were boring through her brain.

"And I have to get back to the office." Since the request for coffee, clearly, had been nothing but a cheap ploy to get himself invited in, Suzy carried the cups through to the kitchen and tipped the contents down the sink. As she returned to the sitting room, a horrid thought struck her. "How long were you planning that?"

"Hmmm? Planning what?"

"That kiss thing."

You bastard, you know perfectly well what

I'm talking about.

"Oh, not long at all. Spur of the moment, really."

He actually had the nerve to smile.

"Not before you came into the office?"

"Look," Leo reasoned, "I didn't know you were going to sit on your Heath bar, did I? And I didn't know you wouldn't have your car with you. I'm good," he added drily, "but I'm not that good. It only became a possibility when you begged me for a lift."

Next time, thought Suzy, *remind me to walk. Even if I'm covered in real dog poo. From head to foot. Just walk.*

"So what about the house?"

"This house?" Leo sounded surprised. "It looks fine."

"Sheldrake House," said Suzy. "Are you still buying it, or was that part of the scam too?"

Leo raised a mocking eyebrow. "What do you think?"

"I think it was all part of the scam."

"Such pessimism!" This time, he actually laughed. "Oh, come on, Suzy, cheer up. I'm still buying the house. I'm not that much of a bastard, you know."

Tuh. "That's a matter of opinion," said Suzy.

■ ■ ■ ■

"So that was Harry's brother." Donna whistled appreciatively when Leo had dropped Suzy back at the office. "Ooh dear, I was right, wasn't I? Exactly your type."

"He isn't," said Suzy with feeling. "He's a ruthless, arrogant, devious shit."

"And when has that ever put you off?" Donna gave her a knowing smirk. "You should have seen the way he was looking at you."

That's nothing; you should have seen the way he was kissing me.

But Suzy couldn't bring herself to say it, not even to Donna. The kiss had been Leo's way of testing her and she had failed with flying colors, hurling herself at him with all the abandon of a large, affection-starved puppy.

Heavens, she had all but wrapped her legs around his waist.

Shameful or what?

"Oh, and Harry phoned while you were out," Donna went on. "He said to clear your schedule on Monday because the people from *Hi!* are coming to take the first round of photos."

"God," said Suzy. "I can just see it: Harry

Fitzallan welcomes us into his lovely hospital room.'"

"He said not to worry about getting your hair done beforehand, because *Hi!* is bringing someone down from London to do it." Donna consulted the shorthand squiggles in her notebook. "And a makeup artist. And a stylist. And a selection of clothes."

"But I don't want to look like Ivana Trump," wailed Suzy.

It all sounded horribly over-the-top. Her mind conjured up a worrying picture of herself wearing a rhinestone-encrusted dress and ultra-bouffant hair. Not to mention ultra-bouffant lips.

"Ivana Trump? You should be so lucky," Donna retorted. "You'd have to lose a few pounds first."

Suzy rolled her eyes. Donna was starting to sound nerve rackingly like Celeste.

The photographer, the hairdresser, the stylist, the makeup artist, and the photographer's assistant weren't the only people to travel down to Bristol on Monday morning.

The man from Tiffany & Co. came too.

"Lucille checked out the rings in your jewelry case to find out the size you'd need," Harry explained with pride.

"Yes, but it's only on loan, for the photo

shoot," said Suzy, to reassure herself. The rings the man from Tiffany's was producing from his heavy-duty briefcase were pretty heavy-duty themselves. There were some serious rocks winking out at her from among the folds of black velvet.

"Not only for the photo shoot." Harry shook his head. "For life."

Alarmed, Suzy said, "You're not serious!"

"Nothing but the best for my future wife." Harry sounded pleased with himself. "Any one of these. It's your choice. Although I must say, I like the look of the heart-shaped one best."

Suzy, her mouth dry, glanced fearfully across at the man from Tiffany's. "How much is it?"

"Don't worry about that!" Harry gestured expansively toward the briefcase. "I want you to choose the one you want. Money is no object!"

The stylist from *Hi!* sighed. "Ooh, I wish someone would say that to me."

Suzy wished Harry wasn't saying it to her. She swallowed and looked at the ring he was sliding onto her finger. She wasn't completely ignorant when it came to good quality jewelry. This ring probably cost twenty thousand pounds. Even assuming that Tiffany & Co. were giving Harry a hefty discount in exchange for the publicity, he was still keen to spend a minimum of ten grand.

On a ring she didn't even want.

The other thing Suzy knew was that it didn't matter how beautiful the ring might be; if you tried to sell the thing back to the shop a week after you'd bought it from them, you'd be lucky to get a tenth of what you'd paid for it.

The heart-shaped diamond was stunning. Harry held her hand up and kissed the tips of her fingers.

"What d'you think?" he said lovingly.

Before Suzy could open her mouth to speak, the photographer and the stylist were nodding in agreement, joining in.

"Perfect, Harry!"

"Yeah, Harry, great."

"Harry?" The receptionist eased herself into the crowded room, carrying a tray of tea and lurid yellow cookies. "Lemon crunch creams all right, love? Ooh, and the physical therapist came around, but I sent her away, told her you were too busy for all that now."

"Thanks," said Harry, his blue eyes crinkling at the corners. "Actually, Doreen, we're a bit cramped in here. Any chance of an empty room where the girls could make a start on Suzy?"

"Don't worry, love. I've already thought of that!" The receptionist planked the tray down next to the briefcase from Tiffany's, slopping tea over the velvet lining and beaming uncontrollably at Harry. "The sluice room's lovely and quiet — she can get herself all gussied up in there."

The gussying up, to Suzy's dismay, took over two hours. First the hairdresser snipped off a few split ends, then went through the heated rollers routine before going completely berserk with the styling spray. Suzy's hair ended up absolutely huge, like a gigantic Dairy Queen ice cream, but — sadly — with the texture of four-day-old Yorkshire pudding.

Next, the makeup artist troweled on more makeup than Suzy had ever had on her face before. Which was saying something.

Now she resembled a drag queen with hair the texture of four-day-old Yorkshire pudding.

"You need a manicure," tut-tutted the stylist.

"My nails are fine." Suzy held them up in protest.

"They might be fine for you," the stylist told her pityingly, "but this is for *Hi!*"

By the time Suzy was ready, the room was even more cramped. The lighting had been set up, silver reflective boards were being arranged at odd angles, and Dr. Hubble, with her sleek dark hair in a new style and her feet in never-seen-before high heels, was busy taking Harry's pulse.

The only thing that cheered Suzy up was the realization that Harry was wearing makeup too.

"Don't say it." He grinned at her. "I look completely ridiculous."

"Not so much as me." Suzy twirled, showing off the hideous, porridge-colored, knee-length linen dress the stylist had insisted on. When Suzy had begged to be allowed to wear her own marigold-orange shirt and short black skirt, the stylist had replied pleasantly, "I think that might look a bit tarty, don't you?"

"Give us a kiss," said Harry, catching her arm as she twirled.

"No kissing!" barked the stylist as the photographer's assistant homed in on them with his light meter. "You'll ruin the lipstick."

"Whose?" Suzy asked innocently. "Harry's or mine?"

CHAPTER 26

It was just starting to rain as Jaz climbed into his car. Next door, he saw Lucille emerge from the house steering her bike with one hand and carrying a guitar case in the other.

He watched her, hatless and coatless, gaze up at the sky in dismay.

Jaz tooted his horn and beckoned Lucille over. "Where are you heading?"

"Just some pub. I sing there sometimes on Monday nights." Lucille looked embarrassed.

"Well, I guessed that much." Grinning, Jaz glanced at the battered guitar case. "Whereabouts exactly?"

Oh well, no big deal. It was no longer a secret, after all, Lucille reminded herself. "Bedminster."

"That's amazing," lied Jaz. "I'm on my way to an AA meeting in Bedminster now. Come on, leave your bike. I'll give you a lift."

The Indian summer had screeched to a halt, hot sun having abruptly given way to cold winds and driving rain. Lucille, shivering in a thin denim shirt and jeans, said, "Are you sure your AA meeting's in Bedminster?"

"Wouldn't say it was if it wasn't." Jaz shrugged and looked amused. "What would be the point of that?"

Lucille was still hesitating. "I'd be stuck for a lift home."

"What time do you finish?"

"Eleven."

"No problem. After our meetings we go out for coffee and a chat. I can pick you up at eleven."

The rain was coming down harder now, dripping from Lucille's eyelashes and darkening her denim shirt.

"Look, it's a pretty rough pub." She paused, wondering how to phrase it delicately. "Sometimes the customers get a bit . . ."

"You mean you'd rather I waited outside for you, in the car. Fine," said Jaz, guessing at once what she was trying to say. "Now please, will you take the bike back into the house and let me give you a lift before you drown?"

The Marshall Arms in the heart of Bedminster wasn't what you'd call classy. Most of the regulars hated her kind of music, Lucille explained, but the landlord — for some reason — was a fan. It was his way, she suspected, of testing his customers' loyalty. Pleasure versus pain. If they wanted to drink in his pub, they had to put up with her songs.

"I used to play in places like that." Jaz was touched by her concern.

"Maybe," said Lucille, "but still promise me you won't come in."

He dropped her off outside the dank, grimy-looking building, then set off across the city to Winterbourne, which was where his AA meeting actually was.

Well, what was a round trip of sixteen miles between friends?

During the course of the evening, several of Jaz's friends asked him how he felt about his ex-wife's involvement with Harry Fitzallan. In their eyes, he saw avid curiosity mingled with concern as they wondered if this might trigger a relapse.

Jaz realized that if he told them the truth — that in his opinion Harry Fitzallan was an idiot and not good enough for Suzy — they would automatically assume he was jealous.

To his intense irritation, therefore, he was forced to smile and crack jokes and tell everyone what a great guy Harry was, and what a perfect couple he and Suzy made.

"She's moving on," said Jeff, who could never resist the temptation to stir things up. "Doesn't that make you feel a bit . . . you know?"

"I couldn't be happier," Jaz insisted. "What my ex-wives get up to doesn't bother me."

Reluctant to let go of the idea, Jeff said, "We haven't seen Celeste for a few weeks. Everything OK between you two?"

"Fine." Jaz stretched and yawned, bored to tears with this interrogation. He glanced at his watch.

"People who think they don't need to come to meetings anymore are playing with fire," said Jeff with a self-righteous air. It had certainly been his downfall in the past.

"She hasn't stopped. She's joined another group closer to home."

This was a lie, but Jaz couldn't be bothered to argue. And since there were dozens of AA meetings being held in the city every single night, Jeff would never know he wasn't telling the truth.

Jeff, an avid gleam in his piggy little eyes, said, "Separate groups, eh? What's brought this on? It'll be separate bedrooms next!"

One of the great things about getting roaring drunk, Jaz remembered, was the way you could say whatever was on your mind. If some idiot was being annoying, you just told them to fuck off, simple as that.

And there was no getting away from it — Jeff *was* an annoying idiot.

But Jaz, being sober, couldn't bring himself to say it. Which was a shame and one of the major disadvantages of giving up the drink.

Instead, he said patiently, "Celeste's fine, I'm fine. We're both fine, I promise."

The meeting was over. Everyone else was putting their raincoats on, getting ready to leave.

"Coming for coffee?" said Jeff, buttoning up his anorak.

"Not tonight." Jaz checked his watch: nine thirty. "There's someone I have to meet."

"Hold up!" snickered Jeff. "Not a female someone, I hope!"

Sometimes, Jaz discovered, you really *didn't* need alcohol.

"Screw you, Jeff," he said pleasantly. "Don't be a jerk all your life."

The Marshall Arms was heaving with bodies when Jaz reached it at ten o'clock, but none of them appeared to be listening to Lucille.

Having slipped unnoticed through the door, Jaz moved to the end of the bar farthest from the makeshift stage, ordered a Coke and sat down in a darkened corner where he could hear Lucille without being seen. The last thing he wanted to do was put her off.

Although anyone who could carry on singing while a group of lagered-up Bristol Rovers' supporters were chanting and hammering their empty glasses on the bar had to be pretty strong-willed.

"Oy, you lot, shut up and give the girl a chance," the landlord bellowed above the noise.

"It's crap!" howled one of the Rovers' supporters with a barbed-wire tattoo circling his fat neck. "Tell her to sing summat we know."

"Like Cher," yelled his sidekick. "Or Madonna, phwooarr!"

"And get your tits out while you're at it." The tattooed one began banging his huge fist on the bar for emphasis. "Yeah, go on! Tits! Tits! Tits!"

Jaz smiled to himself, instantly transported back to the old days of hecklers in filthy backstreet pubs. It was something he missed almost more than the later years of adulation and hero worship. He wondered how Lucille would handle this.

The next moment, he instinctively ducked down as Lucille strode into view — but there was no need to hide; her attention was fixed unswervingly on Barbed Wire.

Swiftly removing the empty glass from his hand, she hauled him away from the bar and led him up onto the stage.

"Tell you what," said Lucille, into the mike. "Why don't you get *your* tits out?"

And she launched without hesitation into "You Sexy Thing," the Hot Chocolate number so memorably featured in *The Full Monty*.

Everyone in the pub let out a great roar of approval. Barbed Wire, thrilled to be the center of attention and grinning like an idiot, gyrated his vast stomach and danced clumsily along to the music. When he finished unfastening his beer-stained shirt and threw it into the audience now gathered around the stage, laughter and wolf whistles rang out, and Lucille murmured into the microphone, "Crikey, they're bigger than mine."

Someone brought a hat around as Lucille was finishing her set. Jaz dropped a ten-pound note in. Barbed Wire, whom he'd observed a couple of minutes earlier throwing in a couple of pound coins, was now leading the singing and clearly yearning to get back on stage. An hour ago he'd been a pain in the neck. Now he was Lucille's greatest fan.

Jaz shook his head in silent admiration. That was the way to deal with hecklers. Lucille definitely had the knack.

She spotted him as she made her way over to the bar for a drink.

"How long have you been here?"

"Two minutes?" Jaz shrugged, reaching into his jeans pocket for loose change. "Just arrived. Let me get you a drink."

"Liar." Lucille broke into a grin. "I saw you being served at the bar an hour ago."

"God." Jaz sighed. "I'd make a useless international spy."

"You would. But you can still buy me a drink. I'll have a Guinness please."

Jaz ordered a Guinness and another Coke for himself.

Watching him, Lucille said, "Is it hard, coming into a pub and not having a drink?"

"Not hard. Just boring. It helps if there's live music." He smiled. "You coped well. Won yourself an admirer into the bargain."

Lucille acknowledged the compliment with a rueful shake of the head. "I coped, but they won. I ended up playing the music they wanted me to play."

"This kind of venue, it's all you can do," said Jaz. "Believe me."

"I know you're right." Lucille took a gulp of Guinness. "It's just . . . singing other people's songs is never going to get me anywhere. But nobody wants to listen to anything I've written myself. I feel like one of those people who stand in the middle of Broadmead shouting about Jesus and the love he can bring into our lives . . . Everyone scuttles away faster than you can say 'nutcase.' "

"The song you were playing when I came in," said Jaz. "That was one of yours."

"Exactly. Nobody was listening to it."

"I listened to it."

"And it wasn't very good." Lucille looked at him. "Was it?"

"You have a fantastic voice. Seriously. Great range, perfect pitch, real depth."

"But the song was still garbage," Lucille prompted. "It's OK, you can say it. I promise not to throw myself off the Suspension Bridge."

"OK," said Jaz. "It wasn't fantastic, no."

"The truth." Lucille's expression was serious. "It was garbage."

Reluctantly, Jaz admitted, "Well, pretty much."

God, being truthful was no picnic. Then again, was there anything worse than being a hypocrite and a liar?

"Thanks a lot."

Appalled, Jaz realized there were tears glistening in Lucille's luminous brown eyes.

He instantly felt terrible. "Oh God, now you're upset —"

"I meant thanks a lot in the grateful sense, not the pissy one." Lucille broke into a watery smile. "It's like going along to a modeling agency and being told there's no way you can be a model because you're only four feet ten. Don't you see?" Reaching across to reassure him, she touched Jaz's wrist. "If anything it's a relief. Now, at last, I can stop trying."

This only made Jaz feel a million times worse. Being honest definitely wasn't all it was cracked up to be. He had trampled on Lucille's dreams and that was unforgivable. Opening his mouth to tell her that when he had been starting out he'd been told he was garbage practically on a daily basis, he was beaten to the tape by Barbed Wire.

"Great stuff, love. That was ace! Clever little girl you got 'ere." Blasting them both sideways with his beery breath, he gave Jaz a congratulatory thump on the shoulder. "Pretty too. You're a lucky bloke."

"Actually —" began Lucille.

"Let me get you both a drink! Pint, mate?"

"Thanks, but I'm fine." Jaz nodded at his pint glass, still two-thirds full.

Barbed Wire gazed at it in horror. "What's that? Coke? Bloody hell, mate, 'ave a proper drink. Oy, Don, get us a couple of pints of Stella!"

"Really, no," said Jaz. "I don't drink."

Barbed Wire, clearly confused, said, "Eh? Why not?"

"I'm an alcoholic."

This was way beyond Barbed Wire's comprehension. He shook his shaven head. "Yeah, but you can have just the one, can't you?"

This, of course, was precisely what Jaz couldn't do. Before you could say "relapse," just-the-one would have turned into just-the-fifty.

"Look," Jaz said easily, "why don't you let me buy you a drink? We've got to leave in five minutes anyway." He swiftly ordered and paid for a pint of Stella.

"Cheers, mate." Relieved to have the situation sorted out, Barbed Wire said, "Bloody good little singer, isn't she?" Giving Lucille a hefty nudge, he went on, "We all thought

340

you was gonna be crap, but you turned out orright in the end. Hey, better give us your autograph, love, case you ever get famous."

The momentary flicker of grief in Lucille's eyes was almost more than Jaz could bear. He turned away, hating himself, as Lucille shook her head at Barbed Wire and said lightly, "Don't worry, no danger of that ever happening to me."

Chapter 27

Next to Jaz in the passenger seat, Lucille opened the manila envelope the landlord had handed her as they were leaving.

Jaz, still feeling rotten, waited until she'd finished counting the money. Overcome with curiosity as Lucille silently pocketed it, he said, "Decent night?"

"Twenty-two pounds eighty-four pence."

"In the hat? That's pretty good."

"Twenty pounds for playing," Lucille corrected him. "Two pounds eighty-four pence from passing the hat around."

Jaz opened his mouth, then closed it again just in time. If he were to tell Lucille he'd put a tenner in, she'd only feel patronized.

Anyway, she'd had more than enough bad news for one evening, thanks to him.

"Look," he tried again, "all I heard was *one song* . . ."

"My best song." Lucille's tone was dogged. "And I told you, it doesn't matter.

I trust you; that's why I asked for your opinion. I'd have really hated it," she assured him, "if you'd lied."

Jaz changed into second gear as they roared up Constitution Hill.

"You do have a terrific voice."

"Thank you," Lucille said gravely. "And you don't have to feel guilty." She broke into a smile. "I'm a big girl, I can take it. I'm glad you told me the truth."

She sounded convincing. If Jaz didn't know better, he might almost have believed her. And he *had* meant it when he'd said she had a terrific voice.

Oh well, there was nothing more he could do about it now. Lucille's nonexistent songwriting skills weren't his problem anyway. The world was full of aspiring singers destined for a lifetime of rejection and failure.

I'm getting soft in my old age, Jaz told himself as he swung the Alfa onto Goldney Avenue. *Like she said, I did her a favor.*

OK, now just forget it.

Two days later, Donna turned pale green behind her computer. Suzy and Rory were too busy sniping at each other to notice.

Rory normally didn't argue, but Suzy's unscheduled disappearances from the office were testing him to the limit. Suzy, in turn, was stressed up to the eyebrows by the situation Harry had landed her in and the endless lies she was being forced to tell.

"Come on," she yelled, "it's not as if I'm skipping out to buy a new pair of shoes or something! Harry's in the hospital, and he wants me to be there with him when the photographers come down from London to take his picture."

"You're losing us business," Rory snapped back. "Our customers are complaining that every time they try to reach you, your phone's switched off."

Suzy almost stamped her foot in frustration. Long hair flying, she grabbed her bag, yanked out her phone, and waved it under Rory's nose.

"It's not always off! It's *on,* OK? See? On! The only time it's off is when I'm in the hospital because when you're in the hospital you aren't *allowed* to have your cell phone switched on!"

"*Exactly,*" Rory hissed, picking up his briefcase and heading for the door.

"Ummm, sorry about this . . ." Donna murmured to no one in particular. Pushing back her chair as the spinning room began to tilt and gather speed, she tried to stand up.

"Sorry about what?" demanded Rory, exasperated. With one hand on the door handle, he turned and looked over his shoulder just as Donna's chair went toppling backward, closely followed by Donna herself, the keyboard from her computer and the two hundred sheets of legal paper she'd been about to load into the laser printer.

"Oh my God," squealed Suzy, trampling all over the scattered sheets as she rushed to Donna's side.

To be fair, it wasn't easy to tell that Donna's complexion was pale green, what with the amount of heavy white foundation she wore. Her black-kohled eyes fluttered for a few seconds as Suzy cradled her head in her lap.

"Call an ambulance," Suzy barked at Rory. "Tell them she's unconscious and burning up. It could be malaria."

Last night she'd caught the end of a movie set in Africa, where the heroine had died of malaria.

"What?" said Rory in disbelief.

"I don't have malaria." Donna, her eyes flickering open, murmured, "I just fainted."

Thankful that she was conscious, Suzy gazed down at her and said, "Heavens, are you pregnant?"

"No, but I ache all over. I think it's the flu."

Flu, yuck. Holding her breath to keep the germs out and casually easing Donna's head from her lap, Suzy said, "You poor thing. Why didn't you tell us you were feeling rotten?"

Still pale and nauseated, Donna nevertheless managed a brief smile. "Couldn't get a word in edgewise."

"See?" Suzy looked up at Rory. "It's all your fault."

"Right, well, that's just brilliant," Rory said when Donna had been dispatched home in a taxi. "How long's she going to be off, a fortnight?"

"You're all heart," Suzy told him. Still on her knees, she was busy gathering together the scattered sheets of paper. "We'll have to get a temp in, that's all." Recalling the last temp they'd employed, she added, "This time, preferably one who can read and write."

Rory shuddered at the memory. He couldn't go through that again. Casually, he said, "What about Fee?"

Suzy shook back her tawny hair and looked up at him from under her bangs. "What about her?"

346

"She helped us out before, didn't she?" Rory forced his voice to stay sounding neutral. "Did a good job, if I remember." I remember. Oh yes, I remember! "You could ask her, couldn't you?"

"Honestly, you've got some nerve," Suzy protested. "Fee offered to help us out for a few hours when we were desperate."

"We're even more desperate now," argued Rory.

"You can't *do* that, though. You can't ask someone to help you out for a whole fortnight. It's like your neighbor calling you over to hold his ladder steady, then five minutes later asking you if you wouldn't mind redecorating his whole house for him. No," Suzy said firmly. "Just because Fee's so good-natured, people are always taking advantage of her, and we're not going to do that. It's too much. We'll just have to hire a temp and keep our fingers crossed."

The words *pot, kettle,* and *very black* indeed sprang to mind, Rory felt, recalling Suzy's remarks about other people taking advantage of Fee's good nature. Talk about shameless.

But he still couldn't believe he was about to do what he was about to do.

It was totally out of character, not like him

at all, but since being seized by the plan, Rory hadn't allowed himself to think of that. Instead, leaving Suzy in the office, he had driven straight to Suzy's apartment and rung Suzy's doorbell. Firmly, several times.

Finally, he rang the bell for Fee's apartment, which was directly below Suzy's.

Fee answered the door wrapped in a green toweling robe and with her hands behind her back.

"I'm sorry. Did I get you out of bed?" Mystified, Rory realized that beneath the toweling robe, she was wearing a T-shirt and sweat-pants, socks, Nike sneakers . . . What on earth was going on?

Fee, blushing slightly, said, "Of course not. Hi, is it Suzy you're looking for? I heard her doorbell being rung."

"I'm desperate to find her." Rory was amazed to discover how easy it was to lie when you had a real incentive. "I know her car isn't here, but I still had to try the apartment. You wouldn't happen to know where she is, by any chance?"

"No. Suzy left for work at the usual time." Fee's green eyes widened. "Has something dreadful happened? It's not Harry, is it?"

"Nothing like that," Rory said hastily. "Just an office crisis." He paused. "Donna's gone down with the flu. We have to get someone in to replace her, and when I phoned DreamTemps all they could offer us was a sixteen-year-old with limited filing skills — and that's probably her nails. Suzy's got the contact number for another agency; that's why I'm so desperate to track her down . . . If we can't get somebody else by midday we'll have to settle for — Good grief, what happened to your *arms*?"

He broke off, staring in horror at Fee's forearms. While he'd been talking, she'd forgotten to keep them hidden behind her back, and now, with the sleeves of her robe falling away, he could clearly see giant white bandages concealing goodness knows what.

Some terrible injury? Or . . . ?

Rory prayed she hadn't been out and gotten herself tattooed.

Going pinker still with embarrassment, Fee promptly tried to shrink her arms into her robe's sleeves, like snails prodded with a stick.

"Oh, it's nothing, really."

Alarmed, Rory said, "Of course it's not nothing! What's going on?" Seizing Fee's right arm, he examined the unusual strip of bandage, then gazed at her in bewilderment. "Did you hurt yourself?"

"No, but I'm just about to." Fee sighed, giving up the struggle to retain a shred of dignity. "Come on in. You can watch if you like."

Still totally mystified, Rory followed her into the apartment.

"I put this on to try to hide my arms," Fee explained, removing her robe. "When the doorbell rang, I thought you were the meter reader. Anyway, here goes."

Peeling a corner of the first bandage away from her skin, she gritted her teeth, visibly braced herself . . . and pulled.

To Rory's utter amazement, there was no sign of blood underneath. Neither — *phew* — were there any tattoos.

"And again," said Fee, screwing up her eyes for a second as she repeated the process on the other forearm.

Still no blood.

Rory, shaking his head, said, "I don't get this at all."

"It's a girl thing." Fee smiled slightly at his innocence. Rolling up the discarded white bandages, she said, "These are called waxing strips."

"Waxing what?"

Rory had never read a women's magazine in his life. He hadn't the faintest idea what she was talking about.

"I have hairy forearms," Fee explained. Honestly, this was worse than imparting the facts of life to a ten-year-old. "I don't like having hairy forearms, so I wax them. You spread hot wax on your arms, lay the strips on top, wait until the wax is set, then rip off the strips. It pulls the hairs out by their roots."

Rory winced. This was all news to him.

"But . . . doesn't that hurt?"

"Not much," said Fee. "Only about as much as childbirth."

"Couldn't you just shave?"

"Stubbly forearms." Fee wrinkled her nose. "Not attractive."

"Oh, right, yes . . . I see . . ." Totally thrown by this waxing business — which just went to show how hopeless he was where women were concerned — Rory tried to remember what he was doing here.

"Poor Donna," said Fee. "Flu, how awful. She'll be off for a couple of weeks."

That was it, Rory thought with relief.

"Well, I'd better make a move." Adjusting his glasses, he backed toward the door. "See if I can track down Suzy and the number of that agency."

Fee, remembering how much she had enjoyed the work last time, said bravely, "I could always be your temp, if you think I'd be good enough."

Yes yes yes! thought Rory.

"No no no," he protested aloud, shaking his head and giving her a look of gratitude mingled with regret. "Oh no, it's a wonderful offer, but I couldn't possibly let you do that. It's far too much of an imposition."

"I'd like to help out," Fee said eagerly. "I can juggle my voluntary work for a couple of weeks —"

"But this time you'd have to let us pay you."

"OK." Her eyes bright, Fee rubbed her tingling pink forearms and said, "When would you like me to start?"

"After lunch?" Rory was overjoyed. His plan had actually worked, and the buzz was even greater than if he'd just sold a house. For the next fortnight Fee would be there in the office. When he walked in each morning they'd smile at each other, say hello, take turns making the coffee, exchange —

"Well, well, speak of the devil." Fee was peering out of the window. "Here's Suzy now."

It could have been intensely embarrassing. Somehow Rory got through it. Suzy shot him a couple of deeply suspicious looks but, miraculously, didn't give him away.

"You've definitely got some nerve." She shook her head at Rory and tut-tutted with disapproval as they left the house together ten minutes later. "Honestly, if I didn't know better, I'd think you fancied Fee."

When they arrived back at the office, Martin was on the phone.

"That's great, seven o'clock at the Greyhound . . . Oh, don't worry about her. I'll just say I've got to work late." He winked at Suzy, who rolled her eyes to heaven.

"Don't look at me like that." Martin grinned at her as he hung up. "It's not as if I'm seeing another woman. Just a few of the guys getting together for a couple of drinks . . . Where's the harm in that?"

"I don't know," said Suzy. "Why don't you ask Nancy?"

"D'oh!" Martin clapped his hand to his forehead. "You said it! You said the *N* word."

"She's your wife."

"She's my nag. Nagging Nancy." He groaned theatrically. "Whose mission in life is to stop me from having even the *tiniest* bit of fun."

Hugely tempted to give him a good slap and tell him to grow up, Suzy glanced at her watch. "Don't you have to be at Carlyle Road by midday?"

"She's got it! By George, she's got it," Martin crowed. "The way you narrowed your eyes just then, and that do-as-you'retold expression . . . Suzy, it's perfect! You're going to make Harry a great nagging wife."

CHAPTER 28

At four o'clock, Fee was alone in the office enjoying herself tremendously. The typing was going like a dream. She had a list of phone messages to pass on to Rory, Suzy, and Martin when they returned from their various appointments. Prospective clients had been dropping in all afternoon and she'd offered them coffee, chatting with them about the kind of property they were after and sending them away with the appropriate particulars . . .

"Hi." Fee smiled brightly as the door swung open again. "Can I help you?"

"You certainly can," declared a startlingly pretty girl with a cloud of dark curly hair. "You could come hold this door open, for a start."

Taken aback by this request, Fee nevertheless did as she was asked. Maybe the girl was struggling with a double stroller or a relative in a wheelchair.

But when she reached the door, Fee saw a cab tick-ticking outside, and the girl energetically hauling a succession of black trash bags off the backseat and out onto the pavement.

What on earth was going on?

"Ummm . . . is this a delivery of some kind?"

This was the trouble with being new to a job, Fee realized. It could be a regular Wednesday afternoon arrangement.

"A delivery? Oh, definitely," said the girl, now throwing the full bags through the open door and into the office. "Special delivery for Martin Lord."

"Er . . . can I ask what it is?"

"All his worldly goods, basically. You're new, aren't you?" said the girl. "I'm Nancy, Martin's wife. Soon to be his ex-wife."

"Oh, good grief." Fee gazed at the small mountain of trash bags in horror. One of them had split open and a tangle of trousers and shirts, like ruptured intestines, was spilling out.

"Don't look so worried. He deserves it." Nancy shrugged and pulled a crumpled envelope from the back pocket of her pink jeans. "He'll probably be thrilled. Could you make sure he gets this?"

Fee's eyes widened. "Shouldn't you give it

to him?"

"Look," Nancy said pleasantly, "Martin's not interested in being married. He doesn't care about me, and he hardly ever sees our children. He's probably got himself another woman, but to tell you the truth, it doesn't even bother me anymore. So you just make sure my husband sees this letter, OK? And tell him not to bother coming around to the house because I've already had the locks changed." As she hopped back into the taxi, she added, "Oh, and I hope he has a nice time tonight, *working late.*"

"What the . . . ? Is this some kind of joke?" Martin demanded when he read the letter two hours later.

"I don't think so. She didn't sound as if she was joking." Fee opened the door leading through to the back room and indicated the pile of shiny black trash bags stacked up against the far wall. "I put your stuff in here."

"I don't believe it! What does she think she's playing at?" Martin stared at the bags, then back at the letter, then angrily at Fee. "What the hell d'you think you were playing at, letting her *do* this?"

Fee, who was a lot braver than she looked, stood her ground as Martin glared at her.

The next moment the glass door flew open, and Suzy and Rory piled into the office behind him.

"I wasn't playing at anything." Fee's gaze was unwavering, her tone ice cool. "According to your wife, you're a lousy husband and father, and you're having an affair with another woman, and she doesn't want to be married to you anymore. Now that's your problem, not mine, so I'd rather you didn't shout at me."

Martin's mouth dropped open in astonishment. With her dark red hair, innocent green eyes, and russet angora cardigan, it was like being savaged unexpectedly by a baby squirrel.

"What's this?" Suzy was instantly enthralled. "Has Nancy kicked you out?"

Exasperated, Martin pushed his hair off his forehead.

"Of course she hasn't kicked me out."

"She has," said Fee. "And she's changed the locks."

"She has *not.*" Martin shook his head. "She's just having a go at me because I called her and said I'd be working late tonight."

"How can you have an affair?" Suzy was utterly disgusted with him. "Nancy's lovely. You've got a beautiful wife, gorgeous children —"

"I'm not *having* an affair!" shouted Martin.

"You know what you're going to need?" Suzy asked conversationally.

"What?"

"A new iron. Your clothes are going to get horribly crumpled in those black bags."

"I know I should feel sorry for him," said Suzy, when Martin had piled the bags into the back of his metallic green Renault Mégane and roared off to talk some sense into Nancy. "But I just can't. He *so* deserves this."

Rory, who had spent the whole afternoon looking forward to coming back to the office, crossed to the door and put up the Closed sign.

"Right, well, I wouldn't say no to a drink." He rubbed his hands and struggled to sound casual. "How about it then, to celebrate the end of Fee's first day . . . Suzy, how does a drink sound to you?"

Suzy sighed and rotated her head and shoulders. "I've got to go see Harry. And I ache all over." She winced, stretching her arms behind her back. "God, how did the muscles in my neck get so scrunched up?"

"Fee?" Rory said hopefully.

"I can't either." Fee looked apologetic. "I've got an evening class at the Folk House. Come on, sit down," she told Suzy, patting the chair next to her. "Let's have a look at that neck of yours."

"Oh, *bliss,*" Suzy murmured as Fee's expert fingers set to work on her bunched-up muscles.

"You know what you're like when you get stressed out," Fee scolded. "Right, now tip your head forward and let your shoulders go."

Suzy, her rippling tawny hair spilling over her face, carried on groaning and sighing in ecstasy as the massage began to take effect. Rory, hunched over his own desk trying to work through a pile of letters that needed signing, tried not to listen but was unable to prevent himself glancing over every now and again. He could only imagine how it must feel, to be massaged like that.

Beneath his suit and crisp white shirt, his own shoulders felt naked and neglected.

I'm tense too, Rory thought longingly, wishing with all his heart that Fee would do the same for him.

"Want to come to the hospital with me?" offered Suzy, pulling off her lime-green shirt as Lucille poked her head around the bedroom door.

"I was just about to ask you if you wanted to come to Leo's new restaurant," said Lucille. "It's the opening night."

Suzy kicked her lilac high heels into the corner of the room and wriggled out of her skirt.

"Is this a joke?" Grinning, she reached for her robe. "Leo's actually invited us to the opening of a fast-food joint? Hey, glitzy! Who needs champagne and canapés when you can have Coke and a burger and fries?"

Lucille started to laugh. "Leo's restaurant isn't like that. They don't do *burgers*. Are we talking about the same Leo here?"

Suzy was taken aback. "Harry said it was. He told me Leo had a chain of fast-food outlets."

As she spoke, Suzy frowned. Harry had described Leo's business in such a derogatory fashion that she hadn't pursued the subject. Nor had she ever discussed it with Leo; being such a concerned, caring sort of person, she had thought he might be a touch sensitive about making his money out of such a tacky venture.

And she deliberately hadn't asked Lucille about the burger bars because she didn't want her to think she was interested in Leo.

"Harry was joking," Lucille explained

361

gently. Roughly translated, Suzy realized, this meant Harry was mocking his brother's business because he was bitterly jealous of Leo's success. "You've heard of the Alpha Bar in Chelsea, right?"

Suzy nodded. Of course she had.

"And there are Alpha Bars in Glasgow, Manchester, Brighton, and Cardiff?"

Light dawned.

"Oh *God*."

"And now there's one in Bristol too," said Lucille.

"So Harry wasn't lying when he said there was a chain of them." Suzy sighed. The Alpha Bars catered to their namesakes, attracting the most glamorous, stylish, and successful clientele from miles around. Immaculate attention to detail, stunning food, and inspired decor — deep purple and dark green marble-mirrored walls were a signature feature — had all contributed to the company's success.

And Leo Fitzallan was the boss.

Well, well, who'd have thought it?

Happily, Suzy said, "Great, yes, of course we'll go. When did Leo invite us?"

At this, Lucille hesitated. Cautiously, she pulled an embossed purple and green card from the pocket of her jeans.

"Well, Leo gave me this last week . . ."

She was prevaricating. Mystified, Suzy reached for the card.

"Lucille Amory *and guest*?" Her eyebrows shot up even more dramatically than her voice. "You mean he didn't even *invite* me? That's all I am . . . *and guest*?"

"I thought he would have." Lucille hastily concealed her discomfort with a so-what shrug. "He must have forgotten, that's all. Anyway, it doesn't matter, does it? We've got the invite here. We can both go!"

Suzy was having trouble getting her eyebrows down again; they felt as if they were lodged up there for good. Indignation wasn't the word for how she was feeling.

This was . . . *outrageous.*

"No, no, really, I'm fine. You go. I have to visit Harry anyway." Belatedly remembering her earlier plans, Suzy headed for the shower.

Not fooling Lucille for a moment, needless to say.

"But I'm sure Leo meant to invite you too. He'd definitely want you to be there," she protested.

"If he wanted me to be there that badly, he'd have put my name on the invitation list," said Suzy. She forced herself to turn and smile at Lucille, to prove that she wasn't the one at fault here. Oh no, this was entirely Leo's doing. Probably to pay her back for accidentally kissing him the other day.

And that had been *all his fault.*

"I feel awful now," wailed Lucille.

"Look, don't worry about it. You go and have a great time. Anyway, Harry's expecting me." To make up for having completely forgotten about him earlier, Suzy vowed to be extra nice to Harry tonight. "I couldn't possibly let him down."

When Suzy reached Harry's room, loaded down with men's magazines and Kit Kat bars, the effect was spoiled somewhat by the pile of duplicate magazines already littering the bed and the mountain of Kit Kats heaped on top of his locker.

"I know. Mad, isn't it?" Harry grinned as he kissed her. "The local radio station phoned up yesterday wanting to dedicate a record to me. When they asked the receptionist what my favorite track was, she thought they said treat. We've had nonstop deliveries of Kit Kats ever since."

"Should have said tins of beluga caviar." Suzy flipped through one of the magazines he'd been looking at. "Where did these come from?"

"One of the staff nurses brought them in

for me."

"One of the pretty staff nurses?"

Harry winked. "Well, I suppose you could call him pretty."

Next moment, Suzy's fingers froze. Incredibly, there was a photograph of Leo in the magazine she'd been idly flipping through.

ELIGIBLE BLOKES — IT'S A TOUGH JOB, BUT SOMEBODY'S GOTTA DO IT!

That was the headline, followed by a series of photos and mini features detailing the histories, lifestyles, and sexual conquests of various British businessmen, sporting heroes, and media types. Dying to read the piece about Leo, Suzy glanced up and saw the expression on Harry's face.

Well, maybe now wasn't the moment.

Instead, she closed the magazine and said casually, "His new restaurant opens tonight."

"I know." Harry nodded, then clasped her hand. "I thought you might have gone along."

Pride wouldn't allow Suzy to admit the truth. Instead, choosing her words with care, she said, "I was invited."

Harry's grip on her hand tightened, causing Suzy to flinch. That was the trouble with great big engagement rings — when someone gave your fingers a squeeze like that, those glittering diamonds really *hurt*.

"Thanks," murmured Harry, his electric-blue eyes gazing into hers.

"Thanks for what?"

He smiled lovingly at Suzy. "You know what I'm talking about. I'm glad you didn't go."

He squeezed again, bringing tears to Suzy's eyes.

Ooh, *ouch*.

CHAPTER 29

At the Alpha Bar, Leo drew Lucille to one side, away from the crush of chattering guests.

"No Suzy?"

"She's visiting Harry." Lucille diplomatically didn't mention Suzy's eruption into orbit upon discovering that she hadn't been properly invited to tonight's launch party. Instead, gesturing around the packed restaurant and bar, she said, "This place is fantastic. It's going to do brilliantly."

"Especially once we get our resident singer." Leo smiled down at her. "How are you fixed for Wednesday and Friday evenings? We can make it a regular thing, two nights a week."

Lucille's stomach did a back flip. Her initial reaction, to jump for joy and stammer out her thanks, died in an instant. *I'm not going to put myself through that anymore, remember?*

From now on she had to forget the dreams that were never going to come true, and concentrate on being practical instead.

Sensible.

Realistic.

And with a regular wage coming in.

Lucille took a deep breath. "It's really nice of you to offer, but I'd be more interested in waitressing five nights a week."

Leo looked shocked. "Why?"

"I'm putting the other stuff behind me." Biting her lip, Lucille prayed her voice wasn't about to wobble. "Giving it up as a bad job."

For once, Leo was lost for words. He knew how much Lucille's singing meant to her; it was what she lived for.

"I don't understand. Look at you." He indicated Lucille's figure, encased in a caramel silk cropped top and matching long skirt split to the thigh. Her beaded braids were fastened up in a topknot, emphasizing her huge brown eyes and swanlike neck. "You've got the face, the body, everything it takes —"

"Except the talent," Lucille said simply.

Leo raised his eyebrows in disbelief. "That's not true. Your voice is amazing."

"Thousands and thousands of people have a great singing voice. If you want people to sit up and take notice, you need a great song." Lucille fiddled with the clasp of her clutch bag, clicking it open and shut, open and shut as she spoke, "I always thought that one day, maybe I'd write one. Now I know it's not going to happen."

"How?" Leo demanded. "How can you know that?"

"Someone gave me their honest opinion."

"Who?"

Lucille shrugged. *Click click, click click.* "Someone I trust."

"Not Suzy, I hope." Horrified, Leo said, "Oh God, tell me it wasn't Suzy!"

The expression on his face was a scream. Lucille started to laugh.

"I promise you it wasn't Suzy. Have you ever heard her singing?"

"I've heard *about* it." Leo shuddered briefly. "And I had a narrow escape once, in her car. Luckily, she had *Riverdance* in the tape deck."

"Luckier than you think," Lucille said with feeling. "Suzy's one of the few people who can and does sing along to *Riverdance.*"

Leo realized she was trying to steer him away from the subject at hand.

"So who told you to give up the music?"

"Someone who knows what they're talking about." Lucille straightened her shoulders and forced a bright smile. "Jaz Dreyfuss."

Leo sighed, because Jaz clearly did know what he was talking about.

Still, what kind of bastard would actually come out and say it?

"Don't look like that," said Lucille. "I asked him to be honest. I don't want to spend the next fifty years waiting for something that's never going to happen."

"You'd rather be a waitress instead." Leo's attention was caught by Gabriella frantically beckoning across the room; there were people over at the bar waiting to speak to him. "Look, we'll have to discuss this tomorrow," he told Lucille. "If that's what you really want, then fine, we'll sort something out." He went on evenly, "But I still think Jaz Dreyfuss could have kept his expert opinion to himself."

"Don't blame him," Lucille insisted.

Leo wondered how she was really feeling, beneath the brave exterior.

"I don't *blame* him," he said. "I just wonder how he can sleep at night."

Jaz couldn't sleep. By three o'clock in the morning he'd given up trying. Next to him, Celeste was out for the count, curled up like a dormouse on her side of the king-size bed with her left hand clutching her right shoulder. When Jaz pushed back the duvet she didn't even stir.

Maybe a swim would help.

Pulling on his toweling robe, Jaz padded downstairs. Yes, a swim, that might do it. Forty lengths of the pool should be enough to stop the endless churning in his brain. Maybe sixty lengths — that would tire him out physically and *force* him to sleep.

Eighty lengths later Jaz eased himself out of the dimly lit pool, his mind still racing unstoppably.

Jesus, it was like being back in the band, realizing that for a laugh someone had slipped speed into your drink.

Except this time drugs had nothing to do with it.

Instead — Jaz ruefully acknowledged — the cause was Lucille.

Naked and dripping, he gazed down at the orange lights shimmering up at him from the bottom of the pool.

The house was utterly silent.

To his left stood the door that would lead him back up the stairs to bed.

Directly ahead of him lay the pool — of course — into which he could always dive once more. Another eighty lengths would surely do the trick. Christ, thought Jaz, pushing both hands through his wet hair and quailing at the prospect. At this rate he'd end up swimming the equivalent of the English Channel in one night.

And then there was the door on the right. All he had to do was make his way along the narrow corridor running parallel to the pool room and open the heavy wooden door at the end of it.

It was what his brain was urging him to do, Jaz realized. It was what *he* wanted to do. But he was terrified, in case it was a trick. What if his brain was only doing it because it was desperate for a drink?

This was crazy, *crazy.* Jaz gritted his teeth. Music was the last hurdle. OK, he'd managed three and a half years. Which was good, of course it was, particularly when you took into account the fact that if he hadn't stopped drinking he'd surely have been dead by now.

But music was his life, it mattered more to him than almost anything. And without it, he knew he was leading an unfulfilled existence. His days were dreadfully empty.

Which was why, needless to say, he spent so much time swimming up and down this bloody boring pool.

"Right," Jaz said aloud, dragging his

toweling robe around him once more. "Let's go."

Because if he didn't, basically, it meant the drink was still ruining his life.

As he made his way along the narrow corridor, it occurred to Jaz that the recording studio might not even *be* there anymore. It had been three and a half years, after all, since he had last visited it.

For all he knew, Maeve could have turfed out all that expensive equipment and transformed it into a launderette.

She hadn't. It was still there, just the same, exactly as Jaz remembered it.

His hands trembled as he closed the soundproofed door behind him. His heart crashing against his rib cage, his throat automatically craving bourbon, Jaz sat down on a swivel chair in front of the mixing desk.

Some part of him had half expected the studio to resemble Miss Havisham's dining room in *Great Expectations,* with inches of dust everywhere and spectacular cobwebs festooned like curtains from every mike stand.

It wasn't a bit like that, of course. Without once mentioning that she ever ventured down here, Maeve had kept the place spotless. Like a mother whose son has left home,

Jaz thought with a brief smile, lovingly keeping his bedroom clean and ready for him in case one day he should decide to move back.

What would any of them do without Maeve?

The urge to get out of the room was powerful, but he'd come this far, and Jaz was damned if he was going to give up now. Forcing himself to stay put, he gazed fixedly at the mixing desk. Next, he ran his fingers over the controls.

He was really sweating now. The connection between songwriting and hard drinking was so powerful he could almost taste the alcohol in his throat. He longed to reach out for the bottle of Jack Daniel's he'd always kept right *there,* on the edge of the console, within uncoordinated groping distance of his left hand.

He'd never written so much as a single note sober.

Christ, more to the point, he couldn't *remember* ever writing a single note. For all he knew, someone else could have written every song in his entire back catalog.

Maeve, perhaps.

OK, maybe not.

Jaz sat there for another hour and a half, refamiliarizing himself with the control desk. He felt like a veteran pilot climbing back into the cockpit of a Spitfire fifty years after the end of World War II.

In theory he could probably still fly the plane, but he didn't try.

Just imagining flying the plane was enough.

When the studio door was pushed open, Jaz didn't hear it. Without touching anything, he was busy running through the process of laying down a track in his mind.

"What are you doing in here?"

Celeste's pale blue eyes were wide with disbelief. She was wearing her *Rugrats* T-shirt as a nightie and her baby fine white-blond hair stuck out all over her head like a dandelion puff.

"What?" Startled, Jaz came crashing back to the present. His own hair was drenched in perspiration and for a split second he didn't seem to register who was standing in the doorway. Then his expression cleared. "Oh, nothing. How did you know where I was?"

"The light was on." Celeste pointed to the glowing red recording light, outside the studio door.

Jaz nodded.

"What time is it?"

"Six o'clock. I woke up and you weren't there." She held out her thin arms and moved toward him, her bare feet making no sound against the soft spongy floor.

"I'm OK," said Jaz. "Really I am."

Celeste shook her head. She hated this room with its walls lined with weird corrugated foam. There were no windows. The smell of latex made her feel sick. Most of all, she didn't want Jaz to start coming down here again.

"You look terrible," Celeste announced. "This isn't doing you any good. Look at you, sweating and shaking. I bet you wanted a drink."

"Maybe I did," Jaz said quietly. "But I didn't have one."

"We're in this together, don't forget." Celeste gave him a sorrowful look. "It's not just yourself you'll kill if you start drinking again. If you relapse, I'll relapse. And if that happens I could be dead in a couple of months."

"I'm not going to relapse." Jaz's knuckles were white as he gripped the sides of his chair.

"You don't *want* to relapse," Celeste whispered, "but you can't guarantee it, can you?" She let out a sob and threw her arms around him. "Oh, please, don't do this. It's not worth it! We could both be dead by Christmas!"

She was hugging him tightly, her head buried against his bare chest. Jaz breathed in the smell of the Organics shampoo in her hair and gazed down at the fragile exposed nape of her neck.

Celeste was so vulnerable, and he owed her so much.

"OK, OK. I'm sorry." He patted her shaking shoulders and eased her to her feet. "Come on, let's go back to bed."

CHAPTER 30

By Friday morning Martin was approaching emotional meltdown. Nancy, true to her word, had changed the locks on their house and refused to open the door when he'd gone around there on Wednesday evening. She was also flatly refusing to speak to him or even listen to his protestations of innocence. Any more of that racket out in the street, their neighbor had brusquely informed Martin, and he'd be arrested for harassment and breach of the peace.

Which was bad news for Suzy in the office, because it meant she had to listen to it instead.

"It's not fair. It's just not *fair*," Martin roared, banging his desk and taking out another cigarette because Suzy had just grabbed the last one out of his hand and stubbed it out.

"So you keep telling us. And if you light that," Suzy warned him, "I'll stub it out on your head."

"But you don't understand! I didn't do anything wrong!"

"Apart from have an affair, you mean."

"I DID NOT HAVE AN AFFAIR," bellowed Martin, almost apoplectic with rage because nobody would believe him. "I go out with the guys, we have a bit of a laugh . . . OK, girls chat us up sometimes, and we might buy them a couple of drinks, but that's as far as it goes, I swear. Oh shit, it's not fair. It's just *not bloody fair.*"

Denied his cigarette, Martin was now venting his rage on the desk instead, kicking it to emphasize every word. He looked dreadful too. Sleeping on the living room floor of his best friend's apartment was clearly taking its toll. His hair was unkempt, there were dark shadows under his eyes, and his suit was crumpled, as if he'd just pulled it out of one of the black trash bags and thrown it on.

Suzy, about to make some sarcastic remark about his appearance and the diminishing likelihood of him being chatted up in the future if he didn't sort himself out fast, was appalled to realize there were tears brimming in Martin's eyes. In the nick of time she closed her mouth and turned away. Irritated by his boring ramblings, she had also been readying herself to tell Martin that he was going to have to pull himself together if he wanted to keep his job. Going around scruffily dressed, reeking of alcohol and incapable of holding any form of conversation unless it concerned Nancy wasn't going to sell a huge number of properties.

But this was more than she could cope with. Suzy, risking a quick glance over her shoulder, saw Martin's Adam's apple bobbing up and down alarmingly.

Oh, help.

Girls cried all the time, girls were easy. When their boyfriends chucked them they had a jolly good blub about it, you gave them a massive hug, and before you knew it, you were both ensconced in the nearest wine bar happily downing bottles of chilled Frascati and swapping what-a-bastard stories.

But men . . . men were different. Men weren't supposed to cry. When they did, Suzy found it downright alarming.

Doubly so, when the reason the man was crying was that his wife had kicked him out because *he'd* been such a bastard.

Up until now, Suzy had thought Martin was simply furious because his wife had accused him — whether rightly or wrongly — of having an affair.

Now, for the first time, she realized he was terrified he may have lost Nancy for good.

Softening instantly, Suzy waited until Martin had recovered his composure.

Well, some of it.

Maybe 40 percent.

"OK, what have you got scheduled this morning?"

Usually scarily on the ball when it came to appointments, it was a measure of Martin's troubled state that he had to resort to his diary.

"Um, Mr. and Mrs. Newman, an appraisal on their garden apartment. Fourteen, Victoria Square, ten thirty."

"Right, I'll see to that." Suzy scribbled it down. "You take a couple of hours off. Go home, have a shower, change your clothes . . . When did you last eat?" Martin looked bewildered.

"Can't remember. Kebab on Wednesday?"

"In that case, have some breakfast."

Jiggle, jiggle went that Adam's apple.

"You said go home. Nancy won't let me into the house."

"The apartment, then. Wherever you've been staying."

Martin said despairingly, "You should see it. That place is a pigsty. There isn't even hot water."

With a sigh, Suzy threw him her keys. At least she knew Lucille was out.

"Spare towels in the linen closet. Iron and ironing board in the closet under the stairs. And there's plenty of food in the fridge. Just help yourself to anything." Hastily, she amended, "Except the Marks & Spencer lemon cheesecake."

Well, she was only human.

For a moment Suzy thought Martin was about to burst into tears again. Luckily, the phone rang, distracting both of them. Clearing his throat and muttering, "OK, thanks," Martin took the call then held out the receiver. "For you."

"It's me," said Harry, sounding jubilant. "Quick, rush out to the convenience store and buy a dozen copies of *Hi!* We're on the cover!"

"OK." If she was covering Martin's appointments as well as her own, Suzy privately wondered if she was going to have time to pee, let alone sit admiring photographs of herself in a glossy magazine.

"And guess what? I'm being discharged this afternoon! Isn't that terrific?"

Oh. *Oh,* thought Suzy, taken aback. So soon? She'd gotten quite used to Harry being in the hospital, the whole visiting routine.

"Isn't this a bit sudden?" She was careful to appear concerned rather than alarmed. "I mean, are those doctors sure you're really well enough to go home? Because you mustn't let them kick you out before you're ready —"

"Sweetheart, it's been ten days." Harry sounded amused. "Of course I'm ready. There's just one small problem."

Problems? Ha, tell me about them.

"Oh? What's that?"

"I can't go home. Too many stairs. The physical therapist said they were too dangerous for someone on crutches and I mustn't risk it. So," Harry said blithely, "OK if I stay at yours?"

Suzy almost dropped the phone.

"But . . . but I've got stairs. I've got loads of stairs. Crikey, I've practically got stairs coming out of my ears!"

Harry, who lived in a small Edwardian end-of-terrace in Westbury Park, said patiently, "Yes, but yours are wide and shallow. Mine are narrow and steep."

Oh Lord, it was happening again, Suzy realized. What choice did she have? She could hardly say no and tell him to go live in a cardboard box instead.

He was Harry the Hero, for heaven's sake. As featured on the cover of the current edition of *Hi!* magazine.

And I'm his loving fiancée, thought Suzy. Her heart sank as she glanced at the vast diamond glittering on her finger.

"Of course you can stay."

"Great," said Harry. "I can leave as soon as the doctor signs my discharge papers. What time shall we say you'll pick me up?"

When Suzy had finished talking to Harry, she realized that Martin was still sitting at his desk in a trance.

"Martin? You can go now."

He looked up slowly, his expression desolate.

"Oh, Suzy, what am I going to do? I *love* Nancy. I love her so much . . . and now I've lost her."

Hmmm, Suzy thought, *I've got the opposite problem. I don't love Harry, and I'm jolly well stuck with him.*

Leo, passing through Clifton, decided on the spur of the moment to drop in on Lucille and find out if she was still serious about not wanting to sing at the Alpha Bar.

Unsure whether she was in, he pressed the bell and waited.

Leo wasn't normally the type to be lost for words, but when the door was eventually opened by a good-looking man he had

384

never seen before, dripping and naked apart from a turquoise bath towel slung around his hips, it was a couple of seconds before he could manage to speak.

"Sorry, I didn't hear the bell at first." Martin indicated his wet hair. "I was in the shower."

"I was looking for Lucille," said Leo.

"She's not here."

"Are you a friend of hers?"

"No." Martin shook his head. "I'm a friend of Suzy's."

"In that case" — Leo's hackles rose instantly — "maybe I could have a word with Suzy."

What the bloody hell did she think she was up to now?

"Can't, I'm afraid," said Martin with a shrug. "She isn't here either. Look, I think my bacon's burning —"

"Why don't I come up," Leo said swiftly, "and leave a note?"

They followed the smell of bacon up the stairs.

"Where's Suzy?" asked Leo.

Martin rescued the bacon, which he'd stuck under the grill before jumping into the shower. Cracking a couple of eggs into the frying pan, he then poured himself some coffee from the pot on the kitchen table.

"Suzy? Oh, she's at work."

From where Leo was standing he had a clear view across the hall into Suzy's bedroom. He knew it was Suzy's because the closet door was wide open, enabling him to see her lilac jacket hanging up, together with the kind of brightly colored shirts and skirts Lucille wouldn't be seen dead in.

Not to mention the rainbow parade of shoes filling the bottom of the closet.

But it wasn't the clothes in the closet that bothered Leo.

It was the man's dark gray suit, white shirt, and orange-and-gray-patterned tie spread out over the unmade double bed.

Still wearing nothing but his turquoise towel, Martin slid the fried eggs out of the pan and onto two slices of thickly buttered toast. He added the bacon rashers, a shower of tomato ketchup, and enough pepper to make Russia sneeze. Realizing that he was being watched with something suspiciously like disapproval, he said, "Have you got a pen?"

"What?" Leo's dark eyes narrowed.

"If not, there's one in the fruit bowl behind you." Keen to get rid of the visitor so he could eat his breakfast and think about Nancy without interruption, Martin said bluntly, "You said you wanted to leave a note for Lucille."

CHAPTER 31

Rory couldn't believe he was doing it again.

Being underhanded.

But he simply couldn't help it. This was all totally out of character for him. His brain kept coming up with these outrageous ideas and his conscience simply wasn't squashing them.

Anyway, it was another case of seizing the moment. He couldn't afford to hang around; it had to be now, before either Suzy or Martin arrived back at the office.

"Ouch," Rory grumbled under his breath.

A bit too far under his breath, evidently, because Fee carried on typing away, unaware that he had said anything at all.

Rory sat back in his chair, stretched both arms above his head, then clutched the back of his neck and exhaled loudly. "Ooh, ow."

Fee stopped rattling her fingers over the keyboard and looked up.

"Are you OK?"

"Sorry, what?" Feigning surprise, Rory said, "Oh, it's nothing. Just my neck." Stoically, he shook his head and winced. "I think I've pulled a muscle."

Silence.

Go on, go on, Rory silently urged. *Offer to give me a neck massage.*

"Oh dear," Fee said uncertainly. "Poor you."

She glanced across at Rory, then looked away quickly as their eyes met. Feeling herself begin to flush, Fee gazed hard at her computer screen and willed her heart to stop thumping quite so loudly.

"It must be stress," Rory hinted, with a touch of desperation. "Pressure of work, that kind of thing."

If it had been anyone else, Fee realized, she wouldn't have hesitated. But because it was Rory she couldn't summon up the nerve to offer. Instead, uncomfortably aware that her ears were still bright red, she said, "Ummm, IcyHot is supposed to be good."

Hopeless, hopeless. IcyHot was the last thing he wanted. *I've gotten it all wrong again,* Rory thought with resignation. *Dammit, why am I such a failure?*

The next moment Suzy burst in through the door.

"What's up with you?" Pulling off her

sunglasses, she looked at Rory, who was still rubbing his neck.

"Nothing. Just pulled a muscle."

"Fee can sort that out for you. She's a genius."

Risking another glance across at Fee, who was looking embarrassed, Rory said hurriedly, "No, really, it's fine. I'm OK."

The last thing he wanted was an audience, particularly when the audience was his wisecracking, smart-aleck sister.

"I know! Let me have a go!" Flinging down her bag, Suzy flexed her fingers with gleeful relish. "I've seen Fee do it loads of times. I promise you, it won't hurt a bit."

"Not a chance in the world," said Rory. "You've watched heart transplants being carried out on *ER,* but that doesn't mean I'd let you near me with a scalpel."

"He's a lost cause," Suzy told Fee with a shrug. "Hopeless. Totally stressed out."

"You should try a relaxation weekend." Bravely, Fee looked at Rory. "They have these fabulous ones in Snowdonia. I've been on a few, and they're great. Really, um, relaxing."

Suzy spluttered with laughter.

"Is this my brother we're talking about? You think he could cope with a whole weekend of relaxing? I'm telling you, Rory'd be pushed to manage a whole hour."

"What do they do there?" Pointedly, Rory ignored her.

"Take things easy. Meditate. Eat. Sleep. Go for long walks."

"Rory's idea of hell," Suzy declared flatly. "You'd have to tie him up and bundle him into the trunk of the car before you'd get him near a place like that."

"It might not be so bad," said Rory. He hesitated. "But I wouldn't know anyone."

"He's joking," Suzy told Fee. "Now if there was a hyperstress weekend, that would be *right* up my brother's street —"

"Maybe I need to learn to relax," protested Rory, feeling reckless.

"I'm going up there in a couple of weeks myself. You could always come along with me, give it a try."

Fee gulped, unable to believe she'd just said that. The words had come blurting out, practically of their own accord.

Rory, equally startled, really wished he wasn't on the receiving end of one of Suzy's incredulous stares.

"Well . . . I don't know." He gulped, chickening out. "Maybe. Um, let me think about it."

"Weird," Suzy announced. "It's like me suddenly deciding to spend a weekend scrubbing out sewers. Or coal mining. Or diving head first into crocodile-infested rivers."

"Look, no pressure. Just let me know if you're interested," Fee told Rory. Then, to change the subject, she grabbed a pile of letters from her out tray. "And you'll need to sign these if you want them to catch the mail."

Maeve, pushing her way into the office, said cheerfully, "Ah, that's great. I hoped I'd catch you here. I was in the convenience store getting myself a quarter of lemon bonbons, and the van driver was just bringing them in, piles and piles of magazines, all with your picture on the front . . . I'm telling you, I almost burst with pride right there in the shop! See?" Maeve held up the just-published copy of *Hi!,* as triumphant as any new mother. "Doesn't she look like an angel? Aren't they just the perfect couple?"

"I look like a Stepford Wife." Suzy winced. When the man from *Hi!* was taking the photographs, she hadn't a chance of looking even remotely like herself. He'd forced her to do that fixed, beauty-queen smile. He'd personally tilted her head to one side and made her keep it at that ridiculous angle. He'd told her to make sure the diamond engagement ring was on show at all times.

"Beautiful," said Fee, glad for the diversion. "Nice of Harry too."

"That boy couldn't have a bad picture taken if he tried," boasted Maeve, who was showing alarming signs of becoming a devoted mother-in-law-type person.

Boy, Suzy thought despairingly. The trouble was, she didn't *want* a boy; she wanted a man.

Martin arrived as they were studying the rest of the sixteen-page spread. He seemed more cheerful this afternoon, Suzy noted with relief. And he was definitely looking cleaner, which was a plus.

"The Fletchers have offered four hundred and twenty for the house in Vyvyan Terrace." Sounding pleased with himself, he glanced at the photos over Fee's shoulder. "Blimey, look at you! Why'd you let them do that to your hair?"

"I didn't have any choice in the matter." Suzy gritted her teeth. Honestly, talk about ungrateful. You save a bloke from getting the sack and lend him your apartment and this is the thanks you get. The moment he feels better he starts mocking your hairdo.

"And that dress. Makes you look about fifty," said Martin with a grin.

"Thank you *so* much."

"It makes her look demure." Maeve's tone was soothing. "Like a proper lady."

"Oh God," Suzy wailed, "I'm supposed to be picking Harry up! He's being discharged this afternoon, and I completely forgot . . . He's staying at the apartment," she explained to Maeve and Fee, "until he's back on his feet."

"And you'll be doing your Florence Nightingale bit? Poor bloke, does he know what he's letting himself in for?" Martin roared with laughter.

Suzy was tempted to roll up the copy of *Hi!* and use it to batter him unconscious.

"Don't you worry, sweetheart." Maeve's eyes lit up at the prospect of being allowed to fuss over Harry and cater to his every whim. "I'll help you look after him — between us we'll treat him like a prince! Oh, and talk about a coincidence, will you take a look at the book I picked up for you not half an hour ago?" Diving into her vast bag, Maeve emerged triumphant with a battered old paperback sporting a fifty pence, Save the Children sticker.

"How to Be the Perfect Wife!" Maeve pronounced, reading the title aloud for the benefit of any dyslexics in the office. "Can you believe it? That's not coincidence; that's fate."

Suzy realized she was mentally bracing herself for Martin's witty riposte. If he said something horrid, she would definitely have to beat him up.

The next moment, hearing a strangled sob, she spun around in her chair.

Tears were pouring unstoppably down Martin's thin cheeks.

"That's what I had." He gulped, his face the picture of misery. "The perfect wife."

When Suzy arrived at the ward, Harry had arranged — surprise, surprise — for more photographers to be there to record his departure from the hospital. It took a good forty minutes of posing on the front steps, kissing every female member of staff good-bye, and presenting Dr. Hubble with a massive bunch of palest pink roses — oh, nice touch, Harry — before Suzy finally managed to bundle him and his crutches into the Rolls.

There was no getting away from it; Harry was clearly addicted to publicity. Actually, it was a wonder he hadn't hired a fly-on-the-wall documentary crew to make a movie of his life.

Suzy kept this thought to herself. No point putting ideas into Harry's handsome but already alarmingly swollen head.

On the way home, she said abruptly, "We aren't sharing a bed, by the way. You'll have to sleep on the sofa."

Harry looked hurt.

"A *sofa*?"

Feeling mean, Suzy said, "It's a very comfortable sofa. Long enough, wide enough, nice and springy . . ."

"Sweetheart, look at me." With his knuckles, Harry knocked the cast on his thigh. "Broken leg, broken arm, cracked ribs . . . I mean, be fair."

"But —"

"No, no, no," Harry protested, "don't say the 'but' word. Look, you've got a double bed. Couldn't we at least share it? I promise not to try anything. All we'd do is sleep!"

"And if I had a Heath bar for every time I've heard *that* old line," said Suzy, "I'd be the size of the Millennium Dome."

"I'm serious. I won't lay a finger on you."

"That one too."

"OK, fine." Harry heaved a long-suffering sigh. "I'll sleep on the sofa."

They both knew that wouldn't happen. Suzy's conscience wouldn't allow it. Harry had to have the bed, of course he did, and if she refused to share it with him . . . Well, it was her own fault for being so prissy.

No prizes for guessing who was going to

end up sleeping where, Suzy thought wearily.
  Good-bye, bed.
  Hello, sofa.

CHAPTER 32

Maeve was in her element that evening, fussing over Harry. She exclaimed delightedly over his glossy dark curls and sparkling blue eyes. She brought over all the food she had spent the afternoon lovingly preparing. She told Harry what a lucky fellow he was to be marrying Suzy, even if she did possess all the domestic skills of a beetroot.

Harry, in turn, flattered Maeve outrageously, made her laugh, and told her she was the best thing to come out of Ireland since Guinness.

You're wonderful, thought Suzy, watching the pair of them together. *No,* you're *wonderful. Oh no no no, I'm not* nearly *as wonderful as* you . . .

"This is mad," Lucille protested later, finding Suzy wrestling to get a clean cover on the spare duvet. "It's your apartment — you *can't* sleep on the sofa."

"Really, I'll be fine. Give us a hand with

this." Suzy's voice grew muffled as the duvet cover fell over her head.

"But you should have my bed. Let me sleep on the sofa. Honestly, I wouldn't mind."

"Maybe not, but I would." Touched that Lucille had made the offer, Suzy emerged tousle-haired from the depths of the cover. "Anyway, it's not going to be forever, is it? Only three or four weeks."

As they began fastening the ends of the duvet together, the doorbell rang. Leaving Suzy on her knees doing battle with the stubborn zipper, Lucille went to answer it.

To her delight, she found Leo on the doorstep.

"Have you changed your mind about the singing?" he asked without preamble.

"No."

"OK. Well, I sacked one of the waitresses tonight, so you can take over if you like. Start at midday tomorrow."

"Blimey." Lucille's light brown eyes widened. "Not if you're the boss from hell. You only opened on Wednesday. How could you have sacked someone so soon?"

"She was treating the place like a dating agency." Leo's tone was brisk. "More interested in chatting up customers than doing any work. So, are you interested?"

"Definitely. Midday tomorrow, I'll be there." Lucille moved to one side, giving him room to pass her. "Are you coming in to see Harry?"

But Leo shook his head. "Can't stop. Ummm . . . what's the name of the guy who passed on my message this morning?"

Lucille gazed blankly at him.

"What guy? What message?"

"Doesn't matter," said Leo. Leaning against the door frame with his hands thrust casually into his trouser pockets he looked thoughtful for a second. "Actually, I wouldn't mind a quick word with Suzy if she's around."

Suzy came clattering down the stairs, out of breath and fresh from her triumphant victory over the duvet cover.

"Hi, Lucille said you wanted to see me. Harry's upstairs."

"I know. He called me this afternoon."

Suzy looked surprised. "And? Aren't you going to come up and say hello?"

"I have to get back to the restaurant. By the way, who was the fellow I spoke to this morning?"

"Haven't the foggiest." Mystified, Suzy said, "Prince Edward? Steve Coogan? Elton John?"

Leo didn't smile. His mouth didn't even

400

flicker. "He was here in your apartment, having a shower and cooking breakfast. Making himself very much at home."

"Oh!" Catching on at last, Suzy said, "You mean Martin. Heavens, I completely forgot he was here . . ."

Her voice trailed away as she realized why Leo was surveying her in that unforgiving manner. Oh no, surely not. Surely he didn't think what she thought he was thinking.

"Right," said Suzy, because he clearly did. "Let's get this straight. Martin is a friend, nothing more. He works for Curtis's, his wife has just kicked him out of the family home, he's staying at a friend's apartment, but it's a complete toilet. Martin was desperate for a shower so I said he could come have one here, and *that is all there is to it.* So I'd be grateful if you'd stop glaring at me, because I've done *nothing* wrong, OK, and I especially haven't done anything to deserve being glared at like that."

During the course of this argument, Suzy had heard her voice gradually rising higher and higher and been powerless to stop it. The harder she tried to convey her total innocence, she realized, the more guilty she sounded. The expression on her face, she also knew, was the expression of someone clearly lying through her teeth but hell-bent

401

on *looking* innocent.

And to add insult to injury, she'd gone bright red.

"If you're having an affair with this man . . ." Leo began softly.

Suzy stamped her foot.

"I'm not having an affair with *anyone*. Ask Martin! Go on," she shouted. "Phone him up now and ask him! He'll tell you I'm not having an affair with him."

"I'm sure he would," drawled Leo. "Out of interest, why *did* his wife kick him out?"

Suzy knew when she was beaten. She would have bitten off her own tongue rather than tell Leo that Nancy had kicked Martin out because she was convinced he was involved with another woman. But she didn't have to. Reading the answer in her eyes, he laughed mirthlessly and shook his head.

"All these men you insist you're just good friends with. Harry might believe your excuses, but I'm not as gullible as he is. I've told you before" — he lowered his voice — "if you hurt Harry, you'll have me to answer to."

Leo left, and Suzy leaned back against the door, marveling at the spectacular mess she'd gotten herself into. For a split second there, she'd actually been tempted to tell him she *was* having a rip-roaring affair with Martin. That way, she could rid herself of the twin burdens of Harry, and the strain of having to live a lie, in one fell swoop.

But there were those two innocent young children to consider, and their trip of a lifetime to Disneyland.

Then there was the effect it would have on Harry. This was his one chance to prove to Leo that he wasn't always second-best.

Oh God, thought Suzy, closing her eyes. Not to mention the other possible complications. Knowing her luck, Nancy would hear the rumor about her and Martin and hire some local thug to dispose of the pair of them.

Harry could go berserk at the news and throw Martin off the bridge.

Or Leo, to save Harry ever finding out about me and Martin, might throw me *off,* Suzy realized with a shudder. She could picture it only too clearly.

Bungee jumping off Clifton Suspension Bridge, without the bungee.

Lucille, appearing at the top of the stairs, said, "Has Leo gone? What are you still doing there?"

Scaring myself half to death, that's all, thought Suzy.

"Nothing."

"What I don't understand is why he came around," said Lucille. "I mean, he's supposed to be at the new restaurant. He's in a tearing hurry . . . Why didn't he just call and offer me the waitressing job?"

Suzy shrugged.

Because he wanted to interrogate me, the bastard. And watch me go red.

Aloud she said, "I don't know."

Lucille, who had clearly taken Leo's visit as a personal compliment, said delightedly, "I start tomorrow! Isn't that fantastic?"

"Fantastic," echoed Suzy, wearily beginning to climb the stairs. *OK, look on the bright side. Be positive. I may be making a bit of a mess of my life, but things could be worse. At least I don't have to work as a waitress in one of Leo Fitzallan's restaurants . . .*

"Suzy, Luce, GET IN HERE NOW," Harry bellowed from the living room.

Oh God. Had he fallen? Was he bleeding internally? Having a heart attack?

"What's wrong?" gasped Lucille and Suzy simultaneously as they piled into the living room.

Harry beamed and upped the volume on the television with the remote control.

"They're showing that piece about me coming out of the hospital on *NewsWest.*"

■ ■ ■ ■

By two o'clock the next afternoon, Lucille was getting into the swing of working in the restaurant at the Alpha Bar. She was serving a table and admiring the domed, mosaic mirrored ceiling along with the customers when she recognized the fractured, upside-down reflections of the two people who had just walked in.

Celeste was wearing a lime-green fluffy angora cropped top, a floaty short skirt the color of sherbet lemons, and silver high-heeled sandals with matching spiral ribbons in her hair. Just right for a quiet Saturday lunch, thought Lucille with a brief smile.

Jaz, in a black V-neck sweater and black trousers, caught Lucille's eye and winked. When the maître d' had ushered them to a well-placed table and finished seating them, he sidled up to Lucille and said, "They want you to serve them."

Spot-lit at the far end of the restaurant, a slender brunette seated at a piano was playing music to eat your lunch by. Sometimes she sang, sometimes she didn't. Most of the songs were her own compositions — Lucille had already asked her — and they were OK, but they weren't great.

405

The brunette, needless to say, lived in hope.

"In a restaurant like this, you never know who could come in," she had confided to Lucille. "One lucky break, that's all it takes. When Mr. Fitzallan called me last night and offered me the job, I was so excited I couldn't sleep!"

Lucille felt sorry for the girl. Thanks to Jaz, she no longer labored under the delusion that one day It Could Happen to Me.

"Our housekeeper has defected," Jaz told Lucille when she arrived at their table. "The only person she's interested in cooking for is the invalid next door. We were forced to come out for something to eat."

"So we thought we'd try this place," said Celeste, gratified to see that they were the center of attention. Gazing around, pretending not to notice the eyes of the other diners on them, she said perkily, "I like it."

Lucille handed them their menus. "How about something to drink while you're deciding what to eat?"

"Great," said Jaz. "Perrier and lime for Celeste, large Scotch for me."

Lucille gave him a look.

"OK." Jaz's mouth twitched. "Make that two Perriers and lime."

He was watching the pianist when she

returned with their drinks, his dark eyes narrowed in concentration as he listened intently to her singing voice. He pulled a face and glanced up at Lucille. "She's garbage."

"Shhh," Lucille hissed, mortified. Subtlety just wasn't Jaz's thing.

"It's true. You're ten times better than her."

"Will you keep your voice down?" squeaked Lucille.

"OK, OK." Smiling broadly, Jaz sat back in his chair and glanced at the menu. "I'll have the seafood risotto, then the saltimbocca with linguine. But don't you wish you were sitting there instead of her?"

The abrupt change of subject caught Lucille completely by surprise; for a heart-stopping second, she thought he meant sitting at the table with him, instead of Celeste.

Even more heart-stoppingly, Lucille discovered, the truthful answer would have been yes.

Not that she'd have admitted it in a million years.

But that was irrelevant, because Jaz hadn't meant that at all. He was — *of course* — talking about the pianist.

"No." Lucille shook her head firmly. "I'm glad I'm not."

Jaz shot her a look of disbelief. "You can't be glad."

"I am. I'd rather be a waitress, far more relaxing. It's like spending a day trapped inside a pair of jeans two sizes too small," said Lucille, "then finally undoing the zip."

"Ugh!" Celeste wrinkled her nose and put down her menu. "Do you mind?"

"So it's 'good-bye, tight jeans,' " Jaz told Lucille with a grin, "and 'hello, crimplene slacks with an elasticized waist.' "

"And stirrups. Don't forget the stirrups," Lucille reminded him.

"Excuse me," complained Celeste. "You're putting me *right* off the idea of lunch."

As they were leaving the restaurant an hour and a half later, Jaz slipped an extra tenner into Lucille's hand.

"You've already tipped me," Lucille protested.

"I know. Give this to the singer after we've gone."

"I thought you said she was garbage."

"She is," said Jaz with a careless shrug.

Oh my God . . .

Lucille shuddered as the realization struck her like a brick. She'd always assumed that people had thrown money into her hat because they'd thought she was good.

It simply hadn't occurred to her that they might have been doing it because she was garbage and they felt *sorry* for her.

"Hey, are you OK?" Jaz was studying her with concern.

Feeling winded, Lucille nodded. There it was again, the Brutal Truth. Still, no point worrying about it; all that music malarkey was well and truly behind her. From now on, waitressing was her thing. She might even give up the dog walking and become a full-time waitress; after all, it would soon be winter and racing across the Downs for hours in subzero temperatures and driving sleet wasn't exactly what you'd call a seductive prospect.

"It's only half past three," said Celeste. "Let's go shopping. I really need some new shoes."

Lucille, who knew for a fact from Suzy that Celeste had over two hundred pairs of shoes at home, struggled to keep a straight face.

"I'm not sure." Jaz frowned. "But I think I'd rather throw myself into a tank of man-eating sharks."

Pouting, sliding her thin arm through his, Celeste said in a singsong, little-girl voice, "Oh, Ja-az, you know you don't mean that."

Jaz rolled his eyes in good-humored resignation.

"OK. Come on, let's go."

"The thing is, I love you," said Leo, his voice throbbing with emotion. "I can't help it, I just do."

"Golly." Suzy swallowed, enthralled, gazing up at him and feeling her fingers curl helplessly around the padded velvet arm of her chair. "But what about Harry?"

"Shhh, first things first. Will you marry me?"

"Of course I will!" The words spilled out joyfully. This time Suzy knew, she just *knew* it wasn't a trick.

"In that case, why don't we let Harry come live with us." Leo moved toward her, his hand reaching out and brushing her hot cheek. "I've thought it all through. He can sleep in a kennel in the garden and we'll pay Lucille to take him out for walks . . ."

Whoa, what's going on here?

Oh, bugger and blast, thought Suzy. *This isn't really happening. I'm having a* dream.

She reluctantly opened her eyes. Oh, yes, it had been a dream all right.

Having closed the office at five, Suzy had driven up to the Sea Walls overlooking the Avon Gorge. She had parked the car, opened the paper bag containing her white-chocolate and fresh-cream éclair from Charlotte's Patisserie and settled down to enjoy both the éclair and the spectacular view in peace.

Just for ten minutes.

Then she'd definitely go home to where Harry was waiting for her, *promise.*

Instead, peering at her watch, Suzy discovered that she'd been asleep for almost an hour. And since there were no padded velvet chair arms for her fingers to tighten around, she had actually been squeezing the life out of her fresh-cream éclair.

There was cream and melted white chocolate all over the seat of the car. Suzy wondered what Leo would have to say if she sent him the bill for having the upholstery steam cleaned.

Well, it was his fault, telling her he loved her like that. He jolly well *should* pay.

Suzy checked her watch again, without enthusiasm. Oh dear, was this how prisoners on day release felt every evening?

Six o'clock, time to go home.

To Harry.

CHAPTER 33

"Suzy, is that you?" Harry's voice drifted down the stairs as Lucille let the front door swing shut behind her.

"No, it's the other one."

"Oh, hi," he said when Lucille came into the living room. "I don't know where Suzy's gotten to. The office shuts at five on Saturdays, and her cell phone's switched off."

"Probably with a client."

Heaving a sigh of relief, Lucille kicked off her shoes and threw herself into a chair. Six hours of waitressing at the Alpha had really taken it out on her feet — weirdly, they ached far more than if she'd run a half marathon.

"Suzy should have phoned, let me know she was going to be late." Harry sounded petulant. "It's not much fun being stuck here on my own."

Accustomed to the bustle of the hospital and the endless attentions of its adoring female staff, Harry was suffering withdrawal symptoms.

"Hasn't Maeve been over?" Lucille rotated her ankles and glanced meaningfully at the coffee table, piled high with enough plates of home-baked cakes and scones to stock a PTA bake sale.

"She has." Harry sighed. "And she's great, I know that, but it's hardly the same. Oh, Jaz phoned, by the way. He wants to see you."

Lucille looked blank. "To see *me*? What about? Jaz already saw me this afternoon."

"He didn't say why. Just asked you to go next door when you got home from work. But not yet," Harry added in alarm as Lucille began feeling around with her feet for her discarded shoes. "You don't have to run over there straightaway."

"Why not?"

"Oh, Luce, don't be mean. Stay and keep me company," he pleaded. "At least until Suzy gets back."

Under pressure, Lucille was forced to stay. She couldn't imagine why Jaz would have called her. It was like taking delivery of a mysterious, exciting-looking parcel and not being allowed to open it. Feeling rather like Harry, she tried calling Jaz back and was frustrated that he didn't answer.

413

"I'd love some coffee," said Harry, who was doubly hampered by the fact that he was on crutches *and* had a broken arm. Making himself a hot drink wasn't a problem, but carrying it anywhere was impossible.

While she was waiting for the kettle to boil, Lucille heard the front door bang again. She almost threw her arms around Suzy in delight when she appeared in the kitchen.

"You're back." Hobbling through from the living room, Harry's tone was accusing. "I didn't know where you were."

Asleep in my car up on the Downs, thought Suzy, *having a saucy dream about your brother.*

Sensibly, she said, "Seeing clients." Then, "Where are *you* going?" as Lucille sloshed boiling water into a cup, heaped in coffee and sugar, and thrust it into Suzy's unsuspecting hands.

"That's for Harry. Just popping next door." Lucille was already halfway out of the kitchen. "Won't be long, OK?"

Astonished, Suzy watched her go. "What was all that about?"

"No idea. Something to do with Jaz. Actually" — Harry eyed the cup in her hand with the air of a persnickety maiden aunt —

"I'd rather have freshly ground than instant."

It was ages before Jaz answered the door. Lucille, who had been on the verge of giving up, was startled by the sight of him.

Jaz's blond hair was looking disheveled, there was a wild, almost feverish glitter in his dark eyes, and beneath the Antiguan tan, his face was tense and drawn.

For an alarming moment Lucille wondered if he was on something. She knew next to nothing about drugs, but wasn't this how people looked when they'd taken speed or coke?

"Hooray," said Jaz, whisking her inside. "About time too."

Or alcohol?

Her stomach lurching in panic, Lucille really hoped he hadn't fallen off the wagon. His voice didn't sound slurred, but maybe he was just brilliant at hiding it.

Oh, please no, prayed Lucille as he towed her across the hall. *Don't let it be that.* Racing to keep up, she strained forward and attempted — surreptitiously — to sniff the back of his neck for telltale alcohol fumes in his slipstream.

The next moment Jaz came to an abrupt halt at the head of the staircase. Lucille promptly cannoned into him from behind, her nose making painful contact with his shoulder blade. "Ouch . . . God, sorry . . ."

"What are you doing?" Jaz swiveled around in surprise.

Oh well, get it over with.

"Your eyes are strange, and you seem a bit weird," Lucille bravely announced. "I wondered if you'd been drinking."

Initial disbelief gave way to amusement.

"No," Jaz told her with a grin. "Nothing to drink."

OK. Next.

"How about drugs?"

His smile broadened. "No drugs either, I promise."

Wondering why he was taking her downstairs, Lucille said, "Where's Celeste?"

"Shopping. I dropped her off after lunch and came straight home."

"I thought you were out. When I called just now, there was no answer."

"You can't hear the phone down here," Jaz explained, leading her past the swimming pool.

"But you heard the doorbell." Lucille frowned.

"In here."

Opening the door on their left, Jaz ushered her through it.

Lucille gasped. "Oh my God, this is your recording studio!"

"See that light?" He pointed to an unlit green bulb fixed to the wall above the console. "When someone rings the front doorbell, it flashes."

"But what are you doing? Suzy said you hadn't set foot inside this room since . . . since . . ."

"I know. I hadn't. But I have now. You can sit down if you like."

Helpfully, Jaz pulled out a swivel chair. "Make yourself at home."

Lucille couldn't sit down. In a flash she realized what this was about.

"Oh, no, no, *no.*" She groaned, mortified. "This was all Suzy's idea. She made you do it, didn't she? She forced you into this . . . Please, really, you don't have to lend me your recording studio, and I will personally *strangle* that girl when I get my hands on her —" Lucille's beaded braids were clattering with agitation as she swung her head from side to side.

"Shhh, stop it. Calm down." Firmly, Jaz said, "This has nothing to do with Suzy, I promise you. Nobody forces me to do anything I don't want to do — and this isn't about me lending you the studio anyway. Now" — he gestured patiently to the revolv-

417

ing chair once more — "all I want is for you to sit down and listen and give me your honest opinion." With a faint smile he added, "Your *brutally* honest opinion."

Lost for words, Lucille sat. She couldn't imagine what she was about to hear. Tucking her hands between her knees she waited for Jaz to fiddle with a tape and gazed around at the state-of-the-art equipment. Then again, what did she know about recording studios? If everything in here was at least three and a half years old, it wasn't likely to be state of-the-art anymore.

Crikey, it was probably antique.

Still, there was an awesome array of buttons, sliding switches, knobs, and dials. Lucille, whose only previous experience with a recording studio had been a musty little closet under the stairs, was deeply impressed.

Then she stopped gazing idly around the room and gave the music her undivided attention, because this was why Jaz had invited her here.

He wants my opinion, thought Lucille, marveling at her own gullibility. It was like Eric Clapton asking Mr. Bean for advice.

"Well?" said Jaz three minutes later when the last notes had faded away.

The tiny hairs on the back of Lucille's neck were standing on end. Glancing down at her knuckles, she saw they were white. Only a very few songs in the world had that genuinely spine-tingling effect on her.

Aloud she said, "Well, I think you're *completely* mad."

Jaz's face was totally expressionless. "Why?"

"Because if you wrote that, I don't understand for the life of me why you never released it. I mean, I know hard rock was your thing, but you could still have put it out as a single." Wide-eyed with amazement, Lucille thrust out her hands. "Look, look at me . . . I'm still shaking! It's that good, don't you see? And I bet you never even considered it for one of your albums, just because it was so different . . . heavens, what a waste!"

"It's for you," said Jaz. "I want you to have it. I want you to record it. Oh Jesus, don't cry."

"You can't do that." Furious with herself, and seriously lacking in tissues, Lucille was forced to use the hem of her primrose-yellow top to wipe her eyes. "You can't give me the best song you've ever written because you feel *sorry* for me."

"No, no, that's not it." Shaking his head,

Jaz pushed his spiky hair out of his eyes. "I don't feel sorry for you."

"You do. You pity me," Lucille retaliated, "because I couldn't write a decent song to save my life! So to clear your conscience, you've decided to dig out one of your old ones, some little number you once effortlessly knocked out in ten minutes when you were smashed out of your mind, and let me have it as some kind of . . . *consolation* prize —"

"But —"

"No, let me finish." Lucille held up her trembling hands, the words spilling out faster and faster. "I mean, I'm sorry if I sound ungrateful, and you probably think you're being really kind, but as far as I'm concerned, it's just patronizing. I feel like a seal who can't balance a ball on my nose, but you've decided to throw me a sardine anyway."

She ran out of breath, pressed her lips together and gazed hard at a section of gray, foam-padded wall, unable to meet Jaz's eyes.

"Finished?" he said at last.

Lucille nodded. "Yes."

"That's it? You're sure?" He raised his eyebrows. "If I start to say something you promise you won't interrupt?"

Oh Lord, I've really upset him now, thought

Lucille. *He thinks I'm a belligerent, ungrateful cow and he's seriously offended.*

A combination of pride and PMS had a lot to answer for. It really did.

Feeling hormonal and lectured to, she tossed back her braids and said, "Fire away."

Oh dear, horribly reminiscent of a belligerent teenager.

"Thank you *so* much," Jaz replied silkily. "OK, d'you see that filing cabinet over there? That's where all my old tapes are kept, in the third drawer down. Songs I started and never finished, songs I decided not to use, ideas for songs that in the end never got written."

"So?"

Good grief, just listen *to me,* thought Lucille, privately appalled.

"*So,*" Jaz drawled with heavy irony, "that filing cabinet isn't where I got this tape from. It hasn't been unlocked for over three years. What you just heard wasn't one of my old songs. I wrote it this afternoon. And for your information I didn't knock it out in ten minutes." He added drily, "There was nothing effortless about it either, I can promise you that."

Lucille's mouth had dropped open as she realized what he was saying. "Oh my God . . ."

"No, please, *don't* interrupt," mimicked Jaz. "It's my turn now, remember? And I didn't do this because I felt sorry for you, OK? I did it because I felt like such a shit the other night. I could have kicked myself when I realized what I'd done, telling you your songs weren't great — it was a terrible thing to say, and I was so ashamed of myself I knew I had to make up for it somehow." His dark eyes were fixed on Lucille's face, his expression intent. "But I didn't just do it for you. You do see that, don't you? If it hadn't been for you, I wouldn't have come back down here. You made me *want* to write another song."

"And now you have," whispered Lucille.

"Now I have. Sober," Jaz added with a brief smile. "And you can't begin to imagine how that makes me feel."

It all fell into place now. Lucille, understanding exactly why he had done it, no longer felt patronized.

Instead, she clapped her hands together and said, "This is *fantastic.*"

"More than fantastic." Jaz began to grin with relief. "It's a bloody miracle."

Longing to fling her arms around him, but not quite daring to, Lucille said instead, breathlessly, "Go on, play it again!"

Jaz did. And this time it sounded even better, like nothing he had ever written before, but slow and melodic, powerful and unbearably moving.

"Still needs a lot of work, of course," he told Lucille when it had ended. "And the lyrics need sorting out. God, you can tell I'm out of practice — did you hear me miss that B flat in the middle eight?"

Lucille nodded. She was still tingling all over in the aftermath of hearing the track again. Jaz's voice was rusty and he'd hit a couple of wrong notes, but in her eyes, the rawness of it only added to the song's appeal.

"So," Jaz said softly. "Will you sing it?"

"Why me? You could sing it yourself." Lucille realized she was having to press her knees together to stop them from knocking like castanets.

"I don't want to. Not interested. I'll write songs, but I won't sing again. And I still want you to have this one, because it's the least I can do to make up for saying what I did the other night."

Lucille willed herself not to start blubbering all over again. The least she could do was accept graciously.

"OK." She smiled, still longing to hug him. "I don't know what to say. Except thank you."

Jaz breathed an audible sigh of relief. "I should be the one thanking you."

Glancing through the glass into the recording area itself, Lucille saw a stool and a mike stand with a set of headphones dangling from it.

"Is that where you sing, in there?"

"Only when there's someone else to press the buttons out here." Jaz flashed her a broad grin. "How about it, then. Ready to give it a go?"

In a daze, Lucille said, "OK," and he led her through to the sound booth. The next thing she knew, Jaz was moving the stool out of the way — "you'll sound better if you stand" — placing the headphones over her ears and carefully angling the mike in front of her mouth.

He retrieved a sheet of hastily scrawled lyrics from his pocket and handed them to her.

"I can't believe you did all this for me," Lucille whispered to herself when Jaz had left the room and was sitting back at the mixing desk.

Immediately, through the headphones, she heard him say with some amusement, "Me neither."

Eek, who thought black girls couldn't blush?

"OK, deep breath now," instructed Jaz,

fingers poised above the console. "Are you ready?"

The mixture of excitement and nerves was too much for Lucille. "No. Stop."

Shaking her head, she pulled an apologetic face at him through the glass. The beads in her hair rattled as she tried to disentangle herself from the headphones.

"What's the problem?" Jaz was looking alarmed.

Damn, thought Lucille, mortified because things like this never happened in the movies.

"I'm really sorry," she told him, "but first I have to pee."

CHAPTER 34

An hour later, listening enraptured to the latest recording of her own voice superimposed on a computer-generated orchestral arrangement, Lucille murmured, "I feel as if I'm dreaming."

"So do I," said Celeste, from the doorway.

Until that moment Lucille hadn't even realized her right knee, tucked up on the seat of the chair, had been resting against Jaz's left forearm. As they sat hunched together side by side over the console, oblivious to everything but the music, she had been absently tapping a plastic Evian bottle on her denim-clad thigh. Now, as Lucille spun around in shock, the Evian flew out of her hand, drenching the front of Jaz's black T-shirt.

"Jesus!" gasped Jaz, because swimming in a heated pool was one thing, but the Evian was straight from the fridge.

"Sorry," Lucille squeaked.

"I think she thought you needed cooling down," observed Celeste. Transferring her attention from Jaz to Lucille she said, "So what's going on? Have you been pestering him to give you the guided tour of his studio? Is that why he came down here the other night?"

Feeling guilty and not even knowing why, Lucille shook her head. "No, nothing like that. I *wouldn't* pester anyone —"

"She didn't," Jaz cut in. "I've written a song. I wanted to hear Lucille singing it."

"You're mad." Celeste sounded resigned rather than jealous. "You'll start drinking again."

"I'm not going to," said Jaz. "Here, come listen to what we've done so far." He patted his knee. "For the first time in almost four years, I've actually achieved something. This is *better* than drinking."

Celeste stayed where she was in the doorway.

"I must go," said Lucille.

"No, you mustn't." Jaz stretched out a hand to keep her there.

"I'm not being polite. I mean I really do need to go." Lucille, who had lost all track of time, showed him her watch. "See? Seven thirty. And I have to pick Baxter up from the restaurant at eight."

"But we're on a roll." Jaz was still buzzing with ideas. "We *can't* stop now."

"There speaks the alcoholic," Celeste murmured. "That's Jaz's trouble. Once he starts he never *can* stop."

Lucille didn't want to stop either, but what could she do? "Baxter needs his run."

"I don't want to lose this." Jaz knew from experience that when inspiration struck, you needed to stick with it for as long as it took. Or, at the very least, until you finished your second bottle of Jack Daniel's and passed out on the floor unconscious. But since that wasn't likely to happen with Evian, he said, "We'll get someone else to take Baxter out."

Oh great, Leo was going to just love this.

"Like who?" said Lucille.

"Celeste could do it."

"Celeste jolly well couldn't," Celeste retaliated at once. "You must be joking! I've been shopping all afternoon, my feet are killing me, and anyway, why should I?"

"Hundreds of pairs of shoes this girl's got" — Jaz turned to Lucille — "and she's yet to find a pair that don't hurt her feet."

"It doesn't matter." Lucille didn't fancy being responsible for a full-scale argument. "I'll be off."

"What about Suzy?" Jaz said suddenly. "She might not mind."

"She could certainly do with the exercise," said Celeste. "A five-mile run would do her the world of good."

Lucille looked worried. "What about Harry? He's not going to be thrilled."

"I'm not asking him to do it," said Jaz.

Suzy and Harry were eating crumpets, playing Boggle, and arguing over which video to watch later when the phone rang.

Clutching the receiver to her ear, Suzy realized she'd never been so delighted to hear from Jaz in her life.

Relief flooded her bloodstream, like biting into a longed for champagne truffle.

"Love to, no problem, I'm your man." Vigorously, she nodded into the phone. "No, no, of *course* I don't mind, I'd be glad to help out, really I would . . . No, don't mention it. Tell Lucille not to worry . . . Oh yes, he's fine about it too! Eight o'clock, no problem. OK, byeee!"

Yes, yesss, hooray!

"Who was that?" Harry looked suspicious. "And what am I fine about too?"

"Jaz. He and Lucille are busy working on something in the studio — isn't that *great*?" Suzy beamed at him as she backed toward the bedroom. "So he wondered if I'd do Lucille a huge favor and take Baxter out for his run tonight. You know these artistic types; once they get started they can't bear to break the momentum —"

"Oh, come on, I don't believe I'm hearing this." Harry's forehead creased in protest. "That's not *fair*. You only just got home, and now you're going out again, leaving me here all on my *own*?"

"Think of Baxter," said Suzy. "How can I let him down?"

"He's not even your dog!"

"Maybe not, but Lucille's my sister. Anyway, it solves one problem, doesn't it?" Reaching for the videos in their rental shop cases, Suzy waggled them at him. "You wanted to watch James Bond; I wanted to see *Notting Hill*. Now we don't have to fight anymore," she went on brightly. "You can watch yours in peace!"

"I wanted us to spend some time together." Harry wasn't to be consoled. "Proper time together. How can we do that if you're never here?"

"I am here. I'm just popping out to do Lucille a favor."

"But I've been stuck here on my own all day!"

In the bedroom, Suzy picked up the extension and dialed Jaz's number.

"Celeste? Hi, it's me. Look, could I have a quick word with Maeve?"

"She's gone out. It's her night off."

"Oh, is it? Damn. I was going to ask her to pop around and keep Harry company for a couple of hours."

OK, so he'd gotten a bit fed up with Maeve earlier, but she was better than nothing, surely.

"Maeve and the rest of her darts team have gone to see the Chippendales taking their clothes off at the Hippodrome," Celeste informed her. "Poor Chippendales, that's all I can say."

"Crikey. I thought she'd been banned from seeing their show after the last little accident with that blond one's jockstrap."

"The whole darts team was banned. That's why they've gone in disguise. Anyway" — Celeste yawned audibly — "she isn't here."

Celeste sounded fed up. Lucille and Jaz were closeted together in the recording studio downstairs. Wondering if she was inflicting a fate worse than death on Harry, but plowing on anyway, Suzy said, "I don't suppose you'd come over for a bit?"

"What? Why should I? What's in it for me?"

"Ummm, gosh, I don't know." Suzy was

431

already casting around in her mind for a suitable bribe. Celeste never did anything out of the goodness of her heart — probably because she didn't keep any *in* her heart.

"I like that scarf you bought the other week," Celeste suggested helpfully. "The silk Georgina von Etzdorf one with the pink and mauve tassels."

Not the three-year-old navy polyester one from Woolworths, sadly. Suzy had paid a fortune for her beloved von Etzdorf.

Honestly, if this was the going rate for babysitting, she was in the wrong business.

In my day, thought Suzy, *it was a tenner for the evening and a handful of chocolate cookies.*

Celeste arrived ten minutes later, as Suzy was preparing to leave. Grabbing Suzy's left hand, she held it up against hers.

"Just comparing diamonds," Celeste bragged. "Ooh, look at that, almost as big as mine!"

Suzy resisted the urge to clank her on the nose with it.

"Now let's compare brains," she told Celeste. "Oh dear, what a shame, not *nearly* as big as mine!"

"Sorry, did you say brains, or backsides?"

Celeste said chirpily as they reached the sitting room.

Death by strangulation with a Georgina von Etzdorf tasseled scarf. OK, so it was still technically murder, but an elegant lady judge with exquisite taste would be lenient, Suzy was almost sure.

"I'll be back by ten," she told Harry.

Harry, stretched out on the sofa with the game of Boggle lying abandoned on the coffee table beside him, grinned up at Celeste.

"Are you my babysitter?"

"Tuh!" Celeste sniffed dismissively. "Only because I'm bored."

Feeling very MI5, Suzy spied on Leo from the dark sanctuary of her car.

She had pulled up on yellow lines across the road from the Alpha Bar. The frontage was all glass, floor-to-ceiling windows, hiding nothing and giving the bar area the appearance of a stage.

To begin with, Suzy had simply sat and admired the glamorous look of the place, all lit up and buzzing with life like the most marvelous party. Then, spotting Leo, her heart had broken into a bit of a canter.

Well, why not? He was wearing his dark blue suit and looking his absolute best as he moved among the guests, doing what he

433

clearly did best, which was meeting and greeting the clientele and persuading them that in coming to the Alpha Bar tonight they had made indisputably the right choice.

It was brilliant, being able to watch him without being watched in return. Heavens, he had a stunning profile . . . not to mention a pretty darn luscious body, Suzy couldn't help noticing as he made his way through the crowd. She tapped her fingers against the steering wheel and hummed along with the music in an attempt to distract her attention . . .

"Kisses for me. Save all your kisses for me," Brotherhood of Man sang jauntily, on her treasured Eurovision compilation tape.

Except he isn't, Suzy thought crossly. *He's doling them out to all and sundry, and he probably doesn't even* know *these girls.*

Still, they weren't the kind of kisses that actually meant anything; just an introductory peck on the cheek type of thing. And it wasn't as if Leo had a lot of choice in the matter, Suzy was forced to acknowledge; these shameless females were lining up, practically *hurling* their cheeks in the direction of his mouth, jostling for his attention like groupies . . .

Which, of course, only made him appear *more* attractive.

It occurred to Suzy that — in comparison — she was going to look a bit of a ninny. She hadn't realized that the Alpha Bar was going to be quite this smart.

Oh well, can't be helped. With a careless shrug, she switched off the tape just as "Making Your Mind Up" (her absolute favorite Buck's Fizz track) was about to start. *Besides, I'd look even more of a twit jogging across the Downs with Baxter in a Prada skirt and six-inch heels.*

Me in the high heels, that is, not Baxter.

Baxter wouldn't wear high heels, because he was a boy.

CHAPTER 35

As she crossed the road, Suzy kept her gaze fixed on Leo and had a silent bet with herself that he'd be great at Boggle.

If she'd still been crazy about Harry, this evening's experience would have come as a crushing blow. Five games played, and the longest word Harry had been able to muster had been *plate.* Suzy's heart had sunk. They simply weren't Boggle compatible. And, like size, it mattered. Oh yes, it mattered a lot. Let's face it, if a man couldn't give you a run for your money in the Boggle department, how could you even *hope* to build a life together?

It simply wasn't possible.

No Boggle, no future. That was all there was to it.

In fact, from now on maybe she should carry a travel-size version around with her at all times — then whenever she met a new man, she could produce it with a flourish and challenge him to a quick game. That way, she could weed out no-hopers on the spot.

Tap-tap. Suzy's knuckles rapped against the plate-glass window, startling half a dozen unamused-looking women and attracting Leo's attention.

Suzy gestured to her legs, then pointed to the door. Grasping the situation in an instant, Leo nodded.

Oh no, he wouldn't have to struggle with Boggle, thought Suzy. *He'd definitely have the knack.*

At the door, Leo greeted her with a broad smile.

"I say, terrific disguise. I almost didn't recognize you with your Nikes on."

If the truth be known, Suzy's Nike sneakers had had trouble recognizing Suzy when she'd unearthed them from the back of the closet. Having been cajoled by Fee into taking part in a charity half marathon last year, she had rushed out and bought the sneakers, plus the rest of the outfit, in a fit of . . . well, idiocy, to be honest. Three days of halfhearted training had been more than enough to bring Suzy to her senses and persuade her that running really wasn't her thing. Writing out a huge check in lieu of participation, she had spent the afternoon of the race cheering Fee across the finish line instead.

With a sigh of relief, Suzy had flung the sneakers into her closet, where they had resided peacefully ever since.

No wonder they'd blinked and looked a bit dazed this evening when they'd found themselves being abruptly hauled back out.

Running? Us?

"Lucille's busy, so I said I'd take Baxter out for his run."

Why did Leo seem to find this so extraordinarily amusing?

"I see." His mouth twitched at the corners as he glanced over Suzy's shoulder at the Rolls, riskily parked on double yellows. "You do know, don't you, that driving slowly with one hand on the steering wheel and the other on Baxter's leash through the window doesn't actually count?"

Suzy blinked. This hadn't occurred to her, but it certainly sounded like an excellent idea.

"Don't worry, you can trust me. This may astonish you, but I do know how to jog."

I just prefer not to make a habit of it, thanks very much. Once every twenty or thirty years, that's plenty for me.

"Did you have to borrow this stuff from Lucille?" Leo was busy admiring the lime-green and silver striped tracksuit top and matching Lycra cycling shorts.

"No, it's all mine." Suzy knew she looked great; modesty aside, she'd never had any complaints about her legs. "What can I tell you," she added with a mischievous smile, "I'm full of surprises."

Leo raised an eyebrow. For a moment she thought he was about to pass some acerbic remark. But it didn't happen; he'd clearly thought better of it. She was, after all, dog walker du jour. Leo couldn't afford to offend her and risk having her flounce off in a huff. Baxter wouldn't be too thrilled if he missed out on his run.

Picking up a phone on the reception desk, Leo asked someone to open the office door upstairs. Seconds later Baxter came bounding down the staircase toward them with his leash in his mouth and the sturdy metal chain clattering against the polished floor.

He looked and sounded like a desperate-to-escape prisoner hampered by leg irons. His tail, whipping around like a helicopter blade, whipped faster still when he spotted Suzy. With a whimper of joy he dropped the leash — a bit dribbly with saliva — on her feet.

"He likes you," said Leo.

Honestly, no need to sound quite *so surprised.*

"He's got taste." Suzy crouched down and greeted Baxter with equal enthusiasm — but much less saliva.

"Lucille takes him for a three-mile run in the evenings," Leo announced.

"Really? I thought I'd take him for a kebab." Suzy beamed up at him. "Just for a change."

"How's Harry?"

Useless at Boggle. "Fine."

"So you'll be back around nine thirty?"

"Unless I get carried away," said Suzy. "You never know, I might start running and not be able to stop."

"I'd better phone John O'Groats and warn them," Leo replied gravely. "Just in case."

It took no time at all for Suzy to remember the number one reason she'd given up jogging. Thankfully, the Downs were both dark and deserted, so there was no one around to see how completely idiotic she looked.

Polystyrene, Suzy decided as she jogged along Ladies Mile with Baxter bouncing joyfully at her heels. If you wanted to transport something fragile, you packed it up in polystyrene to stop it getting jiggled about and damaged en route.

What some genius needed to do was invent a polystyrene bra, or a breast shield or something, which would encase and totally immobilize the bosoms of women who would love to run but just couldn't stand the pain.

But seeing as it hadn't been invented yet, Suzy was forced to jog with her hands crossed in front of her chest to provide the polystyrene-bra effect.

She was getting some funny looks from Baxter, but that was OK — he wouldn't tell Leo.

"So, Baxter, what d'you think of Gabriella?" Suzy panted. This was the great thing about dogs; they couldn't blab. "She can't really be that nice, can she? There must be something about her I can hate."

In reply, Baxter found a stick lying in the long grass. Picking it up, keen for Suzy to throw it for him, he jostled her legs and managed to scrape the sharp end painfully across the back of her knee.

"Ouch!" yelped Suzy, taking the stick and hurling it as far as she could. "You see, I've gotten myself into a bit of a mess here. I've stopped liking Harry, for a start."

In the pitch-blackness, Baxter was having trouble finding his stick. She could hear him snuffling around in search of it, crashing

441

through the undergrowth. Every now and again she glimpsed a swish of his tail.

Talking her problem through with Baxter didn't seem weird at all, Suzy discovered. It actually felt quite soothing, quite therapeutic.

Keeping to the road, raising her voice so he could hear her, she went on loudly, "The thing is, Leo's the one I really like. I didn't mean it to happen, but it has. And the way I feel about him is completely different from the way I used to feel about Harry. In fact, I've never felt like this about *anyone* before."

Panting with exultation, Baxter raced through the grass toward her. With the stick dangling rakishly from one side of his mouth, he looked like Groucho Marx chomping on a cigar.

Suzy retrieved it and flung it once more into the ink-dark sky.

"Actually, it's quite scary," she yelled after him. "He thinks I'm dreadful. A disgrace. Certainly not good enough to marry his precious brother. And I don't even *want* to marry Harry. Oh God, Baxter, what am I going to do?" Suzy's voice rose to a wail. "How can I stop feeling this way about Leo Fitzallan? I keep fantasizing about him, you know. All the time! I wonder what he looks like with all his clothes off. What if I'm falling in love with him, for heaven's sake? How can I stop myself falling in love with someone who doesn't love me back?"

"Screw him!" yelled a male voice from the depths of the bushes, and Suzy felt her heart leap into her throat. Whinnying with terror, stumbling backward in shock, for a deranged moment she wondered if Baxter was able to speak after all.

Then again, maybe not. The next second, as if he'd been fired from a cannon, a startled Baxter shot out from the bushes and all but threw himself into Suzy's arms.

Oh marvelous. Well done, Baxter. Such *a brave dog.*

At the same time, gales of raucous laughter were shaking the bushes from which Baxter had exploded. A second male voice shouted out, "Yeah, give the guy a road test. He might be useless!"

A very flamboyant male voice, Suzy registered.

"One quick go, could be all you need to get him out of your system," rejoined the first voice. Also decidedly flamboyant.

"He might have a dick the size of a peanut."

"Might be a speed merchant," the second chimed in. "All over before you've even started. God, I *hate* it when that happens."

"Might be gay. What did you say his name was, Leo Fitzsomething? Hmmm, can't say it rings any bells, but if you like, I could ask around."

More cackles of laughter from the depths of the bushes. The gay couple clearly found this hugely amusing.

At least the darkness was all-encompassing. Suzy, glad they couldn't see how furiously she was blushing, was gladder still that they couldn't see her face.

OK, so she'd been *heard* saying something hugely embarrassing, but at least they couldn't identify her. She was anonymous.

Relax, thought Suzy, the flat of her hand pressed hard against her breastbone as she tried to persuade her frantically thudding heart to slow down. Good grief, how could jogging possibly be healthy when it led to stuff like this happening to you?

A car, looming up behind her, caught her in its headlights. Instinctively, she raised one arm, shielding her face from the hecklers in the hedge.

Next — and rather cleverly, Suzy felt — she announced in a clear voice, "Come on, Buster. Time we were off."

"Aha!" the first voice crowed in triumph. "Hear that? She's scared we'll recognize her

— a minute ago she was calling the dog Baxter!"

"Kill," Suzy muttered under her breath. "Kill him, Baxter. Go on, *please.*"

But Baxter was far too busy whimpering and pressing his big hairy body against her legs to be any kind of a hero. Nudging the bunch of keys in Suzy's hand, all he wanted to do was get back to the sanctuary of the car.

CHAPTER 36

"Decided against John O'Groats then," Leo remarked when Suzy returned his cowardly dog to him twenty minutes later.

"Baxter had a good run."

Not to mention the shock of his life, thought Suzy. *Not to mention the shock of* my *life.*

Leo was watching her, she realized. "You look worn out."

"Thanks." A frazzled wreck, more like. Suzy ran her fingers through her hair and privately vowed never to confide in a dog again as long as she lived.

Particularly not a dog as cowardly and lacking in sensible advice as Baxter.

Or any gay couple hiding in nearby undergrowth.

Screw him indeed. The very idea.

"Come on," said Leo when Baxter was happily ensconced once more in his basket upstairs in the office. "I'll buy you a drink."

Now that was more like it.

"Am I allowed in?" Suzy plucked doubtfully at her outfit. "Won't people look at me?"

"You know as well as I do," Leo said patiently, "that everywhere you go people look at you."

"Yes, but a fluorescent green tracksuit top and Lycra shorts . . ."

"If anyone says anything, I'll just tell them you're eccentric."

"Oh well, just a quick one then," Suzy said happily.

And blushed.

The restaurant and the bar were both heaving by this time. Leo's security staff was turning people away at the door, but Martin had somehow managed to get in earlier. Now, surrounded by four stunningly beautiful girls, he spotted Suzy and — excusing himself for a moment — made his way over to greet her.

For an idiotic second, Suzy was pleased to see him.

"There's Martin," she told Leo excitedly. Now she had the opportunity to prove that nothing seedy or illicit had been going on between Martin and herself, and that his presence in her apartment yesterday had been totally aboveboard.

"Leo, phone," called the girl he had earlier introduced to Suzy as his PA. "It's urgent."

Leo touched Suzy briefly on the shoulder, murmured, "Won't be long," and disappeared upstairs to take the call.

"Suzy, Suzy, Suzy," sang Martin, reaching her at last and trailing an affectionate index finger down her cheek. "Am I glad to see you! Oh yes, and am I especially glad to see you in that outfit. You know what your legs are? Spectacular, that's what. There's just no other word for them. Let me get you a drink, a massive drink to celebrate your heavenly legs."

He was absolutely plastered, needless to say. Suzy's heart sank like a stone. If she was going to produce Martin as her star witness in order to prove her innocence, she would have preferred him to be sober. Not that he was swaying or slurring or anything, but Suzy could tell how drunk he was — after all, it was practically her specialty. Tomorrow, she knew, Martin would wake up with a clonking hangover.

"Who are you here with?" She skillfully steered the conversation away from the subject of her legs.

"No idea." Martin shrugged helplessly. "Can't remember their names. Mandy, Sandy, Candy, and Bandy . . . Something like that, anyway. Costing me a fortune, I know that much. Six quid a shot, those cocktails they're drinking. I mean, they're nice enough girls, but where am I going to find a bank to rob at this time of night?"

Beneath the brash veneer, the effortless good looks, and the oh-so-charming smile, he was unhappier than ever. Glancing over at the four girls now giggling among themselves, Suzy was able to sum them up in a flash. Blond, divorced, in their thirties, endlessly trawling the clubs and wine bars in search of fresh entertainment, they took men for whatever they could get. Spotting Martin on his own, they had latched on to him like burrs. Or praying mantises, thought Suzy with a shudder. He wouldn't stand a chance against that predatory lot.

"Listen to me." She gave Martin a long look. "Is this the way to get Nancy back?"

The winning smile slid off his face in an instant. "Nancy doesn't want me back."

"Maybe not right now. But she might change her mind. If you can manage to convince her *you've* changed."

"I love her." Martin's face began to crumple, and Suzy pinched the back of his hand, hard. *"Ow."*

"Don't cry. Nancy certainly won't want you back if she hears you've been seen

449

around town with girls like that."

Martin couldn't speak. He hung his head and shook it slowly, considering what Suzy was saying to him. To her relief, through the considerable haze of alcohol, it appeared to be sinking in.

The next moment she was almost sent flying as Martin threw both arms around her. Hanging on to her gin and tonic for dear life, Suzy joked, "Steady on there. I nearly spilled my drink."

Crikey, it was like being hugged by a bear cub that didn't know its own strength.

"You're right," Martin mumbled, his face buried in her neck. "You're always right. Thanks."

He smelled of Gaultier aftershave and whiskey and sounded like a small lost boy. Feeling incredibly sorry for him, Suzy patted his shoulder.

"Hey, cheer up. Want me to take you home?"

Martin lifted his head a fraction. He looked hopeful. "Your home?"

"Sorry, we're full. No room at the inn. But I can give you a lift back to your place. Better than staying here," she prompted.

Across the room, the praying mantises were glaring at her. Suzy glared defiantly back.

"OK." This time, Martin raised his head properly and smiled. Then he kissed her, somewhat damply, on the mouth. "You're amazing, you know? I mean, really. You're the best."

Suzy didn't need to turn around to guess who was standing behind her. The icy waves of disapproval tumbling over her shoulders could only emanate from one man.

"C'mon, let's go." Martin was busy sliding his arm around her waist. Glancing up and vaguely recognizing Leo, he said cheerfully, "Hi! How are *you*? My lucky night, eh? She's taking me home!"

"He's very drunk," Suzy told Leo. Annoyingly, of course, Martin wasn't looking drunk at all.

He didn't sound it either. Not even tipsy.

"What she means is, she's crazy about me and can't wait to get me into bed." Martin gave Leo a man-to-man wink. "I tried saying no, but she won't listen — you know what these girls are like once they make up their minds." Heaving a dramatic sigh as Suzy hauled him away, he called over his shoulder, "Oh, it's a dirty job, but somebody has to do it . . ."

"I should kill you," said Suzy as she shoveled him vigorously into the passenger seat of the Rolls.

Martin looked astonished. "Why? Who *was* that guy anyway? I know I've seen him somewhere before."

Honestly. *Hopeless.*

"My apartment? Yesterday?"

"That's it!" Martin exclaimed. "Came to see Lucille. Is he her boyfriend?"

"No, you big jerk." Suzy fastened his seat belt for him, though why she was bothering she couldn't imagine. "He's Harry's brother."

"Hi, I'm back — ooh, pizza," Suzy exclaimed. "Yum, my favorite!"

It wasn't, but she was so hungry she could have eaten the carpet.

"What happened to ten o'clock?" As he spoke, Harry glanced across at Celeste. "You said you'd definitely be back by ten."

"And it's half past one *in the morning,*" said Celeste.

Déjà vu. Suzy frowned, wondering why this all seemed so very familiar. Ah, yes, that was it. She was fifteen again, creeping home in the early hours and being interrogated by her mother because apparently it was fine for Blanche to disappear for months on end, but if *she* dared to be thirty minutes late, all of a sudden it was a hanging offense.

452

"I stayed on for a drink at the Alpha Bar. Got to chatting with Leo."

"Leo phoned here two hours ago, to let you know he'd found your hair clip," Harry replied frostily. "He seemed surprised you weren't home yet."

Why do I even bother to lie? Why didn't I just tell them the truth in the first place?

All she'd been trying to do, Suzy reminded herself, was keep things simple. Simple and uncluttered. And did it ever work out that way? Of course not.

"Martin was there, drunk as a skunk and on the verge of getting himself into all sorts of trouble. I offered to give him a lift home. Then he invited me in for coffee, but all he really wanted was someone to talk to. Which is why I've spent the last four hours listening to him ramble on about his wife and children and how miserable he is. I drank three black coffees because they'd run out of milk. I've eaten seven peanuts and half a shortbread cookie because that's all the food they had in the apartment. And we didn't have sex. Now, can I finish off that pizza, or would you rather I phoned and ordered my own?"

"Help yourself," said Harry. "No need to get belligerent. I only asked."

"I'll go." Celeste, on the sofa next to him,

453

stretched her matchstick arms and yawned.

"Look, I'm sorry," said Suzy, "but you didn't have to stay this late. Harry can be left on his own, you know."

"S'alright." With a shrug, Celeste searched under the sofa for her sequined mules. "We enjoyed ourselves. It was fun."

Surprised that Celeste knew what fun was — boredom was far more her field of expertise — Suzy said, "Really?" and tried not to look too astonished. "What did you do?"

"Loads. Read our horoscopes in *Cosmopolitan*."

Wow.

"Didn't bother with the videos," Harry said happily. "We watched *Dumb and Dumber* on TV instead."

Ooh.

Celeste giggled. "That was really funny."

Hmmm.

"And we chatted. For ages."

"About ourselves. And about you. And" — Celeste played her trump card — "we played Boggle."

Excuse me?

This time, Suzy was genuinely astounded. Boggle? Celeste? The girl who thought *Roget's Thesaurus* was a breed of dinosaur?

"OK, I'm off. See you around," Celeste told Harry with a vague smile.

"Pop over any time," Harry said generously.

Just don't always expect a von Etzdorf scarf, thought Suzy, spotting the pink tasseled ends trailing from Celeste's unfastened Prada bag.

Feigning exhaustion once Celeste had left, Suzy changed out of the silver-and-green Lycra outfit, showered, and got ready for bed.

OK, ready for sofa.

"Come on, you can do better than that," Harry chided when she planted a businesslike good-night kiss on his cheek.

"Harry, you already know this because I've already told you. I don't love you, I'm not going to marry you, and the sooner you break the news to *Hi!* magazine, the better."

"But *I* love *you,*" Harry insisted, unperturbed. "And I'm going to make you change your mind."

His calmness was infuriating. It was like trying to convince a Jehovah's Witness that you really *really* didn't believe in God. Suzy abruptly changed the subject.

"Did you and Celeste really play Boggle?"

"Not properly. She just mucked about with the letters for a bit." Harry was so handsome he even looked gorgeous when he was yawning like a hippo. "OK, sweetheart. Night."

The bedroom door closed. As Suzy shook out her pale pink duvet, arranging it over the sofa, she spotted the Boggle case on the floor underneath the coffee table.

So that was Celeste's idea of playing Boggle.

Carefully positioned on the four-by-four grid, the lettered dice proclaimed:

S U Z Y
H A Z A
V A S T
A R S E

Laughing to herself, Suzy slid under the duvet and fell asleep.

CHAPTER 37

"Crikey, what time is it? I didn't hear you come in last night." Blearily, Suzy half opened her eyes as Lucille put a cup of tea down in front of her and sat on her feet.

"That's because I didn't come in last night. I've just gotten back."

"God, I feel as if I've had about four hours' sleep." Suzy groaned and tried to stretch her legs. "What's the time?"

"Twenty past six."

"Huh? In the evening?"

"In the morning," said Lucille.

"Nooo!" wailed Suzy, her eyes snapping open in horror as she realized that outside it was still dark. "I *have* only had four hours' sleep! How could you *do* this to me? It's Sunday," she whimpered, "and you've woken me up . . . What did I ever do to deserve this?"

To add insult to injury, Lucille wasn't looking remotely apologetic. Her eyes were bright, her breathing rapid, and she was positively fizzing with excitement.

"Sorry," lied Lucille. "I just had to talk to someone. Here, drink this." She shoved the mug of tea into Suzy's trembling hands. "It'll make you feel better."

A lousy cup of tea? That's *supposed to make me feel better*?

"Twenty past six, twenty past six on a Sunday," Suzy moaned. "What have you been *doing*?"

"I've been with Jaz." Lucille's whole face was aglow as if she'd swallowed a lightbulb. "All night."

Oh God, she had that look in her eyes. That unmistakable *look* . . .

Slopping tea in all directions, Suzy jack-knifed into a sitting position.

"Never! Never! You're kidding me!" It came out as an incredulous rising squeal. "You mean you actually HAD SEX WITH JAZ?"

"Are you out of your *mind*?" Appalled, Lucille clapped a hand over Suzy's mouth. Harry was lying in bed less than twenty feet away. Imagine the embarrassment if he woke up and overheard. "Of course I didn't have sex with Jaz! How can you even *think* that?"

"Gosh, you're rough," Suzy grumbled

when Lucille took her hand away at last. Exercising her squashed lips, making sure they were still in one piece, she said defiantly, "Well, you look as if that's how you spent the night. You're all . . . lit up."

Then again, maybe Lucille was bluffing. *Not telling the truth,* thought Suzy, *rather like I haven't told her the truth about me and Harry.*

"We've been in the recording studio," Lucille explained.

Lovely. Nice bouncy floor, Suzy recalled. All those layers of sponge laid down to deaden the acoustics meant the studio was fabulous for romping around in.

"Will you *stop* that?" demanded Lucille, intercepting the naughty smile on Suzy's face. "Jaz has written a song and he wants me to sing it. We've spent the whole night working on it . . . I'm so excited I don't think I'll ever sleep again! Watching him at the control desk is so, *so* amazing — oh, Suzy, it's just been the best night of my life!"

"Blimey, all that and you didn't even have sex," Suzy marveled.

"I know." Lucille was hugging her knees, dreamily swaying along to the song playing in her head.

"So how did you get Jaz over his music block?"

"I didn't. He did it all by himself."

"Go on then." Well and truly awake now, Suzy gave her a nudge. "Sing it for me."

Lucille was on such a high, she didn't need to be asked twice. Shaking back her braids, she took a deep breath and began:

I need to let you know
I can't let you go
You leave me with no alternative
You see it's our affair
And I can't bear to share
Your love — yours to take and mine to give
Because I'd die, I'd die, I'd die for you
If you asked me to
You're my angel, my miracle, my reason to
   liiive —

"For crying out loud," yelled Harry from the bedroom. "It's not even half past six! Will somebody let that bloody cat out?"

"Always been a bit grumpy in the mornings," whispered Lucille. "Hates being woken early."

Suzy, her spine still tingling from the effect of the song, thought how ironic it was that at last she'd discovered something she and Harry had in common.

Still, if she was awake he could jolly well wake up too.

"Ignore him. It's fabulous. Sing it again,"

she told Lucille.

The next fortnight passed by in a blur for Suzy. Summer was well and truly over now, autumn had swept in with a vengeance, and she had never been so busy or worked so hard. Fee, still covering for Donna in the office, was working like a Trojan but still learning the ropes. Martin didn't have his act together yet and was an absolute waste of space. A more brutal employer might have sacked him on the spot, but Suzy knew that if this happened to Martin, it would be the last straw. It fell to her, therefore, to conceal his utter uselessness from Rory and carry out most of Martin's work herself. Bizarrely, she was only able to do this because Rory didn't appear to be firing on all cylinders either. For some reason these days he was totally distracted, frequently in a muddle, and — in the office at least — barely capable of stringing together a coherent sentence.

Weird.

Nor were things what you'd call normal at home. Like musical chairs gone mad, everyone appeared to have switched places.

"It's surreal," Suzy told Leo when he came into the office to let her know that the mining search had been completed on

Sheldrake House. "I can go for days on end without seeing Lucille — she spends every spare minute next door in the studio with Jaz."

"And you're here," said Leo. "So who's looking after Harry?"

"Weirder and weirder." Suzy rolled her eyes. "You won't believe this. Celeste."

"You mean she pops over every now and again?"

"I mean she's practically moved in! For some reason they've totally hit it off. It's one of those bizarre pairings, like peanut butter and honey sandwiches. You think they won't go together, but somehow they do."

Leo gave her an odd look. "And you don't mind them spending so much time together?"

Mind? Suzy was on the verge of hooting with laughter at the very idea. She hastily composed herself. "You mean am I jealous? Oh, I don't think Celeste's too much of a threat." She smiled confidently at Leo. "Harry and I are getting on just fine."

Honestly, it was a wonder her nose wasn't the size of a telescope.

"Maybe I should drop in on him." Leo glanced at his watch. "I could spare ten minutes."

Don't put yourself out too much, thought

462

Suzy. *He's only your brother.*

Aloud she said, "Feel free."

Harry was in the middle of having his hair washed when Leo arrived.

"Celeste has to do it for me," he explained with a grin, his head bent over the bathtub while Celeste massaged shampoo into his scalp. "I mustn't get water inside the cast on my arm."

The temperature may have dropped outside, but inside Suzy's apartment, it was tropical. The central heating was on maximum, Harry was wearing a pair of shorts and nothing else, and the outline of Celeste's pert little breasts was clearly visible through her flimsy white cotton dress. The way her rosy nipples were brushing against Harry's shoulder blades as she reached for the conditioner was also pretty visible. Leo, leaning in the doorway of the bathroom, listening to the interplay between the two of them, marveled at their brazenness. Feeling neglected by their respective partners, Harry and Celeste were clearly determined to get back at Suzy and Jaz.

They were flirting and not bothering to hide it. Leo doubted whether it actually meant anything to either of them. The chances were, they were both bored and it was nothing more than an entertaining way of passing the time.

"I just saw Suzy at the office. From the sound of it, she's putting in pretty long hours," he remarked when Celeste had left the bathroom in search of fresh towels.

"Don't worry about me." Harry gave him a meaningful smirk. "I'm having a great time."

"So I see."

"Celeste's quite a girl." Harry couldn't resist it. If becoming engaged to Suzy Curtis had been a monumental ego boost, cheating on her was even more of one. Not that he *had* cheated on her, of course — with this number of fractures it was pretty much a physical impossibility, just now — but mentally, that was what he was doing.

And what was so terrible about that?

See, Leo? I can play that game too, thought Harry, his smile triumphant. *I'm no longer second-best.*

Returning from the linen closet with her arms full of clean towels, Celeste pulled the damp one from around Harry's shoulders and let it drop carelessly to the floor. With a sensuous rhythm and her tongue held playfully between her teeth, she began to rub his hair dry with a fresh towel.

"OK?" stage-whispered Celeste. "Not too hard?"

"You're a wicked girl," Harry told her with a grin.

"There, all done. You can have a blow-dry in a minute. Now, Leo." All innocence, Celeste turned around to face him. "What would you like?" She paused. "Tea? Coffee? A proper drink?"

"Thanks." Leo glanced briefly at his watch. "But I have to get back to work." To Harry, he added, "I just dropped by to see how you were."

"Oh, bearing up," said Harry with a broad wink. "Making the best of things."

Behind him, trailing a finger lightly down his bare back, Celeste murmured, "I'll second that."

The reason Rory was having such trouble concentrating in the office was that all he could think about was his upcoming weekend in Wales with Fee. As Friday had drawn nearer, his powers of rational thought had begun to crumble like cake. At home, like a prisoner counting down the days to his release, he had a calendar with larger and larger crosses on it in red felt pen. In the square marked Friday, October 11, he'd written *YES!* and circled it wildly about fifteen times in anticipation.

Needless to say, it was the kind of calendar entry you'd die rather than let anyone else see, but since Rory lived alone and couldn't remember the last time he'd invited someone into his home, his embarrassing secret was safe.

And now it was Friday, October 11 — after what seemed like months, it had finally arrived — and he was so wound up with excitement he could barely speak.

Lucky it's a relaxation weekend we're going on, thought Rory. *Crikey, hope it works.*

"I'm all packed and ready to go," Fee told him cheerfully when he arrived at the office after lunch.

Rory stowed his weekend cases beside the filing cabinets. He could have left them in the trunk of the car but hadn't been able to resist bringing them in so that every now and again he could glance over at them and experience that *ziiing* of excitement in the pit of his stomach.

Just three more hours before they could leave. He would change, in the back room, out of his business suit and into a suitably casual Aran sweater and dark green corduroys. They would stop off at Fee's apartment to pick up her cases. Then, by five thirty they'd be off, across the Severn

466

Bridge and into Wales, all the while chatting easily to each other in the car. Oh yes, the flow of conversation would be effortless, and just to make sure of this Rory had already prepared a list of suitable topics.

And by six thirty, he thought with a surge of joy, we'll be driving through the glorious Brecon Beacons, exclaiming over the scenery, following the snaking path of the River Wye . . .

"Hope you've packed your long johns," Suzy announced, coming off the phone and eyeing first the cases then the steel-gray clouds outside. "It's not a four-star hotel you're staying in, you know. From what Fee's been telling us, the place sounds more like Colditz."

I don't care, I don't care. As long as we're together, that's all that matters, thought Rory rebelliously. *In fact, the colder the better. Then maybe I'll be able to help to keep her warm . . .*

"Now you're sure you'll be able to manage without us," he said aloud, sounding concerned but not meaning it for a millisecond. Like it or not, they'd just *have* to manage.

"Oh, we'll struggle through somehow." Suzy smiled to herself because Rory didn't even realize that for the past fortnight, she'd been running the business practically single-handed. "And Donna's back tomorrow. We'll cope."

Rory wasn't bothered about the temperature of the hotel, but the prospect of Colditz-style food was off-putting. Never mind, they could eat out, he'd take Fee somewhere exquisite and romantic . . . Was Franco Taruschio's famous Walnut Tree restaurant anywhere near Snowdonia?

"Blimey, look who's here," Suzy marveled as the door swung open and Jaz came in. "The Creature from the Blacked-Out Basement! What are you doing out in daylight — are you sure all this fresh air won't make your skin shrivel up and drop off?"

Everyone laughed, except Jaz.

He turned to Fee with a look of compassion on his face.

"Oh God, what is it? What's happened?" Fearfully, Fee clutched her throat.

"I'm sorry, darling. Now, it's nothing horrific, but your mother's had a bit of a fall and slipped a disk. Your father called just now. She's in the hospital in Bournemouth, and he wants to know if you can get down there this evening."

"No," croaked Rory, aghast. *"No."*

CHAPTER 38

Fee gazed over at Rory. He was as white as a sheet. Poor thing. Of course, it had only been six weeks since Blanche had died. Hearing that something had happened to her mother must have brought all those terrible memories flooding back.

"It's all right." Impulsively, she crossed the office and gave Rory a quick, fierce hug. "Really, it's OK. She isn't going to die. She's had a fall, that's all. A slipped disk."

Poor Rory. She could feel him trembling all over. It occurred to Fee that if he was reacting this emotionally, Suzy might be upset too.

With a worried glance across at Suzy, she said, "How about you? Are you all right?"

Suzy looked amazed. "Of course I am! Why wouldn't I be?"

"I said I'd come tell you," said Jaz, "and you'd call him back. He's at the hospital, at this number." Taking a scrap of paper from his shirt pocket, he handed it to Fee, who picked up the phone.

Rory's weekend was collapsing before his very eyes. It felt like his whole world. He listened to Fee's conversation with her father. She sounded calm, practical, and completely in control as she assured him that yes, she could be in Bournemouth by six o'clock.

Nooo! Rory longed to yell. *You don't have to go right away, surely? It's only a slipped disk. That's not serious. Couldn't you just leave it until Monday?*

Please.

He didn't say it, of course. The only noise to escape from his throat was a kind of strangled whinny. Thankfully, it was barely audible.

Although Suzy did raise an eyebrow and give him an odd look.

Fuck, thought Rory, who never ever swore, even to himself. *Fuck, fuck, fuck . . . FUCK.*

"You look like one of the undead," Suzy cheerfully informed Jaz, while Fee was still on the phone. In fact, in his crumpled black shirt and trousers and with his dark, heavily shadowed eyes burning like coals in his pale face, Jaz gave the impression that he hadn't eaten or slept for a week.

Then again, she had never seen him look

470

happier or more alive.

Jaz grinned broadly at her. "It's going so well. You wouldn't believe it."

Jaz could hardly believe it himself. Now that he'd started writing songs again, he was unable to stop. Ideas were spilling out of him like lemmings hurtling over the edge of a cliff. And most amazingly of all, he had Lucille there with him to put her own unique twist on the music. Writing songs might not be her forte — OK, it *wasn't* her forte — but personalizing and interpreting them in ways Jaz had never even imagined was most definitely where her talents lay. Together, they were creating something so incredible it took his breath away.

"That's great," said Suzy, who didn't pretend to understand the writing process but was pleased for him anyway. "I'm really glad."

Great? Great? How could anything *be great?* Rory, jerkily polishing his glasses on his sleeve, was having trouble containing the lump in his throat. Disappointment swirled around him like dense fog. Much as he still longed for it to happen, he knew he had to face up to the fact that Fee was unlikely to put off visiting her hospitalized mother until after the weekend.

"OK, Dad, I'll meet you at the ward. See

you at six. Bye." Fee put the phone down and shook her head. "Well, that's me booked for the next month."

The next month? Nooo!

Fee sighed. "Poor old Mum."

Poor old me, thought Rory.

"Will she be in the hospital for long?" said Suzy.

"No, but she'll need looking after when she gets out. And of course my father will need looking after in the meantime. He's the really helpless one," Fee added drily. "That's where I'm really going to have my work cut out. I don't think he could even make himself a cup of tea."

Then it's about time he bloody learned, Rory silently howled.

"If you're catching the train, I'll give you a lift to the station," said Jaz, feeling heroic. Battling through the Friday afternoon rush hour to Temple Meads would keep him out of the studio for at least another hour.

I could do that, thought Rory, sitting up suddenly. It wasn't much, but it was better than nothing . . . In fact, he could offer to drive Fee all the way to Bournemouth!

"Don't worry," Fee told Jaz, "I'll drive. I'm going to need my car down there anyway."

Rory's shoulders slumped once more.

"Ah, well, so much for our relaxation weekend." Fee gave Rory an apologetic little smile. "Sorry about having to stand you up."

"No problem." Rory forced himself to sound casual. "No problem at all. Some other time, perhaps."

At the tone of his voice, Fee's eyes grew round with alarm. "But you can still go. You mustn't miss out just because I have to. You'll love it, I promise!"

I won't, I promise!

"Please don't cancel because of me," Fee begged. "The people there are great. You'll get on with them like a house on fire . . . and it'll do you *so* much good . . ."

It won't, thought Rory, *because I won't be there.*

"OK, maybe I will," he said, purely because she was looking so worried. The last thing he wanted to do was make her feel guilty.

But seriously, why would he be even remotely tempted to go alone? Without Fee there, what *would* be the point?

"I know what you're doing," Celeste announced. She turned to face Harry as he hobbled into the kitchen behind her.

"Oh yes?"

473

"*Oh* yes. And I know why you're doing it too."

Behind her, steam billowed from the spout of the kettle as it came to a boil.

"Waiting for a cup of tea?" guessed Harry. "Because I'm thirsty?"

"Flirting with me," Celeste corrected him mildly. "Because you want to make Suzy jealous."

Harry moved toward her, his crutches making rhythmic clunking noises against the tiled floor. He sounded like Long John Silver.

"Really? Is that what you think?"

Celeste's nostrils twitched involuntarily. Heavens, his just-washed hair smelled gorgeous.

"Oh yes, that's exactly what I think," she murmured, her thin elbows resting on the countertop behind her. Her breasts, jutting forward, were clearly visible through the flimsy white cotton of her dress.

"Well, you're wrong," said Harry. "OK, maybe it started out that way, but not anymore." He moved another step — *clunk* — closer. "So how about you? Why have you been flirting so outrageously with me? Just to pay Jaz back for abandoning you? Or . . . ?" He paused, the corners of his mouth beginning to twitch.

"Or what?" breathed Celeste. Heavens, her heart was breaking into such a *gallop.*

"Or do you think you might be experiencing the same feelings as me?"

She smiled. Harry knew as well as she did exactly what had been taking place over the course of the last couple of weeks. And you had to give him his due; he'd handled it brilliantly, like a pro.

The timing was spot-on, Celeste decided with a little shiver of appreciation. At first, they had flirted with each other for the sheer hell of it, really just for something to do to pass the time.

Then, after the first few days, had come the temptation to take things further. And by *not* doing so, the flirtation had become all the more delicious.

By the middle of the second week, the sense of anticipation was almost unbearable; they had reached a state of barely controlled frenzy. Every look and smile and teasing remark was enough to set off another spasm of longing.

And now, just as Celeste had begun to wonder if she could stand another day — even another *hour* — of nothing happening, it finally *had* happened.

Harry had made his move.

Yesss!

God, this was going to be fantastic. She just knew it.

"Well?" teased Harry, still apparently waiting for an answer.

Ha, as if he didn't already know!

Pushing herself away from the marble countertop, Celeste took a step forward. Lifting her face, she brushed her lips oh-so-lightly against the left-hand corner of his mouth.

Harry shuddered and sighed. What Celeste didn't realize — and how ironic was this? — was that all this putting-off-the-moment business had been Suzy's idea.

And Suzy, he had to admit, had been right. Exasperating, but right. Her six-week rule might be extreme — two weeks had been as far as Harry had been able to stretch to — but he certainly understood now why she did it.

He had never been so aroused in his life.

As Celeste kissed him again, her gaze fell upon the montage of photos stuck haphazardly to the bulletin board next to the kitchen door. There was Suzy, dressed up as a fairy at some debauched party last Christmas. And there she was again, tanned and tawny-haired in an emerald-green bikini, with one arm draped around Jaz's neck and the other waving — heaven knows why — a gigantic pair of wellington boots.

Suzy and Lucille, screaming with laughter, together on the sofa.

Suzy in bed with a hangover, caught with her hair all over the place and baggy, morning-after eyes like Deputy Dawg.

Suzy, poured into a shimmering gold evening dress, caught on camera at some gala event or other, pinching the bottom of a well-known rugby player.

Suzy, Suzy, bloody Suzy, thought Celeste. She always had to be the center of attention, didn't she? Nothing was ever allowed to happen unless it involved Suzy.

"What are you thinking?" Harry murmured against her neck.

"Honestly?" Celeste caught her breath as he trailed his warm tongue along the delicate line of her collarbone.

"Mmm, honestly."

"OK. I'm here, kissing Suzy Curtis's fiancé." She grinned and raised a playful eyebrow. "Don't you think that's pretty cool?"

Harry frowned.

"Is that the only reason you're doing it?"

"Of course not. I'd feel this way about you whomever you were engaged to. But you have to admit," Celeste told him with a provocative nudge of her hips. "It's an added bonus."

CHAPTER 39

Now that she knew the sale of Sheldrake House was definitely going through, Suzy had to arrange to have it cleared of her mother's possessions. The contracts had been signed, and the closing would take place toward the end of October.

Leo, who planned to have the garden landscaped and was keen to make a start before the temperature plummeted still further and the ground froze solid, had already asked Suzy for permission to allow the firm of landscape gardeners access to the garden on Sunday. Since this was her only free day, Suzy decided she may as well turn up too, and start sorting through everything. All the unwanted furniture would go to auction. Most of the smaller stuff she could donate to local thrift shops — and hope that Maeve wouldn't buy it back. Then there were the thousands of books, the closets full of clothes, the miscellaneous contents of the attic, the garage, the store room . . .

Actually, Suzy realized, she could do with a bit of help.

Or even a lot.

Except Rory couldn't give her a hand, because he was away on his relaxation weekend. Which, God knows, he certainly needed.

Julia didn't sound thrilled to hear from Suzy.

"Why me?" she said irritably. "I thought you were in charge of selling the house?"

"They're Mum's things. I thought you'd want to help. There might be some stuff you'd like to keep."

"There won't be," said Julia, who had already been through Blanche's jewelry case like a one-woman plague of locusts. She'd also scooped up all the best paintings, claiming that money was irrelevant; she wanted them for their sentimental value. "Anyway, I'm busy on Sunday. We're having a lunch party for sixteen."

"OK," said Suzy. "Never mind. I expect Lucille will be able to help."

She heard a kind of reverse hissing sound as the air was sucked sharply in through Julia's teeth.

"Not her! Oh no. I'm sorry. You can't do that."

"Blanche was her mother too."

Julia snorted. "Maybe so, but Sheldrake House was never her home. No, no, Suzy, we grew up there. She didn't. The thought of that Lucille person in *our* house, picking through *our* mother's things like some kind of vulture . . . No, sorry, absolutely not. I'm afraid I just can't allow it."

Suzy was on her knees in the drawing room surrounded by woody-smelling tea chests and mountains of books when she heard familiar footsteps in the hall behind her.

"I saw your car in the drive," said Leo, "and the front door was open. Making a start on the sorting out?"

"There's loads to do." Suzy puffed her hair out of her eyes and lifted a teetering pile of books into the nearest tea chest. A cloud of dust billowed up, making her sneeze. She wiped the sleeve of her orange sweatshirt across her forehead, leaving behind a dusty gray smear. After four backbreaking hours, she was still only on the second room.

"All on your own?"

"Rory's away. Julia's busy." She paused. "So's Lucille."

Lucille had instantly concurred with Julia's decision.

"She's absolutely right," Lucille had announced, upon hearing Suzy's story of the phone conversation with Julia. "It's your family home, with your family's things in it. I'd just feel like an intruder."

Suzy had nodded and smiled in a noncommittal fashion and hated herself for even wondering if Lucille really meant it, or if she just couldn't bear the thought of missing out on yet another fourteen-hour stint in the recording studio with Jaz.

"You've got your work cut out," Leo observed now.

"You don't say. I thought it would only take a few minutes."

Oops. Suzy realized she was in danger of getting belligerent. It was clearly going to be one of those days.

Leo, meanwhile, was pushing up the sleeves of his charcoal-gray sweater.

"I could give you a hand if you like."

He had really nice hands. Rather lovely forearms too. It was a generous offer, but Suzy wasn't in the mood. Hopelessly jittery and on edge, she didn't trust herself not to snap and start screeching at him like a fishwife for no reason at all.

She hadn't the faintest idea what was

making her feel this way, but she knew the one thing she really couldn't cope with right now was Leo being kind to her.

"It's OK." Suzy shook her head. "I'm fine on my own. Anyway, you're busy too."

He looked at her. "Are you all right?"

No, go away! Just stop interfering and leave me alone!

Aloud she said, "Perfect."

Then she picked up a book and frowned, as if deep in concentration. It was a travel guide to Peru. Which was all very well, but had Blanche even *been* to Peru? Had she ever actually traveled farther afield than Bournemouth?

Rain began to rattle like stones against the drawing room windows. Outside, the sky was a darker gray than Leo's sweater. Suzy was glad; the weather suited her mood.

Leo, clearly humoring her, said, "I'm going to get wet out there."

You'll get wet if you stay in here, thought Suzy, *because I'll throw my can of Dr Pepper at you.*

Oh, good grief, what is the matter with me today?

When she looked up, Leo had gone. She was alone once more.

With her mother's books.

Across the Sahara on a Camel.

Oh, right, highly likely.

The Beauty of Fiji.

Yes, Mum, but do you actually know where Fiji is?

Through the Rain Forest.

The rainy Forest of Dean, presumably.

Oh, what was the point of this? Why was she even bothering?

Suzy gathered the books into her arms and swept them into the tea chest. She kept going until the floor was clear and the tea chests full. The whole lot could go to the thrift shop. Who knows, Blanche's travel guides might even end up being bought by people who were actually interested in traveling to Patagonia and Pompeii and Peru.

Suzy made her way irritably around the drawing room, slapping yellow Post-it Notes on all the items the auctioneers were coming to pick up tomorrow.

It was lunchtime, but she wasn't hungry. Standing at the sash window, drumming her fingers restlessly against the radiator beneath it, Suzy watched Leo out in the garden, deep in discussion with the landscape gardener who surely must have better things to do on a Sunday. The icy, driving rain had soaked them both to the skin, but it suited Leo better than it did the other

484

man, who had a pinched red face and thinning ginger hair plastered to his scalp. He was also wearing a pair of unfortunately tight beige trousers.

Leo might look good in his dark blue Barbour and jeans, but he must still be frozen. It occurred to Suzy that if she wanted to do a nice thing, she could go through to the kitchen and make the two men a coffee. Black, because there was no milk, but with cognac splashed in to warm them both up.

At that moment Leo stretched out an arm, encompassing the weeping cherry trees her father had loved so much. As he spoke to the landscape gardener, making brisk, get-rid-of-these gestures with his hand, Suzy felt her own fingers clench with annoyance around the bars of the radiator.

It had taken her father years to get the garden just as he'd wanted it. How *dare* Leo Fitzallan come swanning in and change everything?

Forget it. Now he definitely wasn't going to get any coffee.

Dealing with the contents of Blanche's closets was weirder than Suzy had imagined. Every single item of clothing conjured up a mental picture of her mother wearing it. Blanche had always loved clothes with a bit of drama and originality to them; everything she had worn had been highly distinctive. Suzy, currently filling her fifteenth black trash bag, wondered if perhaps she should take these to some thrift shop out of Bristol. It might feel a bit odd, suddenly spotting someone in the street wearing a pair of her mother's trousers or one of her flower-bedecked hats.

At the sight of Blanche's sapphire-blue velvet evening dress, yet another image sprang into Suzy's mind, like the next color transparency clicking up onto a screen. Her mother and father, celebrating their thirtieth wedding anniversary. Throwing a huge party — Blanche's idea, of course — to celebrate thirty years of married bliss.

Ha!

Into the bag it went with all the rest of the stuff.

Coats next, then shoes.

Suzy had no intention of stopping until she'd finished.

"OK if I put the kettle on?" shouted Leo up the stairs.

Cheek.

"Go ahead."

Damn cheek, Suzy thought indignantly when he appeared in the bedroom doorway five minutes later with a steaming cup. Offering it to her, he said, "Ready for some coffee?"

"Oh, I see." Suzy's shoulders stiffened. Her voice came out sounding jerky and strange. "So you just thought you'd make yourself at home, did you? It didn't occur to you that it might have been polite to ask me first, before you helped yourself to coffee that didn't belong to you?"

Oh dear. Losing it, losing it . . .

Leo gave her a measured look.

"I knew I was going to be here for a few hours," he said calmly. "So I brought along a jar of coffee and a pint of milk."

Oh. Blast.

This is where I'm supposed to smile and say sorry, Suzy thought, *and apologize for overreacting.*

But she couldn't bring herself to do it.

Her teeth were too gritted, for a start. Actually, they felt as if they'd been welded together with superglue.

"So, do you want this?" Leo held out the mug in a just-take-it kind of way.

Suzy, who had finished her can of Dr Pepper two hours ago and could have murdered a coffee, decided she didn't much care for his patronizing tone and ever-so-slightly long suffering manner.

Pointedly, turning her back on Leo, she

said, "No thanks."

By three o'clock it had stopped raining. Suzy, stacking the bulging trash bags on the landing ready for collection tomorrow, looked out of the window and saw the landscape gardener pacing around the garden sticking a thin metal rod into the wet ground at intervals and making notes in a notepad.

What was Leo planning to do with the garden anyway? The gardener was picking up a spade now. As she watched, he thrust it into the corner of a flower bed, dug up a spadeful of earth, and pushed the metal rod into the ground again.

Frustratingly, it reminded Suzy of something from the dim and distant past — but she couldn't remember what.

Oh well, forget it. On with the show. Attic next.

CHAPTER 40

Blanche had kept the two halves of her life efficiently compartmentalized. There were no clues anywhere to her other existence. Suzy, who hadn't expected to find any, marveled at her mother's ability to keep her two families so entirely separate.

The junk in the attic would be easy to dispose of, at least. There was nothing up here that couldn't be dealt with by the house-clearance firm. Slapping lime-green Post-it Notes on all the boxes, bags, ancient lampshades, and assorted rolls of carpet, Suzy wiped her hands on the sides of her leather jeans and heaved a sigh of relief.

There, done. Hooray.

As she climbed down the stepladder, Suzy wondered if she was alone in the house. She'd been upstairs for hours. Leo and the landscaper were probably long gone by now. Not wanting to get his head bitten off — again — Leo had clearly thought better of venturing upstairs to say good-bye.

But when Suzy reached the kitchen, she saw him sitting at the scrubbed-oak table with his long legs stretched out in front of him, drinking coffee and studying the plans left by the landscape gardener.

"Oh." She hesitated in the open doorway. "I didn't know you were still here."

"Why? Were you hiding up there until I'd gone?"

"No."

Leo tapped his own cup. "Coffee?"

"No." Suzy shook her head. All she wanted to do now was get home. She needed a long bath, a massive glass of wine, and a jolly good cry.

"Kettle's just boiled," said Leo. Almost smiling, he added, "I'd be more than happy to lend you some of my milk."

Something inside Suzy went snap.

"Look, will you *please* stop humoring me?" she bellowed. "I've spent the whole of today being a bad-tempered bitch, OK? I know I have, and you know I have, so all this offering-me-cups-of-coffee stuff is just getting on my *nerves*. I mean, what is it, Be Nice to Suzy Day and nobody remembered to tell me?"

There, if that didn't get a reaction, nothing would. She felt that pressure-cooker sensation welling up again inside her rib cage. Her hands were on her hips, her fingers digging into the leather of her jeans. Every muscle in her body felt as taut as a coiled spring. Any minute now, Suzy realized, she was in danger of going *boiiing,* like Tigger.

"OK," said Leo, "if you want to put it like that. It is Be Nice to Suzy Day."

"Ha! Be *Unnaturally* Nice."

He shrugged. "It's a rotten job."

"But somebody's got to do it, and you drew the short straw? Oh, bad luck," jeered Suzy.

"I meant having to clear out the house. Sorting through your mother's possessions." Leo remained calm. "It's an emotional experience. You're bound to be upset."

Opening her mouth to protest, Suzy abruptly closed it again.

Was that it? Could that really be the reason she'd spent the day feeling so awful?

Oh no, surely not. It *couldn't* be that.

"I'm not upset. I'm absolutely fine," Suzy declared frostily. "Why should clearing out my mother's things be an emotional experience? Heavens, it's not even as if we were that close!"

Her voice sounded high-pitched and weird. How embarrassing. Desperate to make a quick getaway, Suzy scanned the kitchen in search of her car keys.

"The reason I stayed on this afternoon is that Roger found something in the garden," said Leo, "while he was checking the quality of the soil. It was buried over there." He pointed through the kitchen window. "Beneath that peony."

Hair like orange cotton candy and a name like Roger, thought Suzy, distracting herself for a second or two. *Crikey, how unlucky was that?*

She knew at once, of course, what Roger had found. Earlier, she hadn't been able to work out why his digging with the spade had triggered off such a sensation of familiarity. Now it came flooding back.

"So what did he unearth?" Beneath her air of flippancy, Suzy's heart was clattering like a giant maraca. "Severed arm? Hidden treasure? Blue-and-gold cookie tin with a picture of a peacock on the lid?"

Swiveling around in his chair, Leo reached for the blue-and-gold tin.

"I didn't know what might be in it," he told Suzy. "So I had a quick look."

He held the tin out to her and she took it, placing it carefully on the kitchen table. Most of the mud had been washed off. The blues and golds were faded and mottled with rust but still instantly identifiable.

Suzy knew exactly what she would find inside. A thin leather dog's collar and leash. A ponytail of her own hair. Photographs cut from magazines, of her favorite pop stars. Photographs of herself, aged ten or eleven — with, needless to say, brutally short hair and a tearful expression. Several broken pieces of cheap jewelry. And, last but not least, a plastic-covered Duran Duran diary.

"I can't believe he found it." Suzy sat down on one of the kitchen chairs with a wobbly smile and a bit of a bump. "I mean, it's not even as if it's a small garden. Of all the sections of earth he could have prodded with his metal rod" — she made a feeble stab at humor — "he had to prod that one."

Leo's smile, understandably, was brief. "Why did you bury it?"

"Posterity." As she spoke, Suzy was already easing off the airtight lid. Everything was there, carefully wrapped in plastic bags, just as she remembered. "I think I got the idea from some kids' TV show. You bury a time capsule, and hundreds of years later, someone comes along and finds it and is enthralled to discover what it was like to be a belligerent teenager in the nineteen eighties."

"Look, I could pretend I didn't open your

diary," said Leo, "but I'm not going to. I needed to find out who it belonged to."

Suzy unwrapped it with trembling fingers. "Did you read every word?"

"Just the first page. Which pretty much said it all. Shall I make that coffee now?"

Miles away — *years* away — Suzy nodded and turned to the first page, the one Leo had already read.

This diary belongs to Suzy Curtis, age 11, Sheldrake House, Sneyd Park, Bristol, England.

January. I don't think my mother loves me. She was here for Christmas, but on Boxing Day, she went again. To Hong Kong for two weeks. I miss her, and I love her, but she can't miss me or she wouldn't go.

And I didn't get a dog for Christmas like I asked for, so spending my pocket money on the leash and collar was a big waste. And my hair looks awful since bloody Julia cut it. If Mummy were here, she could have taken me to the proper hairdressers. I look stupid with short hair, and now everyone is going to laugh at me —

Reaching the end of the page, Suzy realized she couldn't bring herself to read any more. Her throat thickened with tears, the eleven-year-old handwriting dissolved and danced before her eyes, and an undignified sob broke the silence in the kitchen.

Honk.

Good grief, she sounded like a goose laying an egg.

HOOONK.

An egg the size of a watermelon.

HONK, HONK, WAAHAAHAAA!

It really was the most appalling noise, but she was powerless to prevent it happening. In a way, it was such a relief to let it all out that she didn't even care.

Suzy had no idea how long she sat there bawling her eyes out like a two-year-old and making a total spectacle of herself. In the background she was dimly aware of Leo, wisely leaving her to get on with it. He moved around quietly, making the coffee, tidying up, and locating a clean tea towel. When Suzy's one and only tissue had been shredded into oblivion, he handed her the tea towel — thankfully one of those soft, absorbent ones, not horrid scratchy Irish linen.

At long last the worst of it was out of her system, the torrent of tears having given way to sniffly hiccups and the occasional shuddering sob. Suzy, immediately regretting the outburst, stood up and went over to the window so she could pretend to be looking out over the garden rather than be forced to meet Leo's unnerving gaze.

Taking a deep breath, she said brightly, "Well, gosh, I think I had a bit of a delayed reaction thing back there. I promise you, I had no idea that was going to happen!"

She couldn't see Leo, but she knew where he was. Behind her, standing by the dresser, roughly fifteen feet away.

"I'm glad it did happen," said Leo.

"Such a girly thing to do, blubbering like that. I'm so sorry —"

"Suzy, there's nothing to be ashamed of. You mustn't apologize."

He was closer now. At a guess, nine or ten feet away. The backs of Suzy's knees began to tremble.

This is like the game we used to play at primary school . . . Grandmother's Footsteps . . .

"I'd forgotten all about that tin, you know. I hardly ever think about the past. I suppose that's why it caught me by surprise; everything came back with a bit of a whoosh."

"I think you needed to do it," Leo told her. "In fact, I'm sure you did. Bottling things up isn't the answer."

Five, six feet away?

Suzy's spine was fizzing like 7UP. She closed her eyes. "I didn't cry when she died."

Silence. She had absolutely no idea how far away Leo was from her now.

I'm going to feel like such a twit if I turn around and find he's gone home.

And then she felt it, the faintest glimmer of warm breath on the back of her neck.

I can't say it, I can't say it . . .

But she knew she must.

"I must be such a horrible person," Suzy muttered, covering her eyes and realizing that the tears hadn't finished with her yet. "Oh God, I'm s-so, so ashamed of myself . . ."

The next moment Leo's arms had enfolded her like a blanket. His mouth inches from her ear, he murmured, "You don't have to be ashamed. Lots of people can't cry straightaway."

"It's n-not that." Glancing down, Suzy saw his hands around her waist, clasped together just beneath her rib cage. As she watched, two hot tears slid down her cheeks and landed like raindrops on his tanned wrist.

"OK." Leo paused. "Did you murder her?"

"No."

"Well, that's good. So what have you done to be so terribly ashamed of?"

Another tear dropped onto the thumb of his left hand.

Then another, and another.

"I'm j-jealous of Lucille." Suzy hung her head. There, it was out. She'd said it at last. She was officially a mean and despicable person.

Now he'll really *hate me.*

"Go on," Leo prompted.

At least he hadn't given her a disgusted whack on the head with the soggy tea towel.

"I know how awful that sounds," Suzy muttered. "I mean, we were the ones who grew up in the big house in Sneyd Park and went abroad for our vacations. Lucille didn't have any of that. She didn't even have a full-time mother, for heaven's sake. But . . . but at least she understood why Blanche couldn't always be there, and she knew Blanche loved her." Oh, this was hard. Biting her lip, Suzy forced herself to go on. "All the time I was growing up, I could sense that my mother was on edge. She did her best to be cheerful, but really she was just doing her duty, counting the days before she could disappear abroad on another of her jaunts. Except now I know it wasn't that at all. She was counting the days until she could be with William and Lucille again, like . . . like . . ."

"Yes?" Leo hadn't moved; he was still holding her.

Suzy sighed. "Like when you're seven and you know you have to finish your vegetables before you're allowed any pudding."

"And you were one of the vegetables?"

"Not even the sweet corn or the asparagus," she said miserably. "I was probably the cabbage. Don't laugh. This isn't meant to be *funny.*"

"I wasn't laughing," Leo promised, turning her around to face him. The corners of his mouth twitched. "Well, not at the way you felt. I just had a mental picture of you sitting on a dinner plate covered in gravy."

"Huh, thanks a lot," said Suzy, miffed.

"Seriously," said Leo, "I can understand why you might feel like that. But you really mustn't."

"Do you hate me now? For being jealous of Lucille?"

He gazed down at her for a long moment. "I don't hate you at all."

Hypnotized by his mouth, Suzy realized that — *help!* — it was moving closer. He was going to kiss her. His hands were moving up her back, and, oh yes, he was definitely going to kiss her . . .

CHAPTER 41

In the nick of time, Suzy realized what was happening. Damn Leo Fitzallan. It was nothing but a trick, yet another underhanded attempt to catch her out and prove what a heartless two-timing hussy she was.

Like a boxer in the ring facing a lethal left hook, Suzy ducked out of range. Deftly breaking the circle of his arms, she shrieked, "Good grief, is that the time? I promised Maeve I'd be back by five. She'll be wondering where I've gotten to! Now, where did I put my car keys?"

"Suzy —"

"I'll take this home with me too." Still gabbling, Suzy reached across the kitchen table for the blue-and-gold tin and squashed the incriminating Duran Duran diary into it before forcing the lid on. "Oh, phone . . . Hello? Yes? Can I help you?"

Too flustered to realize that the ringing cell phone she'd picked up was Leo's and not hers, Suzy was taken aback when a fuzzy but astonished-sounding female voice said, "I'm sorry, who's speaking please?"

For a split second she couldn't think. Then it came back to her.

"Suzy Curtis of Curtis and Co. If this is a property inquiry —"

"Suzy, *hi*! It's Gaby," the fuzzy female voice exclaimed delightedly. "What are you doing answering Leo's phone?"

What?

"Oh! God, sorry, I thought it was mine! Hang on." Suzy felt a rush of color sweep like a tidal wave up her neck. "He's right here. I'll pass you over —"

"No need," Gaby cut in cheerfully. "I've worked it out now. You're both still over at the house. Look, I'm on the train. I just called to let Leo know we'll be pulling into Temple Meads in five minutes, so if he could come pick me up, that'd be great. If he's too busy, I can get a cab."

"No, no, he's not too busy." Suzy looked at Leo, who was still standing over by the window. Imagine if she hadn't dodged out of the way in time; he'd still have been busy kissing her senseless when the phone had begun to ring.

And unlike Harry, who was only a pretend fiancé, Gaby Price was the Real Thing.

"Sure?" said Gaby. "Because it's no problem, if you've still got stuff to do."

"Absolutely sure," Suzy replied firmly. "We're finished here anyway. He'll meet the train."

"There won't be anywhere to park." Leo's tone was brusque. "Tell her to wait outside, next to the taxi stand."

"Didn't you ever see *Brief Encounter?*" said Suzy. "Don't be so lazy. Meet her on the platform. Far more romantic."

Rory phoned Suzy at home on Sunday evening on the pretext of needing to check that the sale of a rather glamorous house in Leigh Woods was still going through.

"Of course it's going through. They're closing on Wednesday. You *know* that."

"Just double-checking," Rory said briskly. "I took a call from a client who was interested in the property."

"Well, he can't have it. Tell him to choose another one."

"Right. Fine. Oh — how's Fee, by the way?"

Subtle or what? Rory thought with a surge of triumph. He'd managed to slip the question in as a kind of ultracasual afterthought. To hear him, no one would ever guess he'd spent the last two hours practicing those exact words in front of a mirror.

"Fee? She just called. Her mum's OK, but she's definitely going to be stuck down there for the next few weeks."

The next few weeks. Suzy made it sound like nothing at all. As far as Rory was concerned, it was a disaster, like having your jaws wired together without warning and being casually informed by the surgeon that you wouldn't be able to eat solid food for the next few months.

"Anyway," Suzy went on, "tell me how it went."

"What?"

"Your relaxation weekend. I want to hear all about it!"

For a split second, Rory hesitated. Should he tell the truth or attempt the bluff? Except he was the world's most hopeless liar, and whenever he tried it, he was always caught out.

Usually by Suzy.

"I didn't go."

"Oh, you're kidding!" Suzy wailed. "Why not?"

Because I couldn't face turning up on my own, Rory longed to blurt out, *because I'd have found it too* stressful. *And I only ever agreed to try it in the first place so I could go with Fee.*

But since he certainly couldn't admit that to Suzy — he was thirty-four years old, for heaven's sake — he said vaguely, "I had things to do. Paperwork to catch up on."

"You mean you couldn't be bothered," Suzy declared crossly. "Oh well, that's just fabulous. Thank you so much for letting me know."

Startled, Rory said, "Why? What difference would it have made to you?"

"Quite a lot, as it happens," Suzy yelled into the phone. "Because I spent the whole day sorting out Mum's stuff, and a helping hand would have been nice, but oh no, Julia was too busy, Lucille was too busy, and —"

"You didn't ask," said Rory, bewildered.

"Because I thought you were *away in Wales!*"

"Look, I'm sorry, but you aren't being fair —"

"Aren't I? Aren't I? So just how fair do you think it is, leaving *me* to do *everything* myself?" Suzy was shrieking now, her rising voice doing painful things to his telephone ear. Taking a step back, unaware that his other foot was resting on the telephone cord, Rory unknowingly yanked the connector out of the wall.

The phone went dead, and he heaved a sigh. Suzy was in a major fit and had

505

slammed down the receiver. Typical of his volatile younger sister to overreact.

Oh well, maybe it was for the best, Rory decided as he hung up. Give her a chance to sleep on it. Dramatic and over-the-top Suzy might be, but at least she wasn't the kind to hold a grudge. By tomorrow morning, with any luck, she'd be fine, back to her usual sunny-natured, happy-go-lucky self.

"I don't believe it," squealed Suzy, staring at the receiver in disbelief. "You utter, utter bastard. How *could* you?"

"How could I what?" Harry called through from the sitting room. "What have I done now?"

"Not you. My brother." Suzy dialed Rory's number, got a busy signal, and realized he was deliberately leaving the phone off the hook. "Bloody hung up on me!"

"My brother hung up on you?"

"No. *My* brother." Despairingly, Suzy pushed her fingers through her hair. What a rotten, lousy day. It surely couldn't get any worse.

"I had a call too, this afternoon," said Harry. "From Terence DeVere."

Suzy, reappearing in the sitting room, said, "Who?"

Harry gave her a how-could-you-have-forgotten look.

"From *Hi!* magazine. They want to know when they can start making the wedding arrangements."

The day *could* get worse, Suzy discovered.

"He phoned you on a *Sunday*?"

Harry shrugged. "They need to firm up the details."

"Go away." Suzy groaned, covering her eyes in despair. "Leave me alone. I don't need this right now."

"But —"

"No, don't. Stop pressuring me." Her voice rose. "I've got a *headache.*"

Sleep was like public transport, Suzy deduced several hours later. It never came along when you were most desperate for it.

She was still awake — and hot and irritable to boot — when Lucille came creeping in at two o'clock in the morning.

Lucille was doing her best to be quiet, but every creaking floorboard sounded like a clap of thunder to Suzy's *en pointe* ears.

"You sound like a baby elephant crashing around," she declared crossly as Lucille attempted to creep around the sofa on the way to her room.

"Sorry, sorry. I was trying not to wake you up."

"Well, you did." In a big huff, Suzy rolled over onto her side, losing most of the duvet on the way.

"Here, I've got it. Let me tuck you in." Lucille bent over apologetically and hauled the sliding duvet back over Suzy's bare legs. "I didn't mean to be so late. We were just having the most amazing session! Jaz wrote another song today. Honestly, you *must* hear it . . ."

"Oh, must I, really?" parroted Suzy, amazed by Lucille's self-centered attitude. Had it not even occurred to her that while she was closeted away in Jaz's recording studio, other people might *not* have been having the best time of their lives?

"What? What's wrong?" Sensing that something was up, Lucille finished tucking the side of the duvet into the gap between the sofa cushions then stepped back, her forehead creased with concern.

"Wrong? Why would anything be wrong?" demanded Suzy. "I spent the day sorting through *our* mother's belongings while you were closeted away with *my* ex-husband. I mean, it's lucky I'm not the suspicious type, isn't it? Otherwise, we could almost see some kind of pattern emerging here."

Even as the words were spilling from Suzy's mouth she was hating herself for even thinking them. But it had been that kind of day. She couldn't *not* say what was uppermost in her mind.

"I don't know what you mean." Lucille sounded startled.

"Oh, I think you do. After all, it's pretty obvious, isn't it? You made Blanche love you more than she ever loved me, and now you're doing the same thing all over again with Jaz."

There were no lights on in the living room, but even in the dim amber glow of the street lamp outside the window, Suzy could see Lucille's eyes widen in dismay.

"That's not true!"

"Isn't it?" Despising herself for being like this but quite unable to stop now, Suzy lifted her head from the pillow. "Well, that's what it looks like to me."

Lucille gasped, clutching her chest. "I can't believe you think that. Blanche didn't love me more than she loved you!"

Suzy's lower lip began to tremble. She bit it, hard.

"If it hadn't been for you, she wouldn't have spent her whole life disappearing for weeks on end."

She wasn't going to cry. She *wasn't*.

"This isn't fair." The multicolored beads rattled in Lucille's hair as she shook her head.

"Why isn't it fair? I've just spent the shittiest day ever, clearing out *our* mother's house . . . and where were you? Cozily tucked up with *my* ex-husband, that's where!"

"Oh, come *on*." Lucille's voice rose. "You make it sound as if we've spent the day in bed! It's not like that at all and you know it!"

"Jesus, what's going *on* here?" The bedroom door flew open and Harry appeared in the doorway, naked apart from a pair of black boxer shorts and leaning heavily on one crutch. "Do you two have any idea how much noise you're making?"

"Don't look at me," Suzy retorted hotly. "It's not my fault. She's the one who's just crept in at two o'clock in the morning because it's taken her this long to peel herself away from Jaz."

"We've been RECORDING A SONG," bellowed Lucille.

"HA!"

"It's OK, just ignore her." Harry rolled his eyes sympathetically at Lucille. "She's been in a pissy mood all night. I tried to ask her a perfectly reasonable question earlier

510

about our wedding, and she almost ripped my head off."

Suzy stared at them both. They were ganging up on her. It was outrageous.

"Oh well, that's hardly the surprise of the century, is it?" she drawled. "I might have guessed you two would stick up for each other. In fact, here's an idea." She sat bolt upright again, unaware that with her hair sticking out all over her head she looked like an indignant parakeet. "First you took my mother, then you started spending practically *every* waking second with my ex-husband . . . so, may as well go for the hat trick, don't you think? Please, help yourself, feel free to have sex with *my* fiancé . . . on *my* bed . . ."

In the dim recesses of her mind, Suzy was aware that she'd gotten completely carried away. For heaven's sake, Harry hopping into bed with another woman would be the answer to all her prayers.

Except, hang on . . . Why *should* it have to be the answer to her prayers? Only some bizarre, totally misguided sense of loyalty had gotten her into this ridiculous mess in the first place. Harry had bamboozled her into going along with the engagement, hadn't he? And she didn't actually *owe* him anything, did she? Bloody hell, all she needed to do was straighten her shoulders, stick out her chest, and tell him to take a running leap.

Metaphorically speaking, of course.

I'll say it. I'll say it right now. I'll —

"Fine." Lucille interrupted her triumphant train of thought. "If that's the way you feel, I'll move my stuff out in the morning."

"Fabulous," said Suzy, stunned but at the same time damned if she was going to start backing down now.

Mother stealer.

"You don't mean that," Harry announced, hobbling toward her.

"I do. And I'm not going to marry you either, so you may as well call that ridiculous magazine of yours and tell them the wedding's off."

"See what I mean?" Harry turned to Lucille with a long suffering expression. "This is the kind of mood she's been in all night."

CHAPTER 42

Lucille had missed her vocation, Suzy discovered the next morning. She should have been in the Special Air Service.

It was six thirty, still pitch-black outside, and Lucille's bedroom was empty. Her belongings, neatly packed and ready to go, were stacked by the door. There was no sign of Lucille, which Suzy frankly found hard to believe. Having spent most of the night tossing and turning on the sofa, too guilty to sleep, she had deliberately waited until now to say sorry because waking up Lucille at some totally unearthly hour would really be rubbing salt into the wound.

Except Lucille had already crept out, as silent as a ghost, at the crack of goodness knows when.

More silent than a ghost, in fact, because didn't ghosts normally flap their white sheets and go *WOO-HOO*?

It was annoying, plucking up this much

courage to apologize to an empty bedroom.

Luckily, Lucille's dog-walking timetable was still there in the kitchen, pinned up on the corkboard.

Outside it was bucketing down with rain. Suzy, making a dash to the car twenty minutes later, reflected that this was definitely the downside to owning dogs. No matter how diabolical the weather, they still wanted to be out in it. Like small children, they just didn't care. As far as dogs were concerned, a torrential downpour just added to the fun.

The Downs were pretty much deserted. It didn't take long for Suzy to spot Lucille jogging along Julian Road toward her with a sopping wet Afghan hound bounding joyfully at her side.

Buzzing down the window, Suzy stuck her head out of the car and yelled, "Luce, it's me. I'm sorry. I can't believe I was so horrible last ni—"

Lucille, her unsmiling face illuminated by the car's headlights and her eyes pointedly *not* making contact with Suzy's, jogged straight past her.

Suzy swiveled around in her seat, her mouth dropping open.

You aren't supposed to do that.

Wrenching open the door, she jumped out

onto the pavement, but Lucille — with the dog in tow — was now sprinting toward the Downs. Suzy knew she'd never catch up to them.

Not on foot, anyway.

Oh well, in for a penny. Leaping back into the car, Suzy executed a swift three-point turn. Accelerating to the end of Julian Road, she crossed Rockleaze — *no cars coming, phew* — drove up onto the grass, and set off across the Downs in pursuit of Lucille.

Highly illegal, of course. If the police caught her, she'd be ticketed for sure. But at least this way there was no escape for Lucille.

Suzy caught up with them in no time at all.

"Go away," shouted Lucille as she pulled alongside them.

"I want to say sorry."

"Well, I don't want to hear it. I don't want to see you."

"Please," Suzy begged, "I feel terrible. At least listen to me."

"No."

"Please."

"Give me one good reason why I should."

"Because I'm an idiot."

"Huh," said Lucille, "I already knew that." She veered abruptly away from the car and

Suzy slammed on the brakes. Clearly, different tactics were called for.

Bribery . . . blackmail . . . abduction . . . ? Yep, they'd do.

Rummaging through the glove compartment, Suzy found the family-size bag of M&Ms she'd stashed away for emergencies, and tore the packet open. Pushing open the driver's door, she rattled the bag of chips into her upturned palm. Fifty feet away, the Afghan hound's ears pricked up.

"Here, boy. Over here. Yum, *chips,*" Suzy called out.

Lucille, who had only just let the dog off his leash, said firmly, "Carter, sit. *Stay.*"

Carter hesitated, hopelessly torn. He knew and liked Lucille, but she couldn't seriously expect to compete with the prospect of chips. "Carter, come on, boy. See what I've got," Suzy wheedled, rattling the chip bag seductively.

Carter looked like a girl caught in a downpour with her boring boyfriend, being offered a lift home by a charmer in a Ferrari. The next moment, he was bounding across the grass toward Suzy, with his pink tongue lolling and his plumy tail wagging like a metronome.

"No!" Lucille shouted, chasing after him.

Yesss, thought Suzy triumphantly, bundling him into the passenger seat and feeding him a big handful of chips.

By the time Lucille reached the car, Suzy had hit the central-locking buttons.

"You can't do this," she warned Suzy through the open driver's window.

"Too late. Just have."

Lucille's hands were on her hips. Her face was expressionless. "I suppose you think you're clever."

"I do, quite," said Suzy.

"This is kidnapping."

"I know. Good, isn't it?" Suzy risked a smile that wasn't returned. "Oh please, Luce, I've got the dog. You have to listen to me now."

"As far as I'm concerned," Lucille said coldly, "you've already said more than enough."

Realizing she couldn't do this through a car window, Suzy unlocked the doors, leaped out, and promptly locked them again. The icy rain hit her in the face like a wet haddock.

"Right, here we go," she announced. "I acted like a ten-year-old yesterday and I'm *totally,* totally ashamed of myself. Seeing all my mum's stuff again had a horrible effect on me. I'm sorry I said what I did. I never meant any of it. And I couldn't bear it if you moved out. I know we're still a bit new to each other, but you're my sister and I love you. And I'm really really really sorry I'm such an enormous idiot."

"Well, you're definitely one of those," said Lucille. Shivering, she pushed her hands deep into the pockets of her unglamorous waterproof jacket.

"Blanche spent her life lying to us." Suzy struggled to explain. "She didn't lie to you. Yesterday when I was clearing out her things, I just felt . . . stupid, I suppose. Like one of those women who finds out her husband's been having a torrid affair for the last twenty years."

There was a long pause.

Finally, Lucille said, "I can understand that." Slowly, she added, "But it wasn't my fault."

Encouraged by this, Suzy said eagerly, "I know, I know it wasn't! I got myself into a state, that's all. Honestly, I could have cut out my tongue when I realized how —"

"And I'm not after your ex-husband."

"I know that too. I never for one minute thought you were," cried Suzy, blinking the rain out of her eyes and realizing that she was wearing hopelessly inappropriate clothes. Her navy wool sweater was drenched and itching unbearably, and her jeans were sodden. She'd be more comfortable stripping down to her bra and panties, except Lucille thought she was quite mad enough already.

"Are you crying?" demanded Lucille.

"What? Me? Of course not!"

Suzy hastily wiped her face before Lucille could do a random testing for saltiness.

"You are."

"Don't be daft. I never cry. You're crying." She pointed an accusing finger at Lucille.

Lucille managed a wobbly half smile.

"No I'm not. Do you really love me?"

Unable to speak, Suzy pressed her lips together and nodded.

"So was that one of those sister-sister arguments you warned me about?"

"Kind of. It's one of those sister-sister arguments you get when one of the sisters is a total crazy."

"That's you," Lucille double-checked. "Not me."

"Oh yes. Definitely me."

Suzy gave her a hug, and Lucille hugged her back.

"If anyone's watching us now" — Suzy's voice was muffled — "they're going to think we're barking mad."

"Never mind them. I think we're barking

mad." Lucille smiled and wiped her eyes again. For someone who insisted she wasn't crying, she certainly wiped her eyes a lot.

"Coming home?"

"I still have a dog to exercise. He's hardly lifted a paw so far." Lucille glanced ruefully over her shoulder at Carter, his long, aristocratic nose pressed against the window of the Rolls as if he was supposed to be there. "Anyway, you still have a fiancé to apologize to."

"What?"

"Harry, remember? You told him last night you weren't going to marry him. Just after you suggested I might like to sleep with him."

Oh Lord.

Suzy made up her mind. It was definitely time to come clean.

Jaz was laughing so much he almost fell off his chair.

Waiting patiently for him to finish — and heroically resisting the impulse to stab him with her fork — Suzy said, "It's not funny, you know."

"Oh, it is, it is." Tears of laughter were actually rolling down Jaz's face. Waving his hand at Maeve he gasped, "Quick, give me some of those paper towels."

"It isn't funny." Lucille tried to make Jaz understand. "Poor Harry, he's going to be devastated when Suzy tells him. He really loves her."

"He'll get over it." Jaz's shoulders began to shake again. "Which is more than I will! I mean, who'd have thought it? Suzy Curtis, scared of nothing and no one, somehow manages to get herself accidentally engaged and can't think of a way of backing out of it because she doesn't want to hurt this bloke's feelings . . . oh, this is priceless!"

Suzy put down her fork, just to be on the safe side.

"That's the trouble, though, don't you see? It isn't priceless," she explained. "We're talking about a deal worth two hundred and fifty thousand pounds."

"Oh well, marry him then," Jaz mocked. "Then you'll be able to put Occupation: Gold Digger on your passport."

"Idiot!" wailed Suzy. "*I* don't want the money!"

"It's complicated," said Lucille, who knew only too well about Harry's feelings of second-bestness where Leo was concerned.

Maeve, holding up a huge bowl of kedgeree, announced, "Can't concentrate on an empty stomach."

Harry might not know it, but this was set

to be one of the more memorable days of his life. Suzy, the one about to make it memorable, was ashamed to discover she was ravenous. Somehow, losing her appetite seemed the least she could do to make up for inflicting so much misery.

"Anyway," Suzy went on, when everyone around Jaz's kitchen table had their plates full, "it isn't just the Leo thing. If the *Hi!* deal doesn't happen, those two children won't get their trip to Disneyland."

"Give me strength!" Jaz rolled his eyes in disbelief. "So *that's* why you can't bring yourself to call off the wedding? How much were they expecting out of it?"

"Ten grand."

"Mad." Shaking his head, Jaz pushed back his chair and left the kitchen. "Completely mad."

"So now you know," said Suzy, to Lucille and Maeve. "If you ever need to confide in a man, pick someone really sympathetic and understanding. Like Donald Trump."

Jaz was back in less than a minute. He put the check down on the kitchen table next to Suzy's plate of kedgeree. It was made out to her, for ten thousand pounds.

"There. Does that solve your problem?"

Lucille knew it was rude to stare, but she couldn't help it. As far as Jaz was concerned, ten thousand pounds was nothing. Loose change, practically.

Heavens, how must that feel?

"I don't want this." Suzy heaved a sigh of frustration. She hated it when Jaz did his flamboyant I'm-so-rich bit.

"You don't want those kids to miss out," Jaz told her reasonably. "Why can't I help?"

"Because it's not your problem! Look, *I'll* make sure the kids don't miss out."

Jaz knew perfectly well that Suzy wasn't one of life's natural scrimpers and savers — she spent money as flamboyantly as she dressed.

"Fine," he said easily. "Do you actually *have* ten grand lying about?"

"She's ten grand pairs of high-heeled shoes scattered around her bedroom," chuckled Maeve. "And some grand designer outfits hanging up in that closet of hers, that's for sure."

"Ha-ha." Suzy groaned. Honestly, for someone who not so long ago had been swooning over Harry in dramatic fashion, Maeve was taking all this with remarkable calmness.

"She has seven hundred and thirty pounds in her bank account," Maeve supplied helpfully. "And a few odd pence. I saw this month's statement in the fruit bowl when I popped over the other day to take Harry a thermos of soup."

"Ah," said Jaz, "but has she been shopping since then? Come to think of it, didn't I spot a couple of Donna Karan shopping bags, on Saturday, in the backseat of her car?"

"OK, OK, I'll *borrow* it." Suzy sighed, picking up the check. Folding it in two, she slid it into the pocket of her lime-green shirt. "Leo closes on Sheldrake House next week. As soon as the money comes through, I'll be able to pay you back."

"Oh God, I hope —"

"What?" Suzy said as Lucille stopped abruptly and clapped a hand over her mouth. "Oh God you hope what?"

Lucille vigorously shook her head. "No, it's all right. I'm sure that wouldn't happen."

"Aaargh!" wailed Suzy, belatedly realizing what she meant. "You think the sale might fall through! That's it, isn't it? You think Harry might be so furious with me that he'll persuade Leo to pull out?"

"Well, something like that." Lucille pulled a face. "Actually, more along the lines of Leo being so furious he decides to pull out. After all," she ventured cautiously, "you and Leo don't exactly have the smoothest of

524

friendships, do you?"

Bugger bugger bugger. The collapse of a sale was one of Suzy's least favorite things anyway. When the property in question was her own mother's house it just made it worse. She couldn't face starting up the whole grindingly slow process again.

"Don't look at me," said Jaz, signaling despair. "You got yourself into this mess. It's nobody's fault but your own."

"The only reason any of this happened in the first place," Suzy protested, "is because I'm such a kind, good-hearted, and generally lovely person. If I was horrible and mean and didn't care whose feelings I hurt, everything would be fine and I wouldn't be in this mess now."

Jaz gave her a who-are-you-trying-to-kid look. "If you'd been honest in the first place, you wouldn't be in this mess now."

"Oh, come on. You know that's not true! I'm *not* a dishonest person," Suzy wailed.

He narrowed his dark eyes and grinned lazily at her across the table. "So what are you going to do?"

She didn't hesitate for a moment. "Complete the sale of the house first. Then tell Harry it's over."

Jaz drummed his fingers on the tabletop and murmured triumphantly, "Ha."

Remembering the I-win-you-lose gesture of old, Suzy reached across and whacked him on the knuckles, hard, with the back of her fork.

"Ow!"

She broke into a smile. "And that's the other reason I divorced you."

CHAPTER 43

The headquarters of the Kessler Music Company was a square, Victorian redbrick building in Islington, north London.

"This is amazing," breathed Lucille, craning out of the cab window to look at the glittering KMC logo above the front entrance.

"Amazing for you, embarrassing for me." Jaz took out his wallet to pay the driver. "I'm about to meet a load of people I haven't seen for three and a half years. And I've never been here sober. I'm not going to recognize anyone."

"As long as you recognize Jerry Kessler," said Lucille.

He grinned. "Jerry who?"

Hanging back for a few seconds, Lucille watched Jaz push his way through the revolving doors and be greeted like a returning hero. If he couldn't remember the names of the girls behind the reception desk, he gave no sign of it as they rushed out to hug and kiss him and exclaim over how great it was to see him again.

"And still alive," Jaz joked. "Who'd have thought it?"

"You're looking fantastic," one of the receptionists declared, giving him an appreciative once-over.

"Not as fantastic as you," confided Jaz. "Your hair's great. And you've lost weight."

The receptionist hadn't, but this only made her happier. If Jaz thought she looked slimmer, that was all that mattered. God, he was so *nice.*

"Sally's away this week," she gushed. "She's going to be *so* sorry she missed you!"

Sally?

"How *is* Sally?" Jaz said warmly. "Give her my love."

"Well done," murmured Lucille as they were whizzed in the elevator up to the fourth floor. "Who was Sally?"

"God knows." Jaz winked at her. "Probably another long lost ex-wife."

Jerry Kessler reveled in his oddity value. His business brain was Sabatier-sharp, his feel for music instinctive. Over the last fifteen years he had turned KMC into a multibillion-pound business and had signed up some of the coolest bands around. Yet with his ruddy cheeks, shaggy hair, and baggy corduroy trousers he looked more like a jolly farmer than the owner of an ultra-successful record label.

Lucille couldn't believe she was actually here, in his football-stadium-size office, shaking the hand of Mr. KMC himself.

"So you're the one who managed to get Jaz back into that studio of his. Good woman." Jerry Kessler gave her a brisk smile of approval "OK, let's hear this tape."

"It's on DAT." Jaz handed over the tiny, high-quality digital audio tape. "But of course we'd rerecord. I want full orchestral backing on the title song."

"Always so modest, so unassuming." Jerry grinned at him. "Speaking of which, how's Suzy?"

"Trust me, you don't want to hear. Chaos, as ever. Now, honest verdict," said Jaz as the tape slotted into the machine on Jerry's desk.

"Trust *me*," Jerry mimicked. "If this stuff you've written is crap, I'll tell you. No point wasting your time or mine."

Superstitiously, Lucille had persuaded herself that if she dressed up for this meeting, nothing would come of it. In order to fool the jinx, therefore, she had worn a faded gray sweatshirt and a pair of ancient black combats. In fact, compared with Jerry Kessler in his battered check shirt and mud-splattered boots, she looked positively chic.

"Sit down, make yourselves comfortable." He waved them over to a huge bottle-green suede sofa.

"I'm fine, thanks." Lucille couldn't bear to sit. She was far too on edge. She thought Jaz's new songs were amazing, but Jerry's opinion was the one that counted.

Jaz, who until now had seemed ultra-relaxed, shoved his suddenly trembling hands into the back pockets of his jeans and said, "I'd rather stand too."

Jerry switched on the tape, and the opening bars of "Miracle" filled the room.

The next moment Lucille's voice, like melted chocolate, spilled out of the speakers.

I need to let you know
I can't let you go
You leave me with no alternative . . .

She could no longer tell whether it was any good, Lucille realized. Still, at least this time, the tape wasn't warped, and she didn't sound as if she'd been locked in a closet.

■ ■ ■ ■

At six o'clock Jerry Kessler's personal chauffeur dropped them back at Paddington.

"I don't think I need the train," Lucille announced. "If I flapped my arms a bit, I could probably just float home."

Even the train station, busy and grimy and tasting of oil and dust, couldn't dampen her spirits. Jerry had loved — truly *loved* — the new songs. He had loved her voice. He had postponed a meeting and taken them to lunch at San Lorenzo. Then, back at KMC headquarters, he had called Dixon Wright, the director of A&R, into his office to hear the tape. Somehow an orchestra, a recording studio, and a top production team had been booked for tomorrow morning. Mind-boggling amounts of money had been discussed.

"You're back," Jerry had declared, clapping Jaz on the shoulder like a farmer patting a prize heifer.

"Lucille's arrived," Jaz had told him, somehow managing to remain upright.

Catching them completely by surprise, the train back to Bristol had left right on time.

"Hell." Jaz sighed. "Don't these drivers

realize we rely on them being late?"

"We could get a burger or something." Lucille pointed out the stand over to their right. Far too excited to eat at San Lorenzo earlier, she was now ravenous.

"A burger." Jaz looked at her, an odd sensation slowly stirring in his stomach. Not for the first time, if he was honest. And it wasn't hunger for a burger either.

"There's the croissant stall if you'd prefer. If you want to be posh about it." Lucille flashed him a grin.

He liked the way she mocked him. Just like Suzy.

"This is mad." Jaz looked at his watch. "By the time we get home it'll be nine o'clock. We need to be back up here first thing tomorrow morning. Why don't we just book into a hotel?"

"Um . . ."

"You're not eating a cheeseburger and fries. Not today." Jaz shook his head. "I'm sorry, I can't let that happen. We'll stay at the Savoy, have a *decent* dinner, get a proper night's sleep . . . then tomorrow we can be at the studio by ten, all ready to go."

"Um . . ."

"It makes more sense. And I don't have to be back in Bristol tonight," said Jaz. "Do you?"

"No," Lucille managed to say finally. She felt as if she'd been asked a question that was actually much more complicated than it sounded. But that was stupid. *She* was being stupid. Staying in London was a purely practical suggestion. Jaz was right, it made absolute sense.

"So how about it then?"

"OK," Lucille added, "but not the Savoy."

Jaz teased, "Oh God, do you absolutely hate it there?"

"It's not that."

"Don't worry about the bill. My treat."

"I didn't mean that either." Lucille tugged at the frayed hem of her ancient gray sweatshirt. "I'm just not sure they'd let me in."

Somewhere in the distance, a clock was chiming midnight. In the ladies' bathroom of the Savoy Grill, Lucille gazed at her reflection in the mirror.

Her hair was fastened up pineapple style. The gold slip dress shimmered like water as she leaned closer to reapply her lipstick. Blinking, she checked that the gold eye shadow hadn't rubbed off or gone blotchy.

It hadn't. *Hooray.*

Then again, it *was* the most expensive eye shadow she'd ever bought. At twenty-two pounds fifty — *yikes!* — it jolly well should stay put.

As for the dress . . . well, that was entirely Jaz's fault. He was the one who had bundled her out of the taxi on Brompton Road — hooray for Thursdays and late opening — and dragged her through the doors of the exclusive little dress shop with the alarming habit of leaving the price tags off its clothes.

"Honestly, Topshop's fine for me." Her protests had made the sales assistants shudder visibly. Just as well she'd had Jaz with her; otherwise, she'd have been out on her nondesigner ear.

Then again, if she hadn't had Jaz with her, she would never have gone in there in the first place. She'd have gone to Topshop.

"Stop fussing," Jaz had told her when she'd tried to stop him from buying her a pair of shoes. "You can't wear your sneakers with a dress like that."

What's happening to me? thought Lucille, gazing at her reflection now in front of the mirror. *Why do I feel as if I'm about to parachute blindfolded out of a plane?*

More to the point, it's midnight, we've finished dinner, and we're heading up to our rooms for that all-important good night's sleep. So why am I standing here in the ladies' bathroom putting more lipstick on?

And more perfume?

Not to mention mascara?

Oh God. Lucille shook her head at her shameless reflection.

As if she didn't know.

Jaz was waiting for her by the elevators. In Harvey Nichols earlier he had bought — in five minutes flat — a black Versace suit, an orange shirt, and a purple tie. Somehow, they went. Jaz, being Jaz, was able to pull it off. Chiefly because he wasn't the least bit bothered whether he did or not.

The last two and a half weeks had been an incredible experience for Lucille. Being closeted in the studio with Jaz, the two of them working so closely together — and with such intensity — had been a crash course in getting to know him. Music was his passion and his enthusiasm was enthralling. Now that he knew he could produce songs without the aid of his cowriters, Mr. Bushmills and Mr. J. Walker, he was unstoppable. He was like a six-year-old boy discovering he could ride his bike without training wheels. Watching him in action sent shivers of exhilaration down Lucille's spine.

And I helped, I really did. He told me he wouldn't have been able to do it without me.

It had been a fabulous day and an even

more fabulous evening. Throughout dinner they had talked and argued and laughed nonstop. Now, as they made their way up in the elevator, the conversation abruptly dried up.

On the third floor, the walk along the thickly carpeted corridor seemed to go on forever.

Jaz had booked adjoining rooms.

Don't invite me in for coffee, Lucille silently pleaded. *Just don't. And don't start telling me it's been a brilliant evening, because I already know that.*

Jaz didn't say either of these things. He didn't say anything at all, just stood there and looked at Lucille. With such silent intensity she thought she might faint.

Finally, reaching out, Jaz touched her right hand, then lifted it to his lips and briefly — as light as a butterfly — kissed the backs of her fingers.

He did this once, then twice, before releasing her hand, nodding good night and turning to the door of his room.

He unlocked it, went in without looking back, closing the door behind him.

And opened it again, less than a second later.

"It's no good," said Jaz with a sigh. "I can't not do this."

Lucille held her breath, her heart rattling against her ribs like a monkey desperate to get out. As Jaz moved toward her, it all seemed to be happening in slow motion. When he was directly in front of her, their bodies not touching but separated by less than an inch from head to foot, he tilted his own head and kissed her, slowly and with infinite tenderness, on the mouth.

Fireworks were going off under Lucille's skin. Keeping his distance physically — even if the distance was minuscule — meant all the sensations her body was clamoring for were concentrated into that one kiss.

It was the most incredible experience of her life.

Not to mention an utterly brilliant seduction technique.

From that moment, Lucille knew there could be no going back.

It was what she'd longed to happen — and simultaneously dreaded happening — for weeks.

"Sorry," Jaz murmured again against her ultrasensitive mouth. "I couldn't not do it. There's only so much temptation a man can be expected to resist."

Lucille nodded, understanding.

"Right." She stepped back. "Good night then."

Jaz stared at her.

"Just joking," said Lucille with a smile.

CHAPTER 44

A truck beeped its horn on the street outside, and Lucille woke with a start. For a split second she couldn't think where she was. Then it all came back in a rush.

The Savoy.

More to the point, Jaz's room at the Savoy.

And even more to the point, in Jaz's king-size bed.

Oh, crikey, we've gone and done it, thought Lucille. *Um . . . twice.*

Tilting her head to one side, she gazed over at the scarily expensive slip dress, lying like a small gold puddle on the floor a few feet away from her own (embarrassingly inexpensive) panties and Jaz's rumpled orange shirt.

Fancy not even hanging up a dress that had cost more than some people's cars. Now that was definitely a rock-chicky thing to do.

Oh God, we actually did it. And it was out

of this world.

The next moment, two things happened simultaneously to make Lucille feel as if the prison gates were clanging shut on her heart.

First, she remembered — *claaang* — where she'd heard that verdict before. A girly gossip with Suzy, weeks ago, late one night over bowls of eye-wateringly hot chili and a bottle of Bardolino. They'd been talking about men and sex — as you do — and Suzy had confided — again, as you do — that basically, in bed, Jaz had always been pretty spectacular. Her actual words, in fact, had been, "He wasn't just a genius song-writer. When it came to sex, he really was out of this world."

Clang-claaang.

The second thing that happened at that moment — as Lucille was realizing just how pyrotechnically Suzy would react if she ever heard about the events of last night — was that Jaz, still fast asleep, grabbed her by the shoulder and shouted out in a voice hoarse with anguish, "No, Celeste . . . *please don't.*"

The prison gates were still reverberating. Frozen with shame and self-loathing, Lucille lay there rigid until his hand slid off her shoulder and his breathing slowed and grew steady once more. Even in his sleep, his subconscious was worrying away, terrified that this one careless lapse might threaten his relationship with Celeste.

He doesn't want to lose her, thought Lucille. *And he's scared I'll blab.*

Last night had seemed so right. She'd actually thought he'd meant it. But he hadn't; of course he hadn't. All she'd been was a bit of fun, a handy diversion, a meaningless one-off.

And I slept with my sister's ex-husband, Lucille reminded herself, without even considering how she might feel about it.

Except she did know how Suzy would feel about it. She knew only too well.

Oh God, what a mess, mess, mess.

When Jaz woke up an hour later, he knew at once exactly where he was.

But the bed was empty. Lucille had gone. So had her panties, but not the gold dress that was now draped neatly over the back of one of the chairs.

Oh dear, had he been snoring? Not the best of starts.

Unable to remember Lucille's room number, Jaz buzzed reception and asked them to call it for him.

"No reply, sir."

"Try again," said Jaz. "Maybe she's still asleep."

But a cold feeling began to uncurl in the pit of his stomach. Suzy had told him Lucille was a light sleeper. If the phone was ringing, she'd wake up at once.

"Still trying for you, sir. Although . . . are we talking about the young lady with the beads in her hair? Gray sweatshirt, black trousers?"

"That's the one."

"She left the hotel a while ago, sir. I saw her going past the desk at, ooh, around six fifteen."

Jaz looked at his watch. It was now seven o'clock.

"Right. Thanks."

Somehow he knew Lucille hadn't gone out for an early morning jog.

It wasn't supposed to happen like this, thought Jaz.

The phone rang twenty minutes later. Snatching it up, Jaz said, "Lucille, is that you? What the hell do you think you're doing?"

He knew it had to be Lucille. Nobody else would have called him so early; they'd all be asleep themselves.

"I'm sorry. I'm sorry it happened." Lucille's voice was strained. She sounded thoroughly disgusted with herself. "The main thing is, you must never, *ever* tell Suzy or Celeste."

Jaz closed his eyes in despair. "What's it got to do with Suzy?"

There was a brief pause.

"Come on." Lucille sighed. "It's got everything to do with Suzy. We made a big, big mistake, and I can't believe it happened, but it did, and you mustn't let it ruin what you have with Celeste, so just promise me you won't tell Suzy —"

"Hey, no, *you* come on," Jaz said, desperate to find out what was going on before she hung up on him. For the last half hour his brain had been working overtime, and one of the especially hideous possibilities was sounding more and more likely by the second. "What are you saying here — that Suzy actually put you *up to this*?"

Silence.

"Jesus!" howled Jaz. "I don't believe it! Suzy can't stand Celeste; she'd love it if we broke up . . . so she persuaded you to sleep with me . . . ?"

More silence. At the other end of the phone, Lucille marveled at his train of thought. If he seriously thought she would have sex with a man purely because her sister had asked her to . . . well, then that meant he seriously thought she was nothing but a prostitute.

"As far as they're concerned, nothing happened," Lucille repeated evenly. "Tell Suzy I'll be in touch."

"What? You have to come back here." Jaz felt sick. "We're meeting Jerry at KMC at ten o'clock."

"Sorry, you'll have to do it without me. My money's running out. Bye."

"No —"

But it was too late; the line had already gone dead.

"Oh, fucking *hell,*" shouted Jaz, only just managing to stop himself from yanking the phone cord out of the wall.

Jerry Kessler had had his legal team working overtime to draw up the contract. Now it was on his desk, all ready to sign.

"Bit of a problem." Jaz knew he may as well come straight to the point. "Lucille and I had a . . . misunderstanding this morning. She's disappeared."

Jerry wasn't easily fazed. He was used to extravagant shows of temperament. Last year, he'd signed a band so outrageously badly behaved they'd made Oasis look like Trappist monks.

"This is her big chance. She'll change her mind," he told Jaz. "Turn up half an hour late, of course, and need a big fuss made over her, but I'm sure we can manage that." He gave Jaz a jovial clap on the back. "We've had enough practice, eh?"

"That's not Lucille." Jaz knew she wouldn't turn up. It wasn't Lucille's style to change her mind. But there was no alternative other than to wait and hope that — for once — she might.

Ten thirty came and went.

"OK, forget her," announced Dixon Wright, the director of A&R. "Who's the big name around here, anyway? You wrote the song," he told Jaz. "You sing it. We'll sell a million copies."

"Not a chance." Jaz shook his head.

"We will! I guarantee it!"

"I mean I'm not recording the song. I wrote it for Lucille. Either she sings it," said Jaz, "or nobody does."

"Christ." Dixon pressed the intercom and shouted to his secretary outside. "Linda? Bring in that bottle of Bushmills, will you?" Taking out a vast emerald-green hanky, he mopped his sweating forehead. "I need a drink."

An hour later, back in Bristol, Lucille let

545

herself into Suzy's apartment. Suzy was at work, just as she'd expected — and had been banking on — and Harry appeared to be out too. When she called his name and tapped on his bedroom door, there was no response. Relieved that Celeste wasn't there with him — God, how could she ever look Celeste in the eye again? — Lucille moved fast. It took her less than ten minutes to pack a couple of bags. After last Sunday's big fight with Suzy, they were getting used to being hauled down from the top of the closet and stuffed willy-nilly with clothes.

OK done. What next?

In the kitchen, Lucille pulled her dog-walking timetable down from the corkboard, called the owners one after the other, apologized, and explained briefly that she had to go away.

Next, she phoned Leo at the restaurant and apologized even more profusely for letting him down.

"What's this all about?" Leo, bless him, sounded concerned. Then his voice grew taut. "Is it to do with Suzy?"

Feeling mean, Lucille said, "Kind of. She's still upset about Blanche. I think a bit of space would do us both good."

Finally, bracing herself, she called Suzy's cell phone.

"What do you mean, you're leaving?" Suzy sounded astonished. "Why? Oh, for God's sake," she suddenly exclaimed, "don't tell me Jaz made a pass at you!"

Lucille shuddered and closed her eyes. Suzy had the alarming ability to get down to the nitty-gritty in no time at all.

"Don't be daft; of course he didn't make a pass at me. This has nothing to do with Jaz."

"Well, good," Suzy declared. "So *why*, then?"

Phew. She'd lied and gotten away with it. Incredible.

"Look, I think we both need a break, that's all." Even as the words were spilling out, Lucille couldn't believe she was still foisting the blame onto Suzy.

I'm such a horrible person.

"We?" Suzy sounded horrified. "As in us? You and *me*?"

"It's just . . . the whole s-situation," stammered Lucille. "Our mother died. A lot's happened . . . It's changed our whole lives . . ."

"For the *better*," wailed Suzy, sounding desolate. "Oh, Luce, please . . . Is this because of all the stuff I said to you on Sunday? Look, where are you? At the apartment? Just wait there, OK? I'm at Kings-

547

weston Court, but I can be home in five minutes —"

"Don't," Lucille said firmly, "because I'm leaving now."

Out of sheer desperation, Suzy shouted, "But what am I going to do about Harry?"

Poor Harry, Lucille didn't even envy him one bit. Falling for Suzy hadn't been the wisest move he'd ever made. God knows, he didn't deserve to be hurt like this.

"Harry's brilliant," she told Suzy. "I hope you realize how lucky you are."

And before Suzy could splutter a reply, Lucille put down the phone.

The front door slammed, and the apartment subsided into silence once more.

"Has she gone?" murmured Celeste, her voice muffled by the duvet over her head. "Can I come out now?"

Harry lifted the edge of the duvet and grinned down at her, plastered to his side in order to make herself as unnoticeable as possible. As far as he was concerned, Celeste could stay down there just as long as she liked.

CHAPTER 45

"OK, it's safe," said Harry.

"Phew. That was close."

Emerging from beneath the bedclothes with her white blond hair ruffled, Celeste playfully kissed her way up his good arm. "What was Lucille doing back here anyway? I could only hear bits."

"She's quit her jobs and gone," said Harry. "She told Leo the music thing wasn't for her after all; she realized she couldn't go through with it. Basically, she's leaving because of Suzy."

"So Jaz could be back." Celeste yawned and stretched her skinny arms. "I suppose we should get up."

But she didn't move.

It occurred to Harry that Suzy could appear at any moment, but he didn't move either. Instead, tilting Celeste's face so she was gazing into his eyes, he realized how drastically his feelings toward her had altered during the course of the last three weeks.

To begin with, it had been lust, pure and simple. Lust combined with the challenge of discovering just how far you could take things with fractured ribs, a broken arm, and a broken leg.

Actually, it had been incredibly erotic, Harry had discovered. Like being handcuffed to a four-poster and seduced, incapable of putting up any resistance.

But then, basically, it had been fun. Nothing more, nothing less.

The fact that their feelings toward each other had deepened so rapidly had taken them both by surprise.

"I love you," he told Celeste now, and she smiled and stroked his shoulder.

"You say it as if you actually mean it."

"That's because I do mean it."

"Jaz sounds so bored when he says it." Celeste rolled her eyes. "Like when someone comes up to him in the street and tells him they're his greatest fan, Jaz says, 'That's fantastic, thanks a lot.' I've heard him say it a thousand times, and all he's really thinking is, 'How fast can I get away from this person?'"

"I'm not thinking that about you," said

Harry. "If anything, I'm thinking it about Suzy."

There, he'd said it, admitted the truth at last. Suzy, let's face it, had turned out to be something of a disappointment, what with her ludicrous six-weeks-before-sex rule and punishing work schedule.

Harry, accustomed to being pursued by gorgeous females who couldn't wait to get him into bed, had been initially intrigued by Suzy's modus operandi, but it hadn't taken long for the novelty to wear off. In all honesty, he would have dumped her by now if it weren't for the deal with *Hi!* magazine.

"How about you?" He kissed Celeste's smooth forehead. "How are you and Jaz getting on, really?"

It was Harry's question, not the answer, that brought a lump to Celeste's throat. The fact that he was interested enough to ask. That was the brilliant thing about Harry, she had discovered. He actually bothered to listen to you, and he really did care how you felt. Harry gave you his undivided attention too — unlike Jaz, who these days always seemed to be thinking of something else.

Celeste wondered how Suzy would react if she were to walk into the bedroom right now and catch them together. Ha, that'd teach her to be so smug!

"Me and Jaz? Up until you came along, I honestly thought we were fine." As she spoke, a tear ran down Celeste's cheek and plopped onto Harry's chest. "But we aren't fine at all. I've been so bored, without even realizing it. God, there's so much more to life than just being with someone because they've got tons of money."

"Don't cry." Harry hugged her, unbearably touched. "There's no need to cry."

"I'm not upset. I'm happy." Celeste sniffed. "Now that I've found you . . . someone who actually listens to me . . . Oh, Harry," she blurted out. "I'd much rather be with a policeman who loves me than with a rock star who doesn't give a damn."

This was serious, Harry realized. Crikey, this was something neither of them had expected to happen.

And, somehow, it needed to be sorted out.

Preferably, before they were found out.

Closing his eyes, Harry thought hard.

Before this went any further, he had some important phone calls to make.

Maeve wasn't having much luck following what was going on in *EastEnders;* she could hardly make out a word above the din in the kitchen.

"You can't fool me." Suzy pointed an accusing finger across the kitchen table at Jaz, who was busy stirring a cup of black coffee to death. "You did something to make this happen. Either did something or said something. Yesterday Lucille couldn't have been happier. Then she went up to London with you and *bam,* everything changes and Lucille disappears off the face of the earth. I'm telling you, if you were horrible to her or said something vile about her singing —"

"I didn't, OK?" Jaz's dark eyes flashed. "I wasn't expecting this to happen either. Anyway, you said Lucille called you. What did she have to say about it?"

"Just some garbage about realizing she wasn't cut out for the music scene. Which is utter twaddle and makes no sense, because music is her whole life, we *all* know that."

"Maybe she decided she didn't want to get involved because of the drinking and drugs." Jaz made it sound plausible. "Dixon Wright was in the office knocking back the Bushmills and boasting about how many lines of coke he'd done the night before."

"Shhh." Maeve was washing up at the sink, her attention riveted on the portable TV. "They slept together last night and they think no one else knows about it. Hah!" she exclaimed happily, scrubbing away at an oven dish. "Little do they know their secret's about to come out!"

Jaz's intestines squirmed like a nest of snakes before he realized Maeve was talking about *EastEnders.*

Sometimes he could have sworn the woman was a witch.

"There's more to it than that," Suzy insisted, piling sugar into her own coffee. "Lucille's not stupid, she already knows music people do coke. I still think you said something to upset her."

Wishing she'd shut up and stop going on and on about it, Jaz shrugged. "Fine, think what you like."

"Just ignore her," said Celeste, who had been listening from the kitchen doorway. "She's just doing what she always does."

"Look," said Suzy, "this is between me and Jaz."

"And you're telling him it's all his fault that Lucille's disappeared. But it isn't, is it?" Celeste smiled sweetly at Suzy. "Harry told me all about it. He was there this morning when Lucille called you. He heard every word. She said you both needed a break, a breathing space to sort yourselves out and come to terms with the whole Blanche thing. Meaning *you* need to sort yourself out and get over the Blanche thing. So you see?" Celeste turned to Jaz. "It really isn't anything to do with you. It's all Suzy's fault and she's just trying to shift the blame onto someone else, as usual." She swung back to Suzy, enjoying every moment of this. "Because you never can admit you've done anything wrong, can you?"

Oh, and by the way, I'm having the most amazing sex with your precious fiancé.

Massively tempting though it was, Celeste didn't add this last bit.

"Dum de da de da, Dee data," went the *EastEnders* theme tune as the closing credits began to roll.

"Ah, there'll be fireworks, mark my words," chuckled Maeve, "when the rest of the square gets to hear about this."

Douglas Hepworth, Blanche Curtis's lawyer, had every sympathy for Lucille. He couldn't imagine how hard it must have been for her, materializing out of nowhere and having to deal with Blanche's children. He wasn't a bit surprised to hear that sharing an apartment with flamboyant, extrovert, superconfident Suzy Curtis hadn't worked out.

"Completion of the sale is scheduled for the twenty-second," he told Lucille.

Today was the eighteenth.

"Tuesday." Lucille worked it out on her fingers. "So how soon could I get my share of the money?"

"If you like, you can have a check on Tuesday afternoon."

Poor girl, she was clearly desperate.

"I would like." Lucille nodded and managed a brief smile. "Very much. Thank you, Mr. Hepworth."

And beautiful. Stunning, even, with those liquid brown eyes, dazzling white teeth, and astonishing legs.

"No problem. And please, call me Douglas."

If Julia said "I told you so" one more time, Suzy knew she would have to slap her.

Hard.

"Well, what did I tell you?" Julia raised her eyebrows in that Maggie Smith way of hers — only higher class, of course — and tilted her head pityingly in Suzy's direction. "It was bound to happen. All she was ever interested in was the money."

Almost. As good as. But, luckily for Julia, not quite the same words.

Suzy's fingers still itched with longing. Next to her, Rory sensed what she was dying to do and shook his head.

"Do you know where she's staying?" Suzy

asked Douglas Hepworth. Desperate for information, she pleaded, "Can you give me an address?"

"I'm sorry," Douglas replied untruthfully. "All I did was write out the check."

"She got what she came for," Julia said with a tight little smile of satisfaction, "and that was it. I shouldn't think we'll hear from her again."

Oh no, thought Suzy, *and it's all my fault. I did this, I drove Lucille away, and all because I was jealous.*

I didn't mean to do it, honestly.

"I told you so," said Julia. "OUCH!"

Wincing and closing his eyes, Douglas decided that Lucille was best out of it. She deserved better than this.

CHAPTER 46

The sale of Sheldrake House had safely gone through. There was no longer any reason to put off the dreaded deed.

The next morning, feeling horribly guilty, Suzy put it off for a few more hours by volunteering to take Harry along for his three o'clock appointment at Frenchay Hospital to have his casts removed.

He was greeted like the all-conquering hero, of course. As far as the besotted nursing staff were concerned, Harry's absence had merely made their collective hearts grow fonder. In their eyes he still had that dazzling star quality — even if his left leg, minus its cast, was now noticeably paler and weedier-looking than his right.

"That's what five weeks of lying around doing nothing does for you," teased the big blond physical therapist, giving his calf a hearty slap.

"Lying back and thinking of England."

Harry winked at her.

"Exactly. Reduces the muscle bulk." The physical therapist grinned at Suzy. "Don't worry; I've got a million exercises here to get him back up to speed. Then it'll be your turn to lie there shouting instructions."

Suzy laughed, playing along with the charade. If the physical therapist was unattached, maybe *she'd* like to throw Harry onto the nearest bed and put him through his sexual paces.

I don't care who does it, just so long as it's not me!

Having heard that he was in the physical therapist department, Doreen, the devoted receptionist, arrived to kiss Harry's feet. Well, not literally, but if he'd asked her to, she probably wouldn't have said no.

"Look at you," Doreen cried delightedly, blushing as Harry gave her a kiss on the cheek. "Handsomer than ever and twice as charming. I hope you're taking special care of him, dear!"

"Oh yes." Suzy nodded and summoned up yet another cheerful smile. "Extra special care."

"Now, Harry, the committee in charge of organizing the hospital's Autumn Fair met last night." Not interested in Suzy's polite rejoinders, Doreen was already rattling on.

"And we voted unanimously that the person we'd most like to officially open the fair would be you!"

Harry looked suitably modest. "Wow. I'm flattered."

Doreen said eagerly, "So you'll do it then? Oh, that's marvelous!"

"Well" — Harry frowned — "hang on a sec. How much would I get paid?"

The room abruptly fell silent, apart from Doreen's sharp intake of breath. Suzy couldn't bear to look.

"Joke," said Harry, breaking into a grin. "Doreen, of course I'll open the Autumn Fair." He took her pudgy hand and gave it a squeeze. "Seriously, it would be an honor."

After another hour of intensive physical therapy, they headed home.

"Did you mean it about getting paid?" Suzy asked casually as she reversed the Rolls out of its parking space.

"Of course not. I'm doing it for nothing, aren't I?"

"Mmm."

Harry's crutches had been reclaimed by the hospital. He had swapped them for a wooden walking stick to help him get around. As he examined the graffiti on the curved handle he said, "Although I think they could have offered *something*. I mean, if they were getting some professional cricketer in to do it, they'd have to pay them an appearance fee, wouldn't they? Bit of a cheapskate thing to do, if you ask me."

Suzy smiled to herself, glad she'd asked. Now she didn't feel nearly so bad about screwing Harry out of his two-hundred-and-fifty-grand deal with *Hi!* magazine.

"Harry, I'm not going to marry you."

"To be honest," Harry went on, paying no attention, "I think Doreen's got some nerve too, giving me her home address so we'll know where to send the invitation to the wedding. I mean, she just assumed we'd be inviting her, and let's face it, why would we *want* to?"

Suzy stopped the car on Frenchay Park Road.

"There isn't going to be any wedding, Harry. I can't do it."

He stared at her. "What?"

"I'm sorry." Untrue, of course. But polite. "We can't carry on pretending it's going to happen, Harry. Be honest, it was only ever a publicity stunt."

"That's not true."

"It *is* true."

"No." Harry shook his head. "I loved you."

Loved. Past tense. Well, that was an encouraging sign.

"We fancied each other," Suzy corrected. "At the beginning, we fancied each other rotten. I admit that. But, Harry, it was never love."

"And my brother was interested in you too," Harry persisted. "But you were with me, not him."

That had been his chief bargaining point, of course. The Leo factor. Harry had been so desperate to prove that he was on a par with his brother that she had agreed — out of the sheer goodness of her heart — to go along with it.

And I'm a real estate agent, Suzy marveled. *I'm not supposed to be gullible.*

Belatedly, her jaw dropped open. "Leo was . . . what? *Interested* in me?"

"Of course. Couldn't you tell?"

NO.

"Are you sure?" croaked Suzy, suddenly finding herself at a loss for air.

"Come on, of course he was interested. Still, don't be too flattered," Harry drawled, spoiling it all. "It was only because you *were* with me. He'd never have noticed you otherwise."

Ouch. So that was how it felt to be a young snail, brutally crushed by a size-thirteen boot.

"So that's it, is it?" Harry went on. "Us. All over. Kaput."

To be honest, he was taking the news more calmly than Suzy had expected.

"I think so," she said cautiously. "Don't you?"

Harry shrugged. "OK, if that's what you want. I don't know how the kids are going to feel about it."

Mikey and Lauren.

"It's OK." Reaching over for her bag, Suzy pulled out her Rich Bitch checkbook (yes, a present from Maeve) and quickly scribbled out a check for ten thousand pounds. At least thanks to her share of the house sale she hadn't had to use Jaz's money.

"I'll pass it on to their mother," said Harry, folding the check and sliding it into his wallet. He didn't say thank you.

"We'll have to tell what's-'is-name from *Hi!* magazine. Terence DeVere," Suzy remembered with a shudder.

"Don't worry about that. I'll speak to him. Actually, if you could drop me back at my place" — Harry checked his watch — "I'll give him a call from there and sort it all out this afternoon."

Suzy was amazed. She hadn't imagined for a moment that this would be so easy.

And to think she'd been dreading it for weeks!

It was like thinking you were terrified of flying, then finally going up in a plane and discovering it wasn't scary after all.

Restarting the engine, Suzy headed happily up Stoke Lane, passing the imposing castle on the left that had once been part of Stoke Park Hospital.

Phew, all over.

"Thanks," she told Harry with a smile of relief.

"S'OK." He shrugged easily. "It wasn't working; we both knew that. I'm not completely insensitive, you know."

"No." Suzy patted his knee. "Of course you aren't."

Harry caught hold of her hand before she could pull it back. His fingers closed around the glittering Tiffany ring, and in one swift twist it was off.

Holding it up like a winning raffle ticket, he said cheerfully, "May as well have this back too."

Having dropped Harry off at his house in North View, Suzy was frustrated to arrive home and discover that there was no one there to hear her momentous news.

No Lucille.

No Fee.

No anybody.

It was a terrible anticlimax.

Oh well, never mind. She could always go next door and tell Maeve and Jaz.

The next moment, as she was gazing out of the front window, Suzy saw Maeve hurrying down the street in her shiny purple raincoat.

Launching open the sash window, Suzy let out a piercing whistle.

"Oh, hello, love. Can't stop," Maeve called up to her. "I'm on my way to bingo."

Nothing, not a nuclear attack, not even a Chippendale in a G-string, could keep Maeve from her bingo.

Disappointed, Suzy yelled, "Is Jaz at home?"

"Gone to AA, love. Over at Winterbourne. Won't be back for hours."

Bugger.

"How about Celeste?"

This was a severe case of scraping the barrel, but Suzy was bursting to tell someone.

"Haven't seen her all day. Gone shopping, I wouldn't wonder. Bye, love. Must dash."

"Maeve, I did it! I've told Harry the wedding's off . . ."

Suzy's voice trailed away as Maeve disappeared around the corner, desperate not to miss so much as a single game.

At least Donna, in the office the next morning, had the decency to be enthralled. "Gosh, and I thought you two were so perfect for each other."

Smugly, Suzy said, "That's because I'm such a great actress."

"Shame, though. I was looking forward to a good party. And my mum's going to be gutted — she's boasted to everyone that my photo's going to be in *Hi!* Donna Hartley," purred Donna in her best *Hi!* magazine voice, "having freely partaken of the exotic alcoholic beverages at the wedding reception, invites us into her lovely bathroom stall to share the moment when she throws up."

"Hmmm." Suzy tapped her pen thoughtfully against her teeth. "Harry was supposed to call them yesterday to let them know the wedding's off. He didn't come home last night. I hope he didn't forget."

This wasn't quite what she meant; it was hardly something you *could* forget. But Suzy had begun to wonder if Harry might not put it off for a while, in the hope that she might change her mind.

So far, he had taken the news suspiciously well.

■ ■ ■ ■

By lunchtime Suzy could stand it no longer. There was no answer at her apartment, or at Harry's. Going through her purse, she unearthed the gaudily embossed card Terence DeVere had pressed into her hand all those weeks ago at the hospital. Then she dialed his number.

While she waited for the phone to be answered, Suzy unwrapped the hot chicken and mushroom pasty she had picked up from the takeout place around the corner. She had just taken her first mouthful when Terence DeVere answered the phone.

"Suzy who? Oh, *Suzy*! Harry spoke to me yesterday, told me *everything*. Darling, I'm so sorry. How are you?"

Crikey. And to think she'd been expecting him to be annoyed about the deal falling through.

"Absolutely fine, couldn't be better," she said brightly.

Now it was his turn to sound surprised.

"Really? Oh well, jolly good. I have to say, I thought you'd be upset about it, but these things happen, don't they? And I must say, it's a neat twist," he confided happily. "You could almost call it a stroke of genius. Our readers'll love it!"

Puzzled, Suzy gazed down at the pasty in her hand.

"Neat twist?"

"Still getting married, just to a different girl." Terence DeVere was chuckling away. "Classic."

Suzy began to wonder if someone had slipped a hallucinogenic drug into her pasty. Chicken and magic mushroom, perhaps.

"You mean Harry?" she said doubtfully. "Harry's still getting married, but to another girl instead of me?"

What girl?

Oh, good grief, thought Suzy, almost choking on her pasty. *Surely not.*

Surely Harry wasn't marrying Lucille!

"Ummm, well, I assumed you knew." Terence DeVere began to backpedal for all he was worth. "When I spoke to them yesterday, they —"

"Who? *Who's* he going to marry?"

"Ah . . . maybe this is a matter for you to sort out between yourselves . . . Suzy, I'm really sorry. There's a call coming through on my other line . . . Have to go. Bye now!"

CHAPTER 47

It took Suzy less than two minutes to reach
Sian Hill. If Harry and Lucille were getting
married, that was absolutely fine by her. The
reason she was in such a rush to get home
was that Terence DeVere had said he'd
spoken to *them* yesterday, which meant
Lucille might be back . . .

The maroon-and-black moving truck was
parked in front of the house, blocking both
Jaz's driveway and her own. This was pretty
weird, since the few cases Harry had
brought with him would have fit into the
trunk of a car, and Lucille had already taken
her things with her when she'd left.

Then a couple of moving men staggering
under the weight of a glossy fruitwood dining table emerged from Jaz's house, followed by Maeve in her apron and slippers.

No, no, definitely not, thought Suzy, more
mystified than ever. *Not Harry and Maeve.*

Parking farther up the road, Suzy jumped

out of the Rolls and ran back toward the house.

Moments later, Celeste came out carrying a dining chair. Spotting Suzy, she yelled over her shoulder, "She's here."

"Maeve?"

"They're in love, darlin'. What can I tell you?" Maeve gave Suzy's arm a reassuring pat. "There's nothing we can do to stop them."

"Oh, hello," said Harry, next to emerge from the house. He leaned on his walking stick, looking both pleased with himself and handsomer than ever.

Suzy shook her head. "Hang on, hang on, I don't get this. You're marrying Lucille and running off with Jaz's furniture?"

"God, you're thick," said Celeste, handing the chair over to one of the moving men and murmuring something to him under her breath.

"I'm marrying Celeste," Harry announced. "We love each other. This time it's the real thing."

"Great," said Suzy, aware of Maeve's fingers exerting pressure on her arm. "Fine. Um . . . does Jaz know?"

"Not yet."

"Where is he?"

"Where d'you think?" Celeste's tone was

lightly mocking. "AA."

One of Jaz's favorite paintings, meanwhile, was being carried out of the house and down the driveway.

"You can't take that," Suzy protested.

"Can if I want. Anyway, who's even going to notice?" As she spoke, Celeste gently stroked Harry's elbow. "All Jaz cares about these days is his precious music."

"I don't believe this is happening." Suzy was still stunned but not unhappily so. It was the unexpectedness of it that had knocked her so dramatically for a loop.

"Oh, come on," drawled Celeste. "You can't be *that* stupid. What d'you think me and Harry have been doing for the last month — watching TV and playing tiddlywinks?"

Um, well, basically yes.

As one moving man carried out a Tiffany lamp, the second appeared with an armful of bottles.

"Beer's up," he announced to his workmates. Winking at Celeste, he popped the lid off a bottle of Beck's. "Cheers, love. I need this."

"Me too," said Celeste, grinning and reaching for one of the beers. Expertly prying the lid off for her, the moving man was about to hand it over when he was knocked sideways and the bottle abruptly wrestled from his grasp.

"Don't," Suzy shrieked, snatching it away and holding the bottle out of reach. "Don't let her have it! Celeste, you mustn't do this!" Spinning around, she gazed in horror at Celeste, then despairingly at Harry. "For God's sake, are you mad? How can you just stand by while someone tries to give her a drink!"

Not that she liked Celeste, but Suzy couldn't allow the girl to do it to herself. Even she wasn't that heartless.

"Oh, please." Celeste rolled her eyes in amusement. "Don't get your panties in a twist. I'm not an alcoholic, right?"

Oh God, she was in denial. Frantically, Suzy wondered if she should call Jaz or an ambulance or something.

"You are. Celeste, you know you are. Believe me, you can get through this. I'll *help* you —"

"Look, it's nice of you to be so concerned, but you're wasting your time." Snatching the bottle of Beck's from the astonished moving man, Celeste drank half of it down in one go. "You see, I'm really not an alcoholic," she repeated calmly. "I never was an alcoholic. I just pretended to be one to get Jaz to notice me in the first place."

■ ■ ■ ■

"Of course, I suspected they were up to mischief," Maeve admitted later that afternoon when Harry and Celeste had left, "but it wasn't until this morning that I knew for sure."

Jaz still wasn't back. Suzy, dunking fruitcake in her tea, said, "You didn't breathe a word! How could you not tell me if you thought there was something going on between them?"

Maeve shrugged and watched a corner of the cake crumble into Suzy's tea.

"You'd have told Jaz. I didn't want him to know."

Astounded, Suzy said, "Why not?"

"Oh, come on, girl, use your brain. If Jaz had kicked Celeste out, she'd have been after him for millions in . . . ah, now, what's it called, something to do with dog food . . . ?"

"Palimony."

"That's the fellow." Maeve nodded comfortably. "But this way she's run off with another man, so Jaz won't have to pay her a bean."

"You are clever." Suzy was filled with admiration.

"I know I am. Unlike you." Maeve nodded across the table as — *plop* — yet another disintegrating wedge of cake splashed messily into Suzy's cup.

"And Harry persuaded *Hi!* to keep the deal going." As Suzy fished out sodden bits of fruitcake with her teaspoon, she marveled at his chutzpah. "Instead of marrying Jaz Dreyfuss's ex-wife, Harry the Hero marries Jaz's future wife instead. You have to admit, it's right up that magazine's alley."

"And Celeste's going to be selling her story as well," said Maeve. "That's why she disappeared yesterday — she was up in London with the head of some PR agency, working out deals. My life of hell with dried-out, dried-up rock star Jaz. Ungrateful little trollop that she is."

"God, poor Jaz." Suzy groaned at the awful prospect. "That is *so* unfair."

The next moment she stiffened as a truly awful thought went *ziiing* like an arrow through her brain.

I finished with Harry, but nobody else knows that. What if he's planning to make out he dumped me so he could be with Celeste?

Aaargh, no, thought Suzy, horrified. *Bloody, bloody hell,* poor me.

Jaz was in the swimming pool, floating on

his back with his eyes closed. The water, heated to blood temperature so he barely knew it was there, lapped gently over his shoulders and chest.

Opening his eyes, he gazed up at the emerald-green ceiling with its hand-painted border of peacocks swishing their flamboyant blue and gold tails. The peacocks had been commissioned five years ago by Suzy. When Celeste had moved into the house she had lobbied hard to have them painted over, but Jaz had stood his ground. Each peacock was different; some looked mischievous, others proud. One was even winking saucily. They all had their own distinct personalities.

Like the women in my life, Jaz thought with a rueful smile.

The next moment there was a loud splash behind him and the spreading ripples rocked Jaz from side to side.

"It's like an elephant jumping into the water," he complained. "Why can't you just dive in quietly like normal people?"

"I like to make an entrance." Beaming, Suzy bobbed up and down in front of him. "Make sure I'm noticed."

"Take it from me: you'll always be noticed."

"Especially if I was to dive in with this

bikini on," said Suzy. "My boobs would shoot out. But if I take a running jump and curl up into a ball, they can't escape."

Jaz checked his watch; it was eight o'clock. "Has Maeve gone out?"

"Just left. Karaoke night at the Hen and Feathers." Suzy paused. "You've been down here for over an hour. How are you feeling, truly?"

Truly? Like I've been let out of prison, thought Jaz.

Without him even realizing it, Celeste had trapped him. When the Lucille thing had come to a head and he had finally acknowledged his feelings for her, he had wondered at the same time how on earth he could ever end it with Celeste. Her apparent reliance on him to keep her from drinking again had been a powerful form of emotional blackmail. Jaz knew, of course, that one should never give into blackmail, but when you also knew you'd never forgive yourself if the worst did happen, it was a lot easier said than done.

So. Celeste wasn't, in fact, an alcoholic. And she'd chosen to leave him anyway.

Which was good news. Excellent news. *Hooray.*

Then again, she wasn't the only one to have run out on him. Lucille had too. Which wasn't excellent at all.

Furthermore, as far as Jaz had been able to make out, Celeste wasn't the chief reason Lucille had run out on him. Suzy was.

And whatever happened, Suzy must never find out what had . . . er, happened last week in his room at the Savoy.

"Hello? Hello?" Suzy was waving a hand in front of his face. She playfully flicked him with water. "Blink if you can hear me."

Jaz flicked water back at her.

"I'm glad Celeste's not an alcoholic," he said. "Now I don't have to feel responsible for her anymore."

"On the other hand," Suzy guessed when he paused, "you're totally pissed off that she's been faking it all these years, pretending to be going through all the same awful stuff you went through."

"That too," Jaz agreed. Rolling onto his side and kicking his way lazily to the far end of the pool, he added, "The ironic thing is, for the last year I've had this recurring dream, that I'm trying to break up with Celeste. She completely flips and threatens to start drinking again. The next thing I know, she's reaching for a bottle and tipping it toward her mouth. I know it's all my fault. I'm desperate to stop her, but I can't. My feet won't move . . ."

"So what happens next?"

Jaz sighed. "I yell out, scream at her not to do it."

"Then?"

"She still won't stop. So in the end I do the only thing I can. Tell her I didn't mean it and that I don't want us to split up after all. And that's it. Celeste puts down the bottle, and we make up. End of dream."

With any luck, he wouldn't experience it again.

"Boring!" Suzy wrinkled her nose. "No flying horses or talking animals or being seduced by mysterious masked strangers?"

"Sometimes I wonder about you. Come on, race you to the other end," said Jaz. "Indian or Chinese?"

"Mysterious masked strangers? Actually, they never speak so I'm not sure, but I always kind of imagined them as Cossacky-type Russians, you know, with rock-hard bodies and those gorgeous Slavic cheek-bones —"

"I'm talking takeout," said Jaz.

CHAPTER 48

The neighbors were accustomed to the sight of Suzy, wearing her toweling robe over a bikini, running barefoot between her house and Jaz's. She seldom bothered to take a change of clothes with her. By the time Jaz arrived back with the takeout, Suzy was sprawled across one of the sofas in his sitting room warbling horribly along to something on MTV. Her tousled hair was still wet, she was wearing a yellow-and-white-striped robe over her orange-and-pink bikini and — having discovered a jar of lime-green nail polish in the pocket of her robe — was now happily painting her toes.

"Peking duck," announced Jaz, holding up the paper shopping bag.

"Hooray. Except I'm afraid you'll have to do all the shredding and rolling. I can't do it," Suzy said apologetically. "My toenails are wet."

Suzy's excuses for getting out of the fussy

and deeply tedious business of shredding the duck breast and rolling it up into tiny pancakes were legendary.

"All right, just this once." Jaz ruffled her wet hair. "And only because I feel sorry for you." She looked indignant.

"You don't have to feel sorry for me."

"Of course I do. You've been dumped by Harry the Hero."

"Oh God." Suzy groaned. "Is that really what people are going to think?"

"They are if that's what he decides to tell them." Enjoying himself, Jaz began unwrapping the steaming paper parcels of food. "And seeing as it's Harry we're talking about, I rather think he might."

"This was supposed to be a *happy* day," Suzy wailed. "And now he's completely *ruined* it."

"Cheer up. Have a Coke."

Grinning, Jaz held out a chilled can.

"You must be joking." Suzy pointed a regal finger in the direction of the kitchen. "Young man, fetch me some wine. Tonight I'm definitely going to get plastered."

"God, you're hopeless," Jaz declared less than an hour later. Raising one eyebrow he added, "Hopeless *and* disgusting."

Suzy ran her finger around the inside of

the Styrofoam carton, determined to scoop out the very last drops of yummy hoisin sauce. This wasn't disgusting; it was simply efficient.

As for Jaz telling her she was hopeless because drinking always went so quickly to her head — ha, well, he was a fine one to talk.

Having licked the hoisin sauce from her finger, Suzy now wagged it at him like a schoolteacher.

"OK," she announced with a bit of a slur. "Good points and bad points. Harry's gone, hooray, that's a good point. I can move back into my own bedroom and sleep in my own bed again, 'nother jolly good point. Ah. But Harry and Celeste have been screwing in it." Reaching for her glass, Suzy frowned and took a king-size slurp of wine. "Which has to be a bad point. A *very* bad point. Bugger, this bottle's empty. Jaz, Jaz, we've run out of wine."

"Wrong," said Jaz. "*You've* run out of wine."

"Bloody hell, this is all Harry's fault. I'll just die if he tells everyone he dumped me." Jerking upright, sloshing ice cold wine down her front, Suzy exclaimed, "You could sort that out! The papers would listen to you if you issued a statement."

"You aren't serious." Jaz shook his head in amused disbelief. "Me, issue a press release announcing that Harry didn't dump Suzy, she dumped him first? Now that would be a really mature thing to do. Remind me again, how old are you? Thirteen?"

Suzy stuck her tongue out at him in mature fashion. "We're going to be a laughingstock. You and me both. I don't know how you can be so calm about it."

Jaz shrugged. Suzy had gotten exactly what she wanted; she was just peeved about the way it had happened. As far as he was concerned, Lucille was all that mattered. Her abrupt disappearance far overshadowed Celeste's departure.

But the one thing he knew he couldn't do was tell Suzy how he felt about Lucille.

"I miss Lucille so much," Suzy cried, making him jump. "Oh God, what am I going to do? My life's a mess, your life's a mess . . . Where did we go wrong?" Her robe was sliding off one shoulder and the belt had come loose. Her brown cleavage deepened as she reached forward to plonk her empty glass on the coffee table. Shaking back her tousled, almost-dry hair she wailed, "I never even slept with him! Do you know how long it's been since I had sex with *anyone*?"

582

Jaz knew. "That French guy, the tennis player."

"Didier." Suzy nodded, remembering. "Didier the Bastard."

At the time, back in June, theirs had been a whirlwind romance. It had taken Didier the Bastard no time at all to persuade Suzy to break her six-week rule. In Bristol for a pre-Wimbledon tennis tournament, he had possessed ravishing good looks, a body to die for, and the kind of French accent that had made Suzy go wobbly at the knees. They had spent a riotous week together. Didier had told her he was single. His friends at the tournament had assured her he was single. A fortnight later, watching him play at Wimbledon, Suzy had seen the camera zoom in on a stunning brunette and had heard the commentator say, "And there's Didier's lovely wife, Sandrine, mother of his three young children . . ."

Which rather explained why Didier hadn't invited her up to Wimbledon to cheer him on from the friends-and-family box.

Suzy had been delighted when he'd crashed out of the tournament in the second round, beaten by a big, ugly German in straight sets.

"Nobody since then," she announced despairingly. "In all that time, not one single solitary bit of sex. I mean, be fair, is that totally tragic or what?"

Jaz was laughing at her. "OK, why don't you tell me who you'd like to have sex with? I'll give them a call and let them know how desperate you are. You never know, one of them might take pity on you. We may be able to get you sorted out."

Swinging her bare legs up onto the sofa, Suzy aimed a quick kick at his ribs. Expertly, Jaz caught hold of both ankles and rested her feet across his lap. Something about the way he gave her knees a reassuring pat started Suzy thinking . . .

"You wouldn't believe how many times I've fantasized about sleeping with you."

Jaz's mouth twitched. "Oh dear, you're well gone, aren't you? Are you sure you want to tell me this? Because I warn you now, I will tease you about it for the rest of your life."

Suzy shook her head emphatically from side to side. "To annoy Celeste, *stupid*. I fantasized about sleeping with you just to *annoy* her."

"And all the time you were fantasizing about it, she was busy sleeping with your fiancé," Jaz concluded with a grin. "Neat twist."

Suzy gazed at him, perilously tempted to

blurt out everything. She longed to be able to tell someone about her feelings for Leo.

And Jaz was here, and he was listening, but she knew she mustn't let herself do it.

For the first time in my life, thought Suzy, *I've met someone who's out of my league. Leo Fitzallan can do better than me. He can have anyone he likes. What's more, he's already got her.*

Perfect, pretty, doll-like, super intelligent, super nice Gabriella.

Next to her, how can I possibly hope to compete?

"You're miles away." Jaz gave her ankles an affectionate tweak. "What are you thinking?"

She couldn't tell him. Too humiliating for words. And it would give him something else to tease her about for the next fifty years.

Fifty years, thought Suzy. *Good grief, and I might* still *be celibate.*

"You have to say something. When I ask you a question, it's your job to reply," said Jaz. "It's only polite."

He was teasing her, idly stroking her knees as he spoke. Oh, how long had it been since she'd last had her knees stroked like that?

"We used to be good at it, didn't we?" Suzy gave him a playful nudge, determined not to think about Leo anymore. "Sex, I mean. We always had great sex." She paused. "So how about it? What do you think? Fancy a quickie?"

Jaz's hand abruptly stopped in midstroke.

"Well?" Feeling reckless, Suzy smiled and shot him a complicit, what-the-hell look. "Just the one-off. No strings, obviously. Mindless sex, that's all I'm suggesting."

"So you can break your drought?" countered Jaz.

"Well, I wouldn't have put it quite like that. But OK, yes. *And,*" she added enticingly, "it would be a lovely way for you to get back at Celeste."

Not to mention Harry.

"A revenge fuck." Jaz nodded. "But I don't want to get back at Celeste. It's over. She's gone. End of story."

Suzy couldn't help noticing his lack of enthusiasm for the idea. To be honest, it bordered on the insulting.

"Am I too ugly?" she demanded. "Is that the problem? Do I physically repulse you?"

"Don't be daft. If it's that important to you, then fine, we'll have sex," said Jaz. He shrugged, then fixed her with his dark gaze. "But I'm telling you now, you need to think seriously about this. It has to be what you really *really* want."

What I really want is to have sex with Leo, Suzy thought miserably, *and I can't, so I'm settling for Jaz instead because he's an old friend and a good sport, and he's here, we get on perfectly well together, and we both know we'd enjoy it.*

And it might make me feel better.

If only I still fancied him. Except I don't. Heaven only knows why, I just don't. And I can't make it happen . . .

"OK now?" Jaz was smiling, because he had always been able to read her mind with stunning accuracy, "Agreed? Better if it doesn't happen?"

"God," Suzy grumbled. "I really hate it when you're right and I'm wrong."

He broke into a grin and ruffled her tortoiseshell hair. "And I love it that you hate it. Otherwise, where's the fun?"

"What I still don't understand" — Suzy frowned — "is why I don't fancy you anymore. I mean, the whole reason we broke up in the first place was your drinking. Now you don't drink, you should be perfect! But the feelings just aren't there. It's mad." She shrugged and shook her head helplessly. "Makes no sense at all. All those feelings . . . where did they go?"

"Look," said Jaz, "I'd love to have a long, involved, philosophical argument with you

587

about the nature of inner emotion. But, basically, you're extremely drunk."

Suzy screwed up her eyes, thinking what a gorgeous word *philosophical* was. If only she could say it.

"I am, aren't I?" She beamed happily at Jaz. "You're right again. Blimey, what a know-it-all."

"We're friends; that's all that matters," Jaz told her. "It'd be a real shame to spoil that."

"Friends. Yes. You're so, so, absolutely right." Clumsily, Suzy leaned over and gave him an affectionate kiss on the cheek. "And as a friend, the very least you can do is run down to the liquor store and buy me another bottle of wine."

"You're going to have quite enough of a hangover tomorrow as it is," said Jaz. "As a true friend, I'm going to make you a pot of coffee instead."

CHAPTER 49

At seven o'clock the following Wednesday, Suzy was working her way through a pile of paperwork when Martin called into the office on his way home, to drop off a set of keys.

"What a waste of time that was." Sighing, he chucked the keys into a drawer, unwound the scarf from around his neck, and perched on the edge of Suzy's desk.

He'd shown a married couple a stunning house in Harley Place, Suzy remembered. She looked up. "They didn't like it?"

"Oh, they liked it all right. Just can't afford it. Bloody tourists. What I need's a drink. Join me?"

"No thanks."

Martin said sympathetically, "How's your day been?"

Suzy threw down her pen and stretched. "My day? Well, what can I tell you? My life is currently unbelievably awful, the papers are full of stories about how I've been dumped by Harry the Hero in favor of a walking, talking brainless little sex toy, my sister's vanished off the face of the earth . . . Basically, my day has been shit."

"You could definitely do with a drink."

Suzy shook her head. "No, really. I'm not in the mood."

Reaching for her hand, Martin pulled her upright. The next moment, he'd grabbed her black velvet coat and pushed her arms into it. Standing in front of her like a grown-up with a recalcitrant child, he began to fasten the buttons. "You're miserable. I'm miserable. Maybe we could cheer each other up."

Suzy, who never ever fastened the buttons on her coat — how *sweet* — smiled at his logic. "Then again, we could form a suicide pact. End it all, together in my car, with a pipe attached to the exhaust."

"You must be joking." Martin looked shocked. "I've seen the cassettes you keep in your car. There's no way I'm going to die listening to New Kids on the Block."

Suzy laughed and he gave her a hug.

"See?" said Martin. "Feeling better already. I mean it; you and I could be good together. We just need to give each other a chance."

■ ■ ■ ■

Viewed from the road outside, the glass-fronted office was lit up like a Christmas tree. Nothing was left to the imagination. Leo, who had been reading about Suzy's humiliating situation and had decided to drop by to see how she was holding up, observed the goings-on in Curtis and Co. with a we-are-not-amused look on his face.

Next to him, in the front seat of the car, Baxter belatedly recognized Suzy and made a violent lunge for the door, scrabbling at the handle in his eagerness to rush over and give her a huge I-still-love-you welcome.

Leo barely noticed. He was watching with mounting horror as Martin Lord cupped Suzy's face in his hands. Any second now and he'd be kissing her . . .

The number of the office was still stored on his cell phone. Rapidly, Leo pressed the appropriate buttons. At least he hoped they were the right buttons; it was hard to tell in the dark.

At last he heard the ringing tone. A moment later — *yes!* — the phone rang in the office across the road. He saw Suzy take a step backward and say something to Martin. Reaching behind her, she picked up

591

the phone.

Leo knew this was the moment he should hang up, but he couldn't bring himself to do it. Some inner compulsion made him wait to hear Suzy's voice. They hadn't spoken to each other for weeks.

"Hello? Curtis and Co."

Baxter, his big hairy ears pricking up, let out a delighted *woof*!

Too late, Leo hung up.

Damn, what was the matter with him? He was behaving like a teenager.

"Gone," said Suzy, with a frown.

"Who was it?" Not that Martin cared.

"No one." Suzy shrugged. "A dog just barked, then the line went dead."

Thanks a lot, dog, thought Martin, who had been about to make his big move. Somehow the opportunity — and Suzy — now appeared to have slipped out of reach.

Canine interruptus, just his luck.

"Hey, are we going to have that drink?" He grinned and spread his hands, attempting to recapture the moment, but it was too late. Suzy was already reaching for her car keys and looking distracted. "It's OK," Martin added eagerly. "I'll drive."

Suzy realized she was thinking of Leo. Probably because hearing that dog barking had reminded her of Baxter.

"Thanks, but I'll pass. Maeve's making one of her roasts, and Jaz has challenged us both to a game of Trivial Pursuit."

"Now that's what I call an action-packed social life. Sa-ad," Martin jeered.

Outside, in the pitch-blackness, a car was pulling away up the street. Suzy, wrapping her thick silver and white scarf around her neck and heading for the door, decided that Martin wasn't so sweet after all.

"Doesn't sound sad to me," she said lightly. "Night."

"Fee called? Really? When? How is she? Did she say she'd call again?"

Donna, bemused, had only mentioned Fee's phone call in passing. She hadn't been expecting quite such an interrogation.

"Er, no. It was just a quick call to say hi, and that she hopes to be back in Bristol soon. She called five minutes ago."

I am the unluckiest man in the world, Rory decided. *If I hadn't been stuck in traffic on Queen's Road, I could have taken that call.*

Eagerly, he said, "Did she sound OK?"

Donna shrugged. "Fine. Asked how everyone was. I told her we were all fine. She wanted a word with Suzy, but I said she was out of the office."

"Here she is now!" Rory exclaimed, leaping out of his chair as the familiar pillar-box red Rolls slid expertly into its allotted parking space outside the office.

"But Fee's already hung up." Donna gave him a worried look. That was the trouble with these people who worked too hard; all of a sudden they could flip and go completely bonkers. "Rory, would you like me to make you a nice cup of tea?" *Preferably decaf.*

An icy blast of air swirled around Donna as the door was pushed open and a middle-aged West Indian woman entered the office. Tall and stylish, she was thoroughly wrapped up against the bitter November cold. Glancing first at Rory, then at Donna, she said, "Ah, out of luck by the looks of things. I was hoping to have a word with Suzy Curtis . . . I believe she works here?"

"Actually, you're in luck," Donna told her. "Suzy's just pulled up outside. Who shall I say —"

"Suzy!" Rory pounced as she came through the door. "Perfect timing! Fee called, wanting to speak to you. Now you can call her back!"

"My name's Merle," the woman told Donna, her voice low-pitched and melodic. "If she could just spare me five minutes, I'd be grateful."

"Suzy, this is —"

"Suzy! Call her now." Rory's gray eyes behind his wire-rimmed glasses were bright with urgency.

"It's OK." Suzy took off her coat, wondering what had happened to make him so jumpy. "I'll call her tonight."

"Why not now?"

"Because there's no hurry, and I'll have more time later. And," she continued patiently, "you're the one who's always whining on about irresponsible people making private calls on company time."

With an air of desperation, Rory spread his arms wide and almost shouted, "Honestly, feel free, I don't *mind.*"

"*So* sorry about this." Donna rolled her heavily kohled eyes at Merle. "She'll be with you in just a sec, I promise. Rory, don't you have to be at that appraisal on Pitch and Pay Lane by two o'clock? Because if you keep the client waiting, Slade and Matthews will be around there with their electronic tape measures quicker than you can say 'lost sale.' "

"I'm going, I'm going," Rory muttered. Suzy clearly had no intention of making the phone call now. Crikey, it wasn't too much to ask, was it? Just to be in the same room while Suzy chatted to Fee on the phone?

"He's in a funny mood about something." Mystified, Suzy gazed after Rory as he stomped out of the office.

"Suzy, this lady would like to speak to you."

"In private?" said Merle with an almost apologetic smile.

More mystery. Unless . . . Suzy caught her breath.

"Is this to do with Lucille?"

Calmly, Merle replied, "It concerns her, yes."

The tiny back room where they made tea and coffee was cramped and chairless. At that moment the front door was flung open again and a bundled-up family of four burst in. Any form of privacy here was going to be in woefully short supply.

"Look, I know it's freezing," said Suzy, "but we'd be better off out of here. We could go for a walk, or" — much better idea — "there's a coffee shop around the corner."

"Let's walk," Merle said comfortably. "Clifton's so beautiful. And it's years since I last visited the bridge."

Together they headed down Princess Victoria Street, toward the Avon Gorge Hotel. Suzy, fidgeting with the fringed ends of her silver-and-white angora scarf, shot surreptitious glances at Merle's elegant legs as she strolled along, to see if they resembled Lucille's.

Finally, unable to stand the suspense a moment longer, she blurted out, "Are you her aunt?"

Merle raised a plucked eyebrow. "Whose? Lucille's?"

"She didn't tell me she had an aunt, but I can't think who else you might be. Was William Amory your brother?"

As she said it, Suzy realized the possibilities were endless. This woman, Merle, was, at a guess, in her midfifties. She could have been William Amory's sister, or his cousin. Or even — blimey — his *wife*.

"I'm not related to Lucille," Merle told her with a smile. "I was a good friend of your mother's."

Suzy blinked. She definitely hadn't been expecting this. "*My* mother's?"

"That's right. Blanche."

CHAPTER 50

Calmly, Merle nodded at Suzy. "This was many years ago, of course. We lived across the street from each other. Well, I suppose I should say I lived across the street from William and Lucille, but Blanche and I became close all the same."

Oh, good grief, thought Suzy, startled. *I really hope you're not going to tell me you were my mother's lesbian lover.*

"We had no secrets from each other," Merle went on. "She confided in me, and I confided in her. I was involved with a married man at the time, so between the pair of us we had plenty to talk about. And we didn't judge each other, which made a nice change."

Suzy blinked. Heavens, she was almost afraid to ask. "So . . . who were you having an affair with?"

Not my father, please.

"Oh, no one you'd have heard of. Just one

of the professors at the university." With a rueful smile, Merle said, "I'm afraid I was a bit of a scarlet woman in my day. Anyway, to bring matters up to date, I've been living in Switzerland for the past five years. I only moved back here a couple of weeks ago. So when I saw the story in the papers last week about Harry Fitzallan I was interested, because of course I'd known his family too, living as they did next door to William and Lucille." She paused. "You can imagine my amazement when I realized that the article I was reading was all about Harry breaking off his engagement to *you.*"

Suzy's nose was pink with cold. Every lungful of air she sucked in came out again as a puffball of condensation. Knowing she was being ridiculous, but too proud to let it pass, she said, "Actually, *I* was the one who broke off the engagement."

Merle looked as if she was trying hard not to smile.

Indignantly, Suzy insisted, "It's *true.*"

"Don't worry, I believe you. Harry always did have an eye for publicity." As they turned right and began to head up the hill toward the bridge, Merle said, "When he was eight, he found my cat. It had gone missing, and I was terrified it might have been run over. I gave Harry a five-pound reward, and he persuaded some guy from the *Bristol Journal* to come around and take his photo. It wasn't until a week later that his brother Leo turned up on my doorstep to return the fiver. Apparently, he'd found out that Harry was the one who'd kidnapped my cat in the first place and hidden it in his dad's garage. Do you know Leo?" Merle said suddenly. "Harry's elder brother?"

"Oh yes." Suzy, breathing deeply, was glad of the ice cold air on her cheeks. "I know Leo."

"Anyway, I was intrigued, naturally. And even more so when I saw one particular photograph in the paper. It was taken on the night of Harry's accident," Merle explained. "You were arriving at the hospital to see him for the first time, no shoes on, looking pretty distraught . . ."

"I remember *that* night." Suzy spoke with feeling. As if she could ever forget.

"And there, turning up at the hospital with you, was Lucille. I recognized her at once and realized the two of you had found each other." Merle glanced across at Suzy and smiled sadly. "The first thing I did was call Blanche's number — I couldn't wait to tell her how thrilled I was that it had all turned out so well. Of course, that was when I found out she'd recently died. The girl who answered the phone told me."

Girl. She meant Gabriella, Suzy realized.

"It was a heart attack. In her sleep."

"Poor Lucille. She must have been devastated. Of course," Merle added hastily, "you both must."

Suzy, changing the subject, said, "Leo Fitzallan bought the house. That was his fiancée you spoke to on the phone."

"Really? She told me that if I wanted to contact any of Blanche's children, to call you at Curtis and Co. But I needed to speak to you face-to-face. I'd love to see Lucille as well, if she's around."

They had reached the knoll leading up to the bridge. The grass, stiff with frost, crunched beneath Suzy's deeply impractical Kurt Geiger high heels. Pushing her hair back from her face with frozen fingers, she said, "Lucille isn't around at the moment. She's . . . gone away."

Merle looked surprised. "Do you not get on?"

"No . . . I mean yes, we do, like a house on fire, but she just needed a break." *From me,* Suzy thought miserably. *Because I'm such an idiot. I drove her away. And now I don't know if she'll ever want to come back.*

"A break?"

"It was all my fault," Suzy mumbled, bitterly ashamed.

"Blanche was always so sure the two of you would get on marvelously." Merle's voice was gentle. "She must have been thrilled."

Oh Lord, more explanations. As they trudged on up toward St. Vincent's Rocks and the Observatory, Suzy ran through the events of Blanche's funeral, Lucille's unexpected arrival, and the subsequent will reading.

When she had finished, Merle nodded easily and said, "That's exactly how Blanche guessed Julia would react. Oh now, will you look at that view? Can you imagine a more beautiful sight? Here, I brought something along for you and Lucille. And Julia too, if you think she'd be interested. Ah, the sun's beginning to come out. Why don't we sit down on that bench over there? I'll admire the scenery, and you can have a quick look through these."

As she spoke, Merle removed a bundle of letters from her bag and handed them over to Suzy.

"No red ribbon. Not love letters then," Suzy joked, twanging the unromantic rubber band holding them together.

"Actually, you'd be surprised," said Merle,

settling herself on the frosty wooden bench and pulling her coat more tightly around her. "They sound pretty much like love letters to me."

After the first few minutes, Suzy forgot Merle was there. Only when she sniffed loudly for the umpteenth time and a wad of tissues was surreptitiously pressed into her hand did she remember she wasn't alone on the bench.

Blanche's familiar black scrawl covered page after page of cobalt-blue writing paper. The letter Suzy was currently reading had been written fifteen years ago. Snippets of sentences jumped out at her, heartbreaking in their intensity.

Oh, Merle, I don't know how I'm going to cope — I love all my children so much. When I look at darling Suzy, and then Lucille, how can I choose between them? If I tried to leave Ralph, I know he'd fight for custody — and win, of course. The thought of losing my beloved babies is unbearable. It would kill me to be without them. So here I am, stuck in eternal limbo . . . My children are my whole life, but what can I do?

"Oh God," Suzy whispered, the words

swimming hopelessly before her eyes. "I never knew. I just never knew. I thought *we* were the ones making her unhappy."

"Not you," said Merle. "Your father."

"But if she left him, she knew she'd lose us?"

Merle nodded. "She was torn. It was agonizing for her. I thought *I* had troubles," she added wryly, "but mine were nothing compared with Blanche's."

"She could have told us the truth after Dad died." Even as she said it, Suzy knew what the answer to this would be. She and Lucille had already worked it out.

"Blanche knew it would destroy Julia." Merle shrugged. "She was tempted to tell you but knew you'd never be able to keep it to yourself."

Suzy shook her head. "I wish she'd trusted me. Maybe I'm better with secrets than people think."

"Then again" — Merle's tone was affectionate — "correct me if I'm wrong, but weren't you the girl who jumped up in assembly one day and announced to the rest of the school that Father Christmas didn't exist?"

Suzy flushed and said indignantly, "That was when I was six!"

"Exactly. And so was the rest of your

class." Merle, trying not to smile, said, "It's called tarnishing your reputation in a major way. According to Blanche, you had many talents, but discretion was never your forte."

Suzy wiped her eyes, blew her nose, and heaved a gusty sigh.

"This makes such a difference, you know. Reading these letters, talking to you about how Mum felt. Really, you have no idea how much better I feel now."

"Well, I'm awfully glad to hear it," said Merle with a grin. "Because you look an absolute sight."

Suzy held up the bundle of letters. "Can I have these?"

"Of course. I could never bear to throw them away. You'll show them to Lucille, will you?"

If I ever find her, thought Suzy.

Aloud she said, "I'll do my best."

As they made their way back down Sion Hill, Merle said, "Well, you're looking better now, I must say."

"You've cheered me up. The past few weeks have been pretty diabolical. You can't imagine." With a rueful smile, Suzy shoved her icy hands deep inside her coat pockets. "I used to think I was the girl with everything, but recently, I've managed to make a complete mess of my life."

Merle looked amused. "No new man lined up to take Harry's place?"

"Nope."

"What, no one? Sparky girl like you? Come on now, there must be some gorgeous fellow you've got your eye on."

"No," said Suzy, shaking her head and thinking, *If only you knew.*

But as much as she liked Merle, there was no way she could bring herself to tell her that the only man currently capable of making her heart beat like a Salvation Army drum was Leo Fitzallan.

Because Leo wasn't the least bit interested in her. And, in all honesty, why would he want to be? He was already taken, thanks very much. About to marry Gabriella, the girl who — let's face it — really *did* have everything.

Including — damn, *damn* and blast — Leo.

CHAPTER 51

Suzy paid a visit to the Alpha Bar the next day, between appointments. Leo, on the phone when she was shown into his office, looked startled to see her. Baxter, who had been sprawled, half asleep under the desk, let out a yelp of welcome and scrambled to his feet. Whining with delight, he buried his head lovingly between her hands and wagged his tail so hard he almost lost his balance on the polished oak floor.

Now this is what I call a coincidence — woof woof. *We were only parked outside your office the other night! Did you recognize my bark on the phone when he called you to stop you from making out with that other fellow? Did you realize that was me?*

"What are you saying, hey? What's this all about?" cooed Suzy, delighted by the welcoming volley of barks.

Leo sent up a private prayer of thanks that she couldn't decipher what Baxter — the blabbermouth — was evidently busy telling her.

"He's wondering if you'd like to take him for a five-mile run. No, Baxter, she wouldn't, so leave it, OK?"

"Oh, darling, I'm busy. Otherwise, of course I would." Regretfully, Suzy sat down and unwound her scarf. Smiling across at Leo — who for a completely mad moment had thought she was calling *him* darling — she went on, "It's just a short visit, but I was passing by, and I wanted to let you know I'm feeling a lot better. After the episode with the box buried in your garden," Suzy explained, because Leo was looking mystified. "When I blubbered like a baby all over you."

Leo nodded briefly. As if he could ever forget. "Well, I'm glad."

"I met Merle Denison."

"Merle? Good grief. How is she?"

Suzy ran through the events of the previous astonishing day. She told Leo all about the letters and managed not to cry once.

"So you see? All those years of feeling unloved were for nothing. A big waste of time. Poor Mum — can you imagine how she must have felt? God, when I think what she had to *go* through."

"So everything's sorted out now," said Leo.

"Except Lucille's disappeared."

At the mention of Lucille's name, Baxter let out another series of yelps.

That's the one! Lucille! Where the buggering hell has she gotten to, anyway? Calls herself a dog walker and I haven't seen her for weeks.

"I know, darling. You miss her, don't you? I do too." Suzy gave his hairy ears a sympathetic rub. Sadly, she confided, "She's gone away and left us and it's all my fault. And it's just *killing* me not being able to say sorry."

Leo wished she'd fondle his ears like that.

He coughed, dismissing the rogue thought, and said, "Actually, I do know where Lucille is."

"You're kidding!" Suzy's green-gold eyes widened in astonishment. "Really? Oh God, this is so brilliant," she squealed, "I can go and see her and grovel on my knees until she forgives me! I'll go this afternoon, the moment I finish work! Is she here in Bristol?"

"Um, not quite." Leo was doing his level best not to smile. "She's staying in a little place called Grand Baie."

"Grand Bay? Is that in Newcastle? Close

to Whitley Bay?"

Good grief, thought Suzy, what on *earth* made Lucille trek all the way up there?

"Not quite," said Leo. "Actually, it's in Mauritius."

"Bloody Mauritius!" Suzy exclaimed, seizing the brochure she had picked up from the travel agent that afternoon and spreading it open on the kitchen table. "Can you believe it?"

"It's where her family is from," Jaz pointed out reasonably. "It looks nice."

"The jewel in the Indian Ocean, it says here! Emerald-green water . . . and Grand Baie is known as the Mauritian Cote d'Azur . . . Ha! So much for me thinking it was next door to Newcastle. I've never been to Mauritius," Suzy said indignantly. She looked over at Jaz. "Have you ever been to Mauritius?"

"Who knows?" Jaz shrugged; in his alcohol-sodden past he had visited plenty of places he had no memory whatsoever of visiting. "Maeve? Have I ever been to Mauritius?"

"No." Maeve's tone was consoling. "You're thinking of Tasmania."

"Right." Jaz broke into a grin. "Of course. Silly me."

"It's so unfair," Suzy wailed, bursting with frustration. "When Leo said he knew where Lucille was, I thought, Brilliant, I'll go straight there. If she'd been in Newcastle I'd have driven up to Newcastle," she fretted. "But Mauritius . . . I mean, for God's sake, what's Lucille thinking about? She could hardly *get* any farther away than that! And I can't take any time off work . . . Dammit, all I've got is her address. There isn't even a phone number . . ."

"Write to her." Maeve was ever practical. "Make photocopies of all those letters your mother wrote to Merle and send them off to Lucille with a nice letter from you."

"They'll take ages to get there," Suzy grumbled. "Anyway, it's not the same."

"Maybe not." Maeve shrugged. "But it's a start."

"Oh, this is horrible!" Suzy banged her fist on the kitchen table. "I can't wait that long. I want Lucille to forgive me *now.*"

"Stop whining." Jaz sighed. "You sound like a spoiled brat."

"Veruca Salt," Maeve said helpfully.

Suzy stared at her. "What?"

"The spoiled brat in *Charlie and the Chocolate Factory.* That's her name. Veruca Salt," Maeve declared happily. "You sound just like her."

Suzy tossed back her hair. "Oh, thanks a lot."

Jaz was enjoying himself immensely.

"Sometimes," he reminded Suzy, just to annoy her, "you have to sit back and be patient. Let things happen at their own pace."

"Ouch!" Maeve let out a bellow of pain.

"Sorry, sorry." Suzy sighed. "I was trying to kick Jaz."

The fringed ends of Lucille's turquoise cotton sarong flapped in the warm breeze as she made her way along the beach. There were new beads in her hair, pink and lilac and silver ones that glittered in the sunlight and danced around her shoulders with every step she took. Reaching the water, she unfastened the sarong and let it fall onto the sand, stepping away from it and carrying on, without pausing, into the emerald-green sea.

Her golden-brown body was flawless. She was wearing a pale blue bikini. Within seconds she was swimming, heading for the diving raft moored a hundred or so feet out in the middle of the bay.

Jaz retreated behind his dark glasses once more and took a swig of iced mineral water from the bottle in his hand. Reaching Grand

Baie last night, he had checked into one of the five-star hotels overlooking the ocean and had been tempted to go searching for Lucille right away.

But it had been midnight, and the flight from Heathrow had lasted twelve hours. Absolutely exhausted, and aware that he might not be looking his best, Jaz had reluctantly changed his mind and crashed in his room instead.

This morning, following a long cool shower and a change into clean clothes, he had set out with butterflies in his stomach and a terrifying amount of hope in his heart to track Lucille down at the address she had given Leo.

She was out, he discovered, when he arrived at the tiny rented room above a souvenir shop in one of the village's dusty backstreets. The white-haired Mauritian woman who ran the shop told him he'd missed Lucille by ten minutes but to try the beach.

So he had.

And he'd found her, spotted her almost at once. Although, as yet, she hadn't seen him.

It was hot, up in the mideighties already, and Jaz was still dehydrated from the flight.

Not to mention nervous. He had, after all, set himself up here in pretty spectacular fashion. Let's face it — it could go horribly wrong.

He really hoped not, but it might. That was the trouble with women; you never knew what the hell they were likely to do next.

Making his way over to the nearest beach-front bar, Jaz ordered another mineral water and sat gazing out to sea, watching Lucille in the distance, diving from the wooden platform and splashing around in the sparkling azure water like a playful dolphin.

Shit, thought Jaz, *I still don't even know what I'm going to* say.

I need words. The right words.

Can't think *of any.*

At the other side of the bar, two girls in matching parrot-pink bikinis giggled and nudged each other. It was, it was Jaz Dreyfuss. His blond hair was shorter, but it was definitely him. And his lips were moving; he was actually talking to himself — that was what years of excessive drinking did for you, ended up shriveling your brain.

Jaz, not even aware that the two girls were watching him, tried to imagine saying casually, "Lucille, hi, fancy bumping into you here."

Ugh.

Or maybe, jokingly, "D'you come here often?"

Jesus. *Awful.* He shook his head in disgust. Why did this have to happen to him now? He was never usually at a loss for words.

Ha! If only Suzy could see me now. She'd never let me live this down.

"Drugs," one of the girls whispered to the other. "See how twitchy he is? He's only drinking water because he's high as a kite on drugs."

"Ah, it's a shame; he'd be really good-looking if only he didn't twitch so much."

"Yeah. Still, wonder if he'd like to buy us a drink?"

Dry-mouthed and oblivious to the attention he was receiving, Jaz watched Lucille swim effortlessly back to the shore and emerge sleek and glistening from the water. Reaching for her turquoise sarong, she shook it out, spread it on the dry sand, then sat down on it and lay back in order to enjoy the sun.

Now what?

Go over to her.

I can't, I just can't.

Don't be such an idiot. Get over there. You've come all this way . . . What's the worst that could happen?

You mean apart from her telling me to piss off?

"He's out of it. Completely out of it," hissed the first girl, slurping the last of her drink up through the straw and making a noise like a gurgling drain.

"Hang on, he's moving . . . He's standing up . . . Aaargh, I think he's coming over . . . Don't look, don't look . . ."

"Excuse me," said Jaz, and the two girls swung their blond heads around in unison and apparent surprise, grinning and chorusing, "Yes?"

But Jaz, humiliatingly, wasn't addressing them. Instead, leaning across the bar and pointing, he said to the bartender, "Could I borrow that?"

The bartender, who was Mauritian and didn't recognize Jaz, shot him a deeply suspicious look. "My guitar? You want to borrow my guitar?"

In the evenings he did Elvis impersonations for the tourists. It bumped up his tips — and his appeal — no end.

"Could I?" Jaz asked politely. "Would you mind?"

"I don't know." The bartender hesitated, sounding doubtful.

Swiftly, Jaz reached into his wallet. Having only arrived last night, he couldn't

616

remember for the life of him how many rupees there were to the pound. Waving a handful of five-hundred-rupee notes, he said, "Just for a few minutes? Please?"

The bartender pocketed the notes before the gullible tourist came to his senses and managed to figure out just how much money he'd handed over — basically, enough to buy a dozen new guitars *and* a boat — and said, "Don't damage it, OK?"

"I won't," promised Jaz.

That is, unless Lucille used it to batter him senseless.

"Oh Jesus, the guy's a complete fruitcake," hissed the second blond. "He's actually going to try to play us a *song*."

CHAPTER 52

Lucille, her eyes closed, listened to the ul-
trasoft *slap-slap* of the waves breaking on
the shore. Flexing her bare feet, she felt the
silver-white sand, as fine as powdered sugar,
sift between her toes. In the distance she
could hear children playing, and farther
along the beach a family was enthusiastically engaged in a game of volleyball. As the
sunlight played on her eyelids, Lucille
listened to the insect-like buzz of a mono-
plane flying overhead. Out to sea, a couple
of Jet Skis began to rev up. And somebody
behind her had switched on a radio . . .

Every tiny hair on the back of Lucille's
neck prickled to attention as she recognized
the song being played . . . or, more ac-
curately, the bare bones of a song she knew
almost as well as she knew her own name.

I need to let you know
I can't let you go

You leave me with no alternative . . .

Oh my God, my God, thought Lucille, beginning to tremble uncontrollably. It was just a voice and a guitar. Jaz's voice. So he'd gone ahead and recorded the song after all. Without her.

> You see it's our affair
> And I can't bear to share
> Your love — yours to take and mine to give
> Because I'd die, I'd die, I'd die for you
> If you asked me to
> You're my angel, my miracle, my reason to
> live . . .

Slowly, slowly, Lucille sat up. Who was she trying to kid?

There was no radio playing behind her.

She turned and gazed over her shoulder, following the direction of the music, until she traced it to the tiny circular beachfront bar with its palm-leaf roof underlit by fairy lights and two of its bar stools occupied by an apparently matching pair of blonds in bright pink bikinis.

And there, sitting at the far end of the bar, was Jaz. He was wearing a crumpled white shirt and his favorite pair of battered old Levi's, and Lucille's heart flipped over like a pancake at the sight of him. No matter how hard she'd tried, she hadn't been able to stop herself thinking about Jaz. And now, like some stupendous miracle, he was actually here.

The next moment her stomach contracted with fear as it occurred to her that one of the bar stool blonds could be Celeste.

It took ten seconds of concentrated squinting before Lucille was able to relax, having convinced herself that it was OK, neither of them were Celeste. Not unless Celeste had spent the last week and a half getting hair extensions, tattoos engraved around her belly button, and a mega boob job.

Barely able to breathe, let alone sing, Jaz watched Lucille head toward him. The guitar wasn't great, but it was adequate, and anyway his fingers knew the chords by heart.

As Lucille moved closer she joined in, her voice husky and hesitant at first, then gaining in confidence as Jaz reprised the chorus. Then, at the other end of the bar, he heard a girl's voice complain loudly. "So how come she knows the words? I've never heard that song before in my life."

Breaking off abruptly, Jaz slid off his bar stool, passed the guitar back to the bartender and — when she reached him —

took Lucille's hand.

When they were out of earshot, Lucille said, somewhat shakily, "Bit of a way to come, isn't it, just to play one gig?"

"I'm particular about my audience." Jaz couldn't help it; he reached out and touched her cheek. She really did have the most flawless complexion in the —

"Don't." Lucille flinched away. "You mustn't. Just because we're here. It's still not fair."

"Celeste's gone." Jaz felt the corners of his mouth begin to twitch uncontrollably. It was no good; every time he thought about it, he wanted to laugh. "She ran off with Harry."

Lucille's eyes widened in amazement.

"You mean . . . *Suzy's* Harry?"

"It's a luurve thing, apparently. They couldn't help themselves. Suzy's furious because it's left her looking like a jilted fiancée. Oh, and Celeste never was an alcoholic — it was just her way of getting to know me. And a lady named Merle Denison came looking for you. She spoke to Suzy and cleared up all manner of problems. I've got a letter here for you, by the way. From Suzy." Digging in his back pocket as he spoke, Jaz rattled on nervously, "So anyway, she's *much* happier now, and she'll be happier still when you forgive her for being such a belligerent, jealous cow."

"Crikey," said Lucille when he finally paused for breath. "Did I just climb out of a Badedas bath?"

Jaz smiled. "I know. A lot's happened. Here's the letter from Suzy."

He handed over the crumpled emerald-green envelope. Lucille gazed at it, then at him. "You came all this way to deliver a letter?"

"I've felt pretty mean, to tell you the truth. Suzy's been blaming herself for your disappearing act. She thinks it's all her fault." Tilting his head to one side, Jaz realized he had to stop wondering what on earth he was going to say, and just go for it. "You shouldn't have run away, you know. What happened between us was never meant to be a one-night stand. I loved you . . . I *love* you," he persisted, his voice beginning to break. "And OK, I didn't know how I was going to end it with Celeste, but that's all over now, I don't have to worry about her anymore. There's nothing to stop us being together. You and me. I mean it, Lucille . . . don't look at me like that, I'm *serious.*"

He was, he really was. A lump the size of a table tennis ball sprang into Lucille's throat, because Jaz was always laughing, joking, and teasing those around him. The one thing he could never be accused of was being serious.

God, what a mess. It meant so much to hear him say it, but she still couldn't let it happen. Oh well, may as well be honest. He'd come a long way. The least she could do was tell him the truth. "Suzy would never forgive me."

Jaz looked astonished. "*Forgive* you? What for?"

"You . . . and me," faltered Lucille.

"I'm sorry. I don't get this at all. Why not?"

God, talk about embarrassing. Unhappily, Lucille shrugged and mumbled, "She just wouldn't, OK? She'd absolutely hate it."

"This," Jaz declared, "is complete nonsense. Either that" — his dark eyes narrowed — "or a last-ditch excuse."

How could he think that? "It's true!" Lucille blurted out. "She *told* me."

"Right." Jaz yanked his phone out of his shirt pocket and dialed a number. "We'll just see about that, shall we?"

"Oh God," wailed Lucille, "you can't call her! This is *sooo* embarrassing."

"Not nearly as embarrassing as flying halfway around the world to ask someone to marry you," said Jaz, "and being turned

623

down flat."

Lucille gasped. "You haven't asked me to marry you!"

"Only because you haven't given me the chance . . . Hello? Suzy? Hi, it's me. Listen, I've got something I need to ask you."

In Bristol, Suzy shouted, "Jaz, where the bloody hell are you? Have you any *idea* how worried we've been? Are you drunk? Did you go out on a bender? Have you been arrested? Jesus, I've been going out of my mind . . . Are you calling from a police cell?"

"Hang on, calm down. Stop yelling at me," protested Jaz. "Of course I haven't been drinking. What on earth made you think that?"

"You said you were off to an AA meeting," Suzy bellowed at him, "and you offered to drop my letter to Lucille into the mailbox on your way there. Except that was two days ago and there hasn't been a word from you since. So what I'd like to know is what the fuck do you think you're *playing* at?"

"Relax, I'm fine. Now listen," said Jaz, winking at Lucille and realizing that he no longer had to worry. "If I told you I was in love with another girl, would you be jealous?"

"What?" spluttered Suzy. "Jealous? Jesus,

why would I want to be jealous?" Suspiciously, she added, "Are you sure you're not drunk?"

"Absolutely sober, I promise. Now, how would you feel if I told you the girl I was in love with was your sister?"

Suzy's screech nearly perforated his eardrum. "JULIA? NO! NO, NO, NO. This has to be a JOKE. You can't POSSIBLY BE IN LOVE WITH JULIA!"

Calmly, Jaz said, "Other sister."

"Lucille? You . . . and Lucille . . . ?" Suzy sounded dazed.

"Would you be furious?"

"I don't get it. Furious about what? Jaz, is this some kind of joke? Are you really in love with Lucille?"

"If you hate the idea," Jaz said gravely, "I'll forget all about it." Ha! *As if.* "Won't even mention it to her. I'd hate to be the cause of trouble between you and Lucille."

"Jaz, are you mad? I'd love it if you two got together! God, that'd be so fantastic."

She'd *love* it, Jaz mouthed at Lucille. *Fantastic.*

"So you wouldn't mind," he double-checked with Suzy, "if I asked her to marry me?"

"OF COURSE I WOULDN'T MIND,

625

YOU BIG IDIOT," Suzy roared in exasperation.

"And you'll tell Lucille that?"

"I promise." With exaggerated patience, Suzy said, "As soon as she gets back from Mauritius, *if* we ever get her back from Mauritius. I'll tell her the very instant she steps off the plane."

"I'm sorry, I can't wait that long. Here." Smiling at Lucille, Jaz slid his free arm around her bare waist, pulling her toward him. "Tell her now."

CHAPTER 53

"Hi," said Fee with a bright smile. "I'm back."

Rory, who was scrabbling on the floor beneath his desk for the pen he had just dropped, jerked upright and hit his head — *clunk* — against the underside of the left-hand drawer.

"Oh, poor you!" Fee cried as, dazed, he made it into a sitting position. "Are you all right?"

"Fine, fine," murmured Rory, feeling sick and faint but somehow ecstatic at the same time. *You're back! At last! I've missed you so much!*

Of course, he didn't actually say that. Instead, he held his breath and quietly quivered with pleasure while Fee examined his head.

"Bit of a dent," she pronounced at last, straightening up. "But no blood."

"Shame." If there had been blood, she

could have mopped it up. "I mean, good," Rory hastily amended. "How are you, anyway? Mother better now?"

"Tons better."

"You're looking well."

"Thanks." Fee blushed. "I just popped in to say hello, see how you all are."

Attempting joviality, Rory said, "All the better for seeing you!" and instantly wanted to die. Only a complete and utter nerd would say that.

Seized with a sudden overwhelming urge to say, "God, sorry, I'm not really a nerd," then realizing that this would only make matters worse, Rory rushed on, "Actually, we've been pretty busy. Managed to sell Harley House at last — ha-ha. And we've handled three apartments in Royal York Crescent in the last fortnight alone!"

Oh, dazzling stuff. Absolutely riveting. Rubbing his head, Rory wondered unhappily if he could plead concussion.

"Still working too hard," Fee remarked, smiling and giving him a tut-tut look. "Suzy told me you missed the relaxation weekend."

"I know. I should have gone. Maybe another time, now that you're back." Rory didn't allow himself to get his hopes up. By now he had surely blown it. The chances of Fee being interested in spending a relaxation weekend away with an uptight workaholic who was also now officially a world-class nerd had to be in the range of zero-to-nil.

"Actually, I don't know if you'd be able to get away" — Fee was pulling her woolly gloves off with her teeth and delving into her bag — "but I've got a leaflet here; there's a great-sounding course in Snowdonia this weekend." Pulling out the skinny brochure, she grimaced and said apologetically, "I suppose that's too short notice."

In a daze, Rory said, "*This* weekend?"

"I know. And it's Thursday already. Oh well, it was just a thought."

"I'm free," announced Rory. "I can make it." He nodded his head vigorously. He would make it if it killed him.

"Are you sure?" Fee looked delighted.

Rory, the great decision maker, nodded again. "Yes."

"So shall I give them a call?"

"Absolutely. Just what we both need, a bit of a break. And this time," Rory told Fee with absolute confidence, "nothing's going to get in the way."

"Can you believe it?" gasped Suzy as she was hurled by a gust of wind through the door of the office the following afternoon. "The middle of November and it's starting to snow! They're giving out weather warnings on the radio: gales, blizzards, the works. My nose feels as if it's dropped off and my fingers have frostbite — I'm telling you, it's like Siberia out there."

"Poor old Jaz and Lucille," Donna remarked sympathetically, "stuck on some rotten beach in Mauritius."

"Sun, sea, and oodles of sex." Suzy sighed. "God, I feel so sorry for them. I mean, why would anyone want to be there when they could be here, experiencing all this?" She waved an expansive arm, indicating the gray, windswept street outside, the huge sticky snowflakes swirling past almost horizontally, the bundled-up passersby struggling to stay upright. "And if this is what we've got in Bristol, imagine what it's like in the wilds of Wales. You're going to have to cancel your trip." She looked over at Rory who was determinedly ignoring her. "You do realize that, don't you?"

Rory carried on furiously rattling keys on the computer. "We'll be fine. Lot of fuss about nothing."

"Rory, you'll never reach Snowdonia. The roads will be impassable. According to the weather forecast we're in for a whole week of this stuff."

"I'm not canceling." Rory's jaw was set in

a stubborn line. "I promised Fee we'd go, and that's it. We're going."

Suzy and Donna exchanged glances.

"But Fee might not *want* to go," Suzy patiently explained. "Not now the weather's gone bananas. Anyway" — she was struck by a thought — "what with it being this windy, they might close the Severn Bridge. Then you wouldn't be *able* to get across to Wales."

That did it. Rory's bags were all packed and ready in the car. Reaching for the phone, he dialed Fee's number.

Funny how he knew it by heart.

"Hi, it's me. The weather's not looking too marvelous, so I thought we might set off early. Or" — he forced his voice to remain neutral — "if you'd rather give it a miss, we'll cancel."

After a moment's hesitation, Fee said cautiously, "Do *you* want to cancel?"

In the office, making a point of ignoring Suzy, Rory gripped the phone. "No. Not at all."

"Oh well, in that case" — Fee sounded as if she was smiling — "I'm game if you are."

Rory breathed a sigh of relief. "I'll pick you up in five minutes."

Another blast of icy air swirled into the office as the door swung open and shut behind him. In no time at all, like Batman, Rory was gone.

"Blimey, he must be desperate," Donna marveled. "He left without even switching off his computer."

"Hmmm." Suzy had begun to suspect that something a bit unusual was going on here. "I can't help wondering just how relaxing my brother's going to find it, spending the weekend halfway up some mountain with his car stuck in a fifteen-foot snowdrift."

The door swung open three hours later, just as they were closing up for the night. By this time it was pitch-black outside and the fat, somersaulting snowflakes were hurtling past the window at breakneck speed.

"Suzy! Goodness, what about this snow, isn't it just fabulous?" Gabriella was laughing as she pulled off her white fake-fur hat and shook snowflakes from her glossy hair.

"Oh. Hi." Suzy instantly felt like a big heifer in comparison. Gabriella was looking tiny and absolutely dazzling in a scarlet wool coat trimmed with the same fake fur as her hat. Her cheeks and nose were a delicate shade of pink, her eyes as bright as diamonds. She looked exactly like someone in a Ralph Lauren ad . . . with the added bonus that if you happened to keel over with a heart attack she'd know all the latest resuscitation techniques.

Dammit, she even smelled gorgeous.

"Fantastic news about Lucille," exclaimed Gabriella. "You must be thrilled for her."

"I am," Suzy agreed. "Really happy. They're going to get married, did you know?"

"Must be catching." Smiling broadly, Gabriella waggled her engagement ring — *flash flash* — then dived into her shiny black Hermès bag and pulled out a couple of envelopes. "That's exactly why I'm here. I was just around the corner speaking to the people who are doing the flowers for our wedding, so I thought I may as well pop in, say hello, and give you your invitation. Lucille's too, if you wouldn't mind passing it on to her when she gets back."

"Lovely," said Suzy, with over-the-top enthusiasm. Opening the heavy envelope, she slid out the embossed, white-on-white card. "Wow! December the twenty-fourth."

"I know, a Christmas Eve wedding. Can you think of anything more romantic?"

Not offhand, no, thought Suzy. *Unless you count* me *marrying Leo . . .*

"Ooh, I love Christmas weddings." Eagerly, Donna said, "So what's your dress like?"

"Heaven." Gabriella was clearly delighted to have been asked. "In fact, I just picked it up from the dressmaker yesterday." Unfastening her coat, she sketched the outline of the dress against herself with her narrow, expressive hands. "Deep-red velvet bodice, cut low like this and this . . . dark green beading around the bustline . . . then a creamy-white satin skirt, very full and coming out like *this* . . . and a dark green velvet cloak with deep-red beading, instead of a veil. Oh, and the cloak's lined with crimson satin, and I've got shoes to match."

"Cool," said Donna, nodding in appreciation. "Plain white's just boring, isn't it? If my guy asked me to marry him, we'd have a real Goth ceremony. I'd wear a big black wedding dress. But yours sounds great too, doesn't it, Suzy? Hello? Suzy?"

"What? Oh . . . oh yes, um, gorgeous."

To her absolute horror Suzy realized she had been busy picturing herself in the dress Gabriella had described. What's more, she couldn't stop. Because she had actually been there, in the church, heading joyfully down the aisle with the organ booming out wedding-type music and Leo, in his tuxedo, turning to smile at her, hardly able to contain the look of love and pride in his dark blue eyes . . . *Oh yes, I'd look amazing in that dress, it would suit me far more than it would suit Gabriella. Wouldn't fit me, of course, seeing as it's a dinky size six and I'm an undinky size twelve, but if you could spread it out on the photocopier and just press the Enlarge button . . .*

OK, getting seriously carried away now. Enough of the fantasy. Cut.

"It all sounds brilliant." Aware that her heart was racing like a hamster on a wheel, Suzy concentrated on appearing normal. Smiling, she said, "Really. Thanks so much for inviting me."

"Don't be daft," exclaimed Gabriella. "Of course you have to be there! Anyway, Leo insisted."

Hmmm, thought Suzy, *probably because he can't wait to rub in the fact that he's getting married . . . and Harry's getting married . . . and even Lucille's getting married.*

And I'm not.

Rory's car was doing its best against the elements, but the elements were on the verge of victory.

"Did you ever see *Bambi?*" said Fee, her knuckles whitening as she clutched at her seat belt.

"Once. When I was about six."

"The bit where Bambi's trying to stand

635

up on the ice, with his legs going in all directions?"

"I think so," said Rory. "Why?"

"Oh, I don't know. It's just the way this car keeps skidding across the road, I'm starting to feel a bit like Bambi."

The Black Mountains of Wales were no longer black. Everything around them was fast disappearing beneath an impenetrable layer of white. The snow, pelting the car, stuck to it like papier-mâché. Sheep, huddling against low drystone walls for shelter, looked every bit as fed up as Rory felt.

"It's only the middle of November," he said despairingly. "This isn't supposed to happen now."

But, of course, Murphy's Law had decreed that it must happen, because he was, officially, the world's unluckiest man.

They weren't going to make it; he knew that for a fact. At this rate, Snowdonia was as out of reach as the Antarctic. If they slid off the road and into a ditch they could be stuck here for days.

"What do you want to do?" said Rory. "Go back?"

"I don't know. I'm not sure we can. I can't even work out where we are on the map," said Fee. "I've had my eyes closed for so long I've completely lost my bearings."

As she spoke, a signpost appeared ahead of them, just visible in the car's headlights but with its signs obliterated by snow. Shifting gears carefully, doing his best to avoid slamming into the post, Rory managed to slow the car to a halt. Leaping out onto the shoulder, Fee cleared the sign with the end of her woolly scarf.

"Hay-on-Wye, four miles." She gasped, jumping back into the car and rubbing her icy hands together. "That'll do me."

She sounded like a hitchhiker relieved to have flagged down a ride. Confused, Rory pushed his slipping glasses up over the bridge of his nose. "You mean . . . you want me to drop you there?"

Turning to look at him, Fee burst out laughing. "Rory, come on. We can't reach Snowdonia, and we can't go back. We're marooned. So why don't we just make the best of it? We'll improvise, have our very own relaxation weekend."

"In Hay-on-Wye?" The worried look began to recede from Rory's face.

"You'll like it," Fee assured him. "It's a beautiful place."

CHAPTER 54

"This is a beautiful place," Rory agreed several hours later. The hotel they had booked into was warm and welcoming, inglenooked and open-fired. Over a magical dinner, they had talked nonstop, and it hadn't been stressful at all. Now, over coffee, he smiled and told Fee, "I'm relaxing already."

"See? No pressure of work. No phones ringing, no belligerent clients to deal with, no houses to sell. You're free to do whatever you want."

Oh, Rory thought longingly, *if only you knew.*

"Anything at all," Fee reiterated, hinting madly and praying she didn't sound like a trollop.

Feeling daring, Rory said, "In that case, I'm going to ask the bartender if I can have a cognac to go with my coffee."

So much for hint-dropping. Exasperated,

Fee said, "That's your trouble. Sometimes you're just too polite. You're the customer, Rory. If you want a cognac, you can have one. You can have as many cognacs as you like."

Rory had his cognac.

Then he had another, to give him some much-needed Dutch courage.

For Rory, who seldom drank, two cognacs was quite a lot.

Finally, as they were about to make their way upstairs, he said, "So, would you say that was a general rule, or does it only apply to cognac?"

Bewildered, Fee said, "I'm sorry?"

"It's the end of the evening. I think we've had a nice time. I've enjoyed myself, anyway." Buoyed up by the alcohol, Rory went on, "And now I'd very much like to kiss you, but I don't know whether I'm supposed to ask you if I can kiss you, or if I should just go ahead and, er . . . do it."

"Oh!" exclaimed Fee, tingling all over. "Well, um . . . gosh, I think you should just do it."

"Not ask first? You're sure?"

"No no no, definitely don't ask first." Leaning back against the heavy oak banister, her fingers curling helplessly around the newel posts, Fee whispered joyfully, "That would spoil the surprise."

"What are you thinking?" Rory asked much, much later.

"Oh, just that it seems a bit of a waste, paying for two huge rooms when we're only going to be using one."

Fee gazed lovingly down at Rory, lying next to her. His gray eyes — for once minus glasses — had lost their anxious expression. His whole face seemed to have softened and relaxed. And as for the rest of him . . . well, who would ever have guessed that beneath those crisp white shirts and conservative suits lurked quite such an impressive body?

Thank you, snow, thought Fee, sinking back against the mountain of pillows and idly stroking Rory's bare torso.

"It's hardly worth canceling," he said. "We're only here for two nights."

In response to this, Fee jumped out of bed. Padding over to the window, she gazed out at the ever-deepening snow. Their room overlooked the main drag, which was looking ridiculously picturesque, like one of those sentimental black-and-white movies starring Greer Garson.

"Two nights?" Fee glanced mischievously at Rory over her shoulder. "You'll be lucky. By the look of this weather, we could be stuck here for quite some time."

"Oh dear, that's terrible." Rory sighed. "You mean we're going to be forced to spend days and days together, learning to relax?"

"Maybe even weeks and weeks." Fee shook her auburn head sorrowfully.

"It's an absolute tragedy." Reaching for her, Rory held out his arms. "Come here," he murmured, pulling Fee gently back into bed with him, "and relax some more."

The world had gone mad. It was, Suzy decided on Sunday evening, like finding yourself in an episode of *The Twilight Zone* where everything seemed normal but clearly wasn't. For a start, this definitely wasn't the real Rory she was speaking to on the phone. It had to be an alien impostor pretending to be Rory. And, to be frank, making a rather poor job of it.

"Well, there we go," he wound up breezily — *breezily,* for heaven's sake. "Not a lot we can do about it, so I guess we'll just see you when we see you."

I mean, how convincing was that? Rory said things like, *See you at ten thirty-five sharp* and *I'll be with you in exactly seventeen minutes.* His whole life was ruled by the clock; punctuality was the key to efficiency in Rory's book.

See you when we see you simply didn't feature in his vocabulary.

And then there was the other thing.

"I don't get this." Suzy frowned at the TV, which was showing the weather report. "There's no snow left in Bristol at all. It just came down in a giant whoosh on Friday and melted on Saturday. You'd never know it had been here."

"Really? Lucky old you. We're still completely snowed in," Rory repeated. "Can't imagine when we'll get out. Still," he went on cheerfully — *cheerfully?* — "can't be helped. I'm sure you'll be able to cope."

"What if I can't?"

"Hmmm? Oh, just make some phone calls, cancel a few appointments."

Suzy goggled. "You're not serious!"

"Hey, it's only a few houses we're talking about." Rory's tone was chiding. "Hardly life and death."

Enough was enough.

"Let me speak to Fee," Suzy barked.

"Sorry, she's in the bath. I'll give you a call during the week, OK? Until then, just go with the flow," said Rory.

Or the alien masquerading as Rory, to be precise.

The world's definitely going mad, thought

Suzy, staring in disbelief at the receiver, which was now going *brrrrr* in her ear.

The alien had hung up.

"Are you sure?" Lucille was having a bit of trouble breathing, she was being hugged so hard. "I mean, I know you were fine about it on the phone, but are you *really* sure you're okay with this?"

Lucille had new beads in her hair to match the new glow of happiness surrounding her like a halo.

"Come on," Suzy protested, "how can I not be thrilled? My favorite ex-husband and my favorite new sister?"

"Well, quite," said Lucille. "Be honest, it must feel a bit odd."

"Look, I want Jaz to be happy. The only reason I could never stop having a go at Celeste was because I knew she wasn't the one for him. She wasn't good enough, for a start." Suzy spread her arms wide. "But this is completely different, because you are!"

More hugs, more squashed lungs, but there was still something bothering Lucille.

"When we argued that time . . ." She paused, hating to have to say it. "You were mad because you said Jaz liked me more than he liked you."

"But I didn't mean it! We're sisters," cried

Suzy, "and we were having our first fight. What did I tell you about fighting with sisters? You say anything and everything that comes into your head, no holds barred. It doesn't *mean* anything; you weren't supposed to take it to heart. You especially weren't supposed to run away to a tropical island practically on the other side of the world . . ."

Tut-tutting as he lugged cases past them into the hallway, Jaz said, "I don't know, all this hugging and making up, it's like being trapped in an episode of *Friends*. Ah, Maeve, there you are. Excellent to see you again. Could we just shake hands and do without all the sloppy stuff?"

"Will you listen to this fellow?" Maeve's shriek rattled the chandeliers as she enveloped him in a mammoth embrace. "All tanned and gorgeous and announcing that he's getting married again, and he thinks he can get away without a proper welcome home!"

"Third time's the charm, what d'you think?" Jaz murmured the words almost under his breath as she went about kissing him noisily on both cheeks.

"I think — *mwah* — you've got it right at last — *mwah* — and about bloody time too," Maeve declared. "If you must know, I saw it coming weeks ago. It half killed me, keeping my mouth shut and letting you figure it out for yourself."

"You're a witch," said Jaz.

"Tuh, nothing so exotic. I just watch the soaps," Maeve boasted. "When you've seen as many as I have, you learn to spot the signs a mile off."

"I'm sooo glad you're both back." Suzy's tone was fretful. "It's been horrible here without you."

Jaz was checking the cars parked outside.

"Where's Fee? I thought she'd be here too."

"And that's another thing." Rolling her eyes, Suzy said darkly, "Something extremely weird has happened to my brother."

"I'm sorry," panted Lucille, tugging uselessly on Baxter's leash as he cannoned through the front door of Curtis and Co. "I just couldn't stop him. We were on our way through Victoria Square when he suddenly started howling and rampaging across the flower beds. I think he realized he was around the corner from your office and decided he wanted to see you."

Well, it was nice that someone did. Deeply flattered, Suzy waggled Baxter's ears and said, "You always were a dog with impeccable taste."

"Just a quick hello, then we have to go," Lucille warned Baxter. "Suzy's busy."

"Actually, I'm meeting a client in Kensington Place." Suzy reached for her bag and stood up. "It's not worth taking the car. Why don't we walk through the square together?"

Great idea, snuffled Baxter, *and just to refresh my memory, is this the drawer where you keep your emergency supply of potato chips?*

They were halfway across the square when two men sitting on one of the benches began grinning and nudging each other like a pair of music hall comedians.

"Do you know them?" said Suzy.

Lucille shook her head. "No, I thought they must know you."

"Hey, Buster," one of the men called out, clicking his fingers.

"No, *wrong.*" The other one shook his head vigorously. "It was Baxter, remember? Hey, Baxter, over here!"

Naturally, idiotically, Baxter bounded over to them like a dopey debutante at a party. He hadn't a clue who these guys were, but if they knew his name, that was good enough for him.

Besides, they might give him some chips.

CHAPTER 55

"Something's still not right," complained the more flamboyant of the two men. He wagged his finger at Lucille and Suzy. "It's the same outfit, definitely, but the wrong one's wearing it."

Mystified, Lucille looked at Suzy.

"Have you the foggiest idea what they're talking about?"

Suzy shook her head. Damn, why hadn't she just donated the lime-green-and-silver-striped tracksuit top and cycling shorts to Oxfam instead of giving them to Lucille?

"It's her. It *is* her. Look at her face!" crowed the second man. "Same dog, same outfit . . . Hey, darling, put us out of our misery. Did you ever manage to get it together with Leo?"

"Ignore them." Suzy turned scarlet and attempted to drag Lucille away. "They're a couple of drunks. They spend their days on park benches hurling abuse at innocent passersby."

"Don't drag me," complained Lucille. "We can't leave Baxter. Anyway, they said something about Leo."

"Come on, you can tell us," urged the first one. He grinned lewdly at Suzy. "Are you still fantasizing about him? Leo Fitzthing-ummy? Still wondering what he looks like with his clothes off?"

"Never mind that." His friend giggled. "What I want to know is did she ever screw him?"

"Ah. Good question. Well?" The first man raised his blond eyebrows at Suzy. "Did you? Because you know you wanted to."

"This is complete bullshit," Suzy muttered, wishing the ground would open up.

"Now stop it. You mustn't deny your innermost feelings," the other one chided. "You told us you loved him."

"I did *not* tell you that," shrieked Suzy, too embarrassed to catch Lucille's eye and wondering how she was ever going to live this down.

"She's right, you know. She didn't tell us. She was talking to herself at the time." Enjoying himself immensely, the first one clutched his heart and declared, "Oh, woe is me. How can I marry Billy when 'tis Leo I truly love?"

"Harry," Lucille corrected him automatically. "Not Billy."

"That's right." The other one nodded, remembering. "It was Harry."

His friend shrugged, patting Baxter and grinning across at Suzy. "OK, but I still think she has a nerve, yakking away to herself like that and accusing us of needing help."

"Well?" said Lucille, clipping Baxter's leash to his collar. The gay couple had sauntered off in the opposite direction, arm in arm and laughing like maniacs.

Suzy, collapsing on the bench they had just vacated, said despairingly, "Damn, I really wish I'd taken the car."

Lucille sat down too, stuffing her cold hands into the pockets of the tracksuit top Suzy had given her. "Is it true? Are you really in love with Leo?"

"No. No. Of course not." Suzy shook her head, then abruptly stopped and closed her eyes. "Yes."

"But —"

"I know. You don't have to tell me. It's a disaster."

"I wouldn't call it a disaster." Lucille hesitated, because of course it was.

"Come on. He's already taken." Suzy

649

opened her eyes and sighed. "By Gabriella, of all people. They're getting married next month and there isn't a thing I can do about it. How much more disastrous can it get?"

Lucille thought for a moment. "Does Leo know?"

"You must be joking! And he's never going to find out! If he did, I'd just die." Suzy swiveled around in a panic. "And if you tell him, then you'll be the one who dies, so don't even think it."

"But he might —"

"No," Suzy interrupted before Lucille could say the words. "He wouldn't. He just wouldn't, OK?" *Don't you understand? He's out of my league.* "And I wouldn't either," she went on, "because he's getting married."

This wasn't the real reason, of course, but there were some things just too hard to admit to. After a lifetime of being able to pick and choose and have any man you wanted, it was a pretty humbling experience falling for one who was unlikely to want you back.

And why would *he want me,* Suzy thought with resignation, *when he's already got Gabriella?*

"I waited until you were on your own," said Celeste. "Can I come in?"

650

"Why?"

"I need to see you. It's important."

"Actually, I was just about to —"

"Please. Please. We really have to talk."

"Won't the doorstep do?"

"Don't mess around. This is serious. Come on, Jaz, let me in."

Jaz hadn't been messing around, but he let Celeste in anyway. Since she was wearing a pink chiffon crop top and a pink-and-white polka-dot skirt the size of a Kleenex, she was in danger of freezing to death if he didn't. She was already shivering dramatically. When the temperature outside fell below zero, normal people wore coats. Celeste's idea of bundling up had always been to throw on a slightly less-transparent bra.

In the kitchen she huddled against the stove, hugging her stomach and pressing the backs of her bare, fake-tanned legs against the heated rail.

"I've been waiting around the corner for Maeve to go out to the shops." Celeste spoke through chattering teeth.

"You'd better have something to warm you up," said Jaz. "Tea? Coffee?" He paused, his gaze unwavering. "Or maybe you'd prefer a brandy."

"You're looking great," Celeste parried,

fluffing up her hair and ignoring the dig. "Really brown."

"Thanks. Why don't you just tell me why you're here?"

"Oh, Jaz." Clutching the chrome rail and shaking her head, Celeste blurted the words out. "I've done the stupidest thing in the world. It's all been a hideous mistake. All I wanted to do was make you jealous, get you to notice me again . . . it was never serious with Harry, he's nothing compared to you."

"Actually," said Jaz, "I already knew that."

"It's over, OK? I just want to come home." Letting go of the heated rail, Celeste moved across the kitchen toward him. "I love you, Jaz. I never stopped loving you for a second." Her pink lower lip jutted out prettily. "We're good together, aren't we?"

Jaz pretended to consider this. "Good at what, exactly?"

"Sweetheart, please. I made a mistake. I've said I'm sorry. Now if you'd just forgive me, can we forget it ever happened?"

Jaz breathed in the scent she was wearing, the kind she knew he liked. "I forgive you."

In response, a single tear of happiness slid down Celeste's cheek.

"Oh, sweetheart, I *knew* it —"

"But that's all." Jaz shook his head as she reached out to him. "You aren't coming back. It's over."

"What?" The penitent pout promptly went into reverse; Celeste's lips almost vanished from sight. "It isn't over. It can't be. I won't *let* it be over —"

"No choice, I'm afraid." Jaz shrugged and glanced at his watch.

"I kept you from drinking all those years!" shrieked Celeste. "The whole reason I didn't drink was to make sure you didn't start again. Don't you see? I didn't stop because I was an alcoholic; I did it because I loved you!"

"Really?" Jaz raised an eyebrow. "Interesting concept. Sure it isn't anything to do with my bank balance?"

"That's not fair!"

"Let's not have a fight about this. It's over," said Jaz. "Go home to Harry."

"He's *boring,*" roared Celeste, "and he hasn't got any *money,* and he thinks it'd be a good idea if I got myself a *job!*"

"Shocking." Jaz was by this time struggling to keep a straight face.

"Don't laugh." Celeste stamped her foot so hard that a pink silk dragonfly fell off the toe of her shoe. "It isn't funny. You'll never find another girlfriend like me, you know."

"Well, that's something," said Jaz.

"You miss me," Celeste whined. "You

can't pretend you don't."

Jaz considered whether to tell her about Lucille. After consideration, he decided he wouldn't.

"Time to go," he said patiently.

"You could end up spending the rest of your life alone." Celeste's voice rose as he maneuvered her out of the kitchen. "You'll be so miserable." Tears were now rolling down her cheeks in earnest. "Dammit, I'm going to be miserable too, and it's *all your fault.*"

"I daresay we'll both cope." Jaz pulled open the front door with a flourish and stood to one side. Lightly, he said, "Remember what they taught us. You just have to take it one day at a time."

It was a toss-up which of them was more alarmed when Lucille answered the door the following evening and saw who was on the front doorstep. In an instant her heart plummeted.

Oh crikey, what now?

"Oh. It's you," Julia said shortly, her gaze roaming everywhere but in Lucille's direction. "I need to see Suzy."

Julia was looking very done-up in a full-length pale yellow silk dress worn under a midnight-blue velvet jacket. Her dark hair was tied back in a ballerina's bun, the makeup had been troweled on, and heirloom jewelry glittered at her ears, wrists, and throat.

Feeling somewhat done-down by comparison in her black sweatshirt and jogging pants, Lucille cleared her throat and waited until Julia was forced to look her in the eye. "Sorry. Suzy's out."

"Oh well, that's typical." Julia heaved a sigh, exasperated by Suzy's selfishness. "Right, never mind, just let me in anyway. I need to borrow something from her closet."

"She should be back soon," said Lucille. "Why don't you come in and wait?"

Julia's stare was positively glacial. "Alternatively, why don't I come in and borrow something from Suzy's closet? She's my sister, you know. It's really not a problem. She wouldn't *mind.*"

Phew, scary.

"OK." Lucille backed toward the stairs. "Come on up."

Diplomatically, she waited in the sitting room while Julia ransacked Suzy's closet.

"Oh God," wailed Julia. "This is hopeless hopeless *hopeless.*"

"What is?" Lucille appeared in the bedroom doorway. The bed was awash with discarded dresses, and Julia was pacing up

655

and down, agitatedly twisting the neck off a padded hanger.

"OK, here's the situation." The words were bubbling up, bursting to get out. Julia evidently had to tell someone, even if the only person available was Lucille. "My husband's boss and his wife have invited us to a charity ball tonight, at the Grand Hotel. Fifteen minutes ago we drew up outside just as they were getting out of their car." The syllables were by this time being spat out separately, like gravel. "And can you believe it, my husband's boss's wife is wearing exactly the same dress as me."

"Wow," said Lucille. "That's incredible. Even the same size?"

"She's a sixteen, I'm an eight." Julia quivered at such an outrageous slur.

Lucille presumed she wasn't talking about their mental ages.

Diplomatically, she said, "So at least you look better than she does."

"I look fabulous," Julia snapped, "and she looks like a tank in stilettos."

"Oh well, isn't that good?"

"What are you, completely mad? It's a *disaster.*" Julia rolled her eyes in despair. "That's why I had to come here, to borrow another dress, but bloody Suzy hasn't got anything that'll bloody fit me, and there

isn't time to drive all the way back to Tet-
bury, and all the shops are closed, and
there's no way in the world I can walk into
the Grand Hotel, wearing exactly the same
dress as Hermione Blunkett Brain!"

"Right. I see," said Lucille. "In that case,
why don't I lend you something of mine?"

It took less than ninety seconds to rifle
through the contents of Lucille's meager —
sorry, *capsule* — closet.

Julia was breathtakingly ungrateful. "You
can't seriously expect me to wear something
like this." Wrinkling her nose in disgust, she
peered at the label of a leopard-print dress
split to the thigh. "Oh, for crying out loud,
it's Topshop."

Tempting though it was to pack Julia off
into the night in a black trash bag and
matching wellies, Lucille bit her lip and kept
her temper. "How about this one?"

Julia's lips curled. "You must be joking.
I'd never wear anything that tacky."

So much for Lucille's favorite amber silk
trouser suit.

Fretfully, Julia flung it down on the bed.
"Haven't you got anything a bit more . . .
designer?"

"This one's by Chanel," Lucille offered,
pulling out a baby-pink jersey tube dress.

"Chanel is spelled Chanel." Julia was

scornful, flicking the label with a manicured nail. "Not Channel. This is utter garbage. Where in heaven's name did you get it?"

"Southmead Market. Eight ninety-nine. I like it." Struggling to keep a straight face, Lucille flipped the dress around to show Julia the lettering on the back proclaiming *Black Girls Do It with a Wiggle.*

"Thank you very much," Julia said coldly. "You're being *such* a help."

"Look, if you want to go to the ball stark naked, that's fine by me. I'm really not that bothered."

"You're supposed to be helping me out here."

"I'm trying to help you out" — Lucille rolled her eyes helplessly — "and all you're doing is getting belligerent and sneering at my clothes."

Good grief, she realized suddenly. *We sound exactly like a couple of bickering sisters . . .*

"What's this?" Her tone petulant, Julia pulled a plain black velvet dress out of the closet. "You've cut the label out."

"Because it scratched the back of my neck," said Lucille. "It's by Donna Karan."

"Don't give me that. You couldn't afford a belt by Jasper Conran, let alone a dress."

"Maeve bought it for me. She found it in

the St. Peter's Hospice shop."

"I've never worn a thrift-shop purchase in my life," groaned Julia.

"It looks nice," Lucille assured her. "Why don't you give it a go?"

The dress looked fabulous. Luckily, Lucille hadn't expected Julia to fling her arms around her, crying, "Thank you, thank you, thank you. I'm so sorry I was horrible to you before. From now on, let's be best friends forever."

Because she didn't.

"I suppose it'll have to do." Smoothing the velvet over her narrow hips, Julia said ungraciously, "I shudder to think how old it must be. Two or three seasons at least."

Waving Julia off into the night — still agonizing that some woman at the ball might recognize it from Jasper Conran's autumn '97 collection — Lucille decided that one day, when the timing was perfect, she would tell her the truth.

Walmart.

CHAPTER 56

Suzy was in her car, on her way back from an appraisal in Abbot's Leigh, when her cell phone rang.

She almost careered off the road and into a tree when she heard who was on the other end of the phone.

"Suzy? Hi, how are you?" Leo's voice sent shivers down the backs of her legs. He sounded as if he were smiling. "Listen, I need you. Desperately."

More shivers. All over this time, darting in all directions like uncontrollable schoolchildren out on a day trip.

How totally weird that Leo should have called at that moment, just as she'd been thinking about him.

Oh, come on, thought Suzy, *who am I trying to kid? I spend 99 percent of my time thinking about Leo . . . he'd be hard pressed to get through to me on the phone during that fleeting 1 percent when I'm not.*

"Ah, but can you afford me?" she said lightly. It wasn't what you'd call a dazzling reply, but it was better than wailing, *Oh Leo, I desperately need you too.*

And so much less embarrassing.

"I could try bribery," Leo suggested. "Would that work? All the chocolate éclairs you can eat?"

Only if you let me lick the melted chocolate off your bare chest.

"What's the problem?" said Suzy, giving herself a mental slap across the face.

"The door to the cellar. I know you gave me instructions on how to open it, but nothing's happening. It really needs to be kicked by an expert."

"OK. Look, I'm in Abbot's Leigh. I'll be with you in fifteen minutes."

As she spoke, Suzy was already pulling off the road. It would only take five minutes to reach Sheldrake House. That left her another ten to redo her hair and makeup.

"OK, now pay attention." Stepping slowly toward the old trap door — like Michael Flatley about to launch into something spine-tingling — Suzy carefully raised her right foot and brought her heel down sharply on the bottom left-hand corner of the weathered oak door. "Then you kick it again six inches farther up . . . exactly *here.* Then you grab hold of the handle" — reaching down, she clasped the iron ring in both hands — "and yank it to the left while turning it to the right . . . Don't forget to keep your foot on that left-hand corner while you're doing that . . . Then take your foot away and *pull.*"

The trap door swung open, and Suzy stepped back, curtsying modestly.

"See? Just like that."

"Bloody thing. I've been trying to get it open for the last hour." Leo's smile was rueful.

"Right, now you have a go." Letting the door drop back in place, Suzy moved to one side. "Remember the routine. Kick, kick, grab, yank, pull."

Twenty minutes of intensive training later, Leo had more or less gotten the hang of it. His footwork wasn't perfect, and his yank-to-the-left-and-turn-to-the-right technique was haphazard, but he was definitely on his way.

"I'll have to get it fixed." Shaking his head, Leo rubbed his dusty hands on the sides of his jeans.

Wishing she could do the same — but suspecting Leo might regard it as an infringement of his personal liberty — Suzy said, "It's only an empty cellar. Will you ever use it?"

"Gabriella has plans to turn it into a gym."

A gym. Of course. Suzy, who couldn't imagine anything more horrible than a gym in your own home, said, "What a fantastic idea. Now, these chocolate éclairs you were talking about earlier, would they be filled with fresh cream or that weird squirty stuff out of a can?"

Paying no attention whatsoever, Leo murmured, "Oh God, your foot."

Gazing down, Suzy saw that a larger than average spider had clambered up her shoe and was now precariously balanced on the toe.

Leo, looking a bit pale, was edging away. "He must have climbed out through the trap door . . ."

"The cellar's always been full of spiders." Bending, Suzy gently scooped the runaway into her hand and set it down on the top of the stone steps leading back into the cellar. "There you go, sweetheart, you'd only get lost up here." Glancing briefly across at Leo, she added, "Or stepped on."

In the kitchen, Leo made a pot of coffee and Suzy demolished a fresh-cream éclair. Just the one, because she didn't want him to think she was a pig. Then, remembering that it didn't matter what Leo thought, because in just a few weeks he'd be marrying someone else anyway, she thought, *What the hell*, and ate another one.

"Not long to go now, before the wedding." She felt obliged to make a feeble stab at conversation as Leo handed over her cup. Reaching across the table had caused his pale gray cashmere sweater to ride up, affording her a glimpse of dazzlingly taut, tanned flesh above the belt of his jeans.

I want to touch *it. I want to know what it feels like,* thought Suzy, going hot all over with lust and shame.

"You're coming?" said Leo.

Gosh, jolly nearly.

Oh no no no.

He's getting married, remember.

To Gabriella.

Mentally giving herself a big pinch in an attempt to restore order, Suzy said sunnily, "Wouldn't miss it for the world. Any excuse for a party. And please," she told Leo, "feel free to invite as many gorgeous eligible males as you like. What with me being such a desperate old spinster these days, I need all the help I can get."

It was meant to be humorous. She'd said it to lighten the mood, that was all. He was supposed to laugh and make some jokey derogatory remark in return.

Leo didn't laugh.

He said seriously, "I spoke to Lucille last night. We had a long chat."

Oh God. All muscular control promptly flew out of the window. Suzy almost dropped her coffee cup. It was a miracle she hadn't wet her pants.

"Why didn't you tell me?" said Leo.

Oh God oh God oh God.

"Whaa . . ." Suzy discovered that her lips were moving in all the wrong directions. "Wha . . . wha . . . whaaa?"

"Why did you never tell me the truth?" Leo persisted.

This was desperate. This was truly diabolical. Maybe it wouldn't be so awful if only he was saying it in a lovey-dovey, Prince Charming kind of way, but he wasn't.

He was looking at her like a scientist observing a wired-up monkey in a lab.

"Oh, come on, I just *couldn't.*" Suzy clenched and unclenched her hands, which had gone all damp and tingly with embarrassment. Whatever else happened, she was definitely going to have to kill Lucille.

"I suppose not. But I wish you had. It would have made a real difference," Leo said quietly.

Duh? It would?

"I didn't respect you," he went on, as Suzy's head shot up. "I knew you weren't really in love with him, and that's what I couldn't stand. I thought you were just in it for the publicity, the money, whatever . . ."

Double duh?

"Hang on, just hang on a second," Suzy blurted out. "What exactly did Lucille tell you last night?"

Leo gave her an odd look. "Everything. About the engagement being a sham. About Harry blackmailing you into going along with it, because it was his big chance to make a sackload of cash. I mean, I always knew Harry envied me, but I never realized he had such a thing about being second best."

Suzy waited, without moving a muscle, for Leo to take a breath before adding, "Oh yes, and of course Lucille told me the great story about you being in love with me. Ha! Gabriella and I had a real laugh when we heard that one."

It didn't happen.

Leo had finished speaking.

Which was great news for Lucille because it meant she didn't have to die a grisly, Hannibal Lecter–type death after all.

And even better news for Suzy herself.

"I felt sorry for him," she told Leo. Miraculously, her powers of speech had returned. "When I realized how much it meant to Harry, I didn't have the heart to say no. And it wasn't as if we were hurting anyone."

"No." Leo looked thoughtful for a second. "No, I suppose you weren't."

"I have to go." As the grandfather clock began to chime out in the hall, Suzy rose to her feet.

"Busy?" Leo smiled slightly.

"Busy. I'm showing a couple a house on Bell Barn Road." Suzy forced herself to concentrate as he helped her into her coat. "Then at three o'clock, I've got an appraisal in Durdham Park. After that, I have to taxi some woman and her four children around half a dozen different properties . . . Oh, the fun never stops."

Her coat was on. Somehow they'd reached the door. Proximity to Leo — and the touch of his hands on her neck as he'd straightened her upturned collar — had caused Suzy's heart to break once more into an undignified gallop.

Terrified in case he could hear it, she made a grab for the door handle. In that same split second, so did Leo.

"Sorry, sorry . . . Um, I've just realized I'm going to be late." Flustered, Suzy ricocheted off the door frame, cracking her shoulder painfully — and audibly — against the wood. "Ooooch, clumsy me, better get a move on . . . Don't forget: kick, kick, grab, yank, pull."

"Absolutely." Leo nodded, then held out his arm, blocking her exit. "Suzy, I need to —"

"Must dash now." Ducking under his arm faster than a Harlem Globetrotter, Suzy trilled, "Give my love to Gabriella, won't you? And I'll see you both at the wedding!"

Except she wouldn't, of course, because she now knew there was no way she could put herself through such an ordeal.

Standing there watching Leo marry Gabriella, Suzy realized sadly, would simply hurt too much.

Oh God, what am I doing *here? I must be mad. What am I doing here?*

In the pew, next to Suzy, Lucille whispered, "Doesn't she look amazing?"

"Who?"

"Gabriella, you twit!"

"Oh. Yes. Amazing."

"Beautiful dress."

"Thanks."

"Not you. I'm talking about Gabriella's dress. Honestly, will you listen to her?"

Lucille shook her head at Jaz. "She's miles away."

Suzy, sandwiched between the two of them three pews from the front, thought, *No, I'm not. I'm right here. But I certainly wish I were miles away. Whatever possessed me to change my mind and come to the wedding after all?*

"Stop sniffing," hissed Jaz. "You sound like a drug addict."

"I'm sniffing because I don't want to *cry*."

And I am a drug addict, Suzy realized with a surge of hopeless sentiment. *Leo's my drug, and I don't know how I'm going to live without him.*

"She's still doing it," Jaz whispered in disbelief. He gave Lucille a nudge. "Have you got a spare tissue?"

Oh, Leo, I should have told you how I felt. Why didn't I ever tell you? Her eyes swimming with tears, Suzy focused as hard as she could on the back of Leo's dark head, silently willing the words to somehow permeate his brain.

But it wasn't working. He wasn't hearing them.

Basically, because they were *silent* words . . .

"Does anybody here present know of any reason why this man and this woman should not be joined together in holy matrimony?"

The vicar asked the question in an almost jaunty fashion. Suzy saw Gabriella, her head in profile, smile briefly up at Leo. It was an intimate, reassuring smile, the kind that signified, "Don't worry, just a couple more minutes and we'll be man and wife." Actually, it was quite a smug smile.

"I do!" Suzy called out, standing up and waving her program like an eager bidder at Sotheby's. Still, she had to make sure she caught the vicar's eye — imagine the embarrassment if he didn't spot her and she had to sit back down again.

But it was OK. He'd definitely noticed. As had the rest of the congregation — a chorus of gasps and oohs worthy of a Victorian music hall was currently echoing around the church.

"Suzy, shut up and sit down," Jaz groaned.

"Sorry, can't do that. You see" — Suzy raised her voice to address her audience, who were by this time agog — "I love that man up there, and I need him to know that before he makes his vows to someone else. Leo, are you listening to me?" He hadn't turned around, but she guessed he probably was. "I love you. Really. More than Gabriella does, I bet. So, look, I'm sorry to muck up the service, and I'm really sorry if this is spoiling your day" — she looked at Gabriella as she spoke — "but I'd much prefer it if Leo married me."

At last, Leo turned to face her. Love and hope surged in Suzy's heart.

"Suzy, stop this. You're making a complete fool of yourself." His dark eyes were filled with sorrow rather than anger. "I mean, let's be honest. Why on earth would someone like me be interested in someone like you?"

"There," hissed Jaz. "Satisfied? *Now* would you like to sit down?"

"No," said Suzy, shaking all over.

"Suzy." It was Lucille's voice this time; she was tugging at her sleeve. "Suzy, stop it. Come on now, it's OK. Everything's fine."

"Fine? Are you mad?" cried Suzy. "How can everything possibly be fine?"

She opened her eyes and gazed, terrified, up at Lucille.

In her nightie.

Not a church, not a vicar, not an irate bridegroom in sight.

Oh, thank you. Thank you, God. Thank you sooo much.

"Blimey," said Lucille, "you were having a bad dream. What was all that about?"

"I . . . I don't know." Prevaricating, Suzy blinked and rubbed her forehead. "Was I shouting? What did I say?"

"You just yelled out, 'No, no,' and waved your arm around in the air a bit."

"Oh, that's it, I remember now. I dreamed I was a member of Parliament in the House of Commons, heckling the prime minister."

Lucille grinned. "You also mumbled something like 'I love that man up there.' "

"I was a very . . . um . . . religious MP," said Suzy. "Talking about God."

"That's all right then." Lucille departed with a cheerful wink. "Just so long as you weren't talking about Leo."

CHAPTER 57

The dream stayed with Suzy, lingering in her mind like an embarrassing faux pas. When, on her way to a viewing three days later, she spotted Gabriella on the pavement waiting to cross Regent Street, she would normally have pulled up and called out a greeting, just to be polite.

But what if Gabriella said, "Oh, by the way, thanks very much for ruining our wedding ceremony." Unnerved by the thought — God, the dream still seemed so *real* — Suzy pretended not to notice Gabriella, turning an abrupt and unnecessary right onto Royal York Crescent instead. She promptly found herself stuck behind a garbage truck set to crawl the length of the road, holding her up for the next twenty minutes.

If not thirty, once the driver of the garbage truck spotted her. Suzy knew from experience he was unlikely to edge out of the way for a bimbo in a Rolls.

Stretching her arms and letting the engine idle in neutral, Suzy watched Gabriella, in her rearview mirror, lug two heavy paper shopping bags across the road before disappearing from view. Two minutes later she reappeared minus the bags, made her way back across the road, and vanished once more.

It took Suzy a good few seconds of mulling over this sequence of events before it dawned on her that Gabriella had been depositing something at the Oxfam Shop.

The garbagemen, meanwhile, were grinning broadly and going about their trash-emptying business in ultraslow motion. They could keep her waiting there all day if they wanted.

Sighing — because they would only regard this as another form of victory — Suzy shifted gears and reversed the car, highly illegally, up the hill and onto Regent Street.

Two hours later, heading back along Regent Street in the direction of the office, Suzy glanced instinctively across at the Oxfam Shop.

The next moment, as recognition dawned, her world slipped into slow motion.

"Ohhh myyy Goood . . ."

Somehow, Suzy managed to park the car, climb out, and make her way jerkily back down to the shop.

There it was, occupying center stage in the window: a wedding dress with a deep-red velvet boned bodice and an ivory satin skirt, teamed with a dark green velvet cloak lined with crimson satin. Dark green beading on the bodice, and deep-red beading on the cloak.

Never Worn, declared the price ticket clipped to the slender waist of the dress. *£75.*

Without even stopping to wonder why she was doing it, Suzy pushed open the door — *jangle jangle* — and went inside.

There was no doubt about it. This had to be Gabriella's dress.

But what was it doing here? Had she changed her mind at the last minute and decided, after all, to go for virginal white?

Or had she — Suzy struggled to keep her clamoring thoughts under some kind of control — simply *changed her mind*?

After ten minutes of standing there in the window like an idiot, fingering the top-quality beading and stroking the soft velvet, Suzy realized she'd been approached by one of the salespeople in the shop.

"Lovely, isn't it?" The woman smiled, her

tone friendly.

"Yes, it is."

"Now I'm not being rude, dear, but I don't think it would fit you."

"No."

"See that tiny waist? Gosh, there aren't many girls who could squeeze themselves into something so small."

I can think of one, thought Suzy.

Aloud she said, "The girl who brought it into the shop . . . Um, did she happen to mention why she was, um . . . you know?"

"Donating the dress to us? No, dear, she didn't say, and I didn't like to ask — although, my goodness, you aren't going to believe it, but this is the very same young lady coming toward us now."

Suzy, trapped in the middle of the window display, could only turn and stare as Gabriella crossed the road and headed steadily toward them.

The door swung open and shut, the bell above it jangling like Suzy's nerves.

"Hello, Suzy," said Gabriella. "Spotted the dress, then? Nice of them to give it pride of place."

"Oh, you *know* each other," Mrs. Oxfam exclaimed in delight, slipping into garden-party mode. "How marvelous, no need for formal introductions then! This young lady

676

was just admiring your lovely dress, although I'm afraid I did have to point out to her that it might be a trifle . . . um . . ."

"Small." Suzy nodded. "Yes, I think we've all figured that one out. Actually, I wasn't interested in it for myself." Turning, forcing herself to look at Gabriella, she said, "What happened? Did you find another dress?"

Mrs. Oxfam was standing between them, still doing her hostess bit, nodding and smiling and showing tremendous interest in the conversation. Any minute now, Suzy thought, she'd start handing around canapés and asking if they'd prefer cream sherry or a nice cup of tea.

Evidently reading Suzy's mind, Gabriella said in neutral tones, "Why don't we go somewhere more . . . How about the café in the covered arcade? Unless, of course, you're horribly busy."

Suzy *was* horribly busy, but wild horses couldn't have dragged her away now.

"Oh!" Gabriella went on, belatedly remembering the shopping bag in her hand. Passing it over to Mrs. Oxfam she said, "I forgot to bring these earlier. Shoes, to go with the dress. May as well have the matching set."

Gabriella insisted on buying the cappuccinos. When she joined Suzy at their corner table in the steamy, aromatic smelling little café overlooking Boyce's Avenue, she said, "I didn't get a look at the price tag in the window. How much are they selling my dress for?"

Suzy piled brown sugar recklessly into her cup. "Seventy-five."

"Gosh, bargain." Drily, Gabriella added, "Seeing as it cost three thousand."

"You could have taken it to one of those designer second-hand shops."

"Can't be bothered. Anyway, it was Leo's money, not mine. The wedding's off, needless to say. I'm sure you've already worked that one out."

Gabriella had paid for the coffee, which surely meant that she didn't hold Suzy responsible. This was a comfort, but Suzy still found herself feeling guilty. Dry-mouthed, she said, "Totally off?"

"Oh yes."

"You mean . . . you . . . ?"

"No, it was all Leo's decision. Nothing to do with me. Except, of course, it was to do with me," Gabriella conceded with a tiny shrug. "Because basically, ultimately, he decided I wasn't what he wanted."

Suzy felt like a cartoon character whose jaw had dropped in shock onto the table.

Surreptitiously, she put a hand up to her mouth to make sure it wasn't gaping open.

"How?" she managed to say at last. "How can you not be what he wants?"

It was outrageous. Unimaginable. Clearly, Gabriella thought so too.

"I know, isn't it the most ridiculous thing? He's met someone else, apparently. All he'll tell me is she's the exact opposite of me."

The exact opposite? As in tiny, elegant, ultra-controlled and super brainy, versus big, flashy, hopelessly impulsive, and super noisy?

Don't even think *it.* Suzy quashed the idea at once; there was such a thing as wandering just too far into the realms of wild fantasy.

More to the point, how was Gabriella managing to stay so eerily calm? Why in heaven's name wasn't she weeping and wailing like a normal person and kicking stiletto-size holes in Leo's car?

"How do you feel about it?" Suzy felt stupid asking the question, but she had to know.

"Me? Oh well, I think Leo's out of his mind, but that's his problem, not mine. He's met some ditzy good-time girl down at that bar of his, no doubt, and decided she's the one for him. So, fine, if he doesn't want to marry me, that's his loss, and I'm certainly glad I didn't waste my time marrying him."

God, this was unbelievable.

"But . . . aren't you upset?"

"I'm not the fretting kind." With another shrug, Gabriella raised her cup to her perfect lips and sipped her cappuccino. Her hands were rock steady; no hint of a tremor. "Mmm, excellent coffee. It's my medical training, I expect," she continued easily. "You learn never to panic, to take everything in stride. When you've experienced the horrors of emergency medicine, you're equipped to deal with pretty much anything. Getting hysterical won't bring Leo back, so why bother getting hysterical? Anyway, I've applied for a thrilling position at a prestigious neuropsychiatric unit in Toronto, so there's that to look forward to."

She actually looked as if she meant it. Still doubtful, Suzy said, "Really?"

"My career's always been incredibly important to me. To be honest, it was a bit of a sticking point between Leo and myself." Gabriella paused to smooth her ice-blond hair back from her even smoother forehead. "Like the children thing. He wanted them, I didn't. Medicine's always seemed so much more vital than churning out the obligatory offspring."

"Oh." Suzy was lost for words.

"Actually, that's a thought. I wonder if Leo's gotten this girl pregnant."

Oh please God, no. I hope he hasn't!

"Anyway." Gabriella flapped her hand dismissively and changed the subject. "You and Harry. Do you think there's any chance you two might get back together?"

"What?" Startled, Suzy said, "Me and Harry? Nooo."

"Poor old you." Gabriella reached across the table and gave her wrist a sympathetic squeeze. "Never mind, chin up. I'm sure you'll find someone else one day."

Swallowing hard, wondering if she'd ever felt more unlovable and spinsterish, Suzy said faintly, "Thanks."

Still in a daze, she arrived back at the office ten minutes later to find the place awash with panties.

"What d'you think?" Beaming happily, Martin conjured a scarlet silk teddy out of a mound of emerald-green tissue paper and held it up.

"Very glamorous," Suzy remarked. "All you need now are the fishnets."

"Oh, you're so funny. This isn't for me, it's for Nancy. They're all for Nancy. We're going to have a Christmas to remember."

Suzy looked at the lilac satin bra and panties, the silver G-string, the transparent black negligee, fuchsia-pink camisole and matching suspender belt . . .

"I didn't know Nancy was working as a hooker these days."

"I spent ages choosing all this." Martin looked distraught. "I thought these were the kind of things she'd like."

In its own small way, Suzy realized, it was a miracle. Last year, Martin had gotten drunk at lunchtime on Christmas Eve and had only remembered as the shops were closing that he hadn't gotten around yet to buying any presents. Racing down to Habitat, he had hammered on their just-shut doors until they let him in. The next morning, lucky Nancy had unwrapped six beige bath towels.

This time around, Martin was agonizing over gifts for his wife and there were still two weeks to go before Christmas.

Correction, thought Suzy. *Estranged wife.*

Furthermore, Martin evidently hadn't heard the rumors yet, but the word was out that Nancy was having a riotous fling with one of the salesmen from the Mercedes dealership on Merchant's Road.

So it could be a Christmas to remember, after all.

"Take these back to the shop," Suzy

instructed, feeling sorry for him. "Buy her something she'll love, like a beautiful black cashmere sweater."

Martin looked horrified. "But that's boring!"

"You're a man, I'm a woman," Suzy told him kindly. "Trust me, it's not."

Suzy knew it was a desperately teenagey thing to be doing, but she couldn't help herself. Leaving the office at six o'clock, she had driven across Clifton, over the Downs and past Sheldrake House.

Just to see if the lights were on, or some such idiotic reason.

To see if Leo was at home.

And he was, which had given her a warm glow in the pit of her stomach. She had seen the lights on as she had approached her old home. Next, and even better, she spotted Leo's Porsche in the drive.

A moment later the warm glow abruptly turned to ice as Suzy glimpsed a second car, just to the left of Leo's. Another Porsche, furthermore, but this time a white one.

It must belong to *her,* Suzy realized, breathless with jealousy. God, how perfect must they be together. They had mix-and-match cars. This one even had personalized plates — and what the letters stood for, heaven only knew.

BEAUTIFUL BODY?

BUXOM BABE?

BOSS-EYED AND BRAINLESS?

Ha! Some hope.

CHAPTER 58

Without stopping to consider whether this was wise, Suzy parked around the corner and crept back up the road. By keeping close to the high stone wall, she remained in the shadows. Reaching Leo's drive, she knew from experience there was no way of creeping up it without making scrunching noises on the gravel. Instead, first silently sliding her feet out of her shoes, she felt her way blindly across the landscaped flower beds.

What she could be stepping on in the pitch-blackness didn't bear thinking about, so Suzy determinedly didn't think about it. Under cover of the shrubs and bushes she crouched, crawled, and tiptoed her way around the side of the house until she reached the sanctuary of the back garden.

The temperature had plummeted as darkness had fallen. The grass, crisp with frost, was icy against the soles of her stockinged feet. But although her teeth were chattering like castanets Suzy barely noticed the cold. All her attention was currently fixed on the drawing room French windows, uncurtained and ablaze with light.

Beyond them, she could see a long, white trench coat flung casually over one arm of Leo's black velvet sofa. And, next to it, an expensive-looking baguette-style handbag, also in white.

Presumably to match the Porsche.

Then, Suzy covered her mouth to stop a wail of anguish bursting out. A girl with long black hair had wandered into view. Long *gleaming* black hair, perfect skin, bright red lipstick, and the body of a model, encased in a gray trouser suit.

She was so beautiful Suzy could hardly bear to look at her.

The trouble was, she couldn't bring herself to look away.

"Aaargh!" shrieked Suzy as someone leaped out of the shadows behind her, thumped the air from her lungs, and sent her flying.

"WOOF WOOF WOOF," Baxter barked joyously, launching himself like a heat-seeking missile at her now supine body. "WOOF WOOF!"

Oh, help . . .

"Shhh, no. Don't bark. *Shhh,*" Suzy whispered frantically, attempting to cover his big, whiskery, slobbery mouth with both hands.

"WOOF WOOF WOOF WOOF WOOF."

"Yes, I know it's me. Hello, sweetheart. But I do need you to be quiet, so shush, *please,* because I really don't want Leo to know I'm here."

"Bit late for that," Leo drawled, from less than ten feet away.

Suzy, still flat on her back, groaned and closed her eyes and considered feigning death.

"Baxter was scrabbling at the front door," Leo explained, "so I let him out." He gazed down at her, mystified. "Suzy, what are you doing here?"

Suzy shook her head. It was no good, she couldn't think of a single reasonable explanation. Typical. After years of improvising dramatically and almost always successfully, her brain had picked this very moment to give up the ghost.

She shrugged, the frosty grass tickling her neck. "Why am I here? I haven't the foggiest idea."

"Come on, sit up." Reaching down and pushing Baxter out of the way, Leo clasped her hand and pulled Suzy to her feet.

Glancing down at them, his tone conversational, he said, "Aren't they cold?"

Suzy shrugged again. She could no longer tell. They were numb, like her brain.

"Never mind. Let's go." As he spoke, Leo put his arm around her shoulder, which was absolute heaven but at the same time deeply humiliating. He was treating her, Suzy realized, like some loopy maiden aunt found wandering in her nightie along the fast lane of the M4.

On the front doorstep she discovered her shoes, waiting for her.

"I thought they were yours, but I couldn't be absolutely sure," said Leo.

"I didn't leave them there."

"WOOF." Baxter, who had retrieved them from the depths of the bushes over by the front gate, wagged his tail with pride.

"I'm not coming into your house." Suzy let out a squeak of alarm as Leo pushed open the door. Until that moment she'd simply assumed he was doing his sympathetic bouncer bit, escorting her off the premises.

"Oh, yes you are. That's why you came here, isn't it? To see me?"

"Oh God, I suppose so, in theory." Suzy tried digging her heels in, without success. "But not while *she's* here."

Ignoring this feeble protest, Leo propelled her briskly across the hall and into the drawing room. The black-haired vision of loveliness was simultaneously putting on her coat, shoveling papers into a leather briefcase, and laughing as she spoke to someone on her cell phone.

"OK, you can stop nagging now. I'm on my way." Hanging up, she snapped shut her briefcase, then — in quick succession — gave Leo a kiss on the cheek, Baxter a pat on the head, and Suzy a dazzling smile.

"Beth, thanks for sorting that out. And give my love to Ellie."

"I will. And don't worry," Beth told Leo cheerfully, "I'll see myself out."

"Sit," Leo told Baxter when Beth had gone.

Baxter gave him a reproachful look and flopped down in front of the fire.

"Who was she?" said Suzy.

"Beth? My accountant."

Still not convinced, Suzy said truculently, "And Ellie?"

"Ellie's her partner. Not business partner. The other kind."

Oh.

The room was blissfully warm, but Suzy was still shivering. Leo had caught her skulking in the bushes just as, months earlier, she had caught Lucille skulking in the bushes.

The difference being, of course, that Lucille had had a jolly good reason for being there.

"So," Leo said finally. "Does this mean you've heard about the wedding being off?"

"I saw Gabriella. She told me everything, about this woman you're seeing. Is she pregnant, by the way? Because Gabriella thinks she is." The words escaped before Suzy could stop them, like lemmings hurling themselves manically over a cliff.

"The other woman?" For a brief moment Leo looked startled, then the corners of his mouth began to twitch. "Well, I certainly hope not."

Suzy, her tone accusing, said, "I thought you wanted children."

"I do."

"So how can you say —"

"Because I haven't slept with her yet."

"Hah!" It came out as a not-very-elegant snort of derision. "And if you'll believe that, you'll believe anything."

"I can assure you," said Leo, moving toward her, "that if I'd slept with you, you would have noticed."

Suzy stopped snorting. She stopped breathing, as the significance of the last few

690

words sank in.

"Gosh," Leo remarked mildly. "Mouth open, but no sound coming out. I do believe she's lost for words. Excellent."

He kissed her, and Suzy's whole world exploded around her. Fireworks were going off in all directions. It was a wonder Baxter wasn't cowering under the sofa with his paws over his ears.

"I'm still confused," she managed to mumble finally, when they both paused for breath. "Gabriella said you were seeing someone else."

"Wrong. I told her I was in love with someone else," Leo corrected.

Suzy heaved a sigh of relief. "And this isn't a joke? It's really me? You're sure about this?"

"I've been sure since the first moment I set eyes on you." He brushed her mouth with his, setting off another carnival of fireworks.

"It's just that I'm not as brainy as Gabriella. I don't actually have all that many exams."

"I think I can cope with that." Smiling, Leo said, "I've heard you're great at Boggle."

"Oh, I am, I am. Definitely great at Boggle." Suzy breathed again. There, she did have some good points.

"And you're terrific with spiders, mustn't forget that."

Happily, Suzy nodded. "Of course. Brilliant with spiders."

"You're the one," Leo said simply. "When you know, you know. Although" — he paused for a moment — "I did hear one rather worrying thing."

"Worrying?" Suzy stepped back in alarm. "What is it? Did Harry say something awful about me?"

"Not Harry. Lucille happened to mention it once. Apparently, you have this strange . . . quirk." Leo shook his head, at an apparent loss. "According to Lucille . . . she said something about . . ."

"Yes? Yes? About what?"

"Well . . . a six-week rule?"

"Oh." Suzy gulped, hoping he wasn't going to hold her to it. "That."

"Is it true?"

"No, no . . . Well, you know, it's pretty negotiable."

"I'm a great negotiator," said Leo.

Good. "Me too."

"I love you."

Shuddering with joy, Suzy reached up and brushed her fingers against his lips. "Me too."

"And actually," said Leo, "it's handy you're here. There's something I really need you to help me with."

"Really?"

"Upstairs."

Still minus her shoes, Suzy allowed him to take her hand and lead her to the staircase. As they reached the landing, Leo steered her in the direction of the master bedroom.

"What kind of help, exactly?"

"Spider," said Leo.

"Oh dear. Big?"

"Very big. And very menacing. It scared me witless."

He pushed open the bedroom door.

"Where?" whispered Suzy.

"On the ceiling. Above the bed."

"I can't see any spider."

"Right over the bed."

"Still can't see it."

Suzy was by this time lying on the king-size bed, her head cushioned by pillows. As she continued to peer up at the ceiling, she felt Leo begin to unfasten the buttons of her pomegranate-pink shirt.

Henceforth to be referred to as her very, *very* lucky pomegranate-pink shirt.

"Leo, I hate to tell you this," Suzy whispered, "but there's no spider on this ceiling."

"No?" Leo shook his dark head in amazement, then slowly smiled, kissing each corner of Suzy's mouth in turn. "We must have frightened him off. What a shame. Oh well, never mind. Now you're here . . ."

ABOUT THE AUTHOR

Jill Mansell lives with her family in Bristol. She used to work in the field of clinical neurophysiology but now writes full-time. She watches far too much TV and would love to be one of those super sporty types but basically can't be bothered. Nor can she cook — having once attempted to bake a cake for the hospital's Christmas Fair, she was forced to watch while her coworkers played Frisbee with it. But she's good at Twitter!

The employees of Thorndike Press hope you have enjoyed this Large Print book. All our Thorndike, Wheeler, and Kennebec Large Print titles are designed for easy reading, and all our books are made to last. Other Thorndike Press Large Print books are available at your library, through selected bookstores, or directly from us.

For information about titles, please call:
  (800) 223-1244

or visit our Web site at:
  http://gale.cengage.com/thorndike

To share your comments, please write:
Publisher
Thorndike Press
10 Water St., Suite 310
Waterville, ME 04901